"WHY, LORD?"

The table lamp crashed to the floor at Anthony's sudden lunge and the room plunged back into darkness. "Why can't I keep this money? I probably earned this much and a hundred times over! You know me, Jesus. You know my heart. I can't take this anymore!" His words were sobs and groans as he fell to his knees, steadying himself with a hand pushed down on a nearby coffee table.

"It's not illegal. I haven't done anything wrong. It was their fault. I'm not breaking the law!"

What about My law?

Anthony quieted at the question that spoke somewhere in his spirit . . .

Like Sheep Gone Astray

Leslie J. Sherrod

West Bloomfield, Michigan

WARNER BOOKS

NEW YORK   BOSTON

This book is a work of fiction. Names, characters, places, and incidents are the product of the author's imagination or are used fictitiously. Any resemblance to actual events, locales, or persons, living or dead, is coincidental.

Published by Warner Books with Walk Worthy Press™

Warner Books
Hachette Book Group USA
1271 Avenue of the Americas, New York, NY 10020

Walk Worthy Press
33290 West Fourteen Mile Road, #482, West Bloomfield, MI 48322

Visit our Web sites at www.Hachette Book Group USA.com and
www.walkworthypress.net
Printed in the United States of America

First Edition: July 2006
10 9 8 7 6 5 4 3 2 1

Warner Books and the "W" logo are trademarks of Time Inc. or an affiliated company. Used under license by Hachette Book Group USA, which is not affiliated with Time Warner Inc.

Library of Congress Cataloging-in-Publication Data
Sherrod, Leslie J.
     Like sheep gone astray / Leslie J. Sherrod.—1st ed.
          p. cm.
     ISBN-13: 978-0-446-69705-7
     ISBN-10: 0-446-69705-2
   1. Clergy—Fiction. 2. African Americans—Fiction. I. Title.
     PS3619.H46953L55   2006
     813' .6—dc22

                                                        2005035453

Book design and text composition by L&G McRee

For my family—past and present

Acknowledgments

All praise and thanksgiving first to You, Lord Jesus. I'm honored to serve You in this way, and I trust that You will get the glory You alone deserve, and that those who read these pages will be drawn closer to You. Thank You for opening doors, for leading the way, for giving grace, for loving me.

How do I even begin to thank everyone who has helped this come to pass? I know there are no coincidences in God's Kingdom and His timing is perfect, so everyone who has crossed paths with me has in some way contributed to the completion of this book. Thank you for the inspiration, the encouragement, and the lessons learned. I'm grateful.

My family deserves a standing ovation for the way you have supported me. Brian, you've given me my dreams—the chance to be a wife, a mother, and a writer. There is no way this book would have been finished without you. Because of your sacrifices, support, and steady pushing, we can both celebrate what God has done. You are a gift and a king to me. I love you.

My children, Neyla and Nathan, you have been the most accommodating preschoolers a writing mother could ask for. I write because of and for you. My desire is to be an example for you to see that following Christ and the passion and purpose He puts in your heart leads to a fulfillment like no other. Mommy loves you and always will.

To my parents, J. Adrian and Maxine Datcher: Thanks for raising me to believe—to know—that I can do all things through Christ Who strengthens me. This book is for you, for believing and seeing it done, even before I knew what to write. Anna "Nana" Datcher, thank you for your prayers and wisdom. You do not know what it means to have a grandmother as hip and as holy as you are. Jocelyn, thanks for being an encouraging sister. Your gifts and talents have pushed me along since childhood. May God bless you and your family.

To my "mother-in-love," Ms. LaVerne Weambe: The gift you have given me in your son is rivaled only by the constant love and encouragement you bring my way. Your smiles and enthusiasm have carried me more than you know. Jenae, Marcus, and all the Sherrods, thanks for accepting me as one of your own. The excitement and support all of you have shown has been phenomenal.

And in the memories of Novella Cole's attention to detail, Robert Cole's storytelling, and John Datcher Sr.'s quiet confidence, I have felt the support and roots only generations past can hand down. To all of my extended family, your prayers and support have been priceless. Thank you.

Special thanks to the following people who said something or gave something, who dreamed with me or just listened, at a time when God knew I needed it: Angela Graham; Yan Gong; Valarie O. Allen; Sonia Brown; Kimberly Taylor; Jackie Cooper; Lisa Beyer; Alexandria Lewis; Stacey Jones; Ms. Marie Harvey; Ms. Lottie Wright; Shalanda Lyons; Cheri Shannon; Burnett Morsell (and the rest of y'all at EBMHP); my MOPS friends, especially Valarie Foster, Kathi Barber, Carla Jackson, and Tuesday Hayes. None of you know how much God has used you in my life.

Complete thanks to my pastor, Bishop Clifford M. Johnson—a man worthy of his title—and the entire Mount Pleasant Church family. Thanks for feeding me, nurturing me, and growing me.

To my publisher, Denise Stinson: I am honored to be associated with such a visionary woman of God. Your heart for His Word and for perfection in ministry has revolutionized the way I view writing. Thank you for the opportunity to live out this calling. You have been a direct answer to a specific prayer. Thanks to my editors, Frances Jalet-Miller, Karen Thompson, and Robert Castillo. Few people know how hard and exhausting this process is. I applaud you and everyone else at Walk Worthy Press and Warner Books. Here's a shout-out to my fellow scribes of the WWP 11: Mata; MaRita; Gloria; Claudia; Collette; Pam; Kristen; Rodney, Olivia, and Aubrey. Also, Ms. Barbara Holmes, Shawnol Jemison, Toni Robinson, and Andrew Foster—thanks for your services along the way.

To my readers: This book would have little purpose without you. Thanks for your support. I've prayed for each and every one of you. Be blessed.

And finally, to dreamers everywhere: I know God has put hopes and visions in your heart, some of which look impossible and seem too far away and out of reach. Seek Him first and His righteousness, and everything you need will be added to you. Don't take my word for it—take His (Matthew 6:19–21, 33; Habakkuk 2:2–3).

Love,

Leslie

Like Sheep
Gone Astray

Prologue

At three A.M. on a Sunday, most of the community of Shepherd Hills sleeps. Perched at a window high above an abandoned corner, an observer notes how quiet and still the town is under the silver moonlight. A phone rings somewhere in the building, breaking the silence of the hushed moment. It is promptly answered amidst stirred dust and cobwebs. The call is right on schedule.

"I don't think he'll go through with it." Fear is in the caller's voice.

"Don't worry. I knew that was a possibility."

There is a long pause before the caller continues. "So how do you expect to pull this off?"

"You're forgetting the most important thing. He doesn't know where the money is coming from."

"What does that have to do with anything?" Impatience has replaced the fear.

"That has to do with everything."

PART 1

~

Sidetracked

~

All we like sheep have gone astray;
we have turned every one to his own way;
and the LORD hath laid on him the iniquity of us all.
(Isaiah 53:6 KJV)

Chapter 1

It was a small church, the kind of white wood frame building that always finds a home on hilly back roads, with forgotten grave markers nestled under its shadow and a steeple that towers higher than the trees surrounding it. The pews were made of the same worn wood grain as the floor, and hymnbooks and Bibles lined each row.

This was the church that had been around long enough to serve as the refuge of underpaid domestics and first-generation steelworkers from now ghost-like train yards. It had been the meetinghouse of civil rights activists and countless committees; the training ground where little black boys and brown-skinned young girls grew to be decent "churched" folk; the sacred ground where God met those willing to walk the straight and narrow way.

The founding members walked to the small sanctuary, some leaving their homes before sunrise to get to Sunday school on time. But on this Sunday morning, cars filled the gravel lot. And instead of the tinklings of an old, out-of-tune piano, synthesized chords from keyboards and guitars flooded out of the windows. The parishioners who came to the eleven-o'clock service walked down brand-new red-carpeted aisles and rested in cushioned seats.

Second Baptist Church of Shepherd Hills was not the only or oldest congregation in the area, but it was respected by many as a Bible teaching, preaching, and believing church.

And it was this respect that Anthony Murdock did not want to lose. From his seat in Pastor Green's small basement study, he could hear the lively service proceeding above him. The opening hymn, "Hold to His Hand," was echoing through the rafters. As the entire church seemed to shake under the weight of many footsteps stomping in time to the music, Anthony felt his heart pounding in his ears. He looked down again at the letter in his hands. His own neat print glared back. He had written it three weeks earlier, and carried it around just as long. This Sunday he would finally give it to him. He would not lose his nerve again. He would give him the letter after morning service. No matter what.

Anthony sat limply in the leather chair, questioning his own resolve. Six months ago, he had been celebrated for his confidence and decision-making skills as the senior marketing director at Shaw Enterprises, the fastest-growing marketing firm in Shepherd Hills. But that was six months ago.

"You prayin'?" A little boy in a junior usher's uniform stood in the cracked doorway. "I don't mean to interrupt, but I wanted to make sure I had your introduction right."

"I'm sure whatever you have is fine." Anthony smiled. He shook his head as the youngster disappeared. An-

thony never did fully understand why the formal introduction always preceded his sermons every fourth Sunday
morning. He had, after all, been a member of Second Baptist Church of Shepherd Hills his entire life, all twenty-
nine years. Most of the people sitting above him had
witnessed nearly every major milestone in his life. His
walk down the church aisle to confess Christ when he was
eight; his subsequent baptism; his high school then college graduation; even his marriage ceremony had been
celebrated in the small reception hall in the basement of
the rickety church. The evening he gave his trial sermon,
the pews had been packed.

Everyone here knows me—at least they think they do.
Anthony's thoughts raced again. He loosened his necktie
a little as the sweat began pooling around his neck.
Taking one last look at the letter, he carefully refolded it
and placed it securely between the pages of his Bible.
They'll all be surprised, he reflected while mopping his
forehead with the handkerchief he kept in his breast
pocket.

With a heaving sigh he stood up, grabbing his sermon
notes. He stared blankly at the pages of his own scribbled
writing, re-tucked his shirt, and headed for the stairs to
make his entrance into the service.

"Lord, I guess this is it. It's all come down to this."

Minister Anthony Murdock, the youth and young-
adult leader of Second Baptist Church of Shepherd Hills,
ascended the stairs and entered the main sanctuary.

The children's choir swayed in purple robes on the
platform facing him, their voices and arms alive with the
latest arrangement by the animated director, who clapped
louder than all seventeen pairs of hands combined. "Let it

shine, Let it shine, Let it shine," they sang with all the breath within them.

Anthony felt a warm flutter inside as he welcomed in the innocence. Entering the sanctuary of his home church was like walking into a grandmother's kitchen. Here, he was satisfied and comforted. Here, he was loved.

As he made his way to the front of the church, he responded to nod after nod that greeted him. Sister Kellye Porter, the assistant pastor's wife, who had taught his childhood Sunday school class. Calvin Holmes, the old deacon who beat him year after year in the annual horseshoe tournament at the church picnic. Councilman Walter Banks, the revered politician who had taken him under his wing and mentored him from his adolescence.

I would not have known success if I had not known these people. Anthony swallowed hard as he smiled at each nod. He knew that the letter tucked safely inside his Bible was the beginning of the end, and they would all be disappointed. *But hadn't it all already ended with that first phone call six months ago?* Before he could answer his own question, the sudden roar of applause shook him.

"Surely the presence of the Lord is in this place! We're having church today!" Pastor Green exclaimed as Anthony took his place on the pulpit.

From his seat, Anthony agreed. He could see the entire congregation. Hands were clapping, feet were tapping, all in a mesmerizing unison with the clanging cymbals of the drum and the shrill chords of the pianist. Floppy paper fans and bold feather hats dotted the sanctuary, as did the cries of "Amen" and "Thank you, Jesus" blurted out by Sister Ethel, Mother Howard, and Brother Oliver. Anthony knew that it was just a matter of time before the rest of the parishioners, most of whom were already standing and rocking along to the music, would join in the growing crescendo of praise.

The deacons sat solemn-faced in their usual front-row seats. A flurry of white prayer caps covered the heads of the missionaries sitting across the aisle from the deacon board. Anthony watched as a bag of peppermints passed back and forth between the two rows of these ladies, most of whom were considered the Mothers of the church.

He imagined for a second that his Great-Aunt Rosa was still sitting among them. He could still smell the oversized buttery biscuits she pulled out of the oven every Sunday after church. *The family used to be so close*, he reminisced, almost tasting the crispy fried chicken and salty collard greens Aunt Rosa put on her dining room table every week between services. He swallowed hard, remembering the series of tragedies during his teen years that seemed to claim everyone near and dear to him. By his eighteenth birthday, Aunt Rosa and his church family were all he'd had left.

"Life don't make sense sometimes," Aunt Rosa used to tell him, "but God still has plans for you. Look at Joseph in the Bible. All the sufferin' he went through was just to get him to a high place. Remember Joseph, and when you ain't got nothin' else, hold on to God and your integrity."

Integrity. The word stung him even as he sat smiling on the pulpit. He had let her down. He had let them all down.

Rosa Bergenson had moved "back home" to South Carolina after Anthony married, but she was still revered as a leading matriarch of the church. A special seat in the front pew was reserved for her every Church Anniversary

Weekend even though the Anniversary Committee members knew her failing health would prevent her attendance. Anthony hadn't called her in months, convinced she would somehow sense his guilt even over the telephone.

"Let the redeemed of the Lord say so! Let the people of God *rejoice!*" Pastor Green boomed, bringing Anthony back into the service.

The entire church was jolted by a wave of electricity as the organist set the keys of his instrument on heavenly fire. Shrieks of "Hallelujah" courted dances of worship. Some of the mothers and sisters of the church swirled around in the aisles while a few of the brothers stomped in jubilee. The senior ushers and nurses raced around frantically with fans and cups of water to assist those overcome by the Spirit.

Anthony allowed his soul to enjoy the warmth, taking in the sweetness from heaven like a dry garden swallowing long-awaited rainwater. He let his feet tap along to the one-two beat of the drum as a growing surge of living waters seemed ready to burst out of him. He stood to lift his hands higher, forgetting that his Bible and sermon notes were still in his lap. With a loud thump they fell to the floor. As he bent down to retrieve his scattered possessions, his eyes caught hold of the letter peeking out of his Bible.

Maybe it's not too late, he considered as he reorganized his papers. *I haven't said anything to anybody, and those who do know would not dare expose themselves.*

He glanced over at Pastor Green, who was basking in the presence of glory. His eyes, normally gentle in character, seemed ablaze in fiery joy as he nodded back at Anthony.

It's not too late! Thank you, Lord! There's got to be another way to handle this. Anthony thought of tearing the letter into small pieces right then and there. Relief rushed within him, nudging away a burden that had been growing far too long.

But then he spotted Terri in the congregation. Her ice blue suit stood out in the warm sea of worshippers. *No matter what.* He remembered his resolve in the study. Anthony refolded the letter, tucked it back into his Bible, and quietly sat down.

Terri Murdock wanted to shove Sister Pearl out into the center of the aisle.

"If this old bat steps on my foot one more time," she mumbled to herself, "this church will see some real laying on of hands."

With a scowl pulling at her full, berry-painted lips, she bent over to wipe the fresh scuffmarks off her new—and expensive—light blue shoes. She checked a rhinestone-and-silver clasp before sitting up and jeering at her jubilant neighbor.

"Thank you, Jesus!" Sister Pearl shouted, oblivious to Terri's rolling eyes. Four-year-old Tyreeka Oliver turned around in her seat, peeking over the edge of the wooden pew to examine Terri and the Spirit-filled, stomping Sister Pearl. Terri flashed the child a large white smile.

"Bless Jesus," she moaned, letting her eyes drift dreamily to the ceiling while waving both her hands. When Terri saw the plaited pigtails of the little girl bobbing in another direction, she rolled her eyes again and snatched her hands back into her lap.

"Just hurry on up with this service," she groaned. She

studied the church bulletin, noting that only a quarter of the planned program had been covered. Offering had not yet been taken. The announcements still needed to be read. And Pastor Green had not even begun his morning remarks. *I hope Anthony gives a short sermon today.* She sighed to herself while glancing at the pulpit.

Anthony sat slouched in his seat, his eyes studying the red carpet. He looked distant and preoccupied, shuffling and reshuffling the papers in his hand. *This is not the same man I met five years ago.* Terri frowned.

She daydreamed about the first time she saw him. She'd just left the office of a client and was headed back to her car when she heard door chimes ringing to her right. There he was, strolling out of the Golden Touch Dry Cleaners and Tailoring in the busy downtown district. From the number and quality of suits he carried, she knew instantly that he was some type of working professional with a lot of money and a lot of class. He walked like he had jazz in his shoes, a syncopated, sure-of-yourself strut that was smooth and easy. She remembered the warm shiver she'd felt when she studied not only his strapping six-two frame, but also his luxurious brown suede overcoat flapping wildly in the wind. She was rendered speechless, and had frozen, before realizing too late that he had disappeared in the congestion.

Terri smiled to herself, thinking how good confidence and cash looked on a caramel-colored brother. Isn't that what she'd almost told him the second time she saw him, at the gym, a week after that first sighting? How she had missed a brother like that working out in her two years of regular exercise she didn't know, but she was not going to let opportunity pass by her again.

By the time they'd finished their conversation outside the locker rooms about how they had both secured their dream jobs through successful college internships and were well on their way up very lucrative career ladders, she knew she had him hooked. The man had money written all over him. Together they would read like *Forbes* magazine, and he knew it. Terri's smile deepened at the memories. Then she looked back up at Anthony sitting on the pulpit, and both her smile and the memories quickly faded and fizzled away.

"Ouch!" Terri hissed, rubbing her foot. "Sister Pearl needs to hurry up and sit down," she mumbled to herself. She sighed in relief as she saw some of the deacons and trustees getting the collection plates.

"At least the service is moving forward now." She rechecked her watch.

". . . And so may I present to some and introduce to others, our very own, Minister Anthony Murdock." The junior usher charged with the introduction crumpled up the index card and hurried back to his seat. A light applause and a string of Amens rippled through the congregation as Anthony took his place behind the lectern.

Beads of sweat formed on his forehead as he stood quietly for a moment, gazing out into the faces of people who thought they knew him. He was careful to avoid Terri's blank stare. After looking up at the balcony and then letting his eyes circle the rest of the church, he began.

"Good morning, church," he started. "I'd like to first give honor to my Lord and Savior Jesus Christ for giving me this opportunity to stand once more before you this morning."

"Amen, amen." A deacon nodded.

"And to Pastor Green, the deacon board and officials, and all the members of this great assembly." Anthony turned to each as he acknowledged them. "And last but not least, I want to give honor to the lady who keeps me going with her words of encouragement and her prayers, my wife, Terri. Won't you stand, baby?"

Anthony thought how phony his own words sounded to him as Terri Murdock quickly stood, her painted lips arched in a full beauty-pageant smile.

"And now to the business at hand." Anthony hesitated. He held on to the lectern with both hands for balance.

"Proverbs chapter four, verses twenty-six and twenty-seven. This message is for the young people, but I believe that there's a word in this for all of us. The scripture says, 'Ponder the path of thy feet, and let all thy ways be established. Turn not to the right hand nor to the left: remove thy foot from evil.'"

"Yes, Lord!" one of the Mothers shouted.

"Here are two short verses that give a lifelong message," he said. "*Webster's Dictionary* tells us that the word *ponder* means to think deeply about, to carefully consider, to weigh. And what must we be considering and weighing? Let's say it together: 'the path of thy feet.' That means that we must be deliberate in our choices. We must carefully think about where our choices will lead us."

"My, my, my." Sister Ethel shook her head.

"My dear children, my church friends, where are you headed this morning? What path are you on? Where are your feet taking you? You and I must examine the road of our lives. But we can't just stop at considering where we are. No, that's not the last verse in the chapter."

The church warmed up again as echoes of "That's right" and "Tell it" and "Amen" bounced off of every wall and out of every corner.

"See, once we consider our path and make sure that we are established in righteousness, then we must not turn in any way. We have got to get on the right path and we have got to *stay* on the right path. It's a constant walk. If you find your foot on the wrong path, standing in a place of evil, God's word tells you to remove it!"

Anthony stopped suddenly, awkwardly.

"That's okay, son!" one of the older deacons shouted.

"Preach, boy!" Another one laughed while slapping his knee. Anthony took a slow sip of water, thinking only of the letter hidden in his Bible. *What will they all say?* he wondered.

He said a quick prayer for strength to continue and picked up his papers again. This time he simply read the rest of his notes, being careful to inflect his voice to a higher pitch every time the audience grew excited. Together, he and the flock of Second Baptist Church of Shepherd Hills finished the sermon. When the invitation was given and the doors of the church were open, salty tears streamed down Anthony's face.

"Ain't our Jesus sweet?" a lady with a large purple hat dipping over her face shouted from the back row. She stomped both her feet on the padded carpet before jumping out of her seat and wiping the tears from her own eyes.

"Yes, He is, my sister," Anthony soberly responded. But only he and Jesus knew exactly why he was crying.

Pastor Green studied Anthony from where he stood at

the far edge of the pulpit. His thumb and forefinger rested on his chin as a wrinkle settled in his forehead. "Father, Father," he prayed softly.

"It's time for the benediction, church," Anthony said with outstretched hands.

"Hallelujah!" a woman shouted. Tyreeka Oliver turned around to peek over the pew once again. "Bless Jesus!" the woman behind her moaned.

Terri Murdock drummed her fingers on the passenger seat of her old Mercedes-Benz. She dropped her head into her hands with a heavy sigh as she noted the growing crowd of exiting parishioners surrounding her husband. The church door was only twenty-five feet away from where she sat waiting in the car, but it had already taken him fifteen minutes to travel only three of those feet.

"You preached today, boy," she overheard Deacon Ellis encouraging Anthony.

Terri rolled her eyes. She did not know when or if she would ever get used to this preaching thing. It was not that she minded the good-church-boy image. If anything, his spirituality, along with his clean-cut features and promising career, of course, had been the clincher in claiming him as the perfect catch—*her* perfect catch. But she had never expected it to get this far.

"Girl, you know this preaching business won't last long," Cherisse, her best friend and confidante, would continually assure her, twirling one of her long neat braids between two fingers. "Anthony's too proud and pretty of a man to *really* believe that this is what God told him to do.

He'll be calling Shaw Enterprises any day now, begging for his old job back. It's just a phase he'll grow out of real quick when he's ready to buy a new Versace suit."

Terri wholeheartedly believed that her friend was right. But six months had passed and Anthony still seemed content with his new job at a small business firm where he was earning less than a quarter of his former near-six-figure income. And he had just recently registered to take even more classes at the local Bible college.

Terri glanced down at her diamond-studded platinum watch and let out an exaggerated sigh. *It's almost one-thirty! I hope Anthony hurries up.* She turned her eyes toward him, hoping to catch his attention, thinking that maybe he would see the boredom on her face and hurry to the car.

"My, my, my, what a word!" Mother Howard embraced Anthony. Terri dropped her head back on the car seat.

"How much longer is this going to last?' she mumbled, checking her watch again. When she finally heard footsteps approaching, she closed her eyes, hoping that Anthony would think she was tired and not stop to talk to anyone else as they pulled away from the parking lot. She sat there for a moment with her eyes closed, listening to each approaching step on the gravel lot, waiting for the driver's-side door to open. When the footsteps stopped and the door did not budge, she slowly peeked open one eye to discover Sister Kellye Porter's face smiling at her through the passenger window.

"Sister Murdock," the sixty-something-year-old wife of the assistant pastor chirped through the glass, "roll down this window so I can talk to you, honey."

The trill of Sister Porter's voice matched the pleasantness on her face. Terri groaned inside but put on her best smile while holding down the power-window button.

"How have you been, dear?" Sister Porter still smiled, a slight gap in her teeth showing through her broad grin. Her round face seemed to bounce with every word she said, causing the gray-streaked, tight curls cluttering her head to spring with every syllable.

"I've been just blessed," Terri said in a singsong voice to match Sister Porter's. The older lady's head still nodded, her smile still widening. "How is Minister Porter feeling these days?" Terri asked politely.

"Oh, our God is working, child. Bernard will be out of that sickbed and back to the work of the Lord any day now, praise Him. Satan will not keep my husband down." Sister Porter was still nodding, still smiling.

"Mmmmm." Terri joined in the nod, looking away, looking for Anthony.

"Honey, I'm not going to hold you long," Sister Porter sweetly chirped. "I've been thinking about you, that's all. I still want you to come over my house some time. I'll call you with my address. Maybe one day we can get together for lunch or bake some cookies and talk, you know, ministers' wives' talk and such."

"That's an idea." Terri smiled. *Anthony, where are you?* she yelled in her mind.

"You remind me so much of myself in my twenties." Sister Porter grinned. Terri managed to stifle a laugh. What on earth could they possibly have in common, she wondered as she quickly studied Sister Porter's plump frame from head to toe. Her red polyester suit screamed against the black-and-gold-striped ruffled blouse and black-and-white-checked pumps she wore. She smelled of Jean Naté and decorative soap.

"Yes, dear, we've got to get together one day while you're still free," Sister Porter continued. "Once you start having babies, it will be a different story," she said with a wink.

This time Terri could not hide her groan. She was sick of people asking her when she was going to "give that nice preacher" a baby.

"Aw, honey, I don't mean to upset you. Children are a gift from the Lord, and in His time, they will come." Sister Porter patted Terri's shoulder.

There was an uncomfortable break in the conversation. Terri twiddled her thumbs for a few moments while Sister Porter, still smiling, sighed a couple of times.

"Amen," Terri exhaled, for lack of anything better to say. Mercifully, Anthony was finally coming to the car. His shoulders slumped as he kicked at the gravel.

"Well, I'll be giving you a call soon, dear heart." Sister Porter was leaving. "Have a blessed evening."

"You do the same, and give my regards to Minister Porter."

As soon as Sister Porter's back was turned, Terri dropped her smile. "Bake some cookies?" she muttered. "Who do I look like, Betty Crocker?"

"Did you say something?" Anthony plopped into the driver's seat. He barely looked up at his wife.

"Nothing. Let's go home." Terri pressed a silver-painted fingernail on the power-window button. She collapsed back in her seat as the window whisked up with a thud.

～

It was only mid-September, but a biting draft was already finding its way up Anthony's coat sleeves and pant legs as he sat quietly behind the steering wheel. He usually enjoyed the drive home from church, especially in the fall when he purposely took the back roads littered with red, gold, and yellow leaves falling from the unending rows of trees.

But today the winding roads reminded him too much of every dizzying curve and zigzag his life seemed to be taking. The smell of burning leaves suffocated his nostrils as he turned back onto the beltway, joining the frenzy of motorists whizzing by familiar green-and-white traffic signs.

"Oh look, they've almost finished that Stonymill light rail extension," Terri said, pointing to a passing construction site. "I don't see why there was such a big fuss about building it."

Anthony swallowed hard but said nothing.

"I heard Shaw Enterprises has an extensive marketing campaign going on for that new station," Terri stated matter-of-factly. "Imagine all the profits they're raking in from that contract," she added, glancing at her husband.

Anthony was absorbed in his own thoughts, only half listening. Terri changed the subject. She began discussing her plans for the coming week, which included an important meeting with a client the next day. If the deal proved successful she would become a partner in the interior design firm for which she worked.

Anthony caught a word here and there of her one-way conversation, but his thoughts began focusing on his morning message. He wondered if anyone had noticed his awkwardness. The sermon rolled through his mind like a videotape.

He remembered feeling like he could not continue—*should not* continue. But he had. And in the midst of the crowd of greeters who praised him after service, he had not been able to give Pastor Green the letter.

The letter! Where was it? He panicked. Terri had grabbed his Bible and notes from him in her usual attempt to rush him out of the church. He could see his Bible now, peeking out of her large leather tote bag. *What if the letter falls out? Is it still hidden in the pages?* Anthony loosened his already limp necktie as he rounded a swerving exit. Terri could not see that letter under any circumstances. Not yet, anyway.

"You're not even listening to me, are you?" Terri suddenly interrupted his thoughts.

"Of course I am, baby. I'm sure the Hendricks Group will love the hanging-gardens theme for their new restaurant venture." Anthony tried to keep his voice light and airy.

"The Hendricks Group? I was talking about my meeting tomorrow with Reginald Savant!" Terri snarled. "This is the most important account I've had in my career and you're not even paying attention! If I can secure the design plans for this hotel deal, do you know what that will mean for us? For *me?*"

"Baby, I—"

"Don't *baby* me," Terri hurled, pushing his offered hand aside. "*Somebody* in this marriage needs to be taking their career seriously! Am I wrong?"

Anthony searched for words, surprised that she was giving him a chance to respond. Her arms were crossed, her eyes glued on his profile, waiting. But as had become the custom over the past few months, nothing but a sigh spoke for him. *What's wrong with me?* It seemed like six lifetimes and not six months ago when he was applauded for his quick speech in important business meetings and deals. He'd had an answer for everyone and everything back then. But these days he could barely look his wife in the eyes.

"Well?" The window was rapidly closing.

Anthony concentrated on the road before him, thankful that the traffic lights were becoming fewer and the houses more spaced out. They would be on their street soon.

"Do you really think God is going to tell a man to leave a great job?" Terri was just starting. "Seriously, it's one thing to feel the need to preach, but does that mean sacrificing everything you ever worked for? You were a commanding businessman, a wonderful black-man success story! You were an ebony king with power! And what are you now? It makes more sense to me that God would want you to be a mover and a shaker in this world and not an old broke country preacher!" Her hands were clutched together so tightly that her knuckles were white.

"Terri! You just don't understand!" Anthony felt the steam leaving him before he even got started. "God does want me to be a mover and a shaker, but not in the way you think." He hoped Terri hadn't caught the question mark in his voice as they rounded a sharp corner. He thought again about the letter and fell silent.

Terri glared at Anthony and threw up her hands. "You're hopeless. You have lost your mind. What am I supposed to do while you try out this preaching thing? Did you ever even think about me?" she demanded, her eyes narrow slits. "You only think about yourself!"

"Terri, baby, this isn't about me or you. This is about what God wants." Anthony did his best to sound confident, but his own concerns nagged his conscience.

They were pulling into their driveway. Anthony stared at the massive pillars along the porch of their home, the two-car garage, and the elaborate marble fountain that Terri had insisted on when she'd picked out the house in a real-estate brochure six months before. She had wanted their residence to resemble a contemporary Mediterranean palace. At the time he had been excited to entertain business partners and clients in the extravagant and ornate estate. Now he just simply wanted a house to come home to.

He sat a moment in the car as Terri slammed her door shut and listened as her high heels punched the landscaped walkway. When she disappeared through the front door, he lowered his head into his hands and rubbed his temples. *I've got to get my Bible out of her bag before she does,* he reminded himself. *I can't take any chances.*

"Sunday dinner just ain't what it used to be." Anthony looked down at his frozen dinner entrée. For a quick second, he envisioned his Great-Aunt Rosa sitting in one of her high-backed cherrywood chairs, laughing in that loud, husky voice of hers, then gulping down her famous stewed tomatoes.

He could picture his mother and older cousin Patrice-with-the-big-out-of-date-afro seated next to her, arguing over whose turn it was to check on the children, making sure they weren't tearing up the basement or the backyard. And then there was Harold, Anthony's stepfather, the only father he ever really knew, sitting in that burgundy armchair smoking his cigarettes, much to Aunt Rosa's disapproval. "Addin' another flame to your destiny, I see," she would say to him.

Anthony smiled at the memories of Sundays past while sitting alone in his study, chewing reluctantly on a tasteless turkey breast. Terri had just left to meet her longtime friend Cherisse for dinner, as had become her custom for the past several weeks. Although he was not particularly fond of Cherisse, he welcomed the couple of hours he would have to himself.

"Just fifteen minutes of normalcy, Lord. That's all I'm asking for," Anthony mumbled between bites of rubbery peas. *What a prayer,* he laughed to himself.

But then another thought sobered him as he eyed a ragged folder sticking out of the papers on his desk. *How long is this going to last?* he wondered. The large black letters printed on the tab of the folder jabbed his conscience like a steak knife. He shook his head in shame, wanting to be rid of the burden, wondering how he'd even gotten through the sermon earlier that day. He thought about Terri and the words she'd said after morning service.

"An old broke country preacher," he mumbled. "Preacher," he repeated quietly, catching a glimpse of himself in a large mirror across the room.

Following their spat in the car, the tension between the two had only gripped them more tightly when they arrived home. Terri had gone straight to her private sitting area to make several phone calls to her friends. Anthony was sure that he heard his name more than once in her whispered conversations.

But he was by himself now. Anthony was determined to let go of the gnawing frustration he felt. He was especially relieved to see that Terri had left her tote bag with his Bible still inside in her sitting room. He decided to finish eating before retrieving the letter. *I've got to get that letter to Pastor Green as soon as possible,* he reminded himself, his eyes falling on the ragged folder again.

When he finished clearing his plate he headed to his planned destination, stopping only once to water some dying plants sitting near the deck. He walked quickly through the hallways, haunted by his echoing footsteps on the golden beige ceramic floor.

When he reached the french doors sealing off Terri's sitting room, he paused for a second. Terri regarded this area as her own personal sanctuary. He had only been in there twice, both times to help Terri move some furniture. He opened the doors, almost expecting an alarm to go off, laughing at himself when none did.

Nearly everything in the room was a shade of orange, from the heavy damask curtains to the oversized leather lounger and the sculptured floor lamp with furry-looking fringes dangling from its shade. Abstract artwork and a collection of ceramic tigers decorated the peach-painted walls and tables. The tamest item in the room was an oblong animal-print rug lying in the middle of the floor.

He picked up a jewel-encrusted picture frame sitting on an end table and studied the lone figure smiling back at him. It was a portrait of Terri, taken shortly after they began dating five years ago, given to him from her as an engagement gift a year later.

"I'm going to make your life so rich," she'd murmured in his ear as she handed him the photograph encased in the two-hundred-fifty-dollar onyx-and-silver frame. Aunt Rosa must have heard her words because she'd been quick with a remark about a man being rich whose treasure was the Lord.

"And it wouldn't do a woman bad to be rich in Him also," she said, smacking her lips on some smoked salmon at their engagement party. Anthony recalled how her comment had frozen the entire room for a second. He had not missed the quiet nods and concerned faces that surrounded her words. He had not missed them, but he chose to ignore them. They did not know Terri like he did, he had assured himself. A woman of intelligence, self-motivated, who was eager to attend Sunday morning service with him during those pre-marriage days, he was sure she had the makings of an excellent wife.

Anthony ran his fingers along the eight-by-ten photo, studying Terri's slender five-foot-three frame, remembering how easy it was to fall for her smile, the way her hips bounced with her quick steps, the silky, long relaxed curls that flowed past her shoulders back then. She had the kind of beauty that left him forgetting to breathe. He was holding his breath at that moment.

This woman is so fine, he thought to himself, shaking his head.

But does she know Me? The thought caught him off guard.

It was always the same question. Anthony put the picture back down on the table. He only wanted to answer one question right then: *Where is the letter?*

Anthony sat down on the upholstered bench where Terri had tossed her bag. He felt a wave of relief as he took out his Bible and began flipping through the thin gold-trimmed pages. But as he kept flipping and no white envelope surfaced, an alarm went off somewhere between his heart and his stomach.

"No! Oh, no!" Anthony groaned as he checked and re-checked to make sure he was not missing it. He turned the Bible upside down and emptied the contents of Terri's bag onto the floor. He searched the rest of her sitting room, but the truth remained. The letter was nowhere to be found.

"Lord Jesus, what do I do?" Anthony cried while rubbing his temples. "Forget the letter," he told himself while picking up the telephone. He dialed and hung up twice before letting the receiving end ring.

"Praise the Lord," a kind, assuring voice answered.

"P-p-pastor Green?" Anthony stammered.

"Anthony, is that you? Is everything all right?" Pastor Green sounded concerned.

"Yes, yes." Anthony paused. "Well, no. I mean, I—I need to talk to you."

Anthony paused again. *I'm not ready for this, not yet,* he contemplated. Pastor Green voiced further concern.

"Anthony, you have been coming into my mind lately. I have been praying for you. Is everything okay?"

"Pastor Green, if you are available, I would like to meet with you sometime tomorrow. There's something you need to know."

They made plans to meet at the church the next evening. Before hanging up, Pastor Green encouraged Anthony.

"You know there is nothing happening in your life that Jesus can't handle. He already knows the beginning and the end. Just stay with Him, Anthony. Just stay with Him."

Anthony hung up the phone and hit the wall with his hand.

"Lord, please don't let Terri find that letter! Please, Lord!"

Chapter 2

The dining area at the Westcott Room in the Quadrangle Towers was already filling with patrons hoping to avoid the Monday lunch rush. Terri was glad that she had arrived forty-five minutes prior to her 11:30 appointment with Reginald Savant. She had skillfully chosen a quiet booth overlooking a garden courtyard her firm had helped design.

She opened her briefcase for a last-minute study of her presentation. Terri was sure that an air of confidence, capability, and creativity would lead to success. Raylin and Blake Interiors was depending on her not to let Reginald leave without signing the contract.

Terri had spoken only with his personal assistant prior to this meeting and never directly to him. A positive and memorable first impression was first on her agenda for this career-defining meeting. She smoothed down the sides of her favorite business outfit, a navy blue suit with a matching crepe scarf. With its subtle plunging neckline and hem that dangerously skimmed her lower thighs, she had always found success when she wore this form-flattering ensemble. She was just reclosing her small compact when she heard the maître d' approaching the table.

"Here's your party, Mr. Savant."

"Thanks, Steve," a silky bass voice answered.

"Mrs. Murdock," the voice continued, "a pleasure to finally meet you. My assistant has advised me that you have been most professional and courteous, and, may I add, very dedicated to our project needs."

Terri noted the full-length lambskin leather coat. She admired the three-piece double-breasted silk Italian suit. She observed the diamond cuff links sparkling above his extended manicured hands and she listened to how his voice nearly sang the words he said. And then he sat down.

"Mr. Savant," Terri began while slowly easing her right hand from his tight grip, "I want to assure you that our firm is committed to helping make your hotel the standard of the industry. We have several ideas and themes for you to consider, based on the projected budget and proposal your assistant sent to us."

"And Mrs. Murdock, I assure *you* that whatever ideas you personally think will work"—Reginald smiled deliciously—"I will strongly consider. Your reputation as a brilliant designer precedes you."

Reginald paused as a waiter put a bread basket and salad bowls in front of them. He took a forkful of lettuce before continuing.

"A woman of your technical and creative caliber on my team is bound to bring the clever taste and luxurious appointments I desire for the Empress Hotel. I've seen your

work at the Palisades Diner." Reginald paused again, his
smile melting into his chocolate brown skin. "Lovely.
Simply lovely."

"I see you've done your research." Terri was pleased.

"Of course. I seek only the best for my projects. The
Empress Hotel is just the beginning of my dream." Reginald put down his fork. "Black America has been disillu-
sioned for too long. We need to see our own succeeding,
and entrepreneurship is the key. Imagine, an international
chain of five-star hotels, black owned and black operated." He looked up as he spoke, his hands animating each
word.

"A man of vision. I like that." Terri's smile deepened.

"So where do we sign? Let's get this business stuff out of
the way so we can enjoy our lunch." Reginald pulled a pen
out of his briefcase.

She saw no need to disagree. Terri presented the forms
and the deal was done. Before the second course was
served, Mr. Savant answered a call on his cell phone.

"I do apologize, Mrs. Murdock, but I must cut our lunch
short." Reginald reached for his coat. "Here's my card.
Call me so we can further discuss the plans."

He scribbled something on the back of the card.

"And here's a number where you can reach me anytime
you want. Day or night." And with a wink, Mr. Reginald
Savant was gone.

"Raylin, Blake, and *Murdock* Interiors," Terri mumbled
gleefully to herself. She studied Reginald Savant's business
card for a second or two before she placed it in her briefcase.

"Definitely a man of vision." A sugary smile lingered
on her lips as she finished her lunch and asked for the
check.

~

The newspaper rattled loudly before he slammed it down on the desk.

"Ain't a good job nowhere," Marvin Tucker mumbled as he leaned back in the squeaky chair. He crossed his lanky arms behind his head. "I've got to find me a real job with real money like you *once* had so I can get out of this dump. Man, what time is it? I'm ready to go!"

"Marvin, we just got back from lunch." Anthony chuckled at his office mate. He pretended to skim the business section of the ruffled paper to hide the wince that shot through him.

Like you once had . . .

"Do you plan on getting any work done today?" Anthony looked back up with a hard swallow. "We still have to develop some advertising ideas for Priscilla Coates's new pet-care business. Here, let me show you some slogans I came up with." He reached for a folder.

Marvin laughed. "Brother, you take everything so seriously. I mean, look at you, sittin' there in your pin-stripe suit and your alligator-skin shoes, trying to come up with some jingle to sell pooper-scoopers."

"Hey man"—Anthony smiled—"the Word says do all things as unto the Lord. He wants excellence. That's what I'm trying to give Him." Anthony's tone sobered as he dropped his eyes. *I'm trying.* The words pierced him. He was not ready to expose his real thoughts and feelings surrounding his current job to Marvin—or to anyone else, for that matter.

"Save the sermon for Sunday, preacher boy." Marvin smirked. "Don't worry, one day I'm going to get right with the Man Upstairs. As soon as I retire my player's uniform, I'm going to put on a choir robe." Marvin kept laughing. "Those singing church sisters can convert me *any* day."

Anthony shook his head.

"Well look"—Marvin reached for his jacket—"I'm going to head back out to the Solomon Grill. You saw how that waitress was looking at me. If anybody asks, just tell them I had an unfinished business deal to attend to." Marvin buttoned his coat.

Anthony looked up from the papers on his desk, a frown tugging at the corners of his mouth. "You're forgetting about the staff meeting we have with Mr. Haberstick in half an hour. You remember what happened the last time you missed a staff meeting?"

"Let's see"—Marvin playfully stroked his goatee—"go see the cutie around the corner? Or old man Haberstick?" Marvin snickered as he stepped out of their office. "I'm not asking you to lie for me. I'm just asking you to be creative."

"Lies, lies, lies," Anthony drummed his pencil on his daily planner. Pastor Green would be waiting for him at the church later that day. The thought sent Anthony's stomach twirling in knots.

"Mr. Murdock." Anthony looked up to see Diane, Mr. Haberstick's assistant, standing in the narrow doorway. "I didn't mean to startle you. I wanted to let you know that today's staff meeting has been cancelled. Mr. Haberstick does, however, want to meet with you sometime tomorrow."

"Thanks, Ms. Martin." Anthony watched as she disappeared into the quiet hallway. The silence was broken every now and then by a quick tapping on a computer keyboard or the unhurried footsteps of a fellow associate.

"A meeting with the big boss can mean only one of two things," Anthony said to himself, getting up to look out the office window. "More work," he sighed, "or no more work at all."

Anthony studied the back of a neighboring warehouse on the other side of the windowpane. Several Dumpsters sat haphazardly around the perimeter. The downtown-skyline view from his former thirty-second-floor executive suite at Shaw Enterprises floated briefly into his memory.

He stood idle a few seconds more, looking around the cramped office. Files, papers, boxes, and computer disks were strewn about, especially on and around Marvin's desk. Anthony sank back down in his chair and spun it around to face a small conference table. In his right hand was the engraved platinum writing pen he had carefully selected to match his former Shaw Enterprises office-suite furnishings. He wiped a smudge off the gold initials before focusing back on his present work.

"I've got to finish on time today," he mumbled as he reached for a stack of papers, the knots in his stomach tightening.

A chilly wind stirred as Anthony left his job at Haberstick Associates promptly at four-thirty. He had an hour and a half before his meeting with Pastor Green, giving him enough time to run home for a quick snack and a shower.

"Good night, Anthony." Mr. Haberstick, the company president, left the office behind him. "Look's like a storm is coming," the older businessman noted. The two walked across the parking lot in offbeat steps as Mr. Haberstick continued. "Diane informed you of my desire to meet with you tomorrow?" Surprisingly, Mr. Haberstick's soft, warbling voice commanded authority.

Anthony nodded.

"Good." Mr. Haberstick smiled. "I have a special account that I want you to handle." He paused for a second before continuing. "I'm sure with all of your past experience this will be easy for you. I will give you more details tomorrow."

Something in Mr. Haberstick's tone sent a tiny shiver through Anthony. He looked at the aging man, his back slightly humped, the sparse gray hairs on his head rippling in the brisk breeze.

"I'm sure you've probably grown bored with the small-scale projects we've been undertaking, but don't worry. There's something in the works that's more on your level. Of all our staff, I am certain *you* will appreciate this opportunity."

The way he stared at Anthony, the way he singled him out, Anthony felt something was wrong. The older man was getting into his car when his wrinkled cheeks stretched into a smirk. Anthony began feeling queasy. *Did he know?*

"I would prefer that you do not discuss this project with any of your colleagues. Based on your past performance at Shaw Enterprises, I'm sure that you *will* accept this challenge."

Mr. Haberstick's voice became more biting with each word. Anthony froze.

"Oh, there is no need for alarm, Mr. Murdock. I would never ask you to do anything that you weren't capable of doing. This project is right up your alley." Mr. Haberstick stopped smiling, his voice barely above a whisper as his eyes bored into Anthony's. "I know about Stonymill, but don't worry. Your secret is safe with me, Reverend."

Anthony watched Mr. Haberstick's car pull away before getting into his BMW. He wiped a finger through the growing layer of dust on the dashboard, barely remembering the obsessive enthusiasm he'd had for keeping the car clean when he'd first purchased it in the spring.

"What's the point?" he whispered, feeling dusty and dirty inside and out. "What kind of witness am I? How did I let it get this far?" Anthony rested his head on the steering wheel. "I'm sorry, Lord! I'm so sorry!"

As he wrung his hands, he realized something else was bothering him. *How did Mr. Haberstick know?*

~

Cherisse Landrick stood over one of the burgundy pillar candles and let the spicy aroma fill her nostrils.

"Mmm, girl, this is perfect." A mischievous smile spread across her face as she stepped back to inspect her work. Terri, sitting on the edge of a loveseat, agreed.

"Cherisse, you have outdone yourself," she said, admiring the warm glow filling the living room. Candles of all shapes and sizes and in all shades of red were skillfully placed on the side and coffee tables and in wrought-iron sconces on the walls.

"Moving the dinner out in front of the fireplace was a great idea," Terri continued, gazing at the bewitching flames. "You really think this will work?" She turned to her friend. Cherisse finished rubbing some spots off the stemware before she sat down next to Terri.

"Trust me," Cherisse replied. "When Anthony gets a

bite of this caviar and a sip of this champagne, he'll re-member just how good success tastes." Her smile deep-ened. "Girl, I'm so proud of you! I remember in college you dreamed of just getting an internship at Raylin and Blake Interiors. Now, look at you. I can't believe you are a partner!" The two shared a laugh and a hug.

Cherisse pushed back her braids as a smirk returned to her honey-brown face. "When Anthony finds out about your day, he's bound to get jealous. You'll see. He will be trying to find a job that outdoes yours, if that's possible. You know how men are."

Terri nodded, although she secretly questioned whether Anthony would really quit preaching and begin focusing his time and energy on making some real money.

"I don't think I'll ever understand why he left Shaw Enterprises." Terri shook her head. "I mean, I know the hours and trips were unending, but to give all that up just to be able to preach at that small-time country church?" Terri got up to check the filet mignon and the rest of the gourmet meal. "I keep telling you that you've got to come see this place, girl. Half of the people there seem like they've never read any other book but the Bible. They don't understand that there's more to life than religion. And then they're so loud and *long* about it. It makes no sense to me that Anthony would keep going to such a backward place."

"Well, girlfriend." Cherisse grinned. "You work your magic tonight and that man of yours will get it together."

"What would I do without you?" Terri smiled again. She and Cherisse had been best friends since their freshman year of college, when they were paired together as roommates. It still amazed Terri how resourceful and creative Cherisse could be, especially when it came to dealing with the opposite sex. As inventive as Cherisse was, though, it surprised Terri that she never seemed able to keep a man longer than three months.

"Everything's just about ready," Cherisse stated while rearranging some flowers on a small table in front of the marble fireplace. "You've got the right lighting, the right music, the right kind of meal for tonight's agenda." Cherisse placed a bottle of vintage wine in a sterling silver ice bucket. "Just remember, this dinner for two is all about making him envious of the success you're celebrating. Everything you say and do should remind him of what he is currently lacking."

"Cherisse, you're a genius. I hope this works." Terri stared at the bottle of wine. Anthony had not had a drink in over a year and a half.

"Of course this will work, girl. Have I ever steered you wrong?" The two laughed again. "Call me tomorrow with the details." Cherisse reached for her coat.

"You don't have to leave just yet. Anthony doesn't get home from work until after six-thirty."

But as Terri spoke keys rattled in the front door. Terri and Cherisse turned to face a troubled-looking Anthony. He stood momentarily in the foyer, his overcoat and scarf still in place, before he slowly turned and walked toward his study. Terri and Cherisse looked at each other, puzzled by his silence and the worry lines in his face.

"Bad day at the office, maybe," Cherisse whispered before grinning again. "Perfect time to talk some sense into him." She headed for the door. "Work it, girl," she said, snapping a finger as she exited. She peeked her head back through the doorway. "And call me when it's all over."

~

Anthony grabbed a ragged folder hidden in his desk. He fumbled through some old receipts and placed a few in his briefcase. Finally, he laid his Bible on top of the stack of papers and closed and locked the leather attaché case. He knew Pastor Green was already waiting for him at the church.

Fear and relief battled within him. Anthony knew what he had to do. He would finally be taking a step to shake this burden by talking with Pastor Green. But he still had to meet with Mr. Haberstick the next day. *Lord, only You know what will happen next.*

The study door crashed open.

"You could have at least asked me about my day." Terri fumed.

"Baby, I'm sorry. I've got a lot on my mind. But you're right. I should have at least said hello." *I can't deal with this right now.* Anthony inwardly sighed.

Terri glared at him a few seconds longer before forcing a smile onto her face. "Anyway, I've prepared a special celebration dinner for the two of us."

"Celebration? A special dinner?" Anthony blinked a couple of times. "You did it, huh? You made partner. Raylin, Blake, and Murdock Interiors." Anthony looked down at his briefcase.

"You still have your coat on. Were you going some-where?" Terri's smile faded.

"Well, uh—I," Anthony stammered. "I did have a—uh—meeting at church. Didn't I see Cherisse here?"

Terri crossed her arms. "Cherisse just left. What meeting do you have at church? I don't remember any an-nouncements yesterday about any meetings tonight."

"It's a special meeting. Pastor Green and I have to meet to talk about—well, things and, uh, church stuff." Anthony looked back down at his briefcase.

"Just this once," Terri whispered as tears filled her eyes. "Just this once, can't you help me celebrate my success? This is a big day for me."

Anthony blew out a long sigh and put his briefcase under his desk. He slowly took off his coat and threw it on the back of a leather armchair. He walked to where Terri stood in the doorway and took both of her hands in his.

"Terri, I am so proud of you. I know that you have worked hard to be named a partner at your design firm, and now your dream has come true. I would be honored to spend this evening celebrating you." Anthony moved both of his hands to her face and wiped a single tear away with his thumb before planting a light kiss on her forehead. "Give me one moment to call Pastor Green. I need to reschedule our meeting."

Terri grinned from ear to ear. "Tonight we celebrate my success. Just think, we could be celebrating your success soon, right?"

"Don't worry about me, baby. Right now, I'm happy for you. Let's just celebrate you." Terri looked up at him. His smile was genuine. As she fell into his embrace, she thought of kicking Cherisse. Her plan was not working.

Pastor Green hung up the phone and rubbed his chin. He knew something was going on with Anthony, because the young man's name had been popping up in his mind for prayer for quite some time. And that petite wife of his, Pastor Green was sure, had something to do with Anthony calling to cancel their meeting. Pastor Green had known she was not too fond of Second Baptist Church the first Sunday Anthony had brought her there.

"There's something about her that doesn't rest with my spirit," the pastor murmured, rubbing his balding head, remembering the look on her face the night Anthony preached his first sermon. "Lord, that boy's got a heart after You. He wants to be right and do right. He seems like he wants to follow You, but his judgment seems to be a little off at times."

Pastor Green looked up, his eyes pleading to the heavens. "Father, I don't know what's going on in that household, or with Anthony, but You do. Whatever it is, Lord, bring peace and order. Let Your will and purposes be done. Brother Anthony has so much potential to shake things up for Your Kingdom. Help him, Lord Jesus, and help his wife. Do what You've got to do to make things right, whatever it takes. Once again, I commit those two into Your hands. In Jesus' name I pray, Amen."

Pastor Green was picking up a roast beef sandwich and reading a thank-you card from a sick congregant when he heard the church doorbell buzz. He quickly gulped down his evening meal, grateful for the Thermos of warm tea his wife had included in the small sack. He was still chewing when he opened the door. A short, burly man in a dark suit entered the vestibule. He took off a pair of shades revealing sharp blue eyes under bushy black eyebrows.

"Pastor Edward Green?" the stranger inquired.

"Yes?" The old pastor finished swallowing.

"My name is Kent Cassell. I'm a detective with the local sheriff's department, assisting with a case headed up by the FBI." Kent flashed a shiny badge while scanning the foyer. "Do you have a moment? I need to talk to you about one of your parishioners, Anthony Murdock."

Pastor Green stood speechless in the evening sunlight trickling through the stained-glass windows.

Anthony tapped a finger along with the soulful ballad playing on the stereo. He studied Terri, who was taking a slow sip from a long-stemmed goblet.

"I always knew that you would succeed at Raylin and Blake—and *Murdock*—Interiors." He smiled.

Terri laughed nervously, searching for something cutting to say, wanting to make Anthony jealous. She looked into his deep brown eyes, but there was too much pride in them to humble him.

"Well," she finally muttered, her eyes dropping to the cold meat on her plate, "I guess this is what the good life is all about, enjoying success." She continued picking at her food, angry and bored with the wasted effort.

Anthony stared at her curiously, wondering if he had made the right decision to reschedule his meeting with Pastor Green. He knew Pastor Green was still at the church. When he'd called to cancel their meeting, Pastor Green had stated that he would be in his study for a few more hours. *Maybe if we finish this dinner soon I'll be able to catch him before he goes home*, Anthony pondered. *It doesn't look like Terri is up to much more celebration.*

A new song droned out of the stereo. The soft drumbeat brought Anthony to his feet. "Can I have this dance?" He reached for Terri's hand. She pulled back and threw her embroidered napkin on the small table.

"Look," she sighed. "I'm tired and I know you originally had other plans for the evening." She plastered a smile onto her face. "Why don't you go and do whatever you were going to do and we can finish this celebration another time."

Anthony tried not to look too eager to leave as he put on his coat and grabbed his briefcase. He barely noticed Terri on the telephone as he closed the front door behind him.

"Cherisse, what's Plan B?"

The crisp fall day had given way to a bitter cold evening. Remnants of a passing rain shower had left behind the aroma of wet, decaying leaves. Anthony turned off the car radio and rolled down his window, listening only to the swish of passing cars over the slick suburban streets and the rampage of his own thoughts. He rehearsed and restructured and rehearsed again in his mind what he would say to Pastor Green. There was no way to pretty up the confession or avoid its consequences.

He thought of Mr. Haberstick and knew that tonight was just the beginning, the first step. He would need to tap into a reservoir of courage he was unsure he had. And that pool of courage would have to last for the coming weeks, maybe months. He thought of Terri. How would she be affected? *I should have thought about all of this six months ago. . . .*

By the time he neared the church parking lot, the sun had completely disappeared into the western horizon. He wondered at the headlights pulling out of the small gravel lot. He did not recall Pastor Green saying he had another meeting tonight. Plus, the dark Crown Victoria did not look familiar. "Must be a visiting clergy friend," Anthony muttered to himself.

Anthony was glad to see both the vestibule and the

basement lights on in the church. It did not look like Pastor Green planned on leaving anytime soon. He stomped down the narrow, red-carpeted steps. When he knocked on the slightly opened oak door of the pastor's study, he was surprised to see Pastor Green looking startled in his chair.

"Anthony!" he exclaimed. "I did not hear you come in. I was just think—" He stopped abruptly, blinking and sighing. "We really need to talk," he continued, concern in his eyes. "Come in." He motioned toward a couch. "Have a seat. Please tell me, what is going on with you these days?"

Anthony sat down on the green sofa. He placed his briefcase on the floor beside his feet. "I hope I'm not disturbing you. I saw another car leaving as I came. Did you have any other meetings planned this evening?"

"Oh no, nothing planned. But I'm glad you have come. I did just have a visitor. His name was Kent Cassell, a detective from the sheriff's office."

Anthony raised an eyebrow. "A detective? Is everything okay?"

"I'm not sure. He asked about you, Anthony."

Anthony felt his heart skip a beat as Pastor Green continued. "He wanted to know how much you had contributed to the fund for the new Sunday school classroom wing. I'm not sure what this is all about, but I know that God is still in control."

Anthony swallowed hard. "Pastor Green," he began, "the reason I wanted to talk to you—needed to talk to you—was to let you know that I'm . . ." Anthony paused and sighed before continuing. "I want to step down from my ministerial duties."

Pastor Green leaned back in his desk chair, his eyes never leaving Anthony's.

"I want to step down," Anthony continued, "at least for now, for a little while, until I finish dealing with a situation that I brought upon myself."

"A situation?" Pastor Green questioned.

"Yes, I—" Anthony was not sure where to begin. "See, six months ago, as you know, I was working for the marketing firm of Shaw Enterprises. I was their senior marketing director and I oversaw every project that came through our door. I made the majority of the hard decisions when it came down to what projects and accounts we would undertake. My colleagues and supervisors respected my choices and, as a result, gave me a lot of leeway. They trusted me to always keep the interests of the company first, above everything else."

Pastor Green nodded. "I knew that you had a powerful and influential position at Shaw. When you resigned, I assumed it was because you were seeking God's direction for your life. I thought maybe God was telling you to leave so you could devote more of your time and energy to His calling for you to preach. I marveled at the speed with which you left your employer, thinking that you were fervently taking a giant leap of faith to fulfill what God Himself had impressed upon your heart. Was there another reason why you left?" Pastor Green's hands were clasped together as if in prayer.

Anthony sat staring at the floor. "When I initially accepted the call to preach last year, God told me that I was going to have to make hard choices, far more difficult than any I had made before at Shaw. I didn't realize then the test that was coming." Anthony drew his eyes slowly back to the pastor's. "You know how serious I've been about being successful."

"There's nothing wrong with having money or status as long as we realize we are *stewards* of whatever He gives us. Everything we have belongs to Him." Pastor Green nodded. "God has already *placed* us in a high status, a heavenly ranking, a position of authority in His Kingdom that comes with being born again. And He gives us blessings—both material *and* spiritual—so that we can add to His Kingdom and enjoy His abundance. Money and status are things God can give us to use for Himself."

Pastor Green leaned forward in his chair. "But they are only of value for His Kingdom when we have the right perspective. That is, God and His purposes and not ours must come first."

"You're right, Pastor," Anthony stated. "I guess that's where I've fallen. Remember that last sermon Minister Porter preached before the cancer really took its hold, the sermon he gave on Luke chapter eighteen, verses eighteen through twenty-seven?"

"I remember." Pastor Green closed his eyes as he spoke. "That was a powerful message. Bernard really brought to life the rich young ruler who asked Jesus what he had to do to inherit eternal life. He had honored the law and he was a good man by our standards. But when Jesus told him to sell all that he had and give to the poor and follow Him, the scripture says the man was very sorrowful."

"As I would be too." Anthony shook his head, a distant look etched on his baby-faced features. "To tell you the truth, I was relieved when Bernard explained how the issue wasn't getting rid of all of his riches to be saved, but rather, the state of his heart. What was more important to him, following Jesus or keeping his money? Had his money and prestige become a hindrance for him to trust and obey God? I listened to that sermon just like everyone else that Sunday. Said 'Amen,' 'Hallelujah,' even did a little two-step when Bernard gave his final point. Then the Lord flipped the script on me that very week, six months ago. He asked me what would I do with my money and my position when it came down to serving Him."

Anthony's eyes dropped to the floor again and landed on the briefcase next to his feet. "Pastor Green, are you familiar with the new Stonymill light rail expansion that is being constructed?"

"Stonymill? Isn't that the project that was causing a big protest among several local civil- and social-service groups a while back? Something about the construction of the tracks interfering with plans to build a proposed community center, mission, and a substance-abuse treatment center?"

"Yes, Bethany Village is what it was called. It was a radical concept developed by some local businessmen and human-service workers that would transform an entire deserted city block into a haven for the young, the old, the poor, and the abandoned."

"That's right! Bethany Village! How could I forget? I donated a lot of money to that cause. A local charitable group, Citizens' Alliance of Shepherd Hills, initiated it, right?"

"Yes, CASH, for short," Anthony mumbled.

"I never did understand why the politicians changed their support for that worthwhile and crucial project," Pastor Green mused. "Only our good member Councilman Walter Banks stood up against the opponents. I always wondered who talked the city board out of approving the final plans."

"I did." Anthony sat quiet for a moment, watching the confusion grow on Pastor Green's face before continuing. "Councilman Banks has been a friend and a mentor to me since my parents' death, and I'm ashamed to admit that I secretly went against him and all he taught me. When AGS Railroad approached Shaw Enterprises about leading their marketing campaign for the station extension to Stonymill Mall, I initially refused. I knew about Bethany Village, and in my heart I knew that it was a noble and necessary endeavor. CASH had even sought our services, but of course they could not offer the compensation that AGS Railroad could.

"I received pressure from both my company and the executives at AGS not only to accept the marketing campaign but also to lobby at the city and state government levels for its completion. In turn, someone anonymously gave me a total of one-point-five million dollars, some of which I used to 'talk' to a few of the politicians who supported Bethany Village.

"I know it was stupid of me to get involved, but all I could see was dollar signs. I didn't think of the illegality or the immorality of bribery and deceit. I justified it by convincing myself that Bethany Village could be built somewhere else. Of course I knew that the planned site for Bethany Village was the best, if not the only, location for it to be built in this area. I guess I just figured that God could open doors for them elsewhere, and I could use the money to do bigger things for the Kingdom. I even tried to donate some of the bribe money I received to CASH, but of course I didn't feel better."

"Anthony—" Compassion sounded through Pastor Green's voice, but Anthony quickly interrupted.

"Pastor Green," he cried, "do you realize that for the past six months I've been living a lie? When I accepted that bribe, I took on the burden of my life. And rather than giving it back, I passed it on, causing others to fall alongside me. I know that God is not pleased. Every day I wake up afraid that the whole thing is going to get out, that the wrong words will get into the wrong ears, the wrong papers into the wrong hands. Could you imagine if the media got involved? How could I preach? I don't know . . . I can't . . . What do I . . ." Anthony's words faded as he bit hard into his lip, his shoulders shaking. "I wasn't thinking about how everything in my life could be ruined, not to mention the plans for Bethany Village. I'm sorry, God. I'm so sorry."

Pastor Green's reassuring voice never quivered, although a slight question remained in his eyes. "I'm sure that you have gone to God to seek forgiveness. Repentance is more than an apology; it's a complete change in direction." He stood up and walked to where Anthony was seated. He patted a hand on his shoulder before continuing. "And you must seek God's direction for coming clean before the church, the community, and the law. God promises to forgive and cleanse us, but that does not always mean that we avoid the consequences of our faults. But He will give us grace to endure them."

As Pastor Green sat down next to him Anthony regained his composure. "I know what I have to do. I've known for quite some time. Talking to you was the first thing, although it took me this long to do it."

"Do you know where the money originated?"

"No," Anthony admitted with a shaking head. "And that's what disturbs me the most. It was an anonymous donation with careful instructions about how to distribute everything. The more I tried to find out who was behind the funds, the crazier my days at Shaw Enterprises became. That, in part, was why I resigned. I took that job over at Haberstick's as a stand-in until I can get this confusion sorted out. Then I'll get back to making some real dough somewhere else without all the unnecessary baggage. My gut was telling me that I'd gotten involved in something much deeper than I'd realized. There's more going on than the bribe. I just don't know what. I was right to quit. I was wrong to leave it at that."

He reached for his briefcase as he continued. "None of the politicians or executives at Shaw or AGS know, but I kept meticulous notes of every transaction and conversation." There was momentary silence as he flipped through some papers.

"You said that you know what you need to do." Pastor Green looked contemplative. Anthony for once did not feel alone in his decision.

"Yes, Pastor Green. I've talked to you. Now, I must talk with the authorities. I need to expose this wrong for what it is. I know there will be some unhappy people before it's all over."

Pastor Green nodded, glancing quickly at the business card Detective Kent Cassell had left on his desk.

"And the money that you kept?" Pastor Green inquired.

"Yes, the money." Anthony blew out a loud breath. "I'm giving everything back, once I find out who to give it back to. I want every penny of it off my hands, even if it means losing everything I have." Anthony sat quietly for a second.

"Pastor Green," he started softly, slowly.

"Yes, Anthony?"

"It *will* mean losing *everything* I have."

"Does Terri know about all of this?"

Anthony blew out another loud, long breath. "No, I never told her anything. She just assumed the extra money came from bonuses and pay raises and enjoyed spending it on furniture for the new house. We've always kept separate accounts so she has no clue how much money I really have. I even tried to play it down, explaining that we could afford to buy only one new car instead of two. You know her tastes. She was so glad to see me turn in my old Mazda for that BMW, she didn't even question or care."

Pastor Green was moving to his knees. "I think it's time that we pray and give this entire situation over to the Lord and ask for His strength to get through the coming season."

"Amen to that." Anthony nodded as he joined Pastor Green on his knees. As the elder minister began a long, spirited prayer for guidance and intervention, Anthony could not quiet the question that had kept him from this necessary meeting for the past six months. *How much will I have to lose to follow You?*

"Help me, Jesus. Please," he whispered.

Chapter 3

Anthony sat rigid in the conference room, his hands clenched tightly together in his lap, his legs stiff underneath the massive table. Somewhere outside, a bird squawked noisily at the midmorning sun. Anthony listened to the screeching solo for a moment before allowing his mind to refocus on the long-winded speech being spewed by Garfield Haberstick.

Diane Martin, Mr. Haberstick's assistant, sat near the head of the table, scribbling down the older man's ideas, comments, and general observations concerning business, plumbing, teenagers, his prizewinning pet dog, and the rest of life. Anthony let his eyes wander around the medium-sized room. Many of his associates—or Garf's Groupies, as Anthony's office mate called them—were taking notes and nodding at Mr. Haberstick's aggressive assertions.

". . . and Haberstick Associates will become the premier marketing corporation of this region." Mr. Haberstick rose to his feet. "Under my leadership, I have watched this company grow from a small office in my basement"—he paced the room with his hands folded behind his back—"to what will soon be a multi-million-dollar powerhouse of the business community here in Shepherd Hills."

Anthony did not miss the wink Mr. Haberstick threw him before continuing the rambling monologue. He tried to ignore what felt like rubber bands tightening around his forehead, but mental strangulation was difficult to disregard.

He thought of Terri, who had been asleep when he'd come home from meeting with Pastor Green the night before. She was still asleep when he'd left early for work at six-thirty that morning. *How long will she sleep so peacefully when she finds out what I have to do?* He had not decided whom he would talk to first, her or Kent Cassell. The detective's business card lay hidden safely within the pages of Anthony's Bible.

And then there was the matter of the missing letter. Anthony was both relieved and unsettled that the letter had not yet been found. What mattered most was *who* found it and Anthony was confident that it would show up in his belongings sooner or later. *If it was mixed up with Terri's things, she would have discovered it by now,* Anthony comforted himself. He knew that if Terri read the letter she'd be happy—ecstatic—that he was stepping down from the pulpit. But when she found out why . . .

Anthony looked at Mr. Haberstick standing beside the conference-room window. He studied the short, hunched frame of the older man, the age spots on his wrinkled hands looking redder in the beaming sunlight. *I'm not going to let this man pull my strings,* he decided. Anthony's confidence took a stab at rebuilding, his headache subsiding in a flurry of affirmation. *My decision six months ago to accept that bribe left me sidetracked. Now, Lord Jesus, I want to get back on the mainline with you.*

Anthony quivered inside as he wondered how much he was about to lose, but his resolve grew slightly stronger as he reflected on how much he had lost already. Peace of mind was worth more than money. Somewhere inside of him, he heard his Aunt Rosa quoting one of her favorite verses, Proverbs 15:16: Better is little with the fear of the Lord than great treasure and trouble therewith.

For the remainder of the staff meeting, Anthony felt like a recharged battery. He even sat back comfortably in the springy, padded chair and shared a secret laugh with Marvin Tucker, who was imitating Mr. Haberstick every time he turned away.

When the meeting ended, Anthony decided to take up Marvin's idea of eating lunch at the Solomon Grill again. Anthony playfully shook his head as Marvin suggested they meet at the receptionist's desk.

"While you go and get your coat"—Marvin smiled— "I'm going to go introduce myself to the new honey working the front desk." He stepped away in a slick sliding motion while gripping the sides of his leather jacket. Anthony shook his head again as he walked toward his office.

As he reached for his coat, he was surprised to see a sealed envelope sitting on his desk chair. He was even more surprised when he saw that the note inside had been handwritten and unsigned. The handwriting did not look familiar. Puzzlement gave way to alarm as Anthony read and re-read the two simple sentences scrawled on the paper.

You meet with Haberstick at two o'clock. You will make the right decision.

Whatever confidence he had claimed for the first half of the day was sucked away like water down a drain.

Terri Murdock sat back in the colossal brown chair, closed her eyes, and inhaled. She loved the smell. It was the smell of newness. New chair, new mahogany desk, new curtains, new pens, new business cards. New office. New title. She ran a finger over the gold nameplate her partners had given her as part of the office suite. They had *expected* her to close the deal that made her partner, she had realized when they'd surprised her with the impressively sized office that morning.

Life is perfect, she concluded as she pulled out some framed photographs from her briefcase to set on her desk. She studied her favorite picture of herself, a snapshot taken shortly after her graduation from college. *Maybe I'll let my hair grow out again*, she considered while studying the framed portrait. She ran her fingers through her current short, layered tresses, trimmed to professional, polished perfection. She placed the picture strategically on her desk before picking up another one. She stared at the framed photo in her hands. Anthony looked back at her, a playful grin pulling on his full lips.

"Life is perfect," she murmured to herself. "I'm not going to let anything mess it up. Not even him." She put the photo back into her briefcase facedown before picking up another picture of her with Cherisse.

"That reminds me," she mumbled to herself while reaching for the telephone. She dialed quickly as a smile returned to her face. Terri played with the phone cord as the phone rang several times, then listened to the greeting that introduced Cherisse Landrick as the accounting manager of Fabian's Catering Service.

She paused a moment before hanging up, assuming that Cherisse had already left to make the trip across town to meet her for lunch. She tried Cherisse's cell-phone number. When another voice-mail message greeted her, she reached for her car keys, deciding to get an early start to ensure a good table for them at the Westcott Room in the Quadrangle Towers. Terri remembered how busy the exclusive restaurant had been the day before, when she'd met with Reginald Savant. She did not want Cherisse to miss the pasta primavera lunch special. *I don't want to miss that special myself.* She chuckled to herself.

Her mouth watered as she drove through the congested downtown traffic, thinking only of the sumptuous meal ahead of her. She parked the old Mercedes-Benz in an underground garage, giving a quick look over for Cherisse's silver Maxima. As she stepped out of the driver's seat, her eyes caught sight of a white envelope peeking from the floor behind the passenger's seat. PASTOR GREEN was printed neatly across the front.

"What's this?" Terri mumbled to herself, reaching back into the car. As her fingers stretched forward to grasp the letter, she heard loud, echoing footsteps coming toward her.

Terri whisked around, hitting her head on the car door.

Even before she could make out the well-defined ebony features in the dim garage lighting, she could smell the familiar aroma of a spicy cologne and the unmistakable scent of leather.

"My apologies, Mrs. Murdock. I did not mean to startle you. Are you okay?" The silky bass voice of Reginald Savant whirled in Terri's ears.

Terri was caught off guard as Reginald wrapped an arm around her, helping her stand upright. *I don't remember him being this tall*, she thought to herself as she stared into his broad shoulders. She tilted her head up to stare into his face. A look of amusement glittered in his dark brown eyes.

"Are you okay?" he asked again, the smile on his lips bewitching.

"Oh—yes." Terri felt awkward as she quickly regained her composure, closed the car door, and began walking toward the garage exit. "I'm fine. How are you doing today, Mr. Savant?"

"My day just got better." Reginald continued smiling, watching Terri walk a few steps ahead of him before rejoining her. "Let me get that door for you." The two were entering an underground corridor that would take them into a lobby in the Quadrangle Towers. As they stepped onto an elevator, Mr. Savant smiled again.

"I must tell you, Mrs. Murdock, I am thoroughly delighted that you will be working with me on the Empress Hotel. I showed some of your preliminary design ideas to a couple of my colleagues. They were equally impressed. Do not be surprised if you hear from some of them. I have quite a few business associates who are venturing out into the world of free enterprise and who are looking for a woman of your merit and ingenuity to help design the way." Reginald smiled deeply before continuing. "Returning to the Westcott Room, Mrs. Murdock?"

Terri nodded her head. "I've convinced a friend of mine to try their pasta primavera with me today. I'm looking forward to sampling some more of their menu."

Reginald's eyes never left hers. "Yes, the Westcott Room offers some of the finest dining downtown. I come here often for lunch and meetings, for both business and pleasure. I'm a firm believer that the two can mix."

The elevator door opened and a large, noisy, well-dressed crowd filed onto the elevator. Reginald stepped closer to Terri. She could almost taste the spicy aroma of his cologne. She looked down at his leather oxfords. *Those shoes had to have cost at least five hundred dollars,* she thought to herself. When the doors opened again, they both walked onto the red-and-gold Oriental rug leading to the Westcott Room.

"My party should be waiting for me, Mrs. Murdock, but we shall see each other again sooner or later. Hopefully, sooner rather than later." As he disappeared in the crowd of diners, another familiar voice sounded behind her.

"Girl, who was *that*? You've *got* to introduce me to him. That's the kind of brother I'm trying to get with."

Terri turned around and grinned at her best friend.

"Cherisse, where have you been? I've been trying to call you for the past half hour!"

Cherisse's face suddenly turned serious. "Terri, we've got to talk. You're not going to believe what I just found out."

Anthony stared at the menu in his hands for the fourth time. Although it was unusually quiet for lunchtime at the

Solomon Grill, he was having a hard time concentrating. *You meet with Haberstick at two o'clock. You will make the right decision.* The sloppily scribbled note haunted him. Who had sent it? What did it mean?

"Look, brother," Marvin Tucker broke into his thoughts. "I don't mind having that fine-looking waitress coming back again and again to our table, but I'm getting too hungry to wait for you to decide what you want. Conchita"—Marvin flashed a golden smile while signaling the waitress—"we're ready to order."

It was not until later, while Anthony nibbled some french fries out of his shrimp basket, that he realized what else was disturbing him. Across the restaurant, in a booth away from the main entrance, was a stocky, broad-shouldered white man in a black suit. He was sipping a mug of hot coffee and reading a newspaper, but Anthony noticed him eyeing him from time to time.

When the man got up, apparently to head to the rest room, Anthony noted his gait, an awkward walk that looked like he was plagued with an old football or war injury. *I've seen that man before*, Anthony thought. *Recently, I'm sure.* He picked up another french fry to munch, but his hand stopped in mid-air. *That man was walking across the parking lot when I got to work this morning, and again just now when I left for lunch! Am I being followed?*

~

Gloria Randall reorganized the papers in front of her.

"Maybe skipping lunch was not such a good idea," she murmured to herself as a low grumble crawled through her stomach. "But at least I'm finished with this filing." She smiled in satisfaction, pausing to look at the tasks crossed out on her lengthy to-do list. "Now I can focus on getting the rest of this typing done." Gloria relaxed in her swivel chair, pleased with the progress she was making with Councilman Walter Banks's files.

This was only her second week, and Gloria was determined to show Councilman Banks he had made a wise decision when he offered her the vacant position during a conversation on the church steps between Sunday services.

As Gloria tapped skillfully on the computer keys, she reflected on how nervous she'd been when she'd told him of her recent training at a technology school, hoping he'd catch on to her willingness to work as he talked to her about how his last secretary had suddenly quit on him; no notice, no note, just up and gone. As a respected public figure, he could not afford to hire another non-professional, and he was highly selective about who would be his new office representative, his executive assistant.

She had done her best to present herself as a hard-working, capable applicant, standing taller than she felt in her secondhand church suit, knowing there were many others with better credentials than her newly earned GED and office-management degree who would covet such a high-profile position. But as had been the case for the past several months, God showed favor on her and blessed her with the job.

Since her recent decision to trust Jesus with her life, Gloria had come to know just what Second Corinthians 5:17 meant when it said, "Therefore if any man be in Christ, he is a new creature: old things are passed away; behold, all things are become new." *I've got a brand-new life, a brand-new job, and a brand-new attitude*. She smiled to herself.

She eyed the cheery greeting card sitting on her desk from her sister. *I am so proud of you. Love, Jackie*. The words sent a warm ripple through her, almost like a bear hug somewhere inside of her. She'd felt the same way listening to Pastor Green the Sunday she decided to join the small congregation of Second Baptist Church of Shepherd Hills. "Some of you have come a long way, traveling winding roads that have left you tired and worn," he'd said in that warm, fatherly tone of his. "It doesn't matter where you were yesterday. I'm glad you're here today. Welcome home."

She heard footsteps behind her and quickly resumed typing before looking up.

"Good afternoon, Councilman. I'm almost finished typing the report you wanted. Is there anything else you need me to do for you today?"

Walter Banks stood quietly smiling for a second as he reviewed some papers she handed him, his friendly face seeming to approve of her diligent work ethic.

"Nothing immediate, Miss Randall." His smile lingered as he headed for the front door. Abruptly he frowned and turned around. "Actually, there is something you can do for me. I'm late for a meeting at the Westcott Room. Can you look up the cell-phone number of a Mr. Reginald Savant on the Rolodex in my office? He's a constituent who's been seeking support for a business of his. Call him for me, please, and let him know that I am on my way." Councilman Banks fixed a hat on top of his balding head and left.

Wasting no time, Gloria found the number and dialed.

"Hello." The rich, bass voice of Reginald Savant seemed

to vibrate through the phone. Gloria quickly relayed the councilman's message, picturing a polished, all-too-fine, good-looking brother on the other end. *Help me, Holy Ghost*, she prayed to herself, trying to keep her mind focused.

"You say the councilman just left?" Reginald spoke softly, making his already deep voice sound like a sultry whisper.

"Uh, yes. He said, I mean, he is—um, on his way now. To the Westcott Room." Gloria wanted to kick herself. *Be professional*, she reminded herself.

"Hmmm," Reginald murmured. "That is unfortunate. I just left there. If you do not mind, Miss—what is your name?"

"Miss Randall. Gloria Randall."

"Yes, Miss Randall. If you can, please let Councilman Banks know that I will have to reschedule our meeting. I do apologize, and I hope this will not diminish his support, but an unexpected, urgent matter has arisen that I must attend to."

"I'll give him the message."

"Thank you, thank you. And Miss Randall, I have another message I need you to pass on to him."

"Yes, Mr. Savant?"

"Let him know that I have fellow contacts who would also like to meet with him at his earliest convenience. His backing is imperative to our progress, so we are expecting nothing less than his full support for all of our plans. Please convey that message to him."

Anthony stared again at the sloppy handwriting. *You meet with Haberstick at two o'clock. You will make the right deci-*

sion. It was one-thirty now. Anthony refolded the note and put it underneath some papers in his desk drawer. Marvin sat across the office at a computer workstation, nodding his head and tapping two pencils to the continuous beat pounding through his headphones.

"Here comes my part! Yes! Aw, man! *Ooh, ooh, yeah!*" He sang, not realizing how loud his voice was over the music blaring from his headset.

Anthony looked at the clock. One-thirty-seven. *I really need to talk to someone.* The note. The man at the Solomon Grill. The meeting with Haberstick. Everything. Anthony was beginning to feel more unnerved. He picked up the phone and dialed Terri's cell-phone number. Her voice mail came on immediately, signaling that the phone was turned off. He dialed Pastor Green's number, first at church, and then his home. Surprisingly, there was no answer at either. *I guess that just leaves You to talk to, huh, Lord?*

Anthony reached for his little green Gideon New Testament. *I need a word from You, Jesus. Some strength, some peace.* He flipped through the thin, worn pages until he reached Hebrews chapter thirteen. "For He hath said, I will never leave thee, nor forsake thee. So that we may boldly say, The Lord is my helper, and I will not fear what man shall do unto me," Anthony read quietly. The sacred words poured like oil into his troubled soul.

~

Kent Cassell took another deep gulp of coffee. The waitress at the Solomon Grill had given it to him just the way he liked it—black, with no sugar, or cream, or any of that other frilly stuff. Kent's wife, Mona, often laughed at him, wondering how he could guzzle down such a bitter-tasting liquid. But even she expected nothing less from a man who had the stamina of a mountain lion waiting patiently to single out and then pounce on his prey.

That was how Kent felt at the moment, sitting in his dark green sedan near the parking lot of Haberstick Associates. He had been working steadfastly on this case ever since the regional office of the FBI had contacted the small sheriff's office of Shepherd Hills.

Kent had been on the verge of becoming sheriff himself nearly a year ago. That is until he began asking questions about some local politicians' fund-raising techniques. It seemed that the more information he got, the crazier his life became. First there were the untraceable phone calls to his home made by a silent caller who hung up as soon as the phone was answered. And then there were the repeated break-ins into Mona's home day-care business that left her feeling jittery and him embarrassed. Here he was a cop, and he didn't even know what was going on or how to stop it.

The final straw was a serious hit-and-run accident that left him with a permanently damaged knee. After the crash the momentum of his investigation seemed to fizzle away, as did any legitimate leads into who had run into his old police cruiser.

Following the accident, Mona's anxiety turned into hysteria. Kent decided to remove his bid for the sheriff's seat, but he kept his internal departmental connections strong and started his own private detective business. Sheriff Malloy, Kent's close friend and former colleague, usually informed him of any new developments before the rest of the department knew anything.

Malloy was the one who'd told Kent about the FBI's inquiry into local political matters. Kent, hungry for justice and closure, immediately took the case full-time. This was personal.

He did not trust politicians. And he didn't trust preachers either. Kent was convinced that both were in it for the money and would do anything to get it.

It was for the simple thrill of the hunt that he let that young minister see that he was being watched while eating lunch at the Solomon Grill. He'd almost laughed when he saw Anthony nearly choke on a french fry, the unmistakable scent of fear permeating the air from underneath that righteous halo.

Kent had stumbled over Anthony Murdock's name a few times early on in his investigation. He was certain that Murdock was part of a growing web of deceit being spun around the town of Shepherd Hills like the silvery lace of a black widow spider. But as with any intricate web, all bugs and lowlife eventually get caught.

"I'm onto all of you," Kent mumbled while massaging his knee. He scanned the parking lot and the front entrance of Haberstick Associates, looking for any sign of Anthony or anything that would provide further direction for the case.

He checked his rearview mirror. A shiny black Jaguar with tinted windows was nestled between two Dumpsters toward the rear of the small office building.

"Funny place to park such a fancy car." He shook his head. As he watched, a young black female in a fur stole jumped out of the passenger's side. She slammed the door shut and started shouting through the window. Out of curiosity, Kent decided to pull his car closer to make out her words. But before he could start his ignition, she jumped back into the Jaguar and it sped off.

"Weirdos." Kent shook his head at the spectacle before turning his attention and thoughts back to the office building.

"Wait a minute! What are you telling me?" Shock filled Terri's voice as she sat across from Cherisse, both of their plates untouched. The dim lighting of the Westcott Room did not hide the expression on Cherisse's face.

"You heard me right, girl. Your man, Anthony, has finally come around to his senses. If what I heard today is true, you two are on the verge of getting millions and millions! I can't believe it! I'm best friends with a millionaire!" Cherisse was grinning from ear to ear.

"This can't be real." Terri sat back in her chair with an elated sigh. "Are you sure you heard right? Start over again."

Cherisse rolled her eyes and sucked her teeth playfully. "I've told you the same story three times this past hour. You're going to make me late. I'm not like you. I have a supervisor to report to when I return from lunch."

"I know, Cherisse, but this sounds too good to be true. I need you to tell me this one more time to make sure I'm hearing you right. Now what happened again?"

"Like I said, I was running some numbers for Mr. Fabian to make sure we were ready for a wedding we're catering this weekend. You know how the business wing at Fabian's Catering Service is set up. I'm in the cubicle closest to the window, with three cubicles next to me, and then there's the door that leads to the hallway where you can either leave the building or go back to the kitchen."

"I know, I know. Get to the good part."

"Anyway, while I was working, I heard what sounded like two men come in and sit in the cubicle closest to the door. I figured they were potential customers Mr. Fabian was about to meet with. Well, before Mr. Fabian came in, they were talking about some meeting that was supposed to be happening at two o'clock today. I wasn't really paying attention because I wanted to finish what I was doing to meet you for lunch on time."

"Like that was really going to happen," Terri joked. Cherisse rolled her eyes again.

"As I was saying, I wasn't paying attention to their conversation until I heard them say something about a Mr. Murdock. Of course, I wondered if they were talking about your Anthony. That's when I heard one of them clearly state, and I quote, 'After today's meeting with Haberstick, Anthony Murdock will be one of the wealthiest young men in Shepherd Hills.' The other man did not sound so certain. He seemed to be questioning something about Anthony. He was talking too low for me to make out what he was saying.

"But the first guy seemed confident. He said, 'Anthony's already taken one and a half million dollars toward our cause. Two million more will go even further, especially for someone who already has the connections we need.' Girl, I almost fell out of my seat."

"Are you sure about this?" Terri looked uncertain.

"Look, I've been trying to get to this part. I have the proof from the horse's mouth, or whatever. Check this out for yourself if you don't believe me." Cherisse pulled a piece of paper out of her handbag. "When they left, I noticed this on the floor. See, it looks like it was torn out of a date book." She held up the scrap for Terri to see.

"Girl, give that to me." Terri snatched it, noted the date in black ink, and then read the slanted handwriting aloud.

"'Anthony Murdock (410) 555-3793, meets at two, gets $2 mil, confirmed by' . . . I can't make out those initials." Terri shook her head at the looped letters that ran together. "But that's Anthony's name, that's our home number, and it looks like it was confirmed. Oh my goodness, Cherisse?" The uncertainty was turning into shock. She flipped open her cell phone and dialed Anthony's work number. When the receptionist informed her that Anthony was in an important meeting with the company president, Terri's jaw dropped.

"Important meeting? Okay, thank you." Terri stared at Cherisse in disbelief as she hung up the phone.

"See, I told you." Cherisse danced in her seat. "You've got all the proof you need, Terri. Your husband has made you a millionaire."

"I guess the Lord really does work in mysterious ways." Terri sat silent for a moment with a fork in mid-air. "And I thought we had a lot of money when he was working for Shaw Enterprises. I was never sure how much he was making there, although it seemed that Anthony was able to get any- and everything I wanted no matter the cost, especially right before he quit. Look at our house! But millions? Girl, I can't believe it!"

Terri shook her head slowly. She took a bite of her now cold pasta primavera before continuing.

"All this time I was upset about Anthony taking that poor man's job at Haberstick Associates. I guess it wasn't that poor after all. He normally tells me about all the accounts he's handling, but I guess he was holding back on me. I didn't realize he was working so hard. He *has* seemed so preoccupied lately. I wonder why he didn't just tell me. After all I've been saying to him? Girl, I almost feel bad, getting on him the way I have been. Millions? Why didn't he tell me?"

"Maybe he wanted to surprise you." Cherisse beamed. Her plate was still untouched. "Girl, I've been trying to tell you that Anthony really is a good man. You were worried about nothing."

"I guess Anthony's been taking care of business all this time and just not letting on. Why didn't he tell me? Millions . . ."

Terri sat speechless for a moment, listening to the endless chatter and clinking glasses around her. A pianist was thumbing quiet jazz notes near an exit leading to the courtyard. Slowly, like a cloud easing its way past the midday sun, the look of confusion and shock left her face.

"Waiter, can I have a bottle of your best wine now, please, along with a new plate of pasta primavera. Make that two new plates." She grinned at Cherisse, ignoring the snarls and raised eyebrows from the patrons the waiter was currently serving. "Girl, I'm about to ask that piano man to play my new favorite song, 'We're in the Money.'" Both of them laughed loudly, singing the catchy chorus, complete with snapping fingers, stomping feet, and lots of giggles.

"Terri"—Cherisse checked her watch—"it's two o'clock. Anthony should be getting that check in his hand right about now."

~

"Have a seat, Mr. Murdock." Garfield Haberstick mumbled. "You have perfect timing." His eyes never left his desk as he fumbled through some papers in front of him. Anthony sat down, praying for strength and wisdom to deal with whatever was coming next. Silence filled the room for a while as Mr. Haberstick continued flipping through the pages on top of his desk. Without looking up, he placed a sealed brown envelope in front of Anthony.

"Inside that envelope," he began, still fumbling with his desk, "you'll find a check for two million dollars. It's a charitable donation to the fund you are about to found called the Black Entrepreneurs Alliance. Now, I know what you are thinking. Two million dollars is a generous gift for your brand-new organization." Haberstick looked Anthony directly in the eyes. "I could have taken the money for myself, but you, Mr. Murdock, are a man of great influence. You of all people know that money is meant to be shared."

Mr. Haberstick slid away from his desk as he talked. He stood and faced the window, his hands folded behind his back as he continued.

"I'm sure you're wondering why I am so enthusiastic about your new foundation. Why would I be so interested in the black businessman's affairs?" Mr. Haberstick turned to face Anthony, a smile forming on his face. "Well, in this day of cultural diversity and political correctness, I've decided to invest my time and talents in upholding the tenets of equal opportunity and diversity in the workplace."

He paused for a second as a slight frown took over his face. "Personally, I could care less whether you're black or white or pink or blue." A grin quickly reformed. "As long as you have some green, I'm willing to do business with you."

Mr. Haberstick hobbled back to his desk and pulled out a leather portfolio. "I have in my hands the future of Haberstick Associates. We have been offered the opportunity to serve as the personal marketing firm to several businesses that will be started by the members of the Black Entrepreneurs Alliance. All of these businesses are separate, but related—a fact that the general public does not need to know."

Mr. Haberstick relaxed in his chair. "I was excited when I was first approached about this opportunity because major"—Haberstick leaned forward in his chair—"I mean, *major*, money is involved in this deal. I actually wondered why Haberstick Associates was chosen for this incredible arrangement. I thought to myself, maybe it's the no-nonsense reputation I hold in this field, or maybe my stubborn attention to profit-making. I thought maybe the business community had finally taken notice of my humble efforts at success."

The smile faded. "It turns out I was wrong on all accounts. But I'm not bitter." Another smile began to form. "Haberstick Associates was picked because of you. You take this check and start the foundation, and I become something I've always wanted to be: a ridiculously wealthy man."

Anthony, who had never reached for the envelope, broke his silence. "I don't understand. What does any of this have to do with me?"

Mr. Haberstick chuckled. "Property acquisition is in the works for the new and upcoming businesses underneath the umbrella of your foundation. The ideal location has been determined to be along the Stonymill light rail expansion project. However, the real estate chosen for the projects conflicts with the plans of a group known as CASH. You are familiar with them, the Citizens' Alliance of Shepherd Hills, are you not, Mr. Murdock?"

Mr. Haberstick's smile never left. Anthony felt a pit open in his stomach. *Please, Lord, not again. I'm still trying to clean up everything from the first go-around.*

"Yes, you remember them. They lost their first battle when the railroad was approved. However, it appears that they are regrouping and willing to put up an even bigger fight with our current plans. From what I hear, a bill is soon to be introduced in city hall that will allow CASH to claim our newfound property."

Haberstick's smile broadened as he softly patted the check. "Of course, Mr. Murdock, as president of your foundation, you can 'talk' to some of our fine politicians and introduce some new and better 'bills' to them. Bills that will help finance the businesses of your organization. Businesses that my company will solely represent."

Anthony swallowed hard. "With all due respect, Mr. Haberstick, I'm not really interested in participating in any part of this."

"You don't understand, Anthony." Mr. Haberstick's voice grew softer. "I'm not *asking* you. A lot is at stake here. Too many people have put great energy, planning, and effort into this to simply stand back and watch it disappear. We are talking about dreams, hopes, aspirations—" Haberstick turned his chair toward the window. ". . . profits."

A long pause stretched between them before Haberstick spoke again. "Anthony, believe me, I understand your hesitation, but you must understand that this affects all of us."

Mr. Haberstick turned to face Anthony again, a quiet smile overshadowing his aged features as he rested his fingertips together. "I'm sure you desire positive outcomes, not negative ones. We are all in the rat race together. And what are we racing for? Power. The power to hold the keys to open and close doors for everyone else. Right now, Anthony, you hold the keys—the keys of power, the keys of persuasion, the keys of politics. Right there in front of you." Mr. Haberstick beckoned to the sealed check in front of Anthony.

"Take that key"—he pointed to the check—"and use it to open the doors for all of us."

Anthony eyed the envelope. "Where did this money come from?"

"That's not important. What *is* important is where it is going. As founder and president of the Black Entrepreneurs Alliance, you have the right to determine the best way to spend this tremendously liberal donation."

"So you're asking me to take this questionable, anonymous gift and use it to buy political influence for whatever you're planning."

"You assume this is my plan. This is bigger than me, bigger than both of us. As I said earlier, there are many who are counting on you. And besides, the donation is not anonymous. That's a signed check. Why don't you look and see who signed it."

Anthony looked again at the envelope.

"Go ahead, Mr. Murdock, open it. See the philanthropist behind the check."

Anthony slowly reached for the brown envelope and took out the check as Mr. Haberstick softly chuckled.

"This makes no sense! I'm not getting involved!" Anthony slammed the check back onto the desk.

Mr. Haberstick suddenly grew humorless. "Remember, Mr. Murdock, you're not being asked."

Anthony jumped to his feet. "And you, Mr. Haberstick, are not hearing me! I will resign from this place before you or anybody else uses me again!"

"That actually may not be a bad idea, you resigning, that is. You'll have more time to devote to your new organization." Mr. Haberstick chuckled.

Anthony glared at Garfield Haberstick for a few seconds before stomping out of the office. The check still sat on Haberstick's desk.

"Lord, what do I do now?" Anthony rested his head in his hands. He was relieved to see that Marvin had disappeared from their office. He wanted some time to sit and think, and the quiet corner office they shared, though cramped and cluttered, was just the retreat he needed. He thought momentarily about his talk with Pastor Green. It was hard to believe that had happened just the night before.

"I thought I could simply confess and give the Stonymill bribe money back, but I see things are about to get even more complicated. When is this going to end, Lord?" he prayed aloud. *More importantly, how is this going to end?* The thought added no comfort.

You know there is nothing in your life that Jesus can't handle. Pastor Green's words echoed in Anthony's mind. As he continued praying and thinking, he began making a list of people he needed to call.

First on the list was Terri. He dialed her number slowly and was surprised to hear her answer on the first ring.

"Hello, baby!"

"Terri?"

"I saw that it was your number on the caller ID and I couldn't wait to talk to you!" Terri sounded ecstatic.

"That's great, honey, because we do need to talk." Anthony perked up his voice to match Terri's rare jubilant mood toward him. She was obviously having a good day and he was not ready to ruin it quite yet. *Wait until she finds out all that we're about to lose,* he thought, and shuddered.

"Maybe we can go out for dinner this evening," he continued. "I've got a lot to discuss with you. There's some things you need to know. I just came out of a meeting that . . . I don't want to get into it right now, but Terri, there's so much I need to tell you. Our lives, our future might— is—going to change."

"Our lives, our future . . . our finances?" She sounded like she was holding her breath.

"Uh, well, yes. Now Terri, I know how important—"

"Oh, baby, I can't wait to talk! Dinner would be perfect. Let's try Romano's. You know they were recently named the finest restaurant in town."

"Uh—" Anthony paused. "Okay." His enthusiasm and courage were waning. "You do deserve at least one good meal at Romano's. Maybe we can pick up where we left off last evening. We still need to finish celebrating your new partnership."

"Oh, we have a lot more to celebrate than just that! I'll call now to make reservations!" Terri's elation must be contagious, Anthony thought as he heard Cherisse giggling in the background. As miserable as he felt, he brightened at the thought that maybe Terri had some good news to share with him.

Next on the list was Kent Cassell. Anthony located the business card and opted to dial the office number rather than the cell-phone number listed. He was surprised when a young woman's voice answered. She informed him that the detective was not in the office, but if it was urgent, he could speak with Sheriff Malloy. Anthony passed, uncertain of what to say, and decided to leave a message for the detective to call him at home.

Anthony stared at the last name on his list. Guilt flooded him afresh as he remembered the signature on the check. Anthony, familiar with the name, could tell the signature had been forged. *What have I done to make someone want to get his name involved and why?*

Anthony reached for the phone once again. It was a number he'd called many times over the years, a number he knew by heart. Halfway through dialing, he slammed down the receiver.

"I can't tell him about all this over the phone. This calls for a face-to-face visit." Anthony headed for the door, dread slowing every step. He knew that there would be no words to ease the blow of his deceptive actions to his mentor, fellow church member, and friend, Councilman Walter Banks. But someone wanted to get him involved in the mix, and Anthony felt responsible for letting the councilman know. Anthony's secrets of the last six months were about to be uncovered, one victim at a time.

Chapter 4

Eric Johnson rose slowly from his knees and sat back down on the brown couch. He ran his lanky fingers over the tattered material of the sofa as he made a mental checklist of what other furniture and equipment the small office needed.

"Lord, I can't stop thanking You for what You've already provided." He raised his arms in gracious surrender. "I can't wait to see what else You're going to do." Eric surveyed the room, admiring the work completed by a team of volunteers. The walls had a fresh coat of eggshell paint and the plumbing had been refurbished. The volunteers had also carried all the furniture up the four flights of stairs to place in the office.

Everything in the office had been donated, including the antique secretary's desk, the three couches, several folding chairs, and an old dinette that would serve temporarily as a conference table. Even the new equipment—the two computers, the telephones, and the patch of beige berber carpet on the floor—had been gifts from various residents of Shepherd Hills. Through strong political backing, the office space itself had been leased at sixty percent below its already low market value.

"And this is just the beginning," Eric smiled to himself, already seeing in his mind the office teeming with workers, staff who would be committed to the cause, prayer warriors who would see this thing through. Eric could already hear the phones ringing off the hook, finan- cial and spiritual support flooding the office to the point that they would have to move into one of those fancy of- fice buildings downtown to administer everything, instead of working out of this forgotten warehouse sitting next to old railroad tracks. Tracks that were being reclaimed as part of the Stonymill project.

Eric refused to be bitter. He was too grateful for the small successes that seemed to be piling up every day. At least here he was near the plot of land Bethany Village was trying to claim. The vision was clear in his mind. This was just the beginning of a ministry that would reach into the gutters and dark corners of Shepherd Hills and bring hope and life to those who felt neglected and forgotten.

He stared down at his arms. They looked like an old man's limbs on a young man's body. Rows of old track marks scarred his cinnamon-brown skin. Scars from dirty needles that had poured heroin into his veins the way sewage pipes chug waste into clean water covered his lanky forearms and legs.

Eric remembered the day when he'd had enough. He remembered the exact moment when he'd cried out to an unseen God from the dark basement of an abandoned crack house. He promised the Jesus he'd learned about in

Sunday school that if he could just be free, he would help bring freedom to someone else with scarred arms and legs. And he would bring hope to someone else's mother who was on the verge of abandoning her children, for it was too late for his mother. And he would give support to some young father so that a child somewhere would know a real daddy's love.

He had cried out to his Heavenly Father from the steps of that broken-down basement and he knew in that moment what it meant to be re-fathered and renewed. And then came the vision of Bethany Village.

Once he was clean inside and out, he'd presented the vision to the Citizens' Alliance of Shepherd Hills. At first the board, made up of several prominent businessmen and community do-gooders, eagerly took on the project, voicing their support to city leaders, pastors, and anyone else who would listen.

But as support from city hall dissipated, so did the fuel for the fire that had at one time kept the small civic group determined to complete the project. After several key businessmen pulled complete funding and support from Bethany Village, Eric was sure that only cold ashes remained where the living vision once stood.

Devastated at CASH's dissolution, he had almost returned to the high that brought him low in the first place. Then he remembered the One who was higher than the politicians and the corporations, and the dying flicker within him sparked into a bold, confident flame.

With the help of the few remaining members of CASH, Eric had obtained the new office space to fan the single flame inside of him. This time he would keep the vision free from political influence. This time he would *start* with the support of the local churches. This time Bethany Village would win.

"First things first," Eric mumbled as he flipped through the long list of names and phone numbers to be contacted, "I need a secretary."

Gloria Randall was typing, letting her skillful fingers run rampantly over the computer keyboard, when Anthony entered the tidy office. She was so absorbed in her work that she did not notice him until he was standing right in front of her desk.

"Sister Randall! Good afternoon! I didn't know you worked here!"

Gloria looked up into the kind, caramel-colored face of the young minister from Second Baptist Church of Shepherd Hills. Even at the end of the business day he looked strikingly fresh and unruffled.

"Minister Murdock!" she exclaimed. "It's good to see you. You preached a wonderful word on Sunday. It had me dancing in the aisles." She laughed before quickly sobering up and removing the syrup from her voice. *This is a married minister*, she reminded herself, quivering at the thought of Terri Murdock's glassy, high-and-mighty stare. *That woman carries a cold breeze with her*. Gloria shivered, but warmed up again as she looked back into Anthony's sunny brown face. *Help me, Holy Ghost*, she prayed for the second time that day.

"Thanks for the encouragement, Sister Randall. I thought I saw that purple hat of yours flopping around the sanctuary." He grinned as he leaned against a mahogany file cabinet.

"What brings you here to Councilman Banks's office

today?" Gloria straightened up in her seat and imagined that her voice sounded as polished as one of those girls working the receptionist desk at the Quadrangle Towers.

Anthony's smile dissipated as he remembered the seriousness of his visit. "I need to see the councilman immediately."

"Mr. Banks is not in right now, but he should be back any minute. You're welcome to wait for him if you want." Gloria beckoned toward a mushroom-colored leather sofa that sat next to the door of the councilman's personal office.

"I'll do that." Anthony sat down as a distant look etched itself onto his perfectly chiseled face. He sat quietly for a moment before flipping through his little green Gideon New Testament. Gloria watched as the tautness in his jawbone relaxed. "Whatever happened to Nikki?" he finally asked, breaking the silence.

"Nikki? Oh, you mean Nikki Galloway, the former secretary. She quit all of a sudden a couple of weeks ago. From what I understand, she was here one day, gone the next. I never met her."

"That's odd," Anthony commented out loud. "She'd been working here for quite a while. I thought she liked her job."

Terri pulled into the parking lot of the Shepherd Hills Town Center Mall. A shiver of excitement tingled up her spine as she scanned the upscale shopping complex.

"The celebration begins!" she shouted to no one in particular. She turned up the radio for the last few notes of Stevie Wonder's "Uptight" pumping through the speakers.

She closed her eyes and let her head and hips move to the music.

"Cherisse, this was a great idea." Terri finally faced her friend as she cut the ignition.

Cherisse was already stepping out of the passenger's side, her "about-business" mode kicking into full gear. "Terri, come on!" she barked, her eyebrows wrinkled in deep concentration. "It's not every day that we get to take the afternoon off to go shopping together! Especially with millions of dollars to spend." Her eyes twinkled with excitement.

Terri emerged from the car as gracefully as the Queen of England. "Slow down, sister. We're only an hour into day one. I can't believe all my dreams have finally come true. First the promotion, and now this."

With the word "this," she opened her arms toward the mall as if she could contain the entire brick-and-steel complex in one open, surrendering embrace. "I feel like a million bucks," she said dreamily.

"Terri, you *are* a million bucks. And as your best friend, I'm going to make sure we look like it. Now come on. We've got a lot of spending to do. Where do you want to start?" Cherisse turned around, expecting to see Terri still leaning against the car door. To her surprise, Terri was already headed for the entrance of Nordstrom, several credit cards in hand.

They started at one end of the mall and worked their way to the other, stopping only once to indulge in tropical fruit smoothies. They cleared several racks at Nordstrom and Express, exchanged severe words with two customers at The Limited, purchased an array of boots and shoes from Nine West, and several suits from Ann Taylor.

Cherisse helped Terri pick out one of the most expensive watches from the mall's premier jeweler and they argued over a pair of Gucci sunglasses until a security guard threatened to escort them out of the store.

With several shopping and garment bags in tow, they settled into a cushy booth at a fifties-diner-themed restaurant located down a quiet corridor inside the mall.

"I never realized how exhausting shopping can be." Cherisse massaged a shoeless foot as a waiter placed tall glasses of ice water in front of them.

"And how hungry it can make you." Terri smiled. She studied the menu, reminding herself of the Romano's dinner planned later that evening with Anthony. "Bring me a garden salad," she commanded the patient waiter. "That's all."

"And I'll take your best cut of steak and potatoes," Cherisse said in a tone just as sober.

"That will be a mushroom swiss burger and a side of fries. Would you like coleslaw with that?" The waiter sounded bored.

Cherisse surveyed the restaurant as if suddenly repulsed by the red-and-white-checked tablecloths, chrome bar stools, and catsup bottles on each table. "Whatever. That's fine. I forgot where we were." She slammed down her unopened menu.

As soon as the waiter turned toward the kitchen they both burst into laughter.

"What a day. I still can't believe it." Terri stirred her ice water with a red plastic straw. "We did all that shopping and I feel . . . I feel . . ." her voice died off.

"Feel what?" Cherisse inquired as she put her shoe back on her foot.

"I feel . . . I don't know. It's not enough. Something is missing." Terri continued stirring her water, her eyes searching the ceiling.

"Hey, we can always go back and get that leather handbag you were looking at." Cherisse readjusted the black scrunchie that pulled her long, golden braids away from her pear-shaped face.

"It's not that. It's—I mean—I'm a multi-millionaire now. Should I still be shopping at the neighborhood mall?" Terri's voice was wistful. "Don't get me wrong. Shepherd Hills Town Center is definitely a first-rate place when it comes to shopping malls. But is it enough for . . . a woman of my class?"

"I see exactly what you mean," Cherisse stated plainly. "What we need to do is plan a shopping trip to New York. Or better yet, Beverly Hills."

Terri sat straight up in her seat as if someone had poured cold water down her back.

"That's it! We could rent a limo—"

"And go cruising down Rodeo Drive," Cherisse cut in, her hands gripping an invisible steering wheel.

"We've got to go to Escada! And Gucci! And Prada!" Terri's words stumbled over each other.

"And don't forget the three Vs!" Cherisse interrupted again.

"Valentino, Versace, and Vuitton!" They laughed together, giving each other a playful high-five.

As Cherisse continued babbling on and on about buying a fur coat from one of the boutiques on Canon Drive and trying on shoes at the Neiman Marcus on Department Store Row, Terri floated in and out of a fairy-tale trance. She could almost feel the smooth glass walls on her fingertips. She could see the gleaming marble and the fiery flash of one-of-a-kind jewels in the Tiffany & Co. showcases. The aromas of French, Italian, and Asian cuisine from world-famous restaurants filled her nostrils. Terri could not believe it. She was going to go shopping in Beverly Hills. Beverly Hills . . .

"Did you hear me?" Cherisse was looking at Terri as if she were possessed.

"Huh?"

"I said that I saw a travel agency on the lower level of the mall. Let's go, girl." Cherisse stood and started collecting their shopping bags.

They were almost at the exit before Terri paused, returned to their booth, and slammed a fifty-dollar bill on the table, right between the salt and pepper shakers. She reconsidered and switched it to a five. "The service here stinks!" she yelled to the waiter bursting out of the swinging kitchen door, their order in his hands.

"Ma'am, ma'am," he called after them. But it was too late. They were already scurrying down the escalator.

As they entered the Golden Fleece Travel Agency, Terri sparkled with another idea.

"I want to do something for Anthony," she declared. "I'm going to book a fourteen-day cruise to the Greek Islands. I've always wanted to go. Plus, I'll be able to buy some authentic Mediterranean rugs from Ephesus for my house."

Terri flipped open her cell phone and dialed quickly. She did not mind when Anthony's voice mail greeted her.

"Hi, baby," she drawled in her most romantic voice. "Just wanted to let you know that I'm looking forward to our dinner tonight at Romano's." She paused as if torn between two decisions. "Oh, what the heck!" she blurted into the receiver. "I also wanted to let you know that I have a wonderful surprise for you! Wait until you find out where I've been today!" she exclaimed as she thumbed through a booklet detailing Mediterranean cruises.

"He'll never guess this one," Terri giggled with Cherisse as she hung up the phone.

Anthony flipped through the latest edition of *Black Enterprise* for the third time. It had been lying there next to him on the sofa outside of Councilman Banks's private office for nearly thirty minutes before he picked it up. The glossy pictures of successful businessmen and -women of color blurred together even more as his anxiety grew.

Gloria shut down her computer and turned on the automated answering service to silence the constantly ringing phone.

"Minister Murdock, I apologize for the wait. I was certain that the councilman said he was on his way back to the office." Gloria's voice was barely above a whisper, as she was somewhat disturbed by Anthony's edginess.

She bit her bottom lip and looked at a brass mantel clock sitting on one of the office suite's black marble fireplaces.

"It's almost five o'clock. Are you sure you don't want me to call him and let him know you're waiting for him?"

Anthony shook his head no as he had done countless times before in response to the same question. He did not want there to be any alarm over the phone. This was too important not to handle face-to-face from the beginning. Images from his meeting with Mr. Haberstick were glued in his mind. He wanted to peel himself—and now the councilman—out of this mess before it became stickier.

BUSINESS LEADERS OF THE YEAR. A fancy title font from the magazine danced in his eyes. "Another brother or sister who's reached the top of the career ladder," he mumbled to himself as he quickly glanced over the microscopic type. He had licked his index finger to turn the page when the words "Shepherd Hills" caught his eye.

It was a picture of a former co-worker from Shaw Enterprises standing next to a couple of Anthony's old directors. Several huge, colorful flower arrangements stood to the right of the young man. The caption announced that the associate was the new executive vice president of advertising affairs following his outstanding success in securing multi-million-dollar marketing deals. *That could have been me*, Anthony reflected sadly for a second.

Then another thought pierced his conscience. *He's reaping the rewards of my deceptive labor for that Stonymill contract.* Anthony quickly remembered that the young man had been an intern working under his direction when he'd accepted the original bribe money.

Why would they give a fairly recent hire so much power? he wondered to himself as he studied the picture again.

"Minister Murdock, maybe I can schedule you to meet with the councilman first thing tomorrow. Let me check his schedule." Gloria spoke softly while reaching for an appointment book, her purse and coat resting in her lap.

"That won't be necessary."

Both Gloria and Anthony turned toward the entrance of the office suite. Councilman Walter Banks stood in the doorway carrying a bag of Chinese food and a stack of napkins. He was a small man, the color of warm bronze, with thinning hair and gold-rimmed glasses that made him look more like a professor or scholar than a politician.

"Anthony, it's so good to see you! I hope you haven't been waiting here long. I got caught up with the president of one of the neighborhood associations. She invited me to a celebration of a new rec center I made sure the city funded. Gloria, can you cancel all my appointments on October ninth so I can make that event?"

The councilman was laying the food on a table and taking off his overcoat as he spoke. "I'm pulling another late night, hence the food. I have enough here if either of you would like some. Anthony"—he patted an uphol-stered chair at the conference table—"please, come sit with me. What brings you by today?"

Anthony nearly stumbled to the seat offered to him by the councilman, the magazine still tucked in his hand. Walter Banks noted Anthony's troubled gait and the glossy pages he gripped in his right hand. He took the magazine and studied the page Anthony had been staring at as Gloria gathered her things and left for the day.

"Another man rewarded for all your hard work. You did a lot for Shaw Enterprises, but someone else claims the credit." Walter shook his head, but then flashed an en-couraging smile. "Don't be down. God has an even greater reward for you than any man can offer. You are following His calling. God's directions do not always make sense to us, but they all lead to perfection. Stay encouraged, son."

Anthony could see the pride shining in Walter's face and hear the warmth in his words. He instantly thought of all the encouragement the councilman had poured on him since the death of his mother and stepfather. The guid-ance, the advice, the back-pats he'd needed to successfully continue with life, graduating valedictorian from high school, then magna cum laude from college. The councilman had been there for him at each major turn, even standing in the aisle reserved for parents on his wedding day, standing right next to his Great-Aunt Rosa. He had been there for his quick rise to business and financial success.

And now he would be here for his fall. Anthony's words came slowly.

"I came to talk to you today . . . because . . . Well, first thank you for all you've done to help me."

Councilman Banks smiled as he gulped down some shrimp fried rice. "I have been blessed watching you mature into the man you are today. It was an honor seeing you work your way up the ranks at Shaw, but it's been an even greater pleasure observing your pursuit after God's will."

"About Shaw, actually that's why I need to talk to you. See, I did some things while I was working there that, well, I know God did not want me to do. A lot of trouble has brewed since then, and now, I think the hole I dug myself into is getting deeper. And someone wants to take you down into my mistakes as well."

Confusion crawled over Walter's face. He laid down his fork as furrows lined his forehead. The furrows deepened when Anthony began telling him of the deceit and bribes of the earlier months. When he learned of Anthony's role in the dismantling of CASH, he first looked expressionless and then heartbroken, sighing heavily several times as Anthony detailed his conversation with Mr. Haberstick earlier that day. It was only when Anthony told him about the forged check that Walter snapped abruptly to attention.

"*Two million dollars?*"

"Whoever signed that check would have to know how close I am to you, and that I would know immediately that was not your signature. It was a sign—confirmation—that this Stonymill deal surpasses what I know."

"In the field of politics, it's easy to make enemies. Especially when you are dedicated to doing the right thing at all costs." Walter rubbed his chin in deep thought. "We just need to find out who. And why."

"I'm sorry I got you involved in this. If I had known—"

Walter waved his hand to silence Anthony. "I would be lying if I said I wasn't disappointed, but right now that's beside the point. That check was no accident. My gut tells me that we've only scraped the tip of an iceberg. When that bill originally was introduced to provide the okay for Stonymill, I got a lot of pressure from several of my colleagues and many business leaders to push for it instead of CASH. When I didn't buckle, even when everyone else did"—he didn't look at Anthony with those words—"I guess someone or some*ones* remembered that and want me to know. As Mr. Haberstick told you, CASH is about to make headlines again in its bid for property along the Stonymill light rail line. I fully intend to support them once again, but I guess someone wants me to reconsider."

Anthony cut through the silence that followed the councilman's words. "I have the business card of a detective Pastor Green gave me. Maybe we can call together to let him know what's going on."

Walter Banks took the card and nodded his head. "That's definitely a start." He picked up the phone and quickly slammed it down. "This might be some kind of trap. Whoever signed my name probably expects us to call this detective. Didn't you say he was asking Pastor Green about you?"

Anthony nodded, the full weight of the matter settling quickly on him.

"I think we need to do some investigation on our own first. Let's find out who's behind all of this and what they are trying to do. That way we'll have a leg up on the culprit when we go to the authorities and you won't just be turning yourself in."

Walter reached for a notepad and a laptop. "First things first: Did you notice what bank was listed on the check? I do most of my finances online, so I could easily not notice a check missing."

"From what I remember, it was Universal Heritage Bank."

"I do have an account there, which I use mainly to keep track of donations and other politically related funds. I like to keep things separated so it all comes out clean and clear in the books." The councilman pecked several keys on the computer. "I'm checking to see if something fishy happened without my knowing. If someone had access to one of my checks, then I need to— oh my!"

Anthony looked where the councilman pointed, his finger frozen in astonishment.

Listed among the activities of the account was a wire transfer of two million dollars posted the day before.

"You need to get that check from Mr. Haberstick. Maybe I'll recognize the handwriting. And I'm going to close this account immediately. I don't want someone having access to my funds. Get that check and bring it here tomorrow so we can study it together and then call that detective." Walter pounded a fist into his hand. "This is crazy. I don't know wh—"

The distinct ring of a cell phone interrupted him. Anthony started to check his phone, but then remembered that he had turned it off hours ago. He had not wanted any disruptions.

Walter checked his suit and pants pockets and then followed the ring to his overcoat, which was draped on the back of a chair.

"Where did this come from?" he asked gravely, his eyes darting back to the office door.

"Hello? Hello? Who's this?" Councilman Banks's eyes widened as he held the phone to his ear. After a few seconds passed, he slowly flipped the phone closed and stared vacantly at it before picking at his cold fried rice.

"Anthony." His voice was hoarse. "I don't know what's going on. Please bring that check here as soon as you can."

She was tired of working for him. Tired of the confusion he brought into her life. Tired of doing his dirty work. Tired of all the lies. One day she was going to tell him that too. She had the whole conversation all planned out. She would look him straight in the eye and tell him that before she took another order from him, he would have to kiss her black behind. And then she would turn her back to him so he could get a good look at her behind leaving the room.

Of course then he would *try* to kiss it and she would remember why she was working for him. Leaving him was impossible, dangerous even. But at least the perks were good.

Nikki was mad that she'd had to leave the fur stole in the car. But even she knew it didn't go too well with the plain-Jane black skirt suit she was wearing. She loved that mink stole. It showed the world her power. She would wrap that dead thing around her voluptuous curves the way she wrapped men around her pinky. She was absolutely irresistible. Or so she would like to think.

Nikki looked down at the hideous long skirt that skimmed her calves and the green wool overcoat she had on instead of the silky mink stole. She turned up her nose at the ensemble. Much too conservative for her taste.

She was on assignment. A new assignment. But then again, when was any assignment ever new? They were all one and the same. Only now they had gotten more complicated, building treacherously one on top of another. She thought of the blocks her three-year-old son, Devin, played with at the day-care center. Each one piled one on top of another, higher and higher, until they all fell down. *All fall down.* Wasn't there a nursery rhyme or something that went like that? Nikki shook her head, dismissing the thought.

She looked down at her red, yellow, and black fingernails. Each nail sported a different lavish design. "Don't be mad 'cause I didn't take them off," she said smugly to herself as she added a drop of glue to one of them.

She knew the nails were too loud and too busy for the image she needed to portray. But it was too late. She had waited until she'd gotten out of the car before she threw off the fur-trimmed leather gloves, brashly exposing all ten colorful tips. She enjoyed slamming that pretty black

Jaguar's door in that man's pretty face. Couldn't say nothing to her. Hmph. It felt good to have some power.

Nikki blew a large pink bubble and then sucked it back into her mouth with a loud *pop!* She realized her mistake immediately and took a quick look around her, hoping that nobody had heard or seen her blow that bubble. She quickly spit the gum out of her mouth, wrapped it in a piece of tissue she found in her purse, and tossed it into the bus-stop trash can. Fortunately, there was no visible living soul within blocks to view her mishap. Who would want to be around this desolate part of town? Even so, she would have to be more careful.

"This task involves subtle sophistication and class," she mimicked his words out loud to herself. "You must be dedicated, sincere, and, above all, convincing."

She rolled her eyes and sucked her teeth. This assignment wouldn't be any different from any other. All men were the same at heart. Weak. Especially when she started working her prizewinning walk. Eat your heart out, Tyra Banks. Nikki knew the exact moment when she had a man where she wanted him. Her mother would tell her that's what got her in all this trouble in the first place.

She'd been sitting at the bus stop for almost two hours and had watched six buses pass. She was just starting to wonder if she should do something to keep from looking fishy when finally he emerged from the building across the street. She knew he was coming to the bus stop. He would be catching the number fifty-seven to Drylaw Avenue, where he would transfer to the twenty-nine. The next bus was coming in three minutes. She would have to work quickly. Nikki didn't even break a sweat.

As soon as he neared the bus stop, she let out a loud,

mournful sob, just as she had practiced. Men were suckers for beautiful women who were crying.

"Ma'am, are you okay?" He rested a foot on the bench and leaned in toward her. His eyes were gentle and sincere, but Nikki was not swayed. She had a job to do.

"Ooohh," she moaned tearfully. "I don't know what to do. I just got laid off and—I'm not going to bother you with my problems." She let her sentence end in a whimper.

"It's no bother, ma'am. I know what it's like to be down and out." He sat down next to her. A good sign.

"That's very kind of you, but I'll be okay." Nikki carefully flickered her wet eyelashes.

"Just got laid off, huh?" He seemed to be looking past her eyelashes and straight into her eyes. Nikki looked down quickly, hoping he had not looked beyond her eyes.

"It's just that I promised my son that we would go to Disney World this year—he calls it Mickey Mouse House—and now, and now—" She broke down in sobs again. "And now, I'm not even sure how I'm going to pay the rent for our *own* house." Was that doubt in his face? Nikki held her breath, kept her eyes on his dusty tennis shoes, and waited. As the seconds grew longer, she deployed her last-resort weapon. Her lower lip, coated with a fresh layer of glimmering red lipstick, began quivering until a full, irresistible pout had formed.

He began fumbling with a dark blue baseball cap, swinging it between his thumb and forefinger. "Well, I actually was about to put out a want ad for a secretary. Do you have any office skills?"

Nikki dabbed the corners of her eyes with a tissue. Black mascara smudged onto the tattered shreds. "Yes, I do. I'm a hard worker, and I will take whatever salary you can offer." This was too easy.

He sighed again as he finally pushed the cap down over his bushy hair. "Okay," he said slowly, "come to room number four-sixteen in the building across the street." He pointed as he spoke. "Come tomorrow morning, nine o'clock sharp, and, well, I guess you can start working. My name is Eric Johnson and my organization is called the Citizens' Alliance of Shepherd Hills. You may have heard of it—CASH for short."

"CASH? Hmmm, I've never heard of it," Nikki lied. "But I can't wait to learn more about what you do. Thank you, Mr. Johnson. I won't let you down." That violin music from the sappy scenes in the movies should be playing now. Nikki fought to hold back laughter.

"Here comes my bus. I'll see you bright and early tomorrow morning, Miss—what's your name?" Eric Johnson rose to his feet and extended his right hand.

"Galloway. Nikki Galloway." Nikki shook his hand and watched him board the bus. She waited until all the exhaust cleared before she pulled her cell phone from her purse and dialed. Easy enough. She smiled to herself. The bus disappeared around a corner farther up the street.

"Suckers. All of you are suckers." She sneered as she hung up the phone. Nikki unwrapped a new piece of gum and within seconds was popping bubbles as loudly as she could.

Anthony replayed the message for the sixth time to make sure he had not missed anything. "Hi, baby. Just wanted to let you know that I'm looking forward to our dinner tonight at Romano's. Oh, what the heck! I also wanted to let you know that I have a wonderful surprise for you! Wait until you find out where I've been today!"

Her words were punctuated with several dramatic pauses and her tone was unmistakably giddy. *A wonderful surprise*, the words swirled around over and over in Anthony's head. He listened to Terri's message one more time before shutting off his phone once again.

A wonderful surprise. Anthony stirred in his seat, nearly oblivious to the smells of basil and parmigiana wafting over from the table across the aisle. A tuxedoed waiter passed him carrying a bottle of white wine. Anthony took a sip of his ice water.

A wonderful surprise. Could it be? *Lord, you know I could use some good news right about now*. Anthony smiled to himself. Where could Terri have been that would leave her so excited? Anthony reached inside his suit jacket for his appointment book to see if he had made any notes about Terri's schedule. September 15. The day was blank. Anthony shook his head with an uneasy smile. He wished the day had been as uneventful in reality as it was on paper.

A wonderful surprise. Anthony remembered how annoyed Terri had been when he'd first raised the topic of children. It was the day after their first wedding anniversary and he had casually joked about having a child to help celebrate their next anniversary. Terri went berserk, accusing him of thinking only of his own selfish wants and not about her career.

"I thought you supported my dreams," she'd yelled for two days.

"You know that I do and I always will," Anthony had reassured her, secretly hurt that his desire to create something eternally tangible out of his love for her had been mistaken as an attack on her dreams.

"Would you like to order an antipasto as you are awaiting your party?" A tuxedoed waiter interrupted his thoughts. "The calamari is especially tempting this evening." The waiter's fake Italian accent amused Anthony.

"I'm fine, thank you." Anthony decided to wait for Terri before ordering anything. He wanted to see if her tastes were changing. *If she orders something way out of the ordinary, then I'll know that her surprise is what I'm thinking it is.* Anthony made a mental note that Terri usually ordered some variation of a pasta primavera dish when they dined Italian.

"Good evening, Anthony."

Anthony looked up from his menu to see Terri standing next to the green-cloth-covered table. She was wearing a black sheath dress with sheer sleeves. Crystals embellished each seam of the dress, tracing up and down her body and along the V-cut neckline. Even in the dim candlelight she was undeniably glowing.

"Baby, you look like you're—" Anthony caught himself as he stood to help Terri to her seat. "It's the dress. It draws out the warmth in your skin, the golden undertones. The dress—it's new, isn't it?" Anthony ran his fingers over Terri's freshly manicured hand. Her skin was still silky from a luxurious day-spa treatment she'd just had along with Cherisse.

"Yes, the occasion called for something new." Terri was all smiles. "I did some shopping today. With all that's happening, you know I had to get a new wardrobe." Terri did not mean to wink, but she could not help it. Being a millionaire had its privileges. You did not have to explain your actions. You just did as you pleased.

Anthony sat back in his seat, his eyes never leaving Terri's. The flickering candlelight seemed to be trapped deep inside her pupils. He could not remember the last time they had looked so deeply into each other's eyes. He did not want the moment to end.

"*Buona sera, signora.*" The waiter with the mock accent had returned. "Are you ready to order? May I interest you in our specials this evening? For antipasti, we have calamari, lightly seasoned and delicately fried in our specially aged olive oil. We also have—"

Terri held up a hand. "Please, just bring the veal scallopini. And I'll also take a small order of the beef, proscuitto, and mushroom dish. And a couple of the lobster tails that come with the seafood marinara special would be nice also." Terri gave a curt smile as she put the menu down.

Both Anthony and the waiter raised an eyebrow.

"Signora, you understand that these are three separate dishes?" His accent was fading. Terri ignored the question. The waiter turned to Anthony.

"And what would you like, *signore?*"

Anthony smiled as a hint of a Brooklyn upbringing sneaked into the waiter's voice.

"I'll have the fettuccine alfredo."

"That's all you're getting?" Terri whispered as the waiter disappeared.

"I'm sure I'll get full watching you eat all of your food." Anthony's stomach was fluttering. *She ordered everything but the primavera.* He was convinced. Terri had to be pregnant. What other surprise would leave her glowing and eating Romano's out of business? His inner suspicions had been right all along. She *was* excited about having children once she knew one was coming. Anthony relaxed. He had never seen Terri so happy.

"So tell me"—she had been watching the smile ease onto his face—"how was your day?"

Anthony thought about all the stories he'd heard about pregnant women and their moods. *Lord, is this the right time to tell her?*

"Well," he began, "things have happened today—actually they've been happening over the past six months."

Anthony looked down as he continued. *Is this really the right time?* "I've made some decisions in the past that I should have told you about. But I didn't. And now things have gotten even more . . ." His voice trailed off as he stared into the reddish orange flame of the elaborate candle centerpiece. *Now, Lord?*

He tried to continue. "Terri, life as we've known it is about to change. I have been wanting to give back—"

"To the community! And to the church!" Terri interjected. She was too excited to wait for him to finish speaking. "And I know you will! But I think that before we make definite plans of what to do from here, we need to spend some time deciding together what's best for . . . for *us*."

Anthony looked back into her eyes. The glowing candlelight still danced wickedly in her gaze. He decided once again to ignore the voice shouting from his conscience. *This is not the time to wreck her world*, he convinced himself.

"Terri." He managed a feeble smile. "When are you going to tell me your surprise?"

Terri grinned as she reached for the leaflet detailing the cruise she'd just booked. She stopped just short of pulling it from her purse. "I tell you what, Mr. Murdock." She had another idea. "I'm not going to tell you right now. I'm going to give you clues every day until Saturday and then you can guess." She bubbled with pleasure at her latest plan. Wealth must bring creativity, she reasoned to herself.

"Can I just guess now?"

"No! That will spoil everything. Let me give you your first clue." Terri tapped her lip for a second and smiled again. "Think relaxation," she blew out a long sigh and closed her eyes.

Anthony shook his head, trying to look confused. Inside he was smiling. *That's easy. Lamaze class.* Anthony shook his head again. The next few days were going to be interesting.

Chapter 5

Cherisse braced herself and yanked as hard as she could.

"Ouch!" She hated plucking her eyebrows. "I don't see how that lady missed this." Cherisse moved closer to the lavatory mirror to ensure there were no other stray hairs. "As much as Terri paid for us to have that facial yesterday, my brow bones should be bald."

It was Wednesday morning and the day was plugging along at its usual workday pace. Slow. Cherisse was still muttering to herself as she reached for the large brass door handle leading out of the ladies' room. One foot was out the doorway when she suddenly stepped back into the small pink-and-teal powder room.

"I assure you, everything will be in place for you exactly how you want it on Friday."

Mr. Fabian's voice echoed down the corridor. Cherisse held her breath as she leaned against the inside of the door, hoping that her employer had not seen her. He had sounded a little annoyed the day before when she'd called in sick for the afternoon. "You didn't sound sick before you left for lunch," he had grumbled on the phone. She had successfully avoided direct contact with him all morning.

"We've had to prepare for bigger occasions in even shorter amounts of time," Mr. Fabian was continuing from the hallway. "As I told you when we met yesterday, expect nothing less than the best from Fabian's Catering Service."

Cherisse relaxed a little as she realized he had not yet turned the corner. There was no way he could have seen her. She kept her ear to the door, waiting for him to leave the area so she could return to her cubicle undetected.

"Mr. Fabian, we have no doubts about your ability to pull this thing off at such short notice. Indeed, you have a reputation for providing perfection in the most demanding of circumstances. I made that observation myself as an attendee of the infamous Evans wedding."

Rolls of laughter filled the hallway as Cherisse's ears perked up. That voice was familiar.

"As a token of our good faith in your services, Mr. Fabian, I want to personally offer you an additional five thousand dollars to assist you with any last-minute preparations."

Cherisse was certain she had heard that voice recently. She remembered the conversation she had eavesdropped on the day before, about Anthony. Was this one of the same men?

"Five thousand dollars? Oh, that is hardly necessary." Mr. Fabian sounded flabbergasted.

"I assure you, it is necessary. There will be other events

in the future we will need you to cater, and I want you to always know and respect the quality of payment we can offer you, Mr. Fabian."

"Oh, please call me Alexander. And I will always be available and at your service."

"Very well, Mr. Fabian. I mean, Alexander."

The voices were fading away. Cherisse pressed her ear harder against the door to make out the end of the conversation, but the door suddenly gave way and she fell flat.

"Cherisse! Are you okay? I'm sorry! I didn't know you were there!"

Cherisse looked up from the floor into the face of a fellow co-worker. "I'm fine, Julie. Thanks for asking." She moaned as she picked herself up off the tile floor and exited quickly into the empty corridor.

As soon as Julie disappeared behind the rest-room door, Cherisse stood on her tiptoes to peer out of the basement hallway window. A shiny black Jaguar was pulling out of the lot. She strained to make out a figure through the tinted glass.

"There you are, Cherisse! I've been looking for you all morning."

Cherisse fell on her bottom again, her thick, golden braids tangled around her face.

"Mr. Fabian!"

"Are you feeling better today, Ms. Landrick? I have a lot of work for you to do. Are you up to it, or are you going to need the afternoon off again?" Cherisse did not miss the disdain in his voice.

"I have the spreadsheets you wanted at my desk." Cherisse quickly stood, smoothed down her new silk shirt, and pushed some loose braids out of her face.

"Nice manicure," Mr. Fabian grumbled. "It looks very—fresh."

Anthony stared at the white block lettering on the glass door before he entered the small office building. HABER-STICK ASSOCIATES. He unbuttoned his coat and readjusted his tie as he walked through the plain beige foyer.

The game plan was simple. Anthony wanted to fish out more information from Haberstick about the check before he took it back to Councilman Banks's office.

"Hello, Marcie," he mumbled to the receptionist. Anthony did not miss her wide-eyed stare as she abruptly stopped talking into her handset. As he walked down the hallway, he noticed quite a few of his co-workers peeking at him from their desks. As he started to greet some of them, they quickly turned away. One associate from the fiscal department even shut her door as he passed by her office.

Lord, what is going on? Anthony changed directions and headed for the small corner office he shared with Marvin. He was surprised to see his office mate sitting at his desk instead of his own. All of Anthony's work files and the personal mementos he had carefully placed on top of the small workstation were missing. Music blared from a small radio hidden somewhere in the cramped room.

"Marvin, you need to turn that down before Haberstick comes in here. Remember what he did to your portable TV?" Anthony smiled, uncertain of what else to say.

Marvin quickly threw the crossword puzzle he was working on into an open drawer. "Whew, it's just you." He exhaled loudly as he reached again for the puzzle. "I didn't care about that busted-up TV anyway. I *wanted* old man

Haberstick to throw it out the window." He studied Anthony before continuing. "I wasn't expecting you today."

"I can see that." Anthony shook his head. He looked around for an empty seat, choosing finally to remove some boxes from one of the chairs. "Why'd you think I wasn't coming in?" He tried to sound casual as he sat down in the squeaky seat.

"Haberstick announced that you got some new job offer you'd be a fool to turn down. I don't know what kind of offer you got to make you leave all your stuff here like that, but I know you're a fool to be sitting back here today in that same old dusty, black, broke chair."

Marvin finally stood and began clearing paper out of his own desk chair. "Sorry about your desk. You know I couldn't let all that good space go to waste." He sat down with a heavy thud, letting the chair spin him around a few times.

Anthony looked at the mass of papers Marvin had piled onto his desk.

"Don't worry. I'll get that stuff." Marvin looked up at Anthony, a sly smile forming on his face. "I know you're probably wondering what I did with all your things. I started to throw them out. You know, you all *big* now. Couldn't even say good-bye to nobody. Just gonna up and leave like that."

Anthony was growing impatient, his eyes scanning the room for his belongings. The music still blared through the radio speakers.

"Yup, I started to throw them all out. That is, until I saw that picture of your wife still sitting on your desk. That's when I knew you were coming back. I didn't know when and I didn't know why, but I knew you were coming back, if not for anything else but for that picture. Shoot, *I* would come back for *that* picture, and that's not even my wife." Marvin laughed, knowing that Anthony had never minded his playful references to Terri's beauty.

Terri. The thought excited Anthony. *Terri and the baby.*

"Anyway, I just got two questions for you." Marvin continued to laugh. "If you're sitting here in this office, who's sitting in the office you are supposed to be at right now? And if you're not going to be sitting in that office, can you hook a brother up?"

Anthony did his best to keep a smile on his face as he entwined his fingers and rested his elbows on his knees. "Trust me, it's not a job you'd want to take. Not for millions of dollars."

"Speak for yourself, man. But back to your stuff. I didn't throw them out, but I think Haberstick did."

Anthony looked up suddenly. "Haberstick was in here looking through my things?"

"Yeah, man. He was in here for a while, looking through your charts and folders, all that stuff. Then he started taking everything out. Even your personal belongings. I don't know what he did with them. I offered to help, so that I could at least know where he was putting them, but he refused to let me touch anything. Did you know that you left your briefcase here when you left like a madman yesterday? He took that too."

Anthony felt the blood rush from his head. *My briefcase! Lord, you know everything I've got in there, from Stonymill and beyond. I need that! It's my only way out.*

Marvin was still talking, unaware of Anthony's alarm. "I'm telling you, man, he was in here a *long* time, reading stuff, flipping through things, giving me the creeps. You know that man wears some ugly, dark suits and smells like old carnations? I felt like I was sitting in a funeral home with him walking around in here. Hold up, here comes my song." Marvin spun away from Anthony, turned up the radio even louder, and began singing and nodding his head.

Anthony still sat rigid in his seat. Haberstick had his briefcase. First the letter and now this. *I'm going to have to keep better track of my things. At least the letter seems to have safely vanished for the time being. But now the briefcase . . .*

Anthony felt a chill as he imagined every possible thing that Haberstick could do with the information inside his beloved briefcase. The receipts, the names, the notes he'd taken from the initial Stonymill deal. All of the things he needed to have on him to talk to that detective asking around about him. Anthony looked at the phone, almost expecting it to ring at that moment. He wondered why he had not yet heard back from the detective. He was certain that the number on the card Pastor Green had given him was the best way to reach him.

Marvin still crooned along with the radio. His eyes were closed as he gripped a stapler in his hand like a microphone and mopped invisible sweat from his brow with some tissue. When the song ended, he cut the volume.

"But anyway, like I was saying, Anthony," he began, spinning around in his chair, "Anthony . . . Anthony?" The office door swung back and forth on its hinges. Marvin was alone. "Where did Anthony go? My singing is not *that* bad."

"Do you mind me making extra copies of these lists, Mr. Johnson? I like to have extras of everything on hand, in case I lose something."

Eric looked up from the box in front of him and smiled weakly. "Sure, Nikki. Whatever you need to do, go ahead and do it if you think it will help."

Eric reached back into the box and began counting the brochures again. They had just been delivered that afternoon and this was the fifth time Nikki had made him lose count.

"Oh, Mr. Johnson, I forgot. Which list is the mailing list of old CASH members and which is the list of the pastors you want me to call?"

Eric threw all the brochures back into the box.

"I tell you what, Nikki. Why don't you let me handle those lists, and in the meantime you can read one of these brochures to get more acquainted with CASH. We have our first church presentation tonight at Second Baptist. It will be good for you to be familiar with the Bethany Village project." Eric was already walking to where she stood at the copy machine.

"Sure, if you think that's best, Mr. Johnson." Nikki clutched the copies in her hand and turned toward the brochures.

Oh Lord, here comes that ridiculous walk again. Eric shook his head to himself. He was the last person to make a judgment on anyone, but he did not know about this Miss Galloway. Something about her seemed a little loose in the head. The only thing she'd perfected so far was showing up late and leaving early. Eric shook his head again and watched as she tripped over the box of brochures and landed dramatically on an old couch.

"Oops." She giggled as one of her legs lay exposed for a prolonged second.

Everyone deserves a chance, Eric reasoned. He'd been

given many chances and had learned along the way not to be too quick to make a judgment on someone. He stared at the old track marks on his arm or, as he called them, his memorials to God's deliverance.

"Thank you, Lord, for another chance," he whispered.

"Oops," Nikki giggled again. This time her blond hair weave had become entangled with a leafy plant hanging over her head. Nikki stopped giggling and batted her eyelids shyly at Eric.

"Lord Jesus," Eric muttered to himself as he started his phone campaign.

"You need to tell me who's behind all of this!" Anthony demanded once again as he glared down at Mr. Haberstick's shiny bald head. The senior businessman was still hunched over, silently scribbling on a yellow notepad in front of him. He had not looked up when Anthony stormed his office, nor acknowledged Anthony's livid greeting.

"Tell me now!" Anthony stood tall, his voice growing louder with each word. Mr. Haberstick put down his pen, reached for a fork, and unwrapped a medium-sized container of potato salad. He rested the plastic bowl on top of a piece of paper with several columns of numbers and symbols. Anthony noticed his own signature at the bottom of the page and knew instinctively that the paper was a crucial document from his missing briefcase.

Anthony closed his eyes and sank into a large upholstered chair facing Haberstick's massive desk. As he rubbed his temples, the old, nagging questions about the Stonymill deal flooded his mind. The receipts that never added up, the names that mysteriously disappeared from his files, the documents he requested from his former boss that were accidentally shredded by some unknown secretary somewhere.

Anthony knew that the bribe that he had accepted— and passed along to decision makers—six months before had been a deceitful, dishonest act on his part. But what disturbed him even more was the slow realization that nobody could tell him where the original money came from. That realization alone prompted him to keep track of every conversation, every meeting, and every dollar touching his hands. *I guess I knew even then that one day I'd want to be free from this hole I dug myself into, and I left just enough rope to get out.* Anthony looked up again at the paper in front of Haberstick with his own signature in red ink at the bottom. *Or just enough rope to hang myself.* He winced inside as Mr. Haberstick finally looked up at him. They looked each other in the eye as Haberstick began stirring a cup of hot tea. The clink of the metal spoon hitting the delicate walls of the antique porcelain teacup filled the silent void in the room.

Anthony cautiously cleared his throat, thinking only of his briefcase. This new ordeal had to be closely related to the events of six months ago. Why else would Haberstick be holding on to his briefcase? The detective would be calling soon, Anthony was sure.

"You want to know who's behind all of this," Garfield Haberstick blurted. There was both a question and a statement in his tone. "I told you yesterday, Mr. Murdock, this is bigger than you and me. Heck, after what I've been stumbling upon lately." His fingers tapped the paper in front of him. "I'm learning that even *I* do not know all the players in this intricate, convoluted game of enterprise and fortune."

Mr. Haberstick rose from his seat and stood in his favorite spot next to the room-length window. A spark of uneasiness escaped from his eyes as he rubbed at a smear on the smooth glass surface. "It's all a game, Mr. Murdock." His voice was a coarse whisper. "And you must"—he turned suddenly to face Anthony again—"you *must* be a dedicated player, because to lose is *not* an option. I, for one, refuse to lose."

A smile formed and then quickly vanished from his thin lips. "I assure you, Anthony, in this game, things are not always what they appear to be. Take that check, for instance."

Anthony had not even noticed that Mr. Haberstick had placed the envelope on the corner of his desk. Anthony softly bit his bottom lip as the genuinely worried face of Councilman Banks flashed in his mind. He thought again about his briefcase, choosing not to mention it in the hopes that Haberstick would think he did not place a high value on its contents.

"I want to see the check." Here, at least, was a restarting point. He would figure out how to get the briefcase later. Anthony knew that the councilman would be waiting for him.

"The check is on the desk." Mr. Haberstick's voice was distant as he surveyed the drab scene outside of his window again.

As Anthony reached for the envelope, Haberstick suddenly turned around and snatched it from under his fingers. "I want you to sign something confirming your acceptance."

"I'm not accepting it. I only want to see it, examine it. You won't give me any answers, so I'll find them myself."

"Examine it, see it, smell it—do what you want with it. But before you do anything, I want you to sign my own receipt. It's good to keep records, isn't it, Mr. Murdock? You never know when they will come in handy." His voice was cold as his fingertips once again brushed Anthony's old documents still resting on his desk.

Anthony tried to look unperturbed as he scribbled his signature on a piece of yellow legal paper that Haberstick handed him. It was a simple handwritten receipt that would not mean anything to anyone outside of the room, Anthony reassured himself.

"Now go!" Mr. Haberstick faced the window again, his hands folded behind his back, his small, hunched frame swimming in his oversized black suit.

As Anthony closed the heavy door behind him, he heard Mr. Haberstick's warbled voice bounce off the hot windowpane glaring in the late afternoon sun.

"I'm not going to lose, Anthony."

Terri loosened the diamond-studded clip in her hair to let the wind whip through her short tresses. The crisp fall air was an invigorating rush to her senses.

"This is unbelievable!" She shouted through the roaring breeze. "I never dreamed a convertible would be this much fun!"

"Well, the Lexus SC 430 has one of the highest customer-satisfaction rates of all luxury sports cars. You sure know how to pick a winner."

Terri smiled at the salesman sitting in the passenger seat. His sun-bleached blond hair and bronzed arms looked as if he had been riding in the convertible with Terri all afternoon.

"When summertime hits, you'll really see how fun this baby is." The corners of his bright blue eyes scrunched up as he smiled.

"Summertime," Terri whispered the word after him. She could almost envision the scores of envious people standing at bus stops and riding in worthless automobiles who would see her in this red, classy thing. A twenty-first-century stagecoach for a queen. Terri could not get the smile off of her face.

"I don't want this test drive to end." Terri was pulling back into the dealership lot. The colorful, neat rows of every imaginable luxury car sent chills through her stomach.

"This is definitely the car I want," she stated as she reluctantly handed the keys back to the salesman. "But I do want to add some more options."

Terri followed the man into an office, where he began punching numbers into a computer.

"Have you decided on what options you want? There's our gold package, and the rear spoiler, the—"

"All of them," Terri quickly interrupted. "I want every single option you showed me in the brochure." Terri felt good saying those words.

The salesman continued punching data into his computer. "That will put the car you want—in red, right—at . . . let's see, $61,190."

"$61,190? Is that all?" Terri looked genuinely disappointed. She wondered how much other millionaires spent on their automobiles.

"Well, we can add our ultimate extended warranty

package in addition to the one offered by Lexus." A greedy smile contrasted with his innocent blue eyes. "You know, what was I thinking? I believe we have a SC 430 in stock that has everything that I talked to you about, and even more. We call it our crown jewel. Everyone wants to see it, but up to now, nobody has been willing to own it."

Terri kept her head high as she noticed everyone in the showroom watching her inspect the car. Her inspection ended with the printed invoice on the window.

"Perfect," she muttered to herself. "This is the car that I want." She pointed, speaking as loud as an indoor voice could carry her. The jealousy begins. She made no eye contact with the other customers in the showroom as she walked with the salesman to another counter.

Terri withdrew a large wad of one-hundred-dollar bills from her purse. She prided herself in having thought to max out most of her credit cards through cash advances.

"I want to make my down payment now." Terri had decided she would get the rest of the money from Anthony and pay off the car the next day.

As her new Lexus was being driven off the showroom floor, Terri took one last look at her old Mercedes-Benz. The car had been a college-graduation present from her parents.

"You've had a good run," she murmured, running her polished fingers over the top of the green wagon. "Up to now, I've never wanted to leave you. But I've got a new image to create. I can't have a vehicle from the last millennium getting me around town."

As she bent down to plant a light kiss on the back windshield, she caught sight of a white envelope peeking out from under the passenger seat.

"I saw this yesterday," she reminded herself. She picked up the letter and traced Anthony's neat print written across the front. "Pastor Green," she read aloud, flipping the sealed envelope around in her hands.

"It's Wednesday, so there's prayer meeting at church tonight." She patted the letter in her palms. "I'm sure Anthony won't mind me dropping this off to Pastor Green."

A wicked smile spread across her face as the gleaming new red Lexus pulled to a stop in front of her.

"Besides," she murmured softly, "those backwards country people at Second Baptist Church need to see what a *real* blessing is."

As Terri clicked down her new seat belt, a black Jaguar slithered into the space beside her. The smooth, polished metal shined so perfectly, Terri could almost see the glint of jealousy from her own eyes reflecting back to her.

"Who is this?" she muttered.

As if in response to her question, the passenger-side window of the black Jaguar rolled down. Terri tried to look away unimpressed, but the voice was unmistakable.

"Mrs. Murdock, we meet again."

Terri tried to smile as she jammed the key into the ignition. "That's a nice car you're driving. Is it new?"

"No, I've had this for quite some time. I come back to this dealership regularly for scheduled maintenance. With a classy car such as yours, you should consider doing the same. It will keep both of you dazzling."

Terri consoled herself with the compliment. "Thank you. I have to go, but I will be talking with you soon. I believe I have a meeting with your staff tomorrow."

"Yes, and I do look forward to meeting with you again,

Mrs. Murdock." Terri noticed that a team of mechanics was nearing his car.

"See you later, Mr. Savant." She began backing out of the space.

"Please, call me Reggie."

Councilman Banks was pacing his office suite in slow, steady strides when Anthony arrived precisely at five-fifteen. Anthony stood unnoticed in the doorway, watching as the councilman walked from one bookcase to another, stopping once to drum fingers on the back of Gloria's empty seat, stopping again to straighten a pillow on one of the wide couches. A door slammed loudly somewhere in the empty corridor.

"Gloria! Is that you?" The councilman suddenly sprang around and, seeing Anthony in the doorway, collapsed into the sofa behind him, his lips tightening into a thin line.

"First the check, and now . . . Gloria," his voice was low and despondent. His eyes reached Anthony's in a trembling gaze. "I don't know where she is."

Anthony still stood in the doorway, trying to make sense of Walter's words.

"I haven't heard from Gloria since early afternoon. All I asked her to do was go down to the clerk's office at city hall and get some files I've been looking for. I wanted to review some of the documents from the whole CASH and Stonymill ordeal for clues as to who's behind all this. It should have taken her no more than forty-five minutes, an hour at the most." His words seemed to fade into the fringed rug at which he was staring.

Anthony looked at Gloria's desk, noticing for the first time the wrapped, half-eaten delicatessen sandwich sitting next to her computer. A document was on the screen and the cursor blinked blaringly at the end of an unfinished sentence. As he observed, a bright screensaver popped onto the large monitor. *PRAISE THE LORD!* The italicized words darted across the blue screen.

"I called her from my cell phone around one o'clock and asked her to get those files for me." Walter Banks continued talking. "When I came back at three-thirty, I expected to see her sitting at this desk, those files in my mailbox. Neither are here and I'm worried. Gloria is a dependable assistant—the best secretary I've had—and not hearing from her is . . . I'm sure she's fine. She probably became very involved in her task and lost track of time. She's a hard worker and I'm certain I'm worrying over nothing." His voice faded into the carpet again before he continued.

"I closed my bank account first thing this morning, but now I'm not sure that was such a good idea."

The politician beckoned Anthony to a small conference room. As they entered, Walter glanced behind them and locked the door. He arched his neck as if giving a quick scan of all the windows and then pointed to a large woven wastebasket sitting next to a burgundy armchair.

"I'd forgotten that to close the account meant taking out all the money. I don't feel safe with it, so I hid it until we talk to the detective. Where's that business card? I want to talk to him before the owner of that money comes looking for us. There. It's in there. Underneath the plastic trash bag." He pointed as if the money was a biological hazard.

Before Anthony could pull out the detective's card, a phone at one end of the room's sole table began ringing.

"That's odd," the councilman mumbled. "Very few people have this number." He glanced at his watch. "And to be calling this late?" Suddenly his eyes brightened as he rushed for the phone.

"Gloria?" he shouted into the headpiece. Anthony watched as deep lines set into the councilman's forehead.

"Who-who is this? What do you want?" Walter whispered before looking bewilderedly at Anthony.

"Money? What money?" His voice held controlled hysteria as he clutched the handset.

"I don't know what you're talking about." He turned to hang up the phone but stopped suddenly in his path.

"My secretary! What have you done to Gloria?" Outrage overtook his shouts. "Who is this?"

There was a long pause.

"Yes, he's here." The councilman turned heavy eyes toward Anthony, who abruptly reached for the phone.

"He'll do whatever you want! Please don't hurt Gloria!" Walter shouted into the handset. "Here, speak to him!"

Anthony's fingers tangled with the cord as Walter tried to hand him the phone.

"It's no use." Councilman Banks spoke gravely to Anthony. "Whoever it was has already hung up." He gently laid the phone into the receiver. "The person demanded that the money be returned or Gloria will get hurt."

"Where's Gloria?" Anthony's head swirled.

"I don't know, and something else is wrong." The councilman reached for the satchel hidden in the wastebasket. As he continued to speak, he began counting out stacks of hundred-dollar bills.

"Whoever it was asked that all of the five hundred

thousand dollars be returned immediately. Only five hundred thousand out of two million! If that's all that they think I have, then who knows about the rest of the money? And for some reason, they want *you* to take the money to the garden courtyard facing the Quadrangle Towers. A briefcase will be waiting on the park bench in front of the fountain. You have thirty minutes to do it, or—or . . ." The councilman's voice faded into a faint whisper. "Gloria, Gloria." He shook his head.

"I'm calling the police!" Anthony pulled out his cell phone.

Walter quickly grabbed his wrist. "No, no! I don't want anything happening to Gloria." He looked despairingly at the stacks of bills remaining in the satchel. "Let's go do what they asked and call the police when all three of us get back. I don't want this much money in my possession anyway. Here's a way to get rid of some of it." His eyes pleaded with Anthony's as a drop of sweat rolled down from his thinning hairline.

Anthony hesitated, his thumb resting on the nine highlighted on the tiny keypad.

"Look, I'll go with you, and if anything looks fishy—anything at all—I'll call the police myself. Please, Anthony, for Gloria's sake! Plus, I don't want all of this money in my hands." The councilman's low voice competed with the loud steam hissing from a nearby radiator.

"Why do *I* have to do this?"

"I don't know, Anthony, but that's what they asked, and I can't call back to get answers. Please do it. I don't want anything happening to Gloria." The councilman rocked from foot to foot. "Let's do this to make sure Gloria's okay and then we can call the police together, if necessary. This is not the kind of story I need on the eleven-o'clock news," he begged.

Anthony looked back down at his cell phone. Several months old, it was outdated already, a rarity for him. He'd worked so hard to gain himself a cutting-edge image—expensive attire and accessories, high-tech toys and technology—but the decision he made six months ago had chunked slowly away at the image he so prized. *An old broke country preacher.* Maybe Terri was right, he surmised. He had spent the past few months creeping through shadows, trying to avoid the spotlight. Working for a low-key firm. Accepting a paycheck he would not have taken as an intern.

Maybe giving back this five hundred thousand was a way out, he convinced himself. No police, no press. A way out. It would be nice to quietly rid himself of the guilt so he could resume a real career with real money and not have to worry about watching his back. Or the councilman's, and now Gloria's. What had he gotten himself into? Maybe this was a way out. *Lord, You said You like decency and order. Well, this might be a decent way to get my life back in order.* He grumbled to himself as he reached for the cloth satchel Councilman Banks extended toward him. In silence, they headed for the office door.

"We need to hurry." The councilman checked his watch. "We only have twenty-four minutes left."

Terri sighed heavily as the congregants sang the chorus about holding on to God's hands for the fifth time. She slowly surveyed the sanctuary, inwardly rolling her eyes at the feverish hand-clapping, joyous shouts and feet tapping on the solid wooden floor. There was still no sign of Anthony, which surprised Terri. He was a regular attendee of Wednesday night Bible study and prayer service.

She turned her gaze to the back of the church, wondering where Pastor Green was. She had hoped to catch him before the service started so she could give him the letter and leave. Pastor Green was taking too long to appear, and the devotional part of the service was almost over. To get up and leave now would at best look rude.

At least her new Lexus was parked in Anthony's reserved space right next to the steps leading to the front entrance. The thought excited her. Terri had made sure that everyone who attended the Wednesday evening Bible study would not miss the cherry-red convertible as they entered, but now the steady stream of arriving parishioners seemed to be slowing. Everyone was already there and had seen her latest "blessing," Terri reasoned as she shifted impatiently in the wooden pew. She listened halfheartedly as the testifying began.

"Givin' honor to God, and my good pastor, and all y'all saints assembled here." Mother Howard began her weekly speech. Terri swatted at a fly as she studied the older woman leaning against a pew, her knobby fingers curled against the wood grain that was the same color as her weathered skin.

"God's been good to me, church!" she shouted. Her thin body almost buckled under the strength of her voice. "He woke me up this morning in my right mind and started me on my way! He put shoes on my feet, clothes on my back, and a roof over my head! I've got to praise Him tonight, saints, 'cause I don't know if this will be my last chance!"

"Amen!" Sister Ethel shouted from her customary front-row seat.

"And I want y'all to help me sing one of them old songs. Hit that drum, boy, to help me keep the beat. My feet can't tap like they used to." Mother Howard motioned the young drummer toward his little black stool. As his sticks hit the snare and his foot pounded the bass, her rich soprano voice swam out over the sanctuary like a fountain of fresh water.

"Jesus is all the world to me. . . ."

Terri sat mesmerized for a moment, amazed at the vital fullness that overtook the older lady's frail frame. As the pianist found the key and the other congregants joined the refrain, Terri watched in respectful awe as Mother Howard stood taller, her wrinkled hands extended upward, her eyes transfixed on the ceiling as if she were looking past the beamed rooftop and had secret viewing access into the inner courtyards of heaven.

A golden ray from the setting sun peeked through a nearby stained-glass window. Hints of pinks, purples, and blues from the painted shepherd on the windowpane filtered through the glass and bathed Mother Howard in their fragile light. She looked ageless in the warm glow as an aura of peace settled gently around her, as gentle as the flittering dust particles exposed by the light around her floating through the air.

"My life, my joy, my all . . ." The richly sung words took on a life of their own, becoming touchable, delicate material of substance and shape.

Terri watched as the jubilance of Mother Howard radiated into the surrounding pews and spilled into each aisle. The shouts, the tears, the Amens of the other congregants seemed to blend in with hers, becoming one voice of wonder, one song of praise. It was as if some secret society of unspeakable pleasures had convened and everyone who knew the password was joining in the ceremony.

A quiet hush rushed into the small sanctuary. Terri studied the smiling, solemn faces, closed eyes, whispering lips, waving hands, and began to feel like a spectator in a back-row bleacher. She could not ignore the fingers of jealousy that ruffled through her conscience and tapped forcefully somewhere in the core of her being as she watched the worshippers seem to snuggle under an invisible blanket of peace. It was a jealousy that poked deeply into an inner place of unutterable longings and desires, and left a far greater imprint than the envy she had felt when she'd seen Reggie's Jaguar.

Terri listened and watched a few seconds longer before the jealousy formed a chokehold around her neck and she felt as though she would be strangled under its tightening grip. She jumped out of her seat and headed for the red-carpeted staircase that led to the basement. A cool sip of water from the rusting water fountain outside the pastor's study would provide some relief, she decided.

As Terri exited the sanctuary, she noticed Sister Kellye Porter, the assistant minister's wife, nodding at her from the back row, her usual grin stretched even wider over her tear-streaked face.

Seated beside her was the assistant minister himself, Bernard Porter, making an unusual appearance from his sickbed. He had not been at the church in months, the ravages of cancer attacking and weakening his once sturdy body. He sat motionless in the pew, his ashen skin loosely covering his wearied frame. As Terri pushed open the foyer door, she noticed him staring at her, a gray cloud blotting the life from his eyes.

"These darn country people and their old-time religion," she mumbled to herself as she let the door swing behind her. "What could they possibly have for me to envy? I'm not sick and I'm not some old, singing, poor woman." She thought about Kellye's ever-constant smiling face and Mother Howard's stirring song as she ran her fingers over the cold metal key to her new Lexus. "I'm the one with the real blessings. I know I've got much more than any of these people will ever dream of having."

Terri walked quickly to the water fountain. As she let the cool stream of water coat her insides, the door to the pastor's study suddenly crashed open, hitting the back of Terri's foot.

"Oops." A woman with a wavy blond hair weave that hung past her shoulders stood facing Terri. She was wearing a plain brown coatdress that clung to her round hips. The high neckline of the dress struggled to contain her large bosom, which showcased a heavy, diamond-studded golden crucifix. A thick, leather-bound Bible protruded from between her brightly painted fingernails.

"Praise the Lord, sister." The stranger's words brimmed with sarcasm. "Sorry about the door. I couldn't wait to go upstairs to hear a word from the Lord, but I didn't realize that you would be in my way. And you still are."

"Excuse me?" Terri was taken aback by the bold, caustic tone. As she looked fiercely into the squinty eyes of the woman, Pastor Green and a tall, lanky man, the color of cinnamon, emerged from the study.

"Sister Murdock!" Pastor Green exclaimed. "I'm glad

to see you here tonight. I've been thinking about you and Anthony. How is everything?"

"Everything is wonderful, thank you. The Lord has been busy blessing us. Anthony's not here yet, but I think he wanted to give this to you." Terri pressed the letter into his palm.

Pastor Green stared at his name written across the front in Anthony's familiar block print.

"Terri . . ." He spoke her name softly, but Terri was oblivious to his questioning gaze. Her eyes had never left the woman standing behind him and the other man. The two women glared at each other, a dark challenge underlying the plastic smiles.

"Were you planning to stay for service?" Pastor Green seemed unaware of the building tension sandwiching him. "Brother Eric Johnson and Sister Nikki Galloway from CASH will be talking about the revised plans for Bethany Village. You've heard of Bethany Village, right?"

Pastor Green searched Terri's unresponsive face as concern deepened on his own. "Anthony's never mentioned Bethany Village to you?"

"It sounds vaguely familiar. Isn't it some program to help those who are in need of some *serious* help?" She was speaking directly to Nikki, her eyes piercing through the curvaceous fake blond's violet-colored contact lenses. Nikki placed one hand on her hip as her fuchsia-colored, heavily lined lips turned into an unmistakable snarl.

"Something like that." Eric chuckled.

"We're here to do the work of Jesus," Nikki piped in, her face suddenly softening into an angelic expression.

"I would love to hear more about CASH and Bethany Village," Terri spoke decisively and sweetly. She was not about to let some church-queen wanna-be outdo her in front of her own pastor. Especially not this clueless thing. Nikki rolled her eyes at the jab.

"Well, let's go upstairs and join the service." Pastor Green, still oblivious to the unspoken squabble, looked troubled despite his warm smile. "It sounds like they're having a time up there," he observed, referring to the stomping and clapping that seemed to be shaking the entire rickety church. The metal folding chairs in the basement hall rattled under the holy quake.

Nikki quickly stepped past Terri, grazing her elbow in the process. "Hallelujah!" she shouted with fire. "Let's go praise the Lord!"

Before Terri could respond in kind, she caught Eric Johnson looking at her. She wondered how much of the undeclared war he had witnessed. With the grace of a debutante queen, she ascended the steps behind Nikki, shouting "Amen, sister!"

As the two men followed the ladies to the sanctuary, Pastor Green could no longer bottle his concern.

"I wonder what Anthony is up to?" he asked aloud, giving one last look at the envelope in his hands before entering the praise-filled service.

Chapter 6

The sun was completing its daily setting ritual and the sky was streaked with its last few stubborn rays. Anthony patted the bulging lump under his coat and rechecked his watch. Councilman Banks, walking with Anthony the few blocks to the Quadrangle Towers, briskly rubbed his hands in the chill of the evening. They strolled together in silence, their heavy footsteps striking the littered cement in rhythmic unison and echoing through the emptying downtown streets.

It was hard to believe that a half hour earlier these same streets had been backed up with beeping and braking automobiles, buses, and taxicabs; hordes of pedestrians crowding the narrow crosswalks at every light change; and noisy street vendors and whistling traffic police adding to the grinding monotony of the now ending business day. Anthony looked up at a large clock ticking from one of the bank buildings. He had only fifteen minutes left to make the delivery.

As an unsettling wind stirred, Anthony clutched his overcoat tightly around his waist. Instinctively he realized that the occasional passersby knew nothing about the satchel of money hidden under his coat, but simply carrying the large sum of money—hundreds of thousands— made him feel vulnerable to the opportunistic eyes he imagined were waiting at every corner, at every alley, at every step.

He examined each person he passed with suspicion: the preoccupied attorney descending the courthouse stairs, the wiry Asian man with the clanging keys locking the metal gate in front of his corner carryout; even the grubby street-lady who never parked her soiled shopping cart caught Anthony's eyes and ears with her disjointed ramblings and warnings about Armageddon.

Anthony noticed that Walter Banks's eyes darted around even more than his own. He waved and nodded politely to passing constituents who recognized him, even stopping once to discuss with a middle-aged woman a new school gymnasium that was being added to a local high school.

Lord, why am I doing this? Anthony battled inside with each footstep. Confusion and fear both weakened and numbed him as he watched a small whirlwind of rustling orange and red autumn leaves scatter on the gray pavement that stretched unending before him.

He glanced over at the councilman. He looked nervous, afraid even. But Anthony knew Walter would never discuss his feelings or fears. True to character, Councilman Banks quickly put a reassuring smile on his face when he realized Anthony was studying him. "Don't worry. I'm sure everything will be okay—once we give back this money. We'll deal with the rest later." He offered another smile before becoming reabsorbed in his own thoughts.

This is crazy. Anybody in town could be behind all this. Who do I trust? Even as the question formed, words from Proverbs whispered gently in Anthony's mind. "Trust in the Lord with all thine heart; and lean not unto thine own understanding. In all thy ways acknowledge Him, and He shall direct thy paths." Anthony stared at the dizzying sidewalks around him, walkways leading to other streets, dirt pathways circling buildings and bus stops.

"Direct thy paths." Anthony thought of the sermon he had given on Sunday. *My dear children, my church friends, where are you headed this morning? What path are you on? Where are your feet taking you?* His own preached words prodded his senses. He had started to turn to Walter Banks and announce that he was about to call the authorities that very moment to end the chaos and deal with the consequences when the garden courtyard of the Quadrangle Towers came into view. Confusion and fear clouded his reasoning once again as they both checked their watches and quickened their steps.

"Only eight more minutes," the councilman muttered, his eyes frantically searching the sprawling bushes and trees that filled the prized city-center square. "You think whoever it is, is here already?" He asked in a tone that expected no answer. Anthony offered none.

Instead he blew out a large breath and watched it roll into a white frost before turning toward the park's large fountain. He could already see the tips of the marble statue's extended fingers. The solid, outstretched hand from the stoic figure that sat in the middle of the multitiered, watery cascade almost seemed to beckon him toward the bench where the briefcase would be waiting.

Councilman Banks stopped in his tracks. "What was that? Did you hear that?"

"Hear what?" Anthony did not break his stride. "I didn't hear anything. You're imagin—" Anthony suddenly froze.

"What, what?" The councilman's voice was a hoarse whisper behind Anthony. "Do you see something? What's wrong?"

"That's *my* briefcase sitting on the park bench!" Anthony rushed toward the wooden seat and picked up the empty black leather attaché case. He ran his fingers over the engraved AMM as if polishing the golden nameplate would answer some of his questions.

"Where is all my stuff? Who has it? What is going on?" Anthony turned to the councilman, who had finally rejoined him.

"Just put the money in it and leave it like they asked! Come on, let's get out of here! I wasn't thinking! I can't afford any trouble! You know how the press and the public deal with politicians. I've worked too hard. . . ." For the first time, Walter sounded truly petrified and heartbroken.

As Councilman Banks spoke, Anthony noticed a police cruiser recircling the block. "I'm getting help right now!" he shouted as he raised an arm to flag down the officer.

Councilman Banks caught his arm in mid-air. "No, not like this! Don't get the police involved in this yet! I can't have people thinking I'm part of some scandal! Please Anthony, put the money in the briefcase and let's get out of here! Or at least wait until I do!" Walter was already backing away.

Anthony watched as the councilman's lean frame disappeared into the shrubbery before turning his attention
back to the street. He quickly stuffed the satchel with the
money into the briefcase and headed to the corner where
the cruiser had stopped.

"Hey!" Anthony waved an arm, but the policeman was
already out of his car and heading toward him.

"Put the bag down, and put your arms in the air!" The
police officer pointed a gun at him.

"Wait a minute! I want to—"

"I said put your arms in the air!" The officer circled
him, both hands on the gun.

"Look, I need—"

"Shut up and get down on the ground!" He approached
Anthony, who slowly complied, a look of utter confusion
on his face.

"A robbery was reported at a jewelry store up the street
a few minutes ago. The owner says that five hundred
thousand dollars was taken from his safe. A man matching
your description was seen leaving the area. You wouldn't
happen to know anything about this, would you?"

The police officer picked up Anthony's briefcase and
dumped the satchel on the ground. A few stacks of hundred-dollar bills fell out, which the officer quickly re-
trieved before greedily digging into the rest of the money.

In the dim streetlight, Anthony made out the badge of
the officer.

"Sheriff Malloy! This isn't at all what it looks like! Let
me explain! I've been trying to contact one of your detectives. I really need to talk to—"

"Save your story for the judge." The sheriff ignored Anthony's pleas as he shackled him to a nearby lamppost.

"Lord Jesus!" Anthony cried, the cold metal of the streetlight chilling his back, his legs outstretched beneath him.

Sheriff Malloy talked into the radio in his cruiser. Long seconds passed before he turned back to Anthony. "Well, well, this is turning out to be a bizarre night after all. A man walking the streets of Shepherd Hills who for some reason happens to have thousands of dollars on him, and a robbery victim who calls back to say he found the money he reported stolen, that it was all a big misunderstanding."

The sheriff eyed Anthony suspiciously as he unlocked the handcuffs. "I can't arrest a man for simply carrying around a ridiculous amount of money, no matter how suspect or strange it looks to me." This he said while patting Anthony down once again. He stopped at his wallet and flipped through it a few times.

"Anthony Michael Murdock," he slowly read the name off of Anthony's driver's license before staring at him with a questioning gaze. "I don't know what you are up to, but I do know that I've been hearing your name a lot over the past couple of months."

"I've been wanting to talk to somebody. I need to tell—"

"I've got to go," the sheriff cut in again as his radio buzzed with activity. "I'm needed elsewhere, but you better watch yourself, Mr. Murdock, because people are watching you." He gave Anthony one last look of disgust before turning away.

"One of your detectives . . . I left a message for . . ." Anthony threw his hands up as the cruiser disappeared into the moonlit cityscape.

"What now, Lord?" Anthony shouted up to the heavens, desperation in his voice.

He kicked at the upside-down briefcase and several stacked bills fluttered out. He stood thoughtful for a moment, then reached to catch the bills before the growing wind could escort them to a trash-filled gutter grate. As he picked up the last stack, he heard a phone ringing somewhere behind him.

Jumping up, he turned to see a pay phone about fifteen feet from where he stood. The ring was unending. With slow steps he walked over to the booth. The glass had been shattered and graffiti covered the metal box.

Dread and curiosity plagued Anthony as his fingers danced along the smooth black receiver. The phone kept ringing, sounding defiant against the quiet, empty street. Finally, he picked it up.

"Hello?"

A muffled voice immediately greeted him.

"Now you know that we're not playing with you, Anthony. Tonight was a mere sample of what we can do to your life. We control what happens to you, so you better start doing what you are told. Try to talk if you want, but you'll quickly see that nobody will listen."

Before the words could register in Anthony's mind, the other end went dead. He stood a long time in the booth, the phone still at his ear.

"If you would like to make a call, please insert the correct change." The familiar voice blared through the speaker, rousing him out of a stupefied daze.

Anthony dropped the phone and stepped slowly out of the booth. He watched the dangling cord sway back and forth several times before pulling up his coat collar and beginning the walk back to his car parked several blocks away.

As the moon slithered through the twisted maze of the starlit sky, the night creatures were already beginning their furtive quests for survival in the streets, alleyways, and backyards of Shepherd Hills.

Sitting in his parked car for almost an hour, Anthony tried to figure out what had just happened. The money was safely hidden in the floor of his trunk until he could figure out what to do with it. Anthony was unsure what to do about anything or how to explain to the detective the fiasco he found himself in the middle of. Turning on his cell phone, he dialed the detective's phone number, which he got off of the business card Pastor Green had given him two days earlier. When an answering machine greeted him, he promptly hung up. He wanted to speak to the detective directly.

Before he turned his phone back off, he noticed that the small screen was flashing ONE MESSAGE WAITING.

It was Terri: "Hi, baby. Sorry I missed you after work today, but I should see you at church. I'm on my way there now. Wait until you see what I got! I'm sure you'll agree that it's something that will fit right into our new circumstances." With that she giggled. The message continued: "Oh, and today's clue to guess my big surprise is, hmmm, let's see: Think gentle rocking under a canopy of stars, on a foamy blanket of blue-green. Bye, baby."

"We're having a boy," Anthony said dreamily to himself. But before he could fully register the mental picture of Terri cuddling a newborn in a blue, celestial-themed nursery, his phone rang, sending sharp vibrations through his hand and arm.

"Hello." His voice was dull, tired.

"Anthony, it's me, Walter," the councilman whispered. "Look, I'm sorry I left you like that, but I started envisioning everything that could have happened. I'm at a dinner so I can't talk long, but I wanted to let you know that Gloria is okay. Wait until you hear what happened. Things are getting crazier. This whole time she was—"

He stopped mid-sentence, his attention obviously turned away from the phone. Anthony strained to make out a voice in the background that Walter was politely acknowledging.

"Anthony," he whispered again. "I think you should get the authorities involved. I'll help any way that I can. Now I'm thinking that returning the money was a bad idea. Did you see anyone come for the briefcase?" Before Anthony could respond, the councilman quickly whispered, "I've got to go. I can't talk right now, but I'll call you as soon as I can." Anthony heard a loud click.

Perplexing, dizzying questions circulated in his mind like the rotating blades of a window fan. One question remained constant.

"Why am I specifically being singled out?" Anthony wondered aloud as he started the ignition. He knew that his role in the original Stonymill deal had been crucial, but that did not explain why so much seemed to be riding on his shoulders six months later.

As he drove through the empty streets, he knew where he was headed without thinking: the only place in Shepherd Hills where he consistently found solace and refuge.

When he turned into the gravel parking lot of Second Baptist Church, he realized that a genuine smile had found its way onto his face for the first time that day. He longed to be in the house of the Lord, surrounded by people whose very presence encouraged him and lifted his spirits. Even though he would only be catching the tail end of the weeknight prayer and Bible study service, he was confident that hope, courage, and direction lay within the small church's gates.

"Must be a visitor," he mumbled, not bothered by the sight of a sporty red convertible parked in his usual space. "Nice car."

He stepped into the small, carpeted foyer and peeked through the doors that led into the sanctuary. He recognized the voice speaking even before he saw the face, and guilt gargled up within him like a sudden geyser spout.

"Bethany Village is God's project." Eric Johnson proclaimed from a plain, wooden podium at the front of the church. "God is all about helping the oppressed, the afflicted, the addicted. He hears the cries of the abandoned, both young and old. He heals the hurts of a million heartaches. And the people of God should do the things of God."

"Amen!" Sister Ethel slammed some dollar bills onto the podium as Eric continued to speak.

"I'm not turning to the government, church, because this is not the government's project. I'm not turning to the politician, because this was not the politician's plan. I'm starting at the steps of the church, under the steeples of the community. I'm asking you to join God's vision today so that every citizen of Shepherd Hills, both the beggar and the billionaire, will see the work of Jesus right in front of their eyes. You heard my testimony, how I almost gave up the vision six months ago when the disease of greed spread throughout our community and priorities were placed on personal gain."

Anthony wondered if Eric could see him peeking through the door. He wondered if he knew about his role in the dismantling of CASH. All of his mailed donations at that time had been returned.

"But as God reassured Habakkuk, he reassured me. He said, 'For the vision is yet for an appointed time, but at the end it shall speak, and not lie; though it tarry, wait for it because it will surely come, it will not tarry.'"

Anthony watched as a blond-headed, pecan-colored woman quickly stood and began passing out pamphlets and collecting donations. He immediately recognized her as Nikki Galloway, the secretary Gloria had replaced. Councilman Banks had quietly endured her "work ethics" for over a year. His heart for the community must have rubbed off on her as she was now working for CASH, Anthony reasoned. Something twisted inside him as he listened to Eric continue.

"There are some who think we will not last, that we will fail like we did six months ago. But I don't believe that our God fails. No, He flourishes in the face of impossibility. Only God can make green grass grow out of cracked sidewalks, where feet trample and no gardener tends. Church, support us with your prayers, sustain us with your funds, and the vision of Bethany Village will come to pass!"

Anthony marveled at the eloquence of a man who had never graduated from high school, who had spent over a decade with his mind asleep under the lull of narcotics. Surely the hand of the Lord was upon his life.

What about my life? Anthony faltered at the thought. He was too ashamed to enter the sanctuary, and sadly turned toward the exit. Before he could push the worn brass handle of the front door, he heard a series of violent coughs and wheezes coming from the basement stairway.

"Is everything okay?" He turned toward the stairwell.

There, on the middle of the steps was the assistant pastor, Bernard Porter, his frail hands weakly gripping the banister. He coughed uncontrollably as Anthony helped him up the rest of the steps and led him to a bench under a large cork bulletin board.

"Anthony, Anthony," he wheezed between coughs. Anthony tried to quiet him, but the man seemed intent on talking, his tired eyes haunted by desperation.

"It's good to see you, Minister Porter, but you need to take it easy. I'm going to go get your wife and a cup of water for you."

As Anthony tried to pull away, Bernard grabbed his wrist and pulled Anthony close to his face. Anthony was surprised at the force of the gesture, but could tell immediately that the effort had taken the remainder of what little energy Minister Porter had as his voice dropped to a breathless whisper.

"I know . . . I know. . . ." he wheezed.

"Take it easy, Minister Porter," Anthony continued to repeat.

"I know your troubles, Anthony."

"It's no trouble helping you." Anthony's concern was sincere.

"No . . . no . . . You must stay . . . here with me. . . ." The elder reverend struggled to get the words out.

"Sit back, Minister Porter. Don't exert yourself." Anthony helped him sit back in the wooden bench.

"I know your troubles. . . . The money . . ."

At that, Anthony froze, his eyes searching the sunken ones of Minister Porter.

"You're wondering why . . . why you . . . why you're in the center of it all." His breathing was becoming more erratic. "I only came tonight . . . to see you . . . to tell you . . . there's something you need to know. . . ."

Anthony was stunned. What was Bernard Porter's connection to Stonymill? He was a preacher. A retired factory worker.

"You need to know . . . about your father. . . ." With the words came another violent episode of coughs.

Anthony frowned. His stepfather had been a postal worker before the accident that had taken his and Anthony's mother's lives. What did he have to do with any of this? Surely Bernard was mistaken, his thoughts confused by the long menu of medications he was taking.

Anthony smiled. "Oh, Minister Porter, don't worry about him. I knew Harold since I was four years old. He—"

Minister Porter cut him off immediately. "Not your stepfather . . . your real father. You need to know that—" A deep cough stifled out his words.

As Anthony patted his back, Sister Porter appeared in the foyer, a rare look of worry etched across her broad features.

"Oh, there you are, sweetheart. When you didn't come back from the rest room I got concerned." She quickly sat beside him and gently rubbed his back. "Thank you, Anthony, for helping him. I told him that he needed to stay home, but he insisted like never before that he come tonight."

"You . . . need . . . to know . . . that . . ." Bernard was still trying to whisper between hacks.

"Hush, hush, sweetheart." The worry lines on Sister Porter's forehead deepened. "I'm taking you home, back to bed where you belong. Anthony, can you help me get him to the car?"

Minister Porter's coughs became more aggressive, strangling any words he frantically tried to force out as Anthony helped him into the passenger seat of the Porters' Oldsmobile.

"I'll come to visit soon," he said as he closed the car door. Bernard Porter's eyes were glued on him and wide with anguish.

Anthony watched them pull out of the parking lot before heading to his own car. *My father.* Charles Anthony Murdock. A man who was only a name to him, not even a face.

Anthony took the long way home. This had to be an answer to some of the questions, although it raised many more. *My father.* He would call Haven Ridge Nursing Home in Sharen, South Carolina, in the morning. His Great-Aunt Rosa might have some answers for him. She was the only person in his twenty-nine years of living he had ever heard mention his real father by name.

Chapter 7

Sharen, South Carolina

Mabel Linstead signed off on the last chart. She'd finished her morning rounds early for a change and wanted to take advantage of the crisp fall air. Many of the residents at Haven Ridge Nursing Home enjoyed sitting out on the patio on clear days when the smell of pine and magnolias floated in the wind, unearthing lost memories and thoughts. A nursing assistant had agreed to help her wheel the residents out of their rooms and onto the cement terrace.

Haven Ridge was an old plantation home near a forgotten end of the Carolina coast. Seagulls mingled with sparrows on the estate, a formidable white-marbled building whose past glory had never been reclaimed. The landscaper did his best to keep down the weeds and wild grasses that peeped in the driveway and grounds, but he could not keep up with the fast-growing ivy climbing over the walls and pillars.

Several coats of paint and careful carpentry had not stopped the spread of cracks and splinters on the outside walls and porches. Despite its dismal exterior, the interior of Haven Ridge was a bright yellow-green. Clean hallways and inviting wallpaper kept the patient areas cheerful and relaxing. Residents were allowed to bring as many photos, knickknacks, and other personal mementos as their shared rooms would allow.

Although the estate was grand in scale, the executive board members of Haven Ridge were determined to keep the population small, giving it a cozy, intimate feel. Each of the home's twenty-three residents were assigned personal volunteers who visited them at least twice a week to keep them company, and keep them lucid and talking. The care was impeccable, the attention revolutionary. Mabel locked up the medicine cart and joined the residents on the terrace.

"Mr. Gregory, you need to keep your shirt on if you want to stay outside." Mabel helped the ninety-one-year-old-man readjust himself.

As she spoke, she kept her eyes on another resident, a woman with long, silver braids wrapped around her high forehead like a coiled hat. Her wheelchair was parked alone in a corner of the patio, and she was singing an old spiritual Mabel did not recognize. She watched as the older lady clapped worn, wrinkled hands together in rough time with the music. Sometimes the singing would stop, but her mouth and hands kept moving.

"Ms. Rosa, would you like a blanket to put over your legs? It's a little more chilly out here than I realized."

Mabel walked over to her as an aide stepped out into the courtyard.

"There's a telephone call for Ms. Bergenson," the young girl shouted from the doorway.

"You up for a phone call today, Ms. Rosa?" Mabel smiled in the woman's face.

"Fifty cents. That's how much they paid Momma for scrubbing their floors every day. Gonna be time to start school soon. I'm going this year. Are you going, Lilly Ann?"

Mabel patted the wrinkled hands before turning her attention back to the aide. "Take a message. Her mind's not up to it today." Sad how a lifetime of memories starts breaking down; Mabel shook her head. Her own mother had wasted away from Alzheimer's too. She continued to warm Rosa's hands.

"It's a family member, a great-nephew. Anthony somebody. Said it's urgent that he speak to her about a relative or something."

Mabel almost staggered off balance. "Tell him that she is not up to phone calls today." Her voice was as icy as the hands she held. The aide shrugged her shoulders and disappeared back into the warm building.

"Some memories aren't worth holding on to," Mabel mumbled to herself as she walked back to the nurses' station. She'd been holding onto a key since Mrs. Bergenson's admission. The drawer it unlocked was largely unnoticed by office and nursing staff. She opened it for the first time that morning, and removed its only content, a torn piece of letterhead with a phone number scribbled across it.

"My payday is a-coming." She gave a quick look around before locking herself into a corner office. "Hope this number still works." She dialed quickly.

~

Terri turned up the radio as she hit sixty-five on the expressway. The morning was filled with promise, she convinced herself. Disappointed that Anthony had not woken up in time to see her new Lexus, she kept a smile on her face as she planned out her day. She would surprise him with lunch, she decided. A turkey club sandwich from Joe's Deli would be the perfect excuse to catch him at his job later that afternoon.

But first she was meeting with Reginald Savant and his team that morning. He had already offered praise for her blueprints and sketches, so she was confident that the rest of his colleagues would also be impressed with her ideas for the Empress Hotel.

"Darn it!" she slammed a fist into her steering wheel. Traffic was coming to a standstill farther ahead. Terri could make out blue and white, red and yellow lights flashing from somewhere in the middle of the upheaval. A large, dark-colored sedan was scrunched against the cement median.

Terri checked her watch and spotted an exit that would let her off before hitting the standstill.

"Ain't going to let some traffic stop me. I'm going to have a *great* day!" She turned off the exit and readjusted her route. The steel-and-glass skyline of downtown was already in view.

"I can't believe the luck I'm having this week." Detective Kent Cassell murmured the words over and over as he paced beside his totaled car. The trunk of his Crown Victoria was tucked into the backseat, making the rear of his vehicle look like a massive accordion, while the front left of the car sat lopsided over the short cement barricade separating the two sides of the expressway. Shattered glass and metal shreds crunched under his feet as he walked back and forth.

"I'm glad you're okay. This could have been a lot worse." Sheriff Malloy stood beside him, patting his shoulder. "We'll find the creeps who did this. Hit-and-runs have become too popular lately." The sheriff surveyed the car once more before looking back at the snaking traffic that had come to a complete stop for several miles up the expressway.

"We need to start clearing out. The morning rush is in full swing." Malloy beckoned at a tow truck. A burly man with long red hair pulled back into a ponytail jumped out of the truck and began his duty.

"I wish I had gotten a good look at the car that ran into me. It happened so fast. I didn't see the color, the license." Kent shook his head. "But you're right. It could have been a lot worse. They didn't get me this time, either."

Sheriff Malloy's head jerked up. "That's right. This isn't the first time you've been involved in a hit-and-run. You're thinking there's someone after you, huh?"

"Look at my week, Gary. I've missed the past couple of days dealing with break-ins at my home office and my wife's day care. Nothing was taken in either case, but it looked like the intruder was searching for something. Mona is simply too shaken up. She's convinced that this is somehow related to my current case and that someone doesn't want me involved. She was scared for me to come back to work today. You should have seen her crying when

I turned my cell phone back on, afraid of what calls I may get."

"I can't say I blame her for being nervous." Sheriff Malloy was getting into a squad car with Kent. "You're a hard worker, Cassell. The best. But even the best detective needs a breather sometimes. You might want to consider taking some more time off, you know, take a vacation, just you and Mona. Get away from all this. I can get some other guys to take over your cases for a while."

"You know I can't leave my work undone. These two days alone that I've missed are eating me up. I feel like I missed something big." Kent's hands were clenched into fists in his lap. His eyes, ever alert, scanned the passing cityscape as the car turned toward the exit that would take them to police headquarters.

"You're too involved." Sheriff Malloy's voice was flat as he stared straight ahead at the roadway. "You need to take care of yourself, your wife, that knee. Take a vacation. Go to Martha's Vineyard. You always said you wanted to go. I'll keep everything under control here."

Kent rubbed his knee. Mona's tear-streaked face sat firmly in his mind as he recalled seeing her cry in her sleep the night before.

"Maybe you're right, Gary. Maybe I do need to take Mona away for a week or two."

Malloy smiled. "I'll get Burke and Morris to cover for you. You can give me your folders when we get to the office."

Kent nestled back into his seat, trying hard to ignore the sour feeling building in his stomach.

~

Terri took in the view from the forty-third floor of the Quadrangle Towers. The people and commuters on the busy street below looked like colorful worker ants marching to the beat of an unheard drum. From where she stood behind the massive glass pane, all of the sounds that accompanied the outdoor morning hustle were silenced to her ear.

"You're early. I like that."

Terri turned around to see Reginald Savant standing in the doorway of the lavishly furnished reception area. A cup of steaming coffee was in his hand. It smelled of hazelnut and cream. He smelled of suede and spice.

"I make a point of ensuring that all of my clients know they're receiving my most attentive care. Your project is important to me." Instinctively Terri knew she was smiling too much, but the sudden vision she was having of his black Jaguar and her red Lexus riding side by side in the streets of downtown was too much. They were both elitists, a king and a queen in the cutthroat world of success.

Anthony should wear a watch like that, don a suit like that. Terri's smile almost betrayed her thoughts as she carefully studied Reginald head to toe. *Anthony's a multi-millionaire now so he should dress like one.* She made a mental note to talk about that with him later. Of course she would wait for him to finally tell her about his "surprise." She wondered why he was waiting so long to share his overwhelming financial-success story with her.

"My team will be joining us in a conference room down the hall." Reginald was also obviously studying her. "As I told you before, my colleagues have already expressed awe at your work, Mrs. Murdock. I assure you that this meeting is nothing more than a platform from which you can further implement your design ideas."

Terri walked with him down the hallway. Standing next to this visionary businessman, dressed in her best black suit, carrying her polished attaché case, she wondered if the incoming office workers could see how important she was. Like Reginald, she did little to acknowledge the passersby who stepped to the sides of the corridor for them.

"I am personally looking forward to your presence at tomorrow evening's function."

Reginald's words caught her off guard. Terri tried to keep a question mark from forming on her face as she played along with this turn in the conversation. What function? she wondered.

"You should be proud of him."

"Who?"

"Anthony. Your husband." There was a flatness in his voice as he spoke these words.

"You know Anthony?" Terri could not hide her surprise. Anthony had never made any indication to her of knowing or meeting Reginald Savant. "How do you know him?"

"I see there's a lot he hasn't told you." Reginald smiled at her curiously. "It's not good when a young man starts keeping secrets from his unsuspecting wife."

"Oh, I'm sure he's just waiting for the right time to tell me whatever he has to share." Terri suddenly felt unsure of something she couldn't quite put her finger on. She hadn't been seeing much of him lately. Was there something more she should know? Was he hiding more from her than information about his new financial status?

"You don't even know about the function, do you?"

"I have no idea what you are talking about," Terri finally confessed with a grin.

"That's surprising. Even if Anthony didn't tell you about it, Fabian's Caterers is helping with the event. Isn't your best friend, Cherisse Landrick, employed by him?"

Terri paused before slowly easing into the cushioned seat offered by Reginald.

"Boy, you really do know a lot about my life."

"As I told you at our first meeting, Mrs. Murdock, I do my research when I handpick my team members. I like to know as much as possible about everyone with whom I have intimate dealings and vested interest."

Before any more could be said, the door to the conference room flew open and several well-dressed ebony businessmen filed into the room, clipboards, briefcases, pens in hand.

"Gentlemen, Mrs. Murdock, let's begin."

Nagging questions were racing through Terri's mind by the completion of the meeting, despite its overwhelming success. The flood of praise and commendation offered by Reggie's team did little to lessen Terri's mounting doubts and fears. Was Anthony purposely not telling her everything she needed to know?

She'd merely guessed that he was about to share with her the story of their new multi-million-dollar status before she cut him off during the dinner at Romano's. What if he really had something else to say? She strained to remember his words from that evening as she crept through the slow-moving downtown traffic.

I really need not worry that something's wrong; Anthony is a preacher. For once the thought comforted her. Preachers don't keep secrets, especially dirty ones, she told herself. Even still, she had not seen him at prayer meeting the night before, and he never mentioned that he had somewhere else to go. Anthony was a faithful attendee of the midweek service as far as she knew, considering she rarely attended herself. Where had he been? Even Pastor Green had seemed concerned, she remembered.

Thinking of the look on Pastor Green's face, she suddenly recalled the meeting Anthony said he had with the pastor that past Monday night. Had he really met with him? Terri thought of how anxious Anthony had looked when he'd left their fireside celebration that night. She'd been asleep when he returned and then he'd left for work in the morning before she could question him. What was Anthony up to? Was he hiding something? *Or someone?*

These were Terri's thoughts as she waited for Joe to call her number at the crowded deli counter. After paying for two turkey club sandwiches, she switched off her cell phone, not wanting to chance a call from him at the moment. The drive to Haberstick Associates was a short one, and the surprise element was crucial to her quickly devised plot.

She did not even park the car. The moment she pulled into the dingy parking lot, she noticed a battered blue Dodge Shadow in Anthony's assigned spot. That was not his car. He was not there. Her instincts told her he had not been there all day. What was Anthony up to? What was he not telling her and why? The questions scared her. But she was determined to get the answers.

～

Anthony managed to pull himself out of bed for good at eleven. Not usually a late sleeper, he'd delayed getting up until after Terri left for work, still unsure how to face her with his ongoing and unfolding drama. After failing to reach Aunt Rosa at the senior home in South Carolina, he'd gotten back in bed, wanting to ignore the rest of the day.

It was the phone ringing that woke him the second time. Groggy from oversleeping, he missed the call, noting the BLOCKED message on the caller ID box. He'd check for a message later.

For now, he planned to visit the Porters. Reverend Bernard seemed anxious to talk to him. Maybe he held a missing piece to the puzzle of how this Stonymill deal that started six months earlier had come back to haunt him even more. Anthony could not imagine how his long-dead biological father was related to his current circumstances, but he hoped Bernard could offer more insight into dealing with the faceless people who were involved in the unending nightmare.

At twelve-thirty he was standing on the front porch of the Porters' small ranch home, waiting for someone to answer his knock. A minivan pulled into the driveway next to the Porters'. Anthony watched with a smile as a couple of redheaded and freckled preschoolers spilled out, followed by a young woman also with curly red hair. She held an infant in one arm, a grocery bag in the other. She greeted him with a tired but courteous smile before disappearing into her home.

Anthony knocked again on the Porters' door, louder, harder. Still no response. Disappointed, he turned to leave. As he unlocked his car door, the neighbor's door flew open.

"Are you looking for the Porters?" The young mother offered another smile, but concern sounded in her voice.

"Yes. Is everything okay?" Anthony feared the answer.

"I'm not sure." The woman's attention was diverted back into her house for a second before she continued. "An ambulance was here around three this morning. I think they took the reverend to the ER. I'm not really sure what's going on, but I haven't seen either him or Mrs. Porter today. They usually sit out on their porch after lunch. I hope everything's all right."

"Thanks for the information. I hope everything's all right too."

The woman disappeared back into her home, leaving Anthony standing alone on the quiet cul-de-sac, not sure what to do next.

Terri blew her nose softly, hoping that no one passing by her office could hear the phone conversation she was having with Cherisse.

"Look, Terri"—Cherisse's voice was soothing over the receiver—"you need to pull yourself together and calm down. I haven't heard you this upset since you thought Marlene Gibbons beat you out for homecoming queen. Remember, junior year, college?"

Terri had to smile at the memory. She remembered how silly she'd felt taking the winning platform to accept her crown and the bouquet of roses with eyes puffy and red from crying. The announcer had mistaken her tears as a sign of joy and had not known what they really were: tears of relief. She had been wrong then; maybe she was wrong now.

"You're stronger than this, girl," Cherisse continued.

"I'm sure you're making something out of nothing. Anthony may or may not be telling you everything, but that doesn't mean he's hiding anything. Remember, we're talking about Anthony, Mr. Goody-two-shoes, the preacher."

"I know." Terri sighed. "But I can't figure out why Reggie Savant seems to know more about what's going on with my husband these days than I do."

"This Reggie character is creeping me out. You said he knows who I am?"

"He knows that you work for Fabian's and that your company is catering whatever function is happening tomorrow night—the function Anthony hasn't told me about."

"That's odd," Cherisse mumbled. "Mr. Fabian must have assigned someone else to oversee that account. I usually know about these things. Unless . . ."

"What is it?" Terri demanded.

"Does Mr. Savant drive a black Jaguar?"

"Yes, he does. Why?"

"Then that's who's been coming back and forth to see Mr. Fabian this week. I should have recognized his voice from that time I saw him talking to you at the Westcott Room on Tuesday. He *is* involved in some event Fabian is catering. I get the impression it's a rush job—an expensive, elaborate rush job."

"That still doesn't explain how he knows Anthony."

"If that's really him, then he was one of the two men talking Tuesday about Anthony getting millions. I have no idea who the other man was. Whoever it was sounded young and polished."

There was a long pause broken only by a few sniffles

from Terri and the new quartz clock on her desk striking one P.M.

"Something isn't right," Cherisse finally conceded.

A new rush of tears burst from Terri. "Cherisse, what do I do?"

"First things first." Cherisse's "about-business" tone was back. "I'm going to get us tickets to whatever is going on tomorrow night. I work for Fabian and you're the wife of an attendee. There's no reason for us not to be there. Pull yourself together, girl. Whatever Anthony's hiding, whatever game he's playing, we'll find out. I'm not going to let some man toy with my best friend."

"Thank you." Terri sounded stronger already. "Call me back when you have some details."

The intensive-care waiting room at Good Shepherd General Hospital was quiet. Anthony sat next to Sister Porter, her hair pulled back in a hurried, gray-streaked bun. Both were silent and staring at a massive aqua-blue aquarium that stretched across one side of the small room. Several fish of different sizes and brilliant colors swam back and forth against the quiet hum of the filtration system.

"Pastor Green should be here soon." Anthony barely recognized his own voice. He kept his eyes on a small blue-and-yellow fish that seemed trapped in an elaborate castle in a corner of the tank.

"They're taking him off the life support at two o'clock. Bernard always made it clear to me that he would not want to stay in a vegetative state." Sister Porter glanced at

Anthony, the look on her face seeming to plead for permission and understanding.

"They"—she pointed to the nurses' station—"are saying there's no brain activity at all. He's only alive right now because of those machines. The stroke that he had last night came when his body was the most vulnerable. He was already weak from all those years of cancer."

"When Pastor Green arrives, we'll pray again. Jesus said that when two or three are gathered in His name, they can . . . He will . . ." Anthony choked against the words in his throat. Sister Porter raised a gentle hand to silence him.

"I was just telling Terri on Sunday that Bernard would be out of his sickbed soon." A tear dripped off her chin as a distant smile formed around her words. "Our God answers prayer, Brother Anthony; not always in the way we think or expect, but always in the way that is best." Tears were pooling atop a black leather handbag resting in her lap.

"Lord knows my Bernard was tired. He needs his rest. I only want him to be whole again. And he will. Today. He'll be resting wholly in the arms of Jesus, the wonderful, perfect Good Shepherd." She nodded at a mural of the hospital's name painted across the adjacent wall.

At 2:07, Sister Porter, Anthony, and Pastor Green surrounded the bed of Minister Porter. The machines were off, the tubes were gone, the room was quiet. Anthony watched Bernard's chest rise and fall a few times before slowly coming to a stop.

"I love you and I'll see you again, sweetheart. Enjoy your rest." Sister Porter planted a soft kiss on her husband's forehead, smiling even as tears streamed down her face.

As Anthony watched the deathbed scene unfold in front of him, he couldn't ignore the frustration creeping alongside his grief. What information was Bernard taking with him as he left to meet his Maker?

Nikki Galloway spoke politely into the receiver, but her face gave a different story.

"Thanks again for letting me know. Have a nice trip." She slammed down the phone before muttering to herself, "I hate that woman."

"Is everything okay?" Eric Johnson looked up from an old computer, which he was using to create address labels. It was nearly three o'clock and much work still remained to be done. Eric had spent most of the day following up behind Nikki's unfinished tasks. She was slowing him down greatly, but he reasoned it was only because it was her first days on the job. She would catch on soon. Hopefully.

"I'm sorry." Nikki wiped the scowl from her face. "It's my son's day-care provider. She's taking off again for another emergency, this time for a couple of weeks."

"I don't mean to get in your business, but it seems like you have a lot of issues with this woman. Are you looking for another day care?"

"Oh, it's really okay." Nikki quickly smiled. "Devin will be four in January so he'll be able to start pre-K. I can wait."

She rolled her eyes as she turned back to the papers she was filing. The truth was Nikki had never liked Ms. Mona or her stupid day care. The lady was too nitpicky and particular and had too many rules to follow, like she was scared the world would fall apart if a parent picked up their child an hour late. Nikki had never wanted to put Devin under her care in the first place, but *that man* had said it was necessary to keep things running smoothly.

"There is no other option," he would tell Nikki every morning that he was there, his hands stroking her slender legs. "Devin being at Mona's keeps us with a foot in the door. If you were to move him now, our duties would get more difficult."

"Are you sure everything's all right?" Eric had an eyebrow raised at Nikki, who suddenly realized she'd been standing there mimicking *that man's* gestures, mouthing his words.

"Oops." She giggled. "I was thinking about somebody." She composed herself again. "I'm running out of file space. Didn't you say there might be some empty file cabinets in another part of this building?"

"Huh? Oh, yeah." Eric adjusted his reading glasses, straining to make out an illegible address on a sign-up sheet from his presentation at Second Baptist Church the night before. "This old building has a lot of office space that hasn't been used in a while. Why don't you check some of the rooms on the sixth floor? I don't think anyone's using that space. If you see some empty file cabinets, let me know and I'll work on getting them down here tomorrow."

Nikki relaxed at the opportunity to get out of the small office of CASH, but cringed when the elevator door opened to the sixth floor. Instead of being sectioned off into office suites, the entire floor lay as an open space. The massive room was in disarray, with furniture, boxes, and paper scattered everywhere. It looked as if it had been abandoned in a hurry years ago. Thick layers of dust and cobwebs covered everything. Nikki spotted some file cabinets in a far corner and carefully stepped over some fallen bookcases and stacked boxes to reach them.

"I hate this job," she muttered to herself as she rolled out a heavy cabinet drawer. It was not empty, she quickly discovered, and began thumbing through the jam-packed files.

"Hmmm, what's this?" A name printed on a folder sounded like one she'd heard before. As she pulled out the file a yellowed newspaper clipping fell out and drifted to the ground. The article featured a picture of a serious-looking man with a large afro and a colorful dashiki. Something about his facial features looked familiar to Nikki. She wanted to pick it up and read the caption, but at that moment something else caught her attention.

"Aaaeee!"

After several minutes of desperate scrambling, flying papers, and ear-piercing screams, Eric Johnson appeared.

"Nikki, are you all right?"

"A rat! I just saw a rat!" She was crying and wheezing from the middle of a pile of broken chairs.

"Whew! I didn't realize this floor was so bad. Sorry I sent you up here by yourself. Here, let me help you up." He continued talking as he helped Nikki to the elevator.

"You know this building used to be a major warehouse back when all these old factories around here were actually up and running. Some of the tracks they used for that Stonymill project were part of the old railroad system that came to this part of town." Eric shook his head as the elevator doors closed.

"This building is as dirty as it is old. You don't know what you may find in here."

~

The crisper in the refrigerator was full of fresh vegetables: spinach, romaine, mushrooms, and green onions. Terri remembered a recipe for salad dressing she wanted to try and began looking for sugar, vinegar, dry mustard, strawberries, and mandarin oranges. She moved noisily about the gourmet kitchen, switching on the blender to make a frozen drink, turning the faucet on full strength to rinse her salad ingredients. She enjoyed the noise and the growing clutter, as it was keeping her mind off of more grating thoughts.

It was nearly seven-thirty, and she was still waiting to hear back from Cherisse. Growing impatient, she threw the torn spinach back into the sink and picked up the phone to call her. She found a message waiting instead.

"Hi, Anthony. Calling to remind you to wear your best tux tomorrow evening. I'm sure you'll look like a million bucks." There was a giggle and then a loud gum-popping sound. "Oops." The caller quickly hung up.

Terri mumbled some select words as she erased the message. She wanted to catch Anthony in a lie. If he truly had nothing to hide, he would tell her why he hadn't been at work today. And what was going on the next evening that she wasn't privy to.

She was chopping strawberries when the phone finally rang.

"I got the tickets." Cherisse sounded out of breath.

"Do you know what's going on?"

"It's some type of big-wig banquet to celebrate the beginning of a new elitist organization called—wait a minute, I wrote it down . . ."

Terri heard some papers shuffling before Cherisse continued.

"It's called the Black Entrepreneurs Alliance. Everybody who's somebody in Shepherd Hills is going to be there."

"Did you have any problems getting tickets?" Terri grew more puzzled.

"No, I didn't. I was right about this being scheduled at the last minute. Mr. Fabian is so stressed he gave me a ticket to come in case he needs my help. When I asked for an extra one, he didn't even question why. It was a mad house at work today. I probably could have gotten more information than I did, but I get the impression that even Fabian's not quite sure what's going on. I think he's only doing it because he was offered a ridiculous amount of money. Or so I heard."

"What time does it start?"

"At seven. And it's at the Diamond Mount."

"The Diamond Mount?"

"You know, the old steelworkers' lodge on Twenty-third Street that was turned into an upscale banquet hall."

"Oh yeah. I think one of my partners designed that project."

"We can meet at my house at six-thirty and go together."

"Sounds good."

"Oh, and Terri, make sure you wear all black. The theme to tomorrow night's occasion is Business in the Black and they want everyone to reflect that."

They finished their conversation with exact details of logistics and what each would wear. As Terri hung up the phone she heard keys rattle in the front door and turned to face Anthony, who stood on the opposite side of the granite breakfast bar.

"Hello, Anthony. What have you been up to?" Terri spoke coldly, not missing the flash of uncertainty that surfaced in his eyes before he dropped his gaze to the floor.

Anthony was quiet for a moment before he answered. "Minister Porter passed today. I'll be in my study."

With that Anthony disappeared, leaving Terri to absorb his words slowly. She collapsed in a stool by the breakfast bar and was still sitting there when the phone's ringing broke the silence a few hours later.

Kent Cassell decided to give one last look through the house and adjoining day-care center before heading to Mona's packed Volvo wagon, where she was waiting. He hated leaving at night, especially on such short notice; but Mona had immediately jumped at planning the trip to Martha's Vineyard the moment he called her that morning to tell her he'd taken the next two weeks off. She'd made reservations for the night at a quaint bed-and-breakfast a few hours' drive away in a small town off I-95. The manager agreed to let them check in by midnight. The Cassells would be taking a long, scenic route to Massachusetts with several stops along the way, including other B&Bs and tourist attractions.

Kent was not comfortable leaving in the middle of an open case, but the look of peace and relief in Mona's eyes, and the assurance by Sheriff Malloy that he would be contacted if absolutely necessary, helped quiet the nagging uneasiness that had been haunting him since the hit-and-run accident earlier that morning.

He walked through the house first, double-checking the new bolts that had been placed on the doors and windows since the last break-in. As he stepped into the adjacent home office he shared with Mona that connected the day-care center to the house, he noticed several of his own business cards scattered on the floor.

"I must have missed these when I helped Mona close the center today." Kent stacked them neatly on his desk and straightened up a pile of scribbled artwork before turning on the alarm.

As he stepped into the car and fastened his seat belt a thought crossed his mind: *Those cards weren't on the floor earlier and Mona never leaves those kids' artwork in a mess like that. Has someone else been in the office this evening?*

"Kent, darling, we're going on vacation. Leave it all behind, please." Mona rubbed the furrow forming on his forehead. He looked into his wife's clear green eyes and ran his fingers through her smooth silver-black hair. She was so pretty.

"Everything's fine, honey. I was just trying to remember when's the last time I've seen you so happy and relaxed." He started the ignition and backed out of the driveway. There was an explanation for everything, he reasoned. It was a brisk, fall evening. An open window could have been the culprit for the disorder in the office.

By the time Kent veered onto the ramp to get on I-95, he was absorbed in one of Mona's hilarious stories about her day-care children. The sound of her laughter in the rushing wind was music in his ears.

Anthony heard the phone ringing and almost did not want to pick it up. Sitting in his study surrounded by Bibles and old business correspondences, he simply stared at the rattling telephone, only guessing at who would be calling at that hour. With all that had been going on lately—the money, the confusion, the unanswered questions, and now Minister Porter's death—he was not in a mood to talk to anyone. Not even Terri. Especially Terri. Even thinking about the baby did little to cheer him. How could he happily welcome a son into a world of chaos he'd helped to create? Things would change for the better soon, he convinced himself. With God's help, things would change.

But the phone was still ringing and Terri was not picking it up either. With a groan, he reached for the receiver.

"Minister Anthony?"

Anthony blew a sigh of relief when he recognized the voice.

"Sister Porter, is everything okay?"

"Oh, yes, considering." Even in her grief, Kellye Porter still sounded peaceful and cheery. "I'm sorry to call so late, but in all that's happened today, I forgot to give you something."

"Sister Porter, you don't have to—"

"No, listen. This is important. I want to honor one of my husband's last wishes. Last night, before he slipped into the coma, Bernard made me promise to give you a bo—" Crashing dishes cut her off.

"Sister Porter, are you all right?" Anthony leaned forward in his seat.

"Whew, I'm not used to being in this old attic. I think it's been years since I've been up here. This is Bernard's trash and treasures. I keep mine in the basement. That's what Bernard called everything up here, trash and treasures. I can't imagine what he has up here that he wanted me to give to you, but he said I'd find it. A green shoe box on one of these shelves. If only I could reach—"

Another crash echoed through the phone line. This time it sounded like collapsing metal.

"I'm okay," Sister Porter piped with a heavy grunt. "Just

got to keep my balance. Bernard always teased me for my clumsiness. I remember once when I was cleaning out the pantry . . ."

Anthony lost track of her words as he held his breath, his mind racing, his heart pounding.

"Sister Porter"—he suddenly cut in—"don't you spend another minute in that attic." He tried his best to sound light. "You've had an unbelievably trying day. I'll come over and get the box first thing tomorrow morning."

"I know it's late, honey, but I feel like I need to get this to you tonight. Bernard looked so disturbed when he was telling me about it. I want you to take it so he can rest in peace. He was . . . I am . . . Please . . . My, Jesus . . ." For the first time that day, Kellye Porter burst into loud sobs.

"It's okay. I'm on my way now."

As Anthony grabbed his coat and car keys, he barely noticed Terri still sitting at the breakfast bar.

"Going somewhere?" she asked coldly.

"Terri!" Anthony felt dazed. "I have to—I mean . . . Look, I can't explain right now. I've got to go. Don't wait up." The door shut behind him.

"Don't wait up!" she yelled at the closed door. "I'm going with you." She waited for his car to reach the end of the driveway before she headed for the garage.

"You haven't even noticed my new Lexus, Mr. Murdock. I don't know where your mind is, but I'm about to find out."

Under the shadow of the moonlit sky, the shiny red Lexus followed behind Anthony like a snake slithering through the darkness.

Chapter 8

It was nearly midnight when the Cassells reached their destination for the night, a quaint bed-and-breakfast that overlooked the Atlantic Ocean. Mona was excitedly putting their clothes away, talking the entire time about what they would do for the next two weeks.

Kent sat listening in an oversized wing chair facing the fireplace in the cozy suite. He rubbed his bad knee, which had been reaggravated in the morning's accident. The manager had been kind enough to leave a box of herbal tea, a small microwave, and two homemade turkey sandwiches. As Kent slowly took in the food and warmth before him, he realized how tired he was, how drained the events of the past few months, weeks—that day—had made him.

"Mona." He smiled as she stopped speaking long enough to fluff some king-sized pillows. "Thanks for getting me out of Shepherd Hills. I didn't realize how much I needed a vacation."

She returned his smile and came behind him, massaging his thick shoulders. "I love you, darling. I'm glad for once that you listened to me. We both needed a break. I'm not going to think about what's waiting for me at home, and neither should you. Now, turn off that cell phone." She wagged her finger as if to scold him, but her voice was soft and smiling.

"I'm a step ahead of you." Kent playfully pulled a lock of her hair. "I turned it off back home and left it in that bag you were packing at your desk."

"Well, I just finished unpacking everything and I did not come across your phone."

Kent shrugged. "Maybe I left it home."

"That would be even better than turning it off." Mona slipped on her nightgown, preparing for a restful night of sleep.

"Yeah, that would be good." Kent said the words even as a feeling of uncertainty resurfaced. He was sure he had placed that phone in an open bag Mona was packing after the last child had been picked up from the day care. He remembered how disheveled the desk had looked when he'd walked through the house right before leaving. He had attributed the mess to wind from an open window, but was it possible that his first suspicion was right? Had someone else been in the office that evening—and taken his phone?

Kent shook his head as Mona disappeared into the bathroom, a toothbrush and comb in hand. It didn't make sense. There were several other electronic devices and valuable items in the home office he and Mona shared. Kent closed his eyes and pictured the small room as he had seen it before leaving. Apart from the stack of paper and business cards that were on the floor, from what he could remember nothing else had been disturbed.

Why would someone sneak in and steal only a battered, out-of-date cell phone? It didn't make sense. Kent was still shaking his head when Mona reappeared at the bathroom doorway, looking refreshed and rejuvenated in the mixture of fire and moonlight. Kent felt himself relaxing again as he took in her ageless beauty. *It was only the wind*, he told himself. *And I must have put my phone somewhere else without realizing it.*

As waves crashed into cliffs below their window, and salt mixed with the smell of burning logs in their nostrils, Kent and Mona began their vacation in the quiet, calming company of one another's arms.

Anthony pulled in front of Kellye Porter's home just after midnight. The porch light was on and the door was ajar.

"Anthony, is that you?"

He followed Sister Porter's voice into the kitchen, where she was sitting at a pine table in front of a bowl of cold chicken and dumplings.

"I can't sleep, I can't eat. I don't know what to do." Her eyes were bloodshot from tears and tiredness. She was still wearing the same plain white blouse and gray skirt she'd had on at the hospital, the outfit she'd pulled on the night before when the ambulance had been on its way.

"Sister Porter, you should just . . ." Anthony did not know what to say. Even after dealing with so many personal tragedies in his own life, he was still speechless when it came to addressing death.

Kellye Porter did not seem to mind the silence. She dabbed her eyes and explained that Bernard's sister and a niece were on their way from out of town to help her with the funeral arrangements, and the pastor and a few members from church would be over in the morning.

"At least you won't be alone," Anthony commented, trying to remove any hint of anxiousness from his voice.

As if Sister Porter had read his mind, she suddenly rose from the high-backed kitchen chair and motioned for Anthony to follow her to the attic. "I did not intend to hold you long, Minister Murdock, so let me point out this box to you. I can't reach it for nothing."

She heaved up the narrow attic staircase. "Like I said, I have no idea what would be so important that Bernard would make me promise to give it to you, but nonetheless there it is, that shoe box on the bottom shelf over there."

She pointed to a bookcase on the opposite wall. It was a small attic, but the floor was an obstacle course of trunks, boxes, furniture, and crates. Anthony could see why there had been so much commotion when Sister Porter called him.

"I hope you have better luck reaching it than I did." Before she could continue to speak, a phone began ringing somewhere in the house.

"Must be another family member." Kellye glanced down at the watch on her arm. "A lot of people are just finding out about Bernard." She scurried away to answer the phone, leaving Anthony to pick his way to the box.

He could hear the muffled sound of her voice as he slowly lifted the lid off the old shoe box. The single item inside was an opened envelope containing a letter, addressed to Bernard Porter.

Anthony slowly opened it and flipped the business-sized letter around in his hands several times before reading the typed print.

January 12, 2003

Steelworkers' Guild #29
409 Central Avenue
Shepherd Hills, MD 29473

Mr. Bernard Porter
7493 Blue Wheel Court
Shepherd Hills, MD 29473

Dear Mr. Porter:

This letter is in response to your request to have your prescription plan reviewed. As is true with all retirees of Toringhouse Steel, prescription co-pays are either 7% or $15 of the purchase price, whichever is less. As your union, we can only petition in your behalf if we have the original employee folder that details the specifics of the union's agreement between employer and employee at that time. As you were last employed over twenty years ago, your file would have been maintained in our former Perkins Street headquarters.

During the move to our new office ten years ago, several employee files were misplaced, or otherwise lost. Unfortunately, your file appears to be among the missing. Therefore we can only help you if you have an original copy of your employee file that includes the date of your hire in 1956. Sorry for any inconvenience.

Sincerely,
SG#29

Anthony groaned in disappointment. What did this have to do with his father—or Stonymill, for that matter? He studied the text again, noting only that the words "former Perkins Street headquarters" had been circled in black ink. Anthony sighed as he refolded the letter and placed it back in the box and placed the box back on the bookshelf. In his illness, Minister Porter must have forgotten where he had placed whatever it was he really wanted Anthony to see. Or maybe there simply was nothing to see at all. Regardless, there was no point in keeping a letter that had nothing to do with him.

"Did you get it?"

Anthony had not noticed Sister Porter's return.

"I found it, but . . . but . . ." Anthony could see hope and satisfaction pouring from Sister Porter's eyes. He did not want to taint an important moment in her grieving by sharing his disappointment. "But I'm not going to keep you up any longer. Thank you for sharing this with me, Sister Porter." He avoided the question in her eyes as they walked back to the kitchen.

"My sister-in-law and niece should be here soon. I guess

I should try to rest before they come. Tomorrow is going to be another long day. Thank you for coming over so late, Anthony. It means a lot for me to know that Bernard can rest in peace." She dabbed her eyes with a tissue.

"Let me know of any way that I can help you." Anthony buttoned his coat.

"You have already helped me so much today." Sister Porter opened the front door for him. He gave her a warm hug before descending the steps.

"Anthony." Her voice quivered from inside the living room. Anthony looked back with a pensive smile.

"Thank you." That was all that was left to be said. Anthony nodded and started for his car. He never even noticed the red Lexus parked at the end of the cul-de-sac.

"I got you now," Terri mumbled to herself. She could not believe her eyes, watching Anthony disappear into an unfamiliar house and leave almost an hour later, his arms embracing another woman. She could not see who the woman was, but she could tell from the departing hug that there was a lot of warmth between them.

She started to call Cherisse. But what would she say? The entire time he had been inside that woman's home, she had contemplated doing some damage to his car, or to that house. But what would she do?

"Jesus!" It was funny how easily that name slipped out when she wasn't sure what else to do, or who else to call.

She watched as Anthony made a turnabout, passed her, and disappeared down the quiet street. That was when she knew what she was going to do.

In one fluid move, she was out of her car and walking to the house. With every step she felt angrier, stronger, even more certain of what she was going to say to this woman. Names and combinations of names—crude words she rarely said out loud—lay on the tip of her tongue like venom. And she was ready to bite. Anthony would be next.

"Open this door!" She pounded loud enough that a few lights were turned on in the neighboring houses. "I said *open this door!*"

"Terri, is that you?" A weak and tired voice came from the other side.

"Do I know you? You better hope I don't know your—"

"Terri!" The door was flung open. Kellye Porter stood in a bathrobe, the strength in her voice betrayed only by the single tear slipping from her eye.

"Sister Porter! Oh my goodness! Oh my goodness! I'm so sorry!" Terri did not realize that her legs had given way until she tasted the fuzzy, plush carpet of the Porters' living room and felt her knees against the cold cement of the porch. "I'm so sorry!" She could not stop weeping.

Sister Porter knelt beside Terri and pulled her head into her lap. Her tears were flowing as easily as Terri's. "It's okay, dear heart."

"I'm sorry. I thought . . . I thought . . ."

"It's okay. I understand." She stroked Terri's head the way a mother coddles her crying child. They sat this way for a while, each trying to comfort the other while re-leasing tears from their own different wells.

Finally Sister Porter rose to her feet, pulling Terri with her. After closing and locking the front door, she directed them to seats on the plastic-covered sofa of her living room.

"Bernard used to sit right on this corner to read the paper until he became ill. I used to get so sick of him reading that newspaper, beginning to end, hours at a time, every single day."

"I'm so sorry, Sister Porter. With all you've been through over the past twenty-four hours, how could you ever forgive me for acting like such a fool?" Terri's eyes were closed, her hands clenched in her lap.

"Oh hush, honey. Don't get me wrong, I'm hurting right now, but it's not because of you. I done lost too much today to be worried about you trying to beat down my door one o'clock in the morning. I told you, I understand. I have—I had—a husband and a part of me wishes I could go banging on heaven's door right now and scream at God for stealing my husband away from me. But I got too much hope and faith to think I'll never see my Bernard again. I haven't lost him, because I know where he is." She sighed, but a trace of a smile surfaced on her tear-streaked face. "I got hope and you got a husband. And a good one, too."

"Sister Porter, I am completely embarrassed. Anthony's been acting so strange lately. I don't know what came over me."

"Honey, marriage itself can be strange at times. I had forty-six years of it and there are still days I can think of that I'll never understand exactly what was going on. You know, in Ephesians, when Paul compared Christ and His believers to a marriage between a man and a woman, he called it a mystery. Marriage is a day-to-day process of becoming one, just like we are daily trying to abide in Christ and letting Him abide in us."

Terri shook her head.

"What is it, honey?"

"Nothing. It's—I mean . . . does everything really have to come down to Jesus? At what point do you just live your life and not get, well, obsessed with religion? Don't get me wrong, I think God is important and should have a place in your life, but there's more to life than going to church. There's work and money and people and issues and—well, everything else."

Sister Porter smiled even with a wet wad of tissues crinkled in her hand. "You're right, Terri. There *is* more to life than going to church. In fact, I'm not even talking about church. I'm talking about a relationship with Jesus. Jesus said He *is* life and that He came so we could have abundant life. So if you don't have Jesus, what do you have?"

Terri shrugged, not sure that she wanted to continue with the conversation. It had been a long, emotional day, and the whole Jesus thing was making her think about more than she wanted.

Sister Porter continued. "When you think of your marriage to Anthony, you don't think of it only as the time you spend eating dinner together. Your marriage is a constant thing, each moment you spend together, your conversations, your feelings, your commitment. You are married whether you are in the same room or not, on the same page or not. For better or worse, you have a relationship with Anthony, just like you have a relationship with Christ—if you have one.

"It's a living, growing, constant thing you choose to get into that affects every decision you make, the way you get through your day, the way you define yourself. And unlike a marriage to a man, Jesus is guaranteed to never leave you, even if you try to get out of it yourself. Going to church is a small part of that relationship, just as eating meals together is a small part of your relationship with Anthony."

Tears refilled Terri's eyes. She could not figure out what nerve Sister Porter was touching, but it reminded her of how she'd felt the night before, watching Mother Howard sing at prayer service.

"Terri"—Sister Porter took her hand as she spoke— "Jesus died for your sins so that you could have this relationship with Him. He rose to confirm His promise of life to you. The Bible says all we have to do is confess with our mouths the Lord Jesus, and believe in our hearts that God raised Him from the dead, and we shall be saved. Now, Terri—"

A loud knock at the front door jolted both of them.

"Oh my, that must be my sister-in-law and niece. It's almost two-thirty. Terri, sweetheart, you need to get home to your husband." They both walked the short distance to the door. Just before Sister Porter opened it, Terri took both her hands.

"Sister Porter, I'm sorry to have bothered you at such a difficult time."

"Oh, honey, it was meant to be. There are no accidents or coincidences in God's Kingdom."

"Thank you. You've given me a lot to think about." Terri was being honest.

The night air greeted them like a cold handshake when Sister Porter opened the door. On the porch stood two women, both shaking and crying from grief.

"Oh, Kellye, I can't stand this! My little brother is gone!" The older woman wept, a wrinkled nursing uniform peeking from underneath her coat. "I left work and drove up here as soon as you called!"

"Mabel, it'll be all right." Terri was almost off the porch steps when Sister Porter thought to introduce the two to her.

"Forgive me, Terri. This is my sister-in-law, Mabel Linstead, and her daughter, Denise, who've come all the way up from Sharen, South Carolina, to help me."

Terri nodded at the weeping trio as she departed. Anthony's Great-Aunt Rosa was from there, she remembered as she started her car. She would let Anthony know that someone from Aunt Rosa's hometown was in Shepherd Hills. Sharen was a small place where everybody knew everybody. It would be good for Anthony to connect with someone who most likely knew his roots.

Chapter 9

Gloria Randall was sitting at her desk promptly at eight-thirty Friday morning, wide awake despite the sleepless night she'd had. Councilman Walter Banks was not due in the office yet, but she was anxious to talk to him. Something was not right, her gut was telling her.

Two afternoons before, while running a routine errand for the councilman at city hall, she had been approached by a young man who'd introduced himself as a journalist wanting information about the councilman's busy schedule and general involvement with his constituents. Having been told by the councilman to be cordial to the media because he worked to maintain a positive, approachable image, she was courteous and open with the young man, answering all his questions about Walter's upcoming engagements and community functions.

She would have thought no more about the interview except that when the man noted the files she had picked up for the councilman, his questions became more intrusive. She had not wanted to be rude, but when an hour had gone by and she found herself giving more detailed information about Councilman Banks's planned meetings and appointments for the next week, she was sure she'd crossed the line herself and wanted to end the conversation immediately.

"How could I be so dumb, giving out that man's personal business like that?" She kept sighing to herself, feeling like she was failing her new boss already and knowing that was not the end of the story.

She had not called the councilman to tell him she was running late; and when she finally had talked to him late Wednesday night he'd sounded relieved, as if he'd been worried about her. She had been able to avoid him all day Thursday as he was busy with meetings outside of the office, but she knew he ran a lighter schedule on Fridays— and this Friday in particular was especially light—making a run-in with him inevitable. She'd stayed up nearly the entire night wondering how she would explain her indiscretion to him. Maybe it was not a big deal, but her instincts were telling her it was.

At almost nine o'clock, just after she'd finished making the coffee and separating mail, she noticed the *Black Enterprise* magazine Anthony had left on the conference table a couple days before. It was open to an article highlighting a local businessman who was being recognized for his achievements.

"Anthony studied this article for a long time the other day," she murmured to herself as she picked it up to get a closer view. "I wonder if he misses that high-roller life he had a few months ago." Nearly every member at Second Baptist marveled at the sacrifices Anthony had made when he'd decided to spend more time pursuing his ministerial calling.

She'd turned the page, still skimming the article, when her eyes grew wide and her jaw dropped. *The man being featured in the story was the journalist who'd asked all those questions the day before.* So he wasn't a journalist. Her mind was racing. Why had he lied? Why did he want all that information? And what was he going to do with it?

"Good morning, Gloria." Walter Banks entered the suite looking glum. He did not have his usual bag of doughnuts or cheery smile. Before Gloria could stammer out a greeting, he disappeared into his office and shut the door behind him. It was obvious that something was terribly wrong.

The councilman must be in some kind of trouble, and it's all my fault. Gloria was not the type of person who left mistakes alone. She was ready to take action, making up her mind what to do as she picked up the phone. Anthony used to work for the firm where that young man was employed. She would call him and get his opinion on the matter. If something was going on with the councilman, she was certain Anthony could help.

Nikki Galloway coughed as loudly as she could into the phone receiver.

"Eric, I'm not going to be able to make it in to work today. I woke up feeling terrible." She followed her words with a long, drawn-out blow into a tissue.

"I'm sorry to hear that, but I hope you feel better soon." Eric truly was sorry. Today was an important day for CASH. He had planned a pivotal meeting to solidify support from both old and new members. The rally was not until the evening, but a lot still needed to be done in preparation.

"Hopefully I'll be able to make it in on Monday, Tuesday at the latest. See you then." She threw those words in there, knowing that if all went according to plan, she might not have to show up at all again. Her assignment at CASH was nearly complete. Although she had not been able to distract Eric (he must be blind or gay, she'd decided), she had made copies of every mailing list, financial statement, and fact sheet he'd handed to her.

And to top off her success, getting that old detective's cell phone when she picked up her son from Mona's day care the evening before had been a breeze. *Those stupid people always leave their office door open.* The Cassells were going to be gone for two weeks, more than enough time to complete the sabotage.

That man is a true mastermind. She sneered to herself, smoothing her hands across the sheets he'd just left. She never knew what to expect from his daily morning visits. Most of the time it was him telling her what to do—a new assignment, an old argument, an ongoing explanation of the plan. And then he'd lead her tiptoeing past Devin's door to her bedroom. She never objected. She couldn't.

But this morning she'd held some of the power; it was her hands that held the cell phone, the copies she'd made, the information she'd gathered. *You may be the mastermind, fool, but you need my help to get things done.*

She wanted to make him beg for what he wanted. She wanted to hear him *ask* for all that she could give him.

But when he began whispering in her ear that he wanted to reward her for all the hard work she was doing,

Nikki acquiesced. Between kisses, he took the phone, the papers, and another piece of her pride.

"You got yourself into this." She could hear her mother's hiss in the old radiators that did little to warm the cheap apartment. As always, the morning ended with him on top, the winner of every argument, the director of every plan. He seemed to make sure of it.

Even as he casually helped himself to her body he talked business. "Anthony is trying to get in touch with Kent and we want to make sure we have the right response when he calls. I'll do my part, you do yours. Don't mess up." The last three words were what he said to her before leaving at six-thirty.

It was nearly nine-thirty now, time to get moving. Eric Johnson of CASH was not the only person with a big agenda for the day.

The orange juice in his glass was warm and pulpy. Anthony had not realized how long he'd been sitting at the kitchen table until he'd taken a sip. Another morning had passed without his crossing paths with Terri. Another day had pressed forward without a word to the detective, a man Anthony felt both fear and relief in approaching. And the past twenty-four hours had only brought more heartbreak, more burden. Dead-end information from a dead man. A bundle of money bound in his trunk. Money of which he knew not the source, or where would be its final resting place.

He had not bothered to call his job, if he still had it. He had not even bothered to get dressed. He was still wearing the rumpled shirt and khakis from the day before, having fallen asleep in his study upon his return from Sister

Porter's house. It had been late when he got in, and he had not wanted to disturb Terri. In her condition she needed the rest. A feeble smile tried to form on his face as he thought of the next clue Terri would give. Why couldn't she just let him guess that she was pregnant?

He was caught up in a daydream about his baby boy when his cell phone rang.

"Brother—I mean Minister Antho—Murdock!"

"Sister Randall?" Anthony was surprised to hear Gloria Randall sounding so anxious.

"I'm sorry to call so early. I got your cell phone number out of Mr. Banks's Rolodex. I did something and now I think Councilman Banks is in trouble. I thought maybe you could help. You're so close to Walter *and* you used to work for Shaw Enterprises."

At her words, Anthony snapped to attention.

"Are you at his office?"

"Yes, but I would rather talk to you away from the councilman. He doesn't know what I did yet, and I want your opinion on how to handle this. Can we meet somewhere during my lunch break?"

Anthony noticed for the first time how low she was speaking into the phone. "Sure, if you think that's best."

"I don't want to take you far from where you work, so if it's okay with you, we could meet at that little diner down the street from your job."

Anthony could not even begin to explain why he wasn't at his job that morning. He only sighed as he agreed to meet her at the Solomon Grill precisely at noon. He only sighed again as he showered and dressed in a suit and tie. He did not want any extra questions before he could get some answers himself.

After fixing the thermostat for the fifth time, Terri sat back down in her thickly padded desk chair. Her office was still too warm. She decided to open one of the windows, flooding the room with the brisk morning air of mid-September. Now it was too cold. She sipped half a cup of coffee, ate a few spoonfuls of yogurt, reshuffled the papers on her desk, and listened to the chirping birds and waterfalls sounding through the relaxation unit she'd bought herself years ago.

Nothing was working. Nothing was right.

After staring blankly at the plans she was working on for Reginald Savant, she made up her mind how to spend the rest of her day. She would do her best to get some work done, and then she would take a long drive in her new Lexus. That thought put some pep into her.

Anthony still had not seen her car. When she'd come in from Sister Porter's home last night, she saw him sleeping in his study. Not wanting to wake him, she'd collapsed in their king-sized bed and left for work before he stirred from his sleep.

Today would be a perfect day to just show him the car. Her plans were being formed even as she concentrated on the sketches before her. She would take a scenic route to Haberstick Associates and surprise him with the car. She would not allow any doubts about Anthony's faithfulness or agendas to overtake her anymore. Last night's embarrassing episode at Sister Porter's house had left her spent. As Cherisse had initially told her, there had to be an explanation for everything.

"I am a millionaire," she said to her reflection in an

oak-framed wall mirror. A smile began to take shape. "I am in a different class now, and I need to start acting like it. Anthony must have a big plan to surprise me with his news about the money, just like I'm going to surprise him with the blessings I've already been able to buy." The smile was more solid as she thought again about the car, the shopping spree, the cruise to the Mediterranean. Beverly Hills.

By noon, she was humming loudly to herself, in full rhythm, knowing that the morning had been productive. She'd finished identifying some fabric swatches that would be used to upholster the furniture in the main lobby of Reggie's Empress Hotel. Wallpaper and borders had been catalogued by suite style; the perfect grain of marble had been picked out to floor the exotic atrium she'd designed for the top floor. Everything was nearly perfect.

"See, Sister Porter," she mumbled to herself, "it's been a good morning, and I didn't have to say the name Jesus once." She shook her head, wondering why people couldn't see that there was more to life than church. Even Anthony was beginning to see the light. She smiled again, thinking about the money with which he was planning to surprise her.

As she sped down a winding back road to Haberstick Associates, she imagined she was in a car commercial. Pure exhilaration. Her sudden good fortune was a rush in her veins.

She was waiting at a traffic light a block and a half from Anthony's workplace when she saw them. They were walking together quickly, looking around as if they did not want anyone to notice them. When the light turned green and the cars behind her started honking, she still did not move. She could not think of any rational reason why Anthony would be leaving the Solomon Grill with Sister Gloria Randall from church and heading in a direction away from his job.

"Before I cause a scene like I did last night, let me pull to the side and come up with a foolproof plan." She parked in an auto-shop lot and dialed Cherisse as she spoke.

"Terri, where have you been? I've been trying to reach you all morning. I know exactly who—"

"He's seeing another woman." Terri cut in before Cherisse could continue.

"Her name's Gloria Randall, right?"

"How did you—"

This time Cherisse interrupted. "Meet me at my house this evening like we planned. I've got a lot to tell you. You're still coming with me to the banquet tonight, aren't you?"

"I wouldn't miss it for the world."

Anthony and Gloria sat silent in his car. He was stunned at the news she'd just shared with him. Why would his former protégé at Shaw Enterprises be so interested in Councilman Banks's affairs, especially after seeing the Stonymill files in Gloria's hand?

"You need to show me the exact files you were copying at city hall that sparked Jevon's interest."

Gloria nodded with her hands wrapped in her lap as they sped off to the archaic building downtown. Now she was beginning to wonder if she had made a big deal out of nothing. Maybe this was all a small matter that she had blown out of proportion. She worried that it would get her fired and Anthony embarrassed.

"Minister Murdock, I have the copies in Councilman Banks's mailbox. Knowing him, he probably hasn't even gotten them out yet and I know he's busy running an errand. I don't want to take you out of your way from work any more than I already have. Why don't we go back to his office instead of going all the way downtown?" She tried to sound reassuring, feeling silly as she noted the tight lines on Anthony's forehead. *I got this man all worried about something that's probably nothing.*

Anthony rubbed his chin in thought before making a U-turn. No need to draw extra attention to himself by signing out the Stonymill files from the clerk's office. Besides, he could make copies of Gloria's copies without intrusion, and have time to study them alone later.

Maybe some answers would be in those files.

It was nearly six forty-five when Terri lifted the large brass knocker on Cherisse's condo door. She waited impatiently, listening to the taps of Cherisse's heels from inside. When the door opened there was a brief smile from both as they admired one another in their classic black ensembles: Terri in a satin form-fitting black gown with a small matching sequined clutch bag; Cherisse in a keyhole top with a flourished mini that showcased her long legs. The smiles quickly diminished as Cherisse locked the door and the two headed down the steps to Cherisse's Maxima. There was business to discuss.

"I met Reginald Savant today," Cherisse began. "Now before we talk about how fine that brother is, I need to show you what he gave me."

Cherisse handed Terri a folded-up piece of paper before letting them both into her car. As she started the motor,

Terri slowly unfolded it to see what looked like a program for the night's events.

"See, right there." Cherisse pointed with an index finger as she pulled onto a main thoroughfare.

Underneath the words THE FIRST ANNUAL BLACK EN-TREPRENEURS ALLIANCE GALA was the name of the guest of honor: Anthony Michael Murdock.

Terri gasped. "He *never* mentioned this to me."

"If you saw the seating chart, you would know why."

"What did you see, Cherisse?"

"The name Gloria Randall was written in the space next to his. You said you saw him with her, so you know who she is already. Who is she, a co-worker, his new secretary?"

"No, girl." Terri was too mad to cry. "She ain't nobody but a member of Second Baptist who's always jumping up and down the aisles all the time. I can't imagine what Anthony sees in her." Terri thought of all the Sunday afternoons when she would see the slightly overweight woman with the straggly cornrows embracing Anthony alongside Sister Ethel, and wondered if and how she had missed something.

"What do I—"

"I'm a step ahead of you. When I saw that Reginald Savant's name was listed at a table right next to the guest of honor, I mentioned how I knew you were working so hard on his hotel project. Girl, you should have seen him beaming. He said he would make sure that you had a seat near him. Anthony's going to meet you face-to-face tonight."

"And I promise you, this meeting is going to be ugly." Terri's arms were crossed over her chest as the silver

Maxima fell into line with the row of luxury cars turning into the valet entrance of the Diamond Mount.

"You know what's funny, Cherisse?"

"What's that?" Cherisse pulled to the curb, where a uniformed valet was waiting.

"When I first met Reginald, he told me he'd done his homework. I knew he knew a lot about me when he mentioned my friendship with you. But he must really know more about my personal life than I do. Did it ever occur to you when he talked about my seating arrangements, that he knew I was coming tonight, but not courtesy of Anthony? I'm going to talk to him, and see exactly what he knows about my life that I don't."

Councilman Banks entered his office suite bleary-eyed at almost seven P.M. He did not look surprised to see Anthony and Gloria sitting at a conference table with a stack of documents in front of them. They'd been sitting there since lunch, highlighting every name and date found on each paper. Anthony had worked in silence most of the afternoon, stopping only to stare at the wall from time to time, as if the answers he needed would suddenly be written there by an unseen hand. Gloria, afraid they were making a big issue out of nothing, looked apologetic when the councilman walked toward them.

"I'm glad to find you here, Anthony. I've been studying these same documents myself all day. Thanks for making copies for me, Gloria, but everything's been so crazy I ended up going down to the records department myself today to make some sense out of this confusion. I think someone is out to make me pay for not supporting the Stonymill project the first go-around, and now they think they can bully me into giving in this time." He collapsed into an armchair as he spoke.

"Mr. Banks, uh"—Gloria looked quickly at Anthony before continuing—"I'm sorry, but I think it's all my fault. When I copied these files the other day, I think I might have given away too much information to a man who I thought was a journalist. He was actually a former co-worker of Anthony's. I apologize for my indiscretion. I did not mean to get you in any trouble."

Walter smiled weakly. "Gloria, no apologies are necessary. This situation extends beyond anything you may or may not have said." He directed his next words to Anthony. "Are you finding anything of interest in those files?"

"Well, I think I've got a better handle on some of the groups and businesses who had or want to have a vested interest in the expansion of the Stonymill light rail line. There are several businesses that have pending building permits along that route, the same area where CASH wants to build Bethany Village." Anthony sighed with his last words. *Lord, why did I let money get in the way of such a needed project as Bethany Village?*

"What businesses did you find?" Walter flipped through a legal pad as Anthony continued.

"There's Blakeman Brothers Tax Services owned by a Christopher and Shawn Blakeman; Coleman's, a high-end jewelry store owned by a man of the same name who wants to open a second location near the expansion stop; a day-trader group operated by a group of local businessmen; the Empress Hotel, CEO is Reginald Savant—my wife just got that project; and a business named Pride and Fidelity. It appears to be some kind of holding company."

"Who's running that last company you named?"

Anthony shrugged. "I've been reading through these papers, but I've only been getting a vague idea of the owner. I get the impression that he or she is foreign, African maybe. The name Razi showed up somewhere near the listing, and it only showed up once."

"Hmmm, somebody who shies away from discovery," the councilman reflected. "That might be a good place to begin investigating."

"I was thinking about talking first to this Coleman jewelry guy." The sting of Wednesday night's setup involving a jewelry store trying to report stolen money was still fresh in Anthony's mind.

"Did you ever get in touch with that detective?"

"I ran into the law the other night, and after that meeting, I feel like I need to have something to present to them that won't leave me looking overly suspicious. I have enough explaining to do about my involvement with Stonymill without looking like I'm the mastermind behind this scheme. I don't know what scares me more—where the money came from or where it's supposed to end up."

Gloria, who had been quiet throughout this interchange, could no longer hold her fears.

"What is going on, Anthony? Are you in some kind of trouble too?" She looked from the councilman to Anthony for relief but was given none. "If you are, I think you probably should call the police or somebody right now."

Anthony was quiet at her words, rubbing fingers briskly over his temples. He looked back and forth between Walter and Gloria. *The police, the press. I may lose my rep-*

utation on top of losing every cent I have. Lord, there's got to be another way, a more quiet way, to come clean.

"What do you think, Mr. Banks?" His eyes pleaded for direction, advice. Hope. There had to be another way.

Walter responded, a fatherly wisdom in his tone, "I think it's your call, Anthony. I'm not sure what to do right now, but I have full faith that if you do what you believe God is leading you to do, everything will be all right. Whatever you think is best, I'm behind you one hundred percent."

Anthony nodded his head at Walter's solemn face. He appreciated the kindness and support extended, but he did not miss the fear in the politician's eyes. It was not only Anthony's life in the balance.

Why did I get involved in this? Anthony sighed for a long moment, waiting to see if direction would suddenly appear in front of him. *Maybe it's all in presentation,* he decided. *If I can get this detective on my side, maybe I won't have to lose everything, right, Lord?* Anthony made up his mind.

"You're right, Gloria. This appears to be bigger than what we can handle. I'm calling that detective right now, for both of our sakes." Anthony nodded at the councilman as he spoke. He found Kent Cassell's number in his wallet and dialed the agent's cell phone. A young woman answered.

"May I help you?"

Anthony paused before speaking. *This voice almost sounds familiar.*

"I need to speak with Detective Kent Cassell. It's urgent."

"Is this Mr. Murdock?"

Where have I heard this voice?

"Yes it is. Did I speak with you the other day, Ms.—?"

"I'm Mr. Cassell's personal assistant, so it's possible that you spoke to me if you've been trying to get in touch with him." The woman talked fast over a piece of chewing gum. "Anyway, Mr. Cassell has been waiting to hear from you and wants you to come meet him immediately at the delivery entrance of the Diamond Mount on Twenty-third Street."

"Can I just—"

"You must be there by seven-thirty. It's the only place he can talk to you."

"Why—"

"He's waiting there for you right now. Good-bye, Mr. Murdock."

Confused, Anthony looked at the phone before slamming it into the receiver.

"I don't understand what's going on. The detective wants me to meet him at the back entrance of the Diamond Mount within half an hour. This makes no sense."

"Look Anthony, I had an important meeting to attend tonight, but in the interest of getting all this resolved, I'll come with you. That forged check, and the money, these phone calls . . ." The councilman rubbed his temples before continuing.

"We can talk to this detective together. Gloria, would you mind coming with us? I know you've only been working for me a couple of weeks, but the detective may be interested in talking with you too. As my executive assistant, you know my schedule and dealings right now probably better than I do. Maybe you can help remove any suspicions he's bound to have about me. You can tell him about that man quizzing you the other day."

"I'll help both of you any way that I can." Gloria hoped she sounded more certain than she felt.

Anthony buttoned his coat with shaking fingers. How was he going to explain himself to this detective?

Eric Johnson looked hopefully at the empty seats before him. It was only five minutes after seven; maybe everyone was simply running late. Standing in the cool basement of one of the members of CASH's home church, he checked and rechecked his watch. Besides a couple of senior residents who steadfastly supported any pro-community action, nobody else had showed up for the meeting.

Mrs. Malburn-Epworth, a local pastor's wife, sat in the front row. A large woman with large gold-and-gray curls framing her heavily rouged face, her eyes followed every small movement Eric made as he paced back and forth in front of the thirty-odd metal chairs arranged before him. Ernest Rutherford was asleep directly behind her. Soft snores competed with the ticking of a large wall clock to fill the small hall with a pestering reminder that nobody was there and the meeting was not moving forward.

In a move of faith-filled optimism, Eric picked up the prearranged stack of papers and handouts from his duffel bag and placed one on each of the empty chairs. With each resonant ping of a staple hitting steel, he grew more aware of a knowing that something was terribly wrong.

This meeting had been planned for two months. It was to be a decisive, action-oriented gathering of CASH's old and new members, united in a spiritual and physical front to secure support for a bill that would be presented before the city council the following week. The bill would secure the location and funding of Bethany Village on a large lot near the expanded Stonymill light rail line. The location was perfect, large enough to accommodate the facilities, close enough to be considered part of the community, but not too close as to warrant objections from neighbors wary about active addicts and homeless persons, discontented youth and teens seeking refuge and treatment.

And, most importantly, it would be near public transportation, in particular, the Stonymill expansion light rail stop currently under construction. When the expansion project plans won over CASH's initial bid for development six months prior, Eric had been devastated. But now he saw it as a demonstration of God's foresight. What had been a major bump in the road was now a blessing to the destination. The plot of land for which CASH was bidding was still in the general area of the original bid, but now it would be near the proposed light rail stop.

With that type of accessibility, and a promise from the city's public transit administrator to donate a few monthly bus and light rail passes for use by Bethany Village clientele, those who needed help would not be limited by a lack of transportation. And, as an added bonus of the delayed blessing, the new blueprints included acres that could be used for an overnight summer camp, providing open fields for penned-up urban youth.

Now they only needed the city council to approve the bill that would let them begin building. Unfortunately for CASH, a multitude of businesses were once again pushing council members to let them use the land for their purposes. Bethany Village was not the only project that would benefit from prime location near the Stonymill light rail stop.

From an economic standpoint, entrepreneurial development made more sense than investing in cast-offs and rejects who would be bringing their problems and not their pocketbooks to the area. But Eric knew that God's economics were not measured by the divvying of dollars, but by the eternal gains of delivered souls.

However, politics and public hearings in Shepherd Hills were not necessarily run by divine counsel. Which was why CASH needed the support of all of its members and volunteers. Which was why this planning meeting and rally was so important.

Eric and the other members of CASH had agreed to pray and fast for the entire week leading up to the meeting. He knew from experience that everyone who signed up on the mailing list would not come. But where was Sister Nichols, the enthusiastic schoolteacher who pulled him aside after a church presentation? And Brother Tomlin, the church trustee who ran a hardware store outside of downtown and wanted to donate building supplies? Where was Mother George, the lady who successfully started and ran a sewing circle for teenage girls, and Brother Philman, a former drug dealer turned barbershop owner, who promised financial and counseling support for the rehab center that was to be a part of Bethany Village?

And what about the politicians who *had* pledged their public support? Did Councilman Banks forget to check his schedule, or had he become engrossed once again in another act of civic heroism somewhere else? But was this meeting not as important as any other and worth attendance?

Eric prayed to squelch the growing heat of discouragement and anger rising within him. People are human, and things do come up, he knew. Brother Philman may be tied up with a customer at his store, Mother George might be home-bound with her arthritic knee, and Walter Banks never stepped down from his public support of CASH even when everyone else had six months ago. There was no reason for him to back down now, Eric reassured himself.

He began meditating on the miracle of Jesus feeding over five thousand people with five loaves of bread and two fish. God can meet the needs of many with the donated resources of a few. Or, as was the case with Jesus and the multitude, the donated resources of one. *One little boy gave up his lunch to Jesus, and here I am one man willing to give up his life for God's use.* Eric smiled to himself, the mustard-seed-sized faith in him sprouting a bud. *And I am not just one; I have two others beside me.* Eric nodded at Sister Malburn-Epworth and the sleeping Mr. Rutherford.

It was nearly seven-thirty; there was no need to keep waiting. As Eric pulled a chair from the front row to face his faithful attendees, a troubling thought occurred to him. Nikki Galloway, his less-than-dependable secretary, had been responsible for mailing out notices and reminders about the meeting. Maybe he should not have left such a crucial task solely in her hands.

"Mrs. Malburn-Epworth, did you receive a reminder about tonight's meeting in the mail?" Eric's question came out slowly, almost hesitantly.

"Oh yes, I received a letter. In fact, I received both letters, the one about the meeting, and the one about you and what you're doing with all our money." There was a coolness in her voice that Eric had heard existed but to date had never heard directed toward him.

"Mrs. Malburn-Epworth, what are you talking about? I don't know anything about a second mailing."

"Of course *you* wouldn't," she hissed.

Ernest Rutherford woke up with a loud snort. "Wh-what's going on? Are we talking about Eric's drug relapse yet?"

Mrs. Malburn-Epworth was frowning intensely, her arms folded tight across her broad chest. "We were just getting started." Her eyes narrowed at Eric's.

"Drug relapse?" There were many desperate people out there who wanted to see a permanent end of CASH, but this was a personal attack that could destroy the credibility and progress of *everything*.

"Mrs. Malburn-Epworth, Mr. Rutherford, whatever you heard or received is a complete lie! Who sent you this second letter?"

"A concerned citizen."

Even as the elder lady puffed out an answer, another question crept into Eric's mind: *Who had access to his mailing list and what else were they planning to do?*

Chapter 10

Girl, can you believe this place? I don't know how much they're paying him, but Fabian really outdid himself this time. Did you see the ice-sculpture garden by the front entrance?"

Terri was only half listening as she and Cherisse gave their coats to a tuxedoed man and received pink tickets in return.

"This is definitely high-class. High-class food, high-class music, high-class atmosphere. High-class brothers." Cherisse smiled warmly at a man passing by who could have been mistaken for Denzel Washington. He smiled back as his eyes generously lingered on her body. "Ooh girl, I'm getting shivers standing here in the hallway. Do you see all the men in there? All the *unaccompanied* men?"

"Uh-huh."

Terri was looking past the clinking wine flutes, the sparkling sea of diamonds and sequined black. She saw the jazz band but did not hear the music. Saw the white-gloved waiters passing by but did not smell the stuffed mushrooms and shrimp they were carrying.

"He's not here yet." She pointed to the place card at the front of the room where Anthony's name stood out like an ink spot on good linen, each letter carefully scripted and outlined in silver glitter. Gloria Randall's name was on the white bone-china plate next to his.

"I'm going to catch him. Them together. And when I do—"

"Mrs. Murdock, I'm glad you made it."

Terri felt the warm embrace of Reggie Savant before she heard his voice. She turned to face him, and for a brief second she forgot the who and the why of her being there. Standing in a collarless black tuxedo, if it were possible, he looked better than his normal perfected, polished state.

"You look absolutely enchanting, Mrs. Murdock." He smiled before turning to her side. "And it's good to see you again, Miss Landrick. I'm glad you both were able to make it tonight."

Cherisse grinned under his gaze. "I have never seen my boss put together a function this elaborate in such a short amount of time. You sure know how to throw a party, Mr. Savant. A man like you capable of planning such an upscale event obviously has impeccable taste."

"I do set high standards." Reggie smiled at Terri for a long second before taking both her and Cherisse's hands. "Come, now, let's join the festivities. Looks like the program's already begun. Our guest of honor should be here soon."

Terri's eyes narrowed at his words.

～

The rear entrance where deliveries were received at the Diamond Mount was far less elaborate than its imposing front. Anthony turned his car into the alleyway, where only a small truck and one of Fabian's vans was parked.

"Must be something going on tonight," Anthony mumbled as the trills of laughter and the scent of alcohol wafted toward them in the beginning night breeze.

"Do you see anyone?" Gloria studied the vehicles parked near the back entrance, fearing what the darkness of the alley held for the three of them. Sitting in the front seat next to Anthony was the only comfort she had in an evening that felt surreal to her. Walter Banks sat behind them, continually removing his gold spectacles, wiping them with the corner of his suit jacket, and replacing them on his oval face.

"What's this detective's name again?" He asked as he readjusted his glasses.

"Cassell. Kent Cassell. I still don't see why I have to meet him here instead of his office or somewhere like that."

He parked the car next to a Dumpster and cut the ignition. All three of them got out and stood quietly for a few minutes, looking around. Music and laughter continued to pour gently into the night air.

"This is crazy. What time is it?"

"Seven-thirty on the dot. Did he tell you where to meet him exactly?"

"His assistant said the back entrance."

The three of them looked at the single white door at the top of the truck ramp. Anthony shook his head before heading for it.

"I'm going to go knock." *Lord, something doesn't feel right about this.*

Walter and Gloria were standing next to Anthony when the door swung open. A small, chestnut-colored man in his mid-twenties greeted them with a warm smile.

"Mr. Murdock, Councilman Banks. You must be Gloria Randall, the councilman's assistant." He grabbed all of their hands in a quick shake. "Wow, I can't believe I finally get to meet all of you personally. They told me you'd be coming in this entrance, and I can understand that, with all your big bucks and clout and all, both of you. You, Mr. Murdock, are the superstar of the evening."

The councilman and Anthony looked at each other, the same puzzled expression on both of their faces.

"I'm looking for Kent Cassell. Are you Mr. Cass—"

"He's here," the man shouted into a walkie-talkie, cutting Anthony off. "You're just in time, Mr. Murdock." He smiled again. "They are expecting you onstage in thirty seconds for the presentation. Your generosity is awesome, man. God bless you, brother. Excuse my rudeness. It's been so insane in here, I forgot to introduce myself in all the rush. I'm Shawn Blakeman. My brother and I were shocked when we found out you were going to support our little homegrown tax business with such a large donation. It means a lot that you would have that kind of belief in us. We hadn't even sent you our portfolio yet."

"Look, I don't know what's going on. I came here to meet with—"

Anthony was cut off by a frenetic call on the two-way.

"We're coming!" Shawn shouted back into the walkie-talkie. He grabbed Anthony by the arm and began pulling him deeper into the building as he continued talking. Councilman Banks and Gloria stood frozen until the man reached out a hand, pulling both of them along also. "Mr.

Banks, we know how much you've been a mentor to Mr. Murdock. It's only fitting that you join him onstage. You might as well come too, Miss Randall, 'cause there's no time to escort you to your seat at the table of honor."

"Now wait a minute—what is going on here? Where are you taking us?" Walter's words were drowned out by the clatter of plates and pans being jostled around the kitchen through which they were being quickly pulled.

Anthony was dazed in the commotion, silently confused as he was ushered past tuxedoed waiters and waitresses, suited men with walkie-talkies, women in long black gowns. It was not until the three of them were suddenly bathed in a bright flood of white light that he realized he was standing on a platform in front of about one hundred well-dressed people. Shawn was gone and an older man with a microphone was now pulling him across the platform. He beckoned, and then grabbed the councilman and Gloria to join them center stage.

The entire place broke into a roaring cheer. Nearly everyone circling the round banquet tables was standing on their feet. Anthony scanned the audience looking for answers, a clue as to what was going on, and why he was in the middle of it. He saw Terri still sitting in the crowd of standers. She was angry. Their eyes locked for a brief second until the spotlight turned on him in a blinding sheet of light. *What is Terri doing here? Does she know what's going on?*

"And here he is, ladies and gentlemen: the benefactor and founder of the brand-new Black Entrepreneurs Alliance, Mr. Anthony Michael Murdock."

The applause grew louder as the jazz band clashed in with a few notes of "He's a Jolly Good Fellow."

"He is joined tonight by our fine councilman, Mr. Walter Banks, who will be providing the BEA with the political backing we need to ensure African-American businessmen and -women have a voice in this city. Miss Randall"—the speaker grabbed her hands and placed them in both Walter's and Anthony's—"you keep up the fine support you've been giving these gentlemen."

Anthony backed away, stunned. The man with the microphone laughed and pulled him closer.

"Not so fast, Mr. Murdock. I've heard you don't like the spotlight, but everyone needs to know about your hard work behind the scenes." He turned to the audience, which still echoed with isolated claps and whistles. With his hands clasped around the microphone, he beamed as he spoke. "As quiet as it's kept, this man has been working hard in the field of marketing, and through his efforts, he's earned himself quite a fortune making sure African-American businesses have equal advertising and exposure—a chance—in our locality."

Anthony noticed Mr. Haberstick sitting at a table near Terri. He was grinning, both hands resting on top of a wooden cane.

"And if that's not enough," the speaker continued, "he has unselfishly decided not only to start up this worthwhile foundation, but also to donate a large part of his hard-earned fortune to each of the businesses that make up the BEA. In an unheard-of public display of generosity in this part of Shepherd Hills, Mr. Murdock has agreed to give $100,000 each to the five cornerstone businesses that make up the Black Entrepreneurs Alliance: Blakeman Brothers Tax Services, Future First Financial, the Empress Hotel Corporation, Pride and Fidelity, and Coleman's.

"All other businesses that apply and are accepted as part of this alliance will be given $10,000 from the endowment funds, and, as I understand, there are already several other businesses pending. Let us all join in a hearty applause once more for the generous efforts of Mr. Anthony Murdock. Because of him, all this is possible."

The crowd stood again, applauding wildly; but this time, Anthony had headed for an exit offstage. Walter and Gloria were close behind him.

"It was all a trap, a ridiculous, well-planned trap that successfully put me publicly in the center of this fiasco. How do I get out of this? I don't even know what's going on. I'm sorry they've got your name in the middle of all this too, Walter. They're using my respect and care for you against me, to get me. And now they're drawing you into this too, Gloria. I just wish I knew who the 'they' was. And Terri . . ."

"We need to pray and ask God for some direction." The councilman followed Anthony out of the rear service entrance. Short puffs of breath punched out his words as he ran behind him. Despite his reassuring words, Anthony could hear fear and uncertainty in Walter's voice as he continued. "God will show us what to do and everything will turn out fine."

But even as he spoke, all three came to a halt at the sight of a police cruiser parked behind Anthony's car. It was Sheriff Malloy.

"Got a call about a car illegally parked in a tow-away zone. Can't say that I'm surprised to see it's you, Mr. Murdock. Didn't I see you the other night?" Even as he spoke to Anthony, his eyebrows were raised at the councilman standing beside him.

"Look, Sheriff, there's something going on and I don't even know how to begin explaining it. I came here tonight looking for—"

"From what I understand, you've been giving out a lot of money to a lot of people. How does a local man like yourself keep coming up with so much money? After our little run-in the other day I checked with the IRS, and they have no records supporting the amount of money you were carrying around with you that evening. Where are you getting all this cash from, Mr. Murdock—enough to be giving hundreds of thousands of dollars away to a select group of people?"

"That's not my money. I don't know whose it is, or where it's coming from. Believe me, Sheriff Malloy, I don't have that kind of cash."

"Oh, don't you?" Sheriff Malloy opened Anthony's trunk and pulled out the satchel of money he'd hidden after the phone-booth call two nights earlier. "Then tell me why I found this in your possession."

"Do you have a search warrant?" Anthony felt pools of sweat gathering around his neck.

"Do I need one? Is there something you're trying to hide?"

"No, I mean, look—I don't know how to begin telling you about the last six months, but—"

"Save the explanations for your lawyer. Just tell me where you got this money, Murdock."

"I can't leave this for you to fight alone, Anthony!"

Both Sheriff Malloy and Anthony were taken aback by the councilman's sudden outburst. Anthony quickly raised his hand to quiet him, but Walter swatted it down.

"No, let me," he said to Anthony before turning to face

the sheriff square in the eye. "Anthony got this money from me. *I'm* the one who doesn't know where it came from."

Malloy looked from Anthony to Walter to Gloria and back to Walter as he continued speaking.

"Look, someone is trying to set *both* of us up by putting our names on money whose source is unknown. Earlier this week, a lot of cash was put into one of my bank accounts by an unknown party, and a check forged with my signature was forced upon Anthony to accept. We don't know who's behind all this, or what their ultimate aim is. We think it has something to do with that Stonymill expansion project that's warring with one of the civic groups, but the trap keeps getting harder to pull out of. Sheriff Malloy, we're hoping you can help us."

The sheriff pulled one end of his red mustache, glaring at the three of them before letting his eyes rest on Walter's.

"So, you actually think I'm going to fall for your sob story about you, a respected political figure, landing a sudden, mysterious financial windfall? And the two of you are just 'lost' in some entanglement that has both of you helplessly controlling all that money? That's just what the public wants to hear: a preacher and a politician taking their tithes and tax dollars to make the poor poorer and the rich richer. And what's your role in all this, lady?" He turned to Gloria. "What's your reward for your compliance in this game of take-and-give?"

"No, leave Gloria out of this! She has nothing to do with any of this whatsoever!" Walter boomed.

"So you are admitting to *something*, aren't you? What is it? Where are you two getting all this money from?"

"No, that's not what I'm saying at all. We need your help, Sheriff! There's a—"

"A scandal that's about to turn this city upside down. I had a lot of respect for you and your work, Councilman, but now I see that you're as crooked as they come. Both of you, all of you."

The sheriff headed back to his cruiser. Before he stepped back in, he turned to face the stunned trio, his eyes singling out Walter's once more. "I wouldn't take any sudden vacations right now. I'm sure both of you will be down at my headquarters in the very near future as I get to the bottom of this. You're not going to keep abusing my tax dollars, or whatever it is you're doing. I hope you have some other employable skills, Councilman, because your politicking days are just about over."

As he sped off, Anthony bowed his head toward Walter. "I apologize for all of this. If I had not been so greedy six months ago, this door to hell wouldn't ever have been open. I'm sorry, Walter. I am truly sorry."

Councilman Banks stared ahead as Anthony slammed his trunk shut.

"What do I do with all this money?" There was no reply. Anthony tightened the strap around the satchel and put it back in his trunk.

∽

"Can you believe that crap?" Terri punched an elbow into a metal paper-towel holder. "I've never felt so humiliated in my entire life! I can't believe he would do this to me! And in front of so many people!"

"Pull yourself together, girl. People can hear you in the hallway."

"Does it matter anymore, Cherisse? Does it really matter?" Terri let out a stifled wail. The two of them were in the handicapped stall of the ladies' room at the Diamond Mount. Cherisse pulled Terri to her and let the wail get choked up in her shoulder.

"It's okay, Terri. You are a proud, black woman with a good job and good sense. You don't need him anyway. Everything is okay."

"How can you say that? Everything is *not* okay!" Terri pushed away, black smudges under both of her eyes. "He had the nerve to have another woman standing next to him on the stage while he's getting honored for a foundation *I* didn't know he started with money *I* didn't know he had. How could he embarrass me like this? It's like I don't even exist—I'm nothing to him. I don't even deserve a place at his table. Did you see all those people turning to look at me?" Terri's words ended with another long sob.

"I don't think too many people were paying you any mind. Think about it: Who in that room even knows you were the honoree's wife?"

Terri let out another wail before cutting it off with her fist slamming the paper-towel holder again.

"I can't stand feeling like this, acting like this. I never thought a man could make me carry on like this. You're right, Cherisse, I need to pull myself together. I'm better than this."

"That's what I'm trying to tell you, Terri. Everything will be okay." She wet some paper towels and offered them to Terri. "Here, fix your face. We've got to go back out there with some dignity."

"What am I going to do?"

"You can always have a little talk with Jesus."

"What? What did you just say to me?"

"You're right, Terri. This is a bad time for a joke."

"Jesus? Why should I talk to him? He's obviously not leading Anthony in the right direction! What the heck is he going to do for me? Huh, Jesus? Where are You now? Where are You? What are You doing to my life?" Terri slid down to the floor, her voice breaking into choking sobs.

"Terri! Terri! Calm down! People can hear you out there. I'm sorry. I was just joking, girlfriend. My timing was terrible. I didn't realize you would take me so seriously. What's gotten into you, girl? Calm down. Calm down."

"I'm so sick of everybody trying to use Jesus to get in or get out of their two-timing schemes. I'm done, Cherisse. I'm finished with trying to understand all that religious crap. I'm not even going to try *a little bit* anymore. Jesus ain't any more real than Anthony's little phony hallelujah self. I see who I've got now, girl. I see it. Me, myself, and I."

"And me. You've got me, Terri." Neither Terri nor Cherisse had noticed Reginald Savant standing in the rest-room doorway.

Uncertainty swept the car clean of any conversation the entire return trip to Councilman Banks's office. Anthony pulled into the small parking lot a little after eight-thirty. When a nearby church bell tolled nine o'clock, the three of them, Anthony, Walter, and Gloria, were still sitting speechless in the midnight-blue BMW.

"I think we need to go inside and discuss strategy." Walter was the first to break the silence. "If the police are not on our side, we need to deepen our own detective work to convince them we're not the bad guys. Or at least come clean about any prior action we may have taken which might not have worked in our favor." Walter's eyes met Anthony's in the rearview mirror.

Anthony could only feel small in his seat. *Why did I accept that bribe six months ago?*

"Gloria, why don't you go on home. Anthony and I can stay here and talk awhile to formulate a quick and effective plan of action. Don't you worry about a thing, Miss Randall. None of this concerns you, so it should not affect you in the least." Walter tried to sound cheery, but even as Gloria unlocked the passenger door and got out of the car, the strain on his face mirrored that of Anthony's.

"Have a nice weekend, Gloria," Anthony managed to mumble. He watched expressionless as she headed in the direction of a nearby bus stop before he jerked back to attention. "Gloria, wait. I can give you a ride home."

"You don't want to stay to figure out what to do next?" Councilman Banks's words were tinged with fear.

"Walter, honestly, right now I just want to go home. Give me a night to clear my head, and I'll contact you first thing in the morning."

Walter sighed before nodding his head. "Okay, Anthony, but we really need to get things straight as soon as possible."

"I know, I just need some time by myself to make sense of all this."

Walter slowly got out of Anthony's car as Gloria got back in. When Anthony turned back onto the boulevard, he could see the councilman sitting on the curb next to his office suite.

"I'm sorry, everyone." He could not think of anything else to say.

After seeing Gloria safely into her apartment, Anthony headed home, landing straight in his favorite leather recliner.

"I don't want to think about anything at all right now." He reached for the remote control and the two-story family room soon began to flicker in a trance of dancing black-and-white shadows. Even with the television muted, he felt a headache brewing. He clicked off the set and sank back into the uneasy darkness of the room.

When was the last time you talked to Me?

The voice, so quiet and tender, cut into his thoughts. He grabbed the remote again and turned the TV back on, this time keeping his thumb on the volume button until the top-of-the-line speaker system thundered under his skin. But the voice did not stop speaking.

When was the last time you talked to Me?

"I don't want to think! I can't pray right now! Not right now!"

When was the last time you talked to your wife?

With those words, Anthony switched off the TV again and the room at once was quiet. He waited, but the silence remained.

"You are the very essence of a Nubian queen, the epitome of black queendom."

Under normal circumstances, Terri would have given Reggie's words a C-minus for effort and a D for effectiveness, but these were not usual circumstances. As she sat on the bathroom floor at the Diamond Mount, feeling alone, humiliated, hair off duty, makeup undone, his words were like breath to her collapsing lungs. She needed to hear them.

"You don't have to sit there hurting. Stand up, black woman."

And she stood.

Cherisse squeezed her hand. "All right, Terri, come on. Let's go. You can stay at my place for the night until we figure out what to do with the hypocrite."

"I've got her." And with those final words, Reggie took Terri by the arm and led her out of the ladies' room. "Come, let's get a drink to celebrate. A toast to new beginnings."

They walked together arm-in-arm through the lobby, back to the main hall, where only a few partyers remained. Terri's feet felt like lead to her, her mind as frozen as the ice swans they passed on their way to the bar. She was oblivious to the scattering groups of two around them, tittering nervously in their games of cat-and-mouse. The last drunk dancers on the hardwood floor moved in and out of focus as if she were seeing them through cracked glass. She did not hear the closing notes of the saxophonist, smell the scattered flower petals that remained on the empty tables, feel the smoothness of Reggie's lips on her forehead as he pressed her closer to his side.

Above all, she did not see the blond-headed woman in the black micro-mini dress staring at the two of them from a corner near the kitchen door. Her bare, pecan-colored arms were drawn tightly across her chest, her mouth spitting out obscenities.

"No, that thing *isn't* trying to take *my* place!" Nikki Galloway stood fuming a few moments, and then a slow smile came over her face. "I ain't taking no more orders from anybody. It's time to do things *my* way."

~

Kent Cassell filled in the last space of the crossword puzzle and then tossed the mini-magazine in the waste-basket. From his seat beside the fireplace in the nine-teenth-century Atlantic-facing Victorian, he could see Mona in the kitchen, cutting slices of tiramisu and scooping vanilla ice cream into bowls for a late-night snack. When she turned toward him with the food on a wooden tray, he quickly put a smile on his face and found an easy compliment to give her. She'd done a good job planning the impromptu trip. He wanted her to feel ap-preciated.

"Those are some pretty flowers you have on that tray."

Mona smiled back with a pleased nod. "I found them in the garden on the other side of the property."

"Ah, I should have known you would sneak back to that spot." Kent smiled, remembering their walk to the shoreline earlier that day. A garden courtyard blooming in autumn colors bordered the path that led to the rocky coast.

"The owners maintain this place so nicely. We'll have to come stay here again, maybe this summer?"

"Yes, maybe." Even as he spoke, a distant look shad-owed his face a second too long for Mona not to notice.

"Kent, darling, please try to relax. We are on vacation. You promised to leave all that stress and worry back in Shepherd Hills. You promised."

"I am relaxed, honey, I really am. If it makes you feel

any better, it's not the job that's on my mind, it's my cell phone. I'm bothered that I don't know where it is." Half of the truth was better than none of the truth, he reasoned.

"Oh, if that's all you're thinking about, why don't you just call the number. If it's only mixed up with our luggage, you'll hear it and the case will be closed. If not, then you know it must still be at home. Where else could it be?"

"You're right," Kent conceded. He took the phone Mona handed him and dialed his cell-phone number.

"Hello?" A young black woman answered on the second ring.

"Hello, who is this?"

"What do you mean, who is this? Who do you think it is?"

"I'm sorry, is this 410-555-2125?"

There was a long pause before the woman slowly answered, "No, it is not. I think you dialed the wrong number, mister. In fact, I'm sure you did."

"Well"—Kent was confused—"I guess I did. Sorry to disturb you." He hung up and dialed his cell-phone number again. This time there was no answer.

Anthony watched in silence as the illuminated clock hands ticked closer to midnight. He was still in the family room, shoes and socks off, suit crumpled around him as he sat on a sofa in complete darkness. *Always remember you're a child of the light.* He could hear his Great-Aunt Rosa's voice piercing the darkness with a simple melody: *Walk in the light/Beautiful light/Walk where the dewdrops of mercy shine bright. . . .*

"God, how did I end up in this place?" His eyes were

dry, his voice a hoarse whisper. He could not stand feeling this low. He needed a break, a change in thought, something, anything, to give his hurting head a reprieve. He grabbed a stack of unopened bank statements and clicked on a table lamp. Usually, a sense of peace would settle on him as he reviewed the balances of his accounts. But this money was not legally his. He knew it, and there was no peace in that knowledge. Most of his savings were what had been left of his share of the bribe money.

In the dimly lit room, Anthony kept flipping through the papers, the statements. There had to be something in here that he could claim as his own. Did he really have to lose it all? He stopped at a statement from his old employer, Shaw Enterprises; a pension fund that had started long before he got involved with the bribery scheme. This money was safe, legally his. Anthony sighed, feeling a small rush at the sight of the current balance. He could cash it in, if necessary. And it more than likely would be necessary. Even after taxes and the penalty for early withdrawal, it was a good balance, a very good balance.

Too good a balance. Anthony noticed for the first time that his former employer had contributed more money to the fund than it was supposed to; not a whole lot, but enough to make a small difference. It was an error, a glitch, Anthony was sure, but an extra two hundred dollars or so nonetheless.

He'd worked hard for Shaw, he assured himself. For all he was going through and for all he was about to lose, there was no reason to worry about correcting a computerized error. It was only two hundred dollars. Shaw was a multi-million-dollar agency. The company would never miss such a small amount. He would even tithe the over-payment, give God back some of the overflow.

Anthony thought of all these reasons and more why he was entitled to keep this money, accept it as a backhand blessing from God, but uneasiness tore at his mind.

"Why, Lord?" As Anthony suddenly lunged to his feet, the table lamp crashed to the floor and the room was plunged back into darkness. "Why can't I keep *this* money? It was their error, not mine! All the overtime I put in there, I probably earned this much and a hundred times over! You know me, Jesus. You know my heart. I can't take this anymore!" His words were sobs and groans as he fell to his knees, steadying himself with a hand pushing down on a nearby coffee table.

"What's wrong with me keeping this money? They'll never miss it. It's not illegal. I haven't done anything wrong. It was their fault. This one ain't on me. I'm not breaking the law!"

What about My law?

Anthony quieted at the question that was spoken somewhere in his spirit. He pulled a Bible from the book-case and found his way back to his knees.

"I need to see." He stood up one more time, flooding the room with the light of a wrought-iron chandelier. Blinking, he remembered standing onstage just a few hours earlier, the spotlight on him, blinding him from everyone but Terri. Terri. Where was she? *She looked angry last night and tonight at the banquet.* Maybe her not being home meant nothing. Maybe it meant everything. *How much does she know?*

He ran his fingers over the dark blue leather cover of

his favorite study Bible. It had been a gift from Terri, given to him for his birthday the year before they married.

"A spiritual book for a spiritual man," she'd said then. He took it as a sign from God that she did indeed have some kind of Jesus-connection, a question a few members of his church family, including his Aunt Rosa and Sister Porter, had raised when they saw her frequenting the congregation with him during those days. He found out much later, during a post-honeymoon spat about him "reading that Bible too much and taking it too seriously," that the gift had been Cherisse's idea, a device to get him to see that Terri had an appreciation for the spiritual.

It is one thing to know about Me, and a completely different thing to know Me.

Anthony knew that God had spoken those words to him about Terri long before he bought the one-and-a-half-carat engagement ring he gave her on Valentine's Day. He knew it, he'd heard it directly from Him, but he hadn't listened. What he'd listened to was the other voice in his head telling him that if she continued attending Second Baptist, she would get to know Him as he did. And that she was a *fine* sister from a good family with the drive and desire to help him reach his lifelong goal of being a millionaire by age thirty.

"I gained the millions, but at what cost?"

Anthony was quiet, reflective, as he bowed his head. "Lord," he prayed, his voice barely a whisper, "I need a word from You. Talk to me. I can't think another thought, or take another step, until I hear a clear, practical word from You. How much have I missed You saying already?" He glanced over at the pension statement.

Anthony sat on the floor next to the sofa and began flipping through the thin pages of his Bible. Highlighter and pen marks zigzagged through verses, colored entire chapters. He stopped at a few random Psalms for encouragement, a couple of Proverbs for wisdom. An hour passed with him reviewing previous notes he'd made in the margins, reading and rereading study commentaries at the bottom of the pages.

It was not until his fingers landed on a familiar Old Testament chapter that he heard that gentle voice speak somewhere inside of him.

Read.

And so he read, underlining words that stood out to him, praying for a clearer understanding of the passage. It was the sixteenth chapter of Judges, the story of Samson and Delilah. Although he was not exactly sure what this late-night Bible study was going to teach him, he was already beginning to feel the excitement of a coming revelation, a truth, a turning point that would get him back on track.

His eyes raced through the story of how Samson, the promised and purposed son of a barren Israelite couple, fell into the traps of the seductress Delilah. He had been born destined to deliver his people from their enemies, the Philistines, and had supernatural physical strength to accomplish that purpose. His strength was promised from God as long as he did not cut his hair, for he was under a special Nazirite vow.

Anthony slowed down when he got to the description of how Delilah pestered him into telling her the secret behind his strength, and then schemed to have his hair cut off when he fell asleep on her knees. Once asleep, the

Philistines overtook him, put out his eyes, bound him, imprisoned him, and forced him into menial labor.

Reaching for a legal pad, Anthony continued to read, sensing a message for him about to break through the sacred words.

Samson was called to perform before the Philistines during one of their religious celebrations at a temple for their god. None of them took notice that Samson's hair had regrown. Blind and humiliated, he asked the young boy who was attending him to place him between the pillars that held up the temple. He prayed and asked God for one last burst of strength, which he used to push the pillars heroically, causing the temple to fall and end his life and the lives of three thousand high-ranking Philistines.

Anthony read the chapter once more before laying his Bible beside him.

"Okay, Jesus, what is it that You want me to know from this?" He sat there twiddling a pen between his fingers for a few moments, and then a deluge of thoughts poured through his mind. He could not write it all down fast enough.

> Samson's passions led him away from the power and calling of God for his life. I've done the same. Money has been my seductress, and I've given it a place and position in my heart that should have been reserved only for God. Like Samson, my temptress lulled me to sleep through deception, trapped and stripped me of my strength, my common sense, and my dignity.
>
> I am awake now and find myself bound, my

reasoning and abilities shackled by my sin. I haven't been able to think clearly, decide clearly, and, like Samson, I was blinded so that I could not see clearly, letting others lead me around in circles for the past six months. My sight, my vision, was taken from me. My vision for my life, for my ministry, for my relationship with my wife have all been darkened ever since I fell for the bait.

When Samson's hair was cut, he lost his supernatural strength and was imprisoned. His identity as a Nazirite was forfeited. My identity was blurred and weakened when I left my First Love to pursue another; my identity as a man, and most importantly as a child of God, was washed out by my willingness to be led astray by dollar signs.

My sin wasn't getting the money; it was loving money to the point of leaving Him, and leaving Him led to weakness, a loss of identity, a loss of sight, and a loss of freedom.

Anthony stopped to look at what he had written. He read it a few times, circling the words *weakness, identity, sight,* and *freedom.* He picked up his pen again.

But just like Samson who still fulfilled his pre-birth purpose, my God-given destiny is not gone. I've been imprisoned mentally, physically, spiritually for the past six months, but regaining strength the entire time.

Sin made me weak, but now in repentance to You, Lord, I am strong. Strong enough to reclaim my purpose in You, Jesus. Strong enough to step back into my God-given place to be the man of God You called me to be.

No more confusion, only confidence. Confidence that You have forgiven me and given me enough supernatural strength to get through all of this. Confidence that even if I still can't see exactly who my enemies are, You will show me how to feel and push my way to victory.

Tonight, the real Anthony Michael Murdock— the strong, decisive, clear-headed warrior for God—is standing by the pillars, ready to topple the whole scheme of corruption that has taken over Shepherd Hills. All for Your glory, all in Your name.

"Father, I repent. I'm sorry. It wasn't the bribe that hurt You. It's been me wanting money more than wanting You. Lord, You know my heart, my desires. Forgive me, cleanse me. You said in Your Word to seek You first, and Your righteousness, and then everything else will be added unto me. So, Lord, right now, I am chasing after You *first*. I receive Your forgiveness, and I trust You to provide my every need, material and otherwise."

Anthony laid down his pen and stood, his arms raised up in praise to the One whose loving kindness has relieved many burdened souls. For the first time in months, he felt genuine joy and peace.

"I'm free." The words themselves released a new wave of hope, a clear view of direction. He sat back down and tore out a clean sheet of paper. He felt truly right with heaven; now to get right on earth.

"Let's start at the beginning." He followed the urge to

map an outline of the past six months, starting with the day the first note showed up in his mailbox at Shaw Enterprises.

That's not the beginning. Anthony's pen froze in mid-air as a new thought came upon him. He had been snagged by the bribe money half a year ago, but that was just the end result of a lusty relationship he'd been having with money. He'd been flirting with the narrow focus of getting rich for years. A verse from First Timothy came to his mind: "For the love of money is the root of all evil: which while some coveted after, they have erred from the faith, and pierced themselves through with many sorrows."

"Ain't that the truth." Anthony shook his head. "It's not *money*, but the *love* of money that's at the root of my problems." Even as he spoke, the word *root* jumped out at him.

Start at the beginning. Anthony closed his eyes and began trying to remember when he'd started craving wealth insatiably. He thought about his career at Shaw Enterprises, when he'd accepted promotion after promotion, focused not on adding to the quality of his relationship with Terri, but on adding to the quantity of his bank accounts. He remembered a few times when he'd used his tithe money to buy some new suits he knew he looked good in. At the time, he justified it by wearing them to church. "I'm wearing my offering to you," he'd prayed as he dropped a buck or two into the church collection plate.

And then there were his college days when he'd picked a major not based on a consulting session with Jesus, but on a quick check of the salary data in the *Occupational Outlook Handbook* from the U.S. Department of Labor. In his high school yearbook, when asked what he wanted to be when he grew up, his answer was there in black and white: Rich. Even then, he'd determined the purpose of his life with no thought of going about it God's way.

"The blessing of the Lord, it maketh rich, and He addeth no sorrow with it." The proverb was underlined in his Bible, but had he really lived by it? If he had embraced God's definition of being "rich," could he have had God's best, without all the baggage?

Anthony stood to stretch. It was nearly five A.M.; he'd been up all night. He left the family room just as the first fingers of the sun began prying through the drawn shades. He set a pot of coffee to brew. Although it was Saturday, he knew a long day was ahead of him. He needed to call Councilman Banks soon.

Start at the beginning. The words still pressed within him.

"How far back do I have to go?" He asked aloud. "My teen years, my childhood?"

And then he remembered.

It was the night before his mother's wedding to his stepfather. Anthony had stayed with his Great-Aunt Rosa as his mother flurried with last-minute details. She'd had a low budget to work with, greatly impeding her dream of a bigger, fancier event. He remembered asking Aunt Rosa why his mother was so mad when she dropped him off, complaining about someone "not even leaving her with a pot to pee in." He could still smell the soft scent of Aunt Rosa's powdery perfume, feel the silk warmth of her housecoat as she pulled him close to her wide bosom.

"Your momma's just mad 'cause your daddy didn't give her the world in a silver-plated basket before he left. For all his promises, he never did provide her real wealth and riches."

Anthony did not remember anything about his father, but he did remember looking into Aunt Rosa's black-wire-framed eyes and saying at that moment the words he would spend most of his life living by: "I'm going to make enough money so that none of us will ever be sad when we're supposed to be happy."

Aunt Rosa looked back at him with a sad knowing in her eyes. "You sound just like your father, Charlie Murdock. He learned the hard way that money don't equal happiness."

Anthony leaned back in his kitchen chair, the memory of that moment as tangible to him as the ceramic bowl filled with apples, bananas, and oranges sitting in front of his face. He thought about a series of sermons Pastor Green had preached a few years back on generational curses, teaching how the atmosphere of a family can allow for the sins of the father or mother to become the sins of the child.

"My father must have been as money hungry as I am. I wonder if he ever got into a mess like me?"

Yes.

Anthony immediately wanted to know everything about his father's finances.

"Minister Porter may have really been onto something." Anthony cut off the coffeepot as he reached for his coat and keys. He left the overpaid pension-fund statement out on the table to address the next business day. I Timothy 6:9–11 was written on it with bright red ink.

"I feel a Samson victory coming." Anthony jingled the keys in his hand. But even as he said the words a realization choked his sentence. For Samson to overcome, he had to go down with the enemy.

PART 2

∾

Man of Steel

∾

For ye were as sheep going astray;
but are now returned unto
the Shepherd and Bishop of your souls.
(I Peter 2:25 KJV)

Chapter 11

Clattering plates and clanking utensils jolted Mabel Linstead awake. She rolled over in the sofa bed her sister-in-law had prepared for her and searched for the clock in the dim light of predawn.

"Five-thirty? What is she doing?" Mabel sat up, feeling for her slippers hidden under a corner of the paisley-print comforter. As she stood she tugged at the heavy blanket, repositioning it, careful not to awaken her daughter, Denise, who was sleeping on the other side of the bed.

A loud metal clang clashed from the kitchen along with a short swish of water. Mabel followed the sound to find Kellye Porter standing by the suds-filled sink, an apron tied over her bathrobe, soaked in splotches of bubbles and water.

"Kellye, why are you worried about them dishes right now?" Her voice had a maternal edge to it. Although both women were well over sixty, Mabel still saw Kellye as the cute little northern girl who married her baby brother,

Bernard, taking him six hundred miles away from his Sharen, South Carolina, home.

"There's going to be more people coming over today than it was yesterday, and I can't have this kitchen looking like this." Kellye's concentration never left the grease she was scrubbing out of an empty pan that had held baked chicken.

True to tradition, church members, friends, and other sympathizers had been steadily flocking in and out of the Porters' home, bringing with them pots and bowls of chicken and ham, greens and potato salad, cakes and pies, and plenty of beverages. In her time of bereavement, cooking for a crowd of grievers was the last thing a newly named widow should be fussing over, and the community answered the call.

"Honey, people are coming here to see you, not your kitchen. Now why don't you try to rest. I doubt that you got much sleep last night, and we have to finish making the arrangements later on today." Mabel squeezed Kellye's shoulder as she spoke.

"I can't just sit. There's too much to do. I still need to gather everything to give to the mortician, and I can't decide between Bernard's blue suit or black one. And then there's the obituary photo. I just can't decide. . . ." Kellye took a deep breath as her eyes drifted to the kitchen table. Dozens of photographs were laid out in neat rows, Mabel noticed for the first time.

"Kellye"—she took her by both arms and with a sorrowful smile looked her straight in the eyes—"please go rest. I can help you with all this. I'll lay out some outfits and pictures while you sleep and you can decide from those later. Okay? Now you go and get some rest."

Kellye gave the kitchen sink and the photos an uncertain last look before heading quietly to her bedroom, closing the door behind her. In slow, hesitant steps, Mabel approached the pine table where her brother, Bernard, smiled up at her from a million different captured memories. Weddings, family reunions, birthdays, lazy summer afternoons. Bernard as a young man, eyes gazing with the bold dare of youth; Bernard as an old man, distinguished and comfortable with the life he'd forged.

Her fingers ran over the glossy finishes, a single tear resting in the corner of one eye as she picked up photos one by one. Bernard standing next to Kellye, sitting with Poppa, cradling Denise; Bernard on the usher board, the deacon board, his trial sermon. Bernard with family from back home, with his Toringhouse Steel co-workers, with people she knew, with many she didn't. Bernard with— Mabel suddenly froze. Her eyes dried of all tears as she picked up an old photo that had been stuck to the back of another, the edges torn and ragged as if time had tried to will the memory away.

Mabel reached for her glasses to get a better look but was interrupted by a soft knock at the front door.

"They're starting early today," she mumbled as she went to greet the first visitor of the morning. She opened the front door to find a young man in his late twenties standing there, a focused fire in his eyes despite his disheveled appearance.

"I'm sorry to be over so early, but I really need to speak to Sister Porter." He looked at her like he was trying to place her face. She knew exactly who he was, instinctively clutching the photograph in her hand closer to her side, away from his eyes and attention.

"I'm sorry, but Kellye just went to sleep and she really needs her rest. I'll tell her you stopped by. What's your name, darling?" Her voice was a sweet sound of southern melody, but her heart was pounding a different tune.

"Anthony. Minister Anthony Murdock. Tell her I came and I'll be back later this morning."

"Oh? Okay." She forced a smile as she closed the door. Padded steps sounded from the hallway.

"Who was that? Was someone just at the door?" Kellye's voice was hoarse, her face a ragged maze of tears and tiredness.

"Oh, I was just checking to see if your paper came today. I wanted to see how they list obituaries up here so I can help you better. That's all, now go on back to bed."

When Kellye disappeared into the hallway, Mabel took another long look at the photo in her hand.

"Don't worry, I'm taking care of everything," she called after her. And then in a softer voice, whispered, "Starting with this." She crumpled up the worn picture and put it in her bathrobe pocket.

It had been a long night and Terri felt it in her feet, her arms, her back, and, most of all, her head. She woke up with a start, sitting straight up and then collapsing under the weight of a piercing headache that wrapped itself around her forehead and reached down to the bones in her neck.

She would have lain there a few moments longer, soaking in the frenzied solos of a few distant birds; but just as she was about to reclose her eyes something caught her attention. What was that abstract painting doing in her bedroom? And why was there a collection of sculptures on her desk? Wait a minute, she didn't have a desk in her bedroom and even if she did, it wouldn't be that one. The minimalist design would clash with her Moroccan-themed bedroom furniture. And if this wasn't her furniture, then—

"Where the heck am I?" She sprang up with a shout. At her feet, in an easy chair facing her, with an easy smile on his face, sat Reginald Savant. Snapshots of the night before suddenly flashed through Terri's mind like a rushed slide show, starting with the anger and humiliation of Anthony's disregard for her and ending with a bottle and a half of Moët at a bar counter with Reggie. She did not remember anything beyond that.

"Oh my goodness!" Her whisper had the impact of a scream as she threw both hands over her mouth.

Reggie, still dressed impeccably in his tux from the evening before, squelched her fears before she even fully expressed them.

"No." He let the word sink in before continuing. "I consider myself a gentleman, and as such, I would never take advantage of a lady caught in a state such as yours last night. The only task fitting for me to do was see you to a safe place."

"And the safest place available was here in your bedroom, right?" As quick as the sarcasm rose, so did the uneasiness in Terri's stomach. She threw a hand over her mouth as Reggie quickly put a wastebasket in front of her.

His smile was wicked as Terri put the can to use. "Well, if I had known that you would have considered my bedroom to be such a safe haven, I would have most certainly taken you there instead of here to my office." He stood as he spoke and with a quick pull, black window shades were drawn, letting a megadose of yellow sunshine spill loosely into the room.

Terri squinted in the bright light, but as her eyes took better focus, she realized she was sitting on an oversized plush sofa, and not a bed. There were several bookcases around her, a computer workstation, and the view out the window was a panorama of downtown glass and steel. In her embarrassment, she did not see Reggie's eyes glued to the delicate motions of her arms and hands setting down the trash can and then smoothing out the wrinkled black gown she was still wearing.

"You are absolutely beautiful." His voice was a whisper as he neared her again. He sat down, pulling his chair as close as possible to her.

"You are quite the charmer, Mr. Savant, giving me a compliment after all I've given is a mess."

Their eyes met in a tense engagement until Terri surrendered to the jitters that were stinging her conscience. Everything felt right and wrong at the same time.

"It's—"

"Saturday morning," Reggie cut her off. "A good time to enjoy the early-bird breakfast buffet at the Westcott Room. Let's go eat, and then . . . and then we can see what other adventures await us this fine weekend day." His fingers lightly tickled her bare arms, stopping gently at her shoulders. "It's a good day for discovery and exploration, leisure and letting go."

The words *letting go* lingered in Terri's head as Reggie planted soft, warm kisses on her hand and arm. She pulled back slowly, shutting her eyes, not wanting to think beyond the moment, blocking out the thoughts of Anthony and the circumstances that had led her to this very un-businesslike meeting in Reggie's forty-third-floor office suite.

"Let's go," she said decidedly, "to the Westcott Room." She jumped to her feet, taking his hand in hers.

Anthony turned up the heat in his car. It was surprisingly cold despite the abundance of September sunshine. The sunlight was just a few hours old, leaving few cars to compete for lane space as Anthony turned onto the highway away from Kellye Porter's home. He had not given much thought to how early it was until after he knocked on her door, and was almost relieved when another woman answered it.

Kellye did need her rest, as it was sure to be an exhausting, trying day for her. Despite the minor crimp in his plan, he was not deterred in his search for information about his father. He was already moving on to Plan B. He would revisit Plan A later.

Anthony settled comfortably in the driver's seat, feeling for the first time in a long time a certainty that he was on the right track. Repentance had opened his eyes to his own heart and God's place in it, giving him an unwavering sense of peace. The burden was lighter, although his mission had taken on an extra assignment.

Now it was about more than revealing the source of the bribe money and coming clean before everyone. He felt a freedom, an exoneration almost, that pinched a nerve of purpose somewhere inside of him. It was as if the journey had taken on the task of resolving a lifetime obsession; a task that had been handed to him and would lead him to a destination of God's design. It was, up to this point, his ultimate undertaking: fighting for his life, his family, his community.

Mr. Haberstick had been right at least about one thing: this was bigger than the two of them. But now the fear and confusion that had surrounded Anthony when he'd heard that statement was gone with the realization that the biggest involvement was from his Lord, and He had a purposed outcome in mind.

For I know the thoughts that I think toward you . . . thoughts of peace, and not of evil, to give you an expected end. The words God spoke in the book of Jeremiah brought assurance to Anthony's heart, an assurance no amount of money could ever buy.

He decided to make a brief stop en route to Plan B. Pastor Green was usually at the church early on Saturday mornings as he prepared sermon notes for Sunday services. Anthony wanted someone to rejoice alongside him in his revival of spirit and purposed direction. He turned off the expressway a few exits before the church with the intent of finding a drive-though serving breakfast. The rumblings of his empty stomach, which he had successfully ignored for nearly twenty-four hours, had ceased their polite request for nourishment. His body now screamed for food, and Anthony was eager to break his forced fast. Pastor Green could probably use a cup of steaming coffee and a hot bacon-and-egg sandwich, Anthony decided as he pulled to a stop at the rear of a short line of other hungry drivers.

Just as he placed his order, his cell phone rang, the shrilling of it almost foreign to his ears as it had succumbed to silence for so long.

"Anthony, what are you doing? Where are you? I

thought you were going to call me first thing this morning?"

Anthony had never heard the councilman sound this anxious. Walter Banks had established a reputation as a cool-headed council member, able to calm the nerves and angry sentiments of the ill-at-ease public at community forums, never breaking a sweat during three exceedingly tight election races.

"Good morning, Mr. Banks." Anthony sounded cheery over the static. "I haven't forgotten you. I was planning to see you this afternoon after I checked a couple of leads. I think—no, I know that I'm on to something. Come to think about it, you may be able to help me with this. It's about my father, Charles Anthony Murdock." Anthony wondered if Aunt Rosa had ever spoken to the councilman about his father.

"Your father? Your biological father? I thought he died—what, over twenty-five years ago? You really think this has something to do with him?"

"I'm sure of it."

"How?"

Anthony could hear the doubt in Councilman Banks's voice. "That's what I'm trying to find out," he asserted.

The councilman sounded like he was shaking his head as he spoke into the receiver. "I don't know, Anthony, but if the Lord's leading you in this direction, then I'm going also. I hate to say it, but I'm feeling pretty desperate. I'll go along with anything that will clear my name of any scandal."

"I'm sorry I got you mixed up in this. You don't know how hard I've been kicking myself over my greed." Anthony pulled up to the pick-up window.

"Son, we all make mistakes, some with more consequences than others. We choose the deed, but not always the result. I can't be angry with you, Anthony. I have to trust the Lord to see both of us through. You're sounding pretty calm this morning, so I guess I need to calm down too."

"Be encouraged, Mr. Banks." Now Anthony was the adviser, the mentor, the friend. "God is still in control. Even if we can't see it, He knows what's going on. Remember, no weapon formed against us will prosper. We're both going to emerge from this as victors."

"Amen. Thank you, Anthony. It's good to know that God will send a word when we need it."

"You don't have to tell me." Anthony chuckled. As he drove away from the fast-food restaurant, he told the councilman of his plans to see the pastor, make some other stops, and then meet with him at his office at two.

He turned onto a narrow street, trying to remember a shortcut he'd found once that put him directly in front of the church. A construction crew slowed his progress, flaggers stopping him as an oversized truck crept toward a water-main break. As he waited for the okay to move forward, a man in a yellow vest securing a sign caught his eye. Anthony nodded at the man, but the sign struck a nerve in him:

CAUTION: DANGER AHEAD.

When another vested man raised a red flag, Anthony set his eyes forward and continued straight ahead.

"I'm Freddy the Fearless Frog and I have come to rescue you from the evil Pond Monster!" A throaty voice thundered from the television set as synthesized theme music rose to a glorious trill.

"Dum-da-da-dum!" A little boy, peanut butter and jelly crusted around his mouth and fingers, jumped to his feet and began to hop in front of the TV.

"Go git 'em, Freddy Frog!" He jumped and shouted and hopped until a loud groan sounded from a nearby queen bed.

"Didn't I tell you to be quiet? I'm trying to get some sleep!" Nikki Galloway pressed a pillow over her head but the light from the window, and the song from the TV, and the stomps of the boy, were beating out any last hopes of sleeping in she had. Wiping crust out of her eyes, she crawled out of the bed and headed for the kitchen, where she plodded from one cabinet to another, slamming first a bowl and then a box of cereal onto a counter.

"Mommy, can I have some?" Three-year-old Devin pressed into her side, his eyes big with hope.

"Here." Nikki pushed the bowl toward him before grabbing another and pouring milk into both. "Hurry up and eat, and then go play with your toys."

"Yeah!" The boy sloshed milk on the floor as he scrambled off.

Nikki gulped down the cereal and then lay across the sofa. "I got too much to figure out today to be bothered," she murmured. She yanked the glittery PRINCESS T-shirt she was wearing as far as it would go down her bare thighs and retightened the scarf on her head. She sat there quiet for a long minute, her mouth scrunched up in an angry scowl. After another minute passed, her face relaxed.

"All right, I know how I'm going to get Miss Thang." She stuck her hand inside the stuffing of one of the sofa pillows and pulled out a cell phone. She turned it on slowly, waiting for the signal to light up. Last night had been a close one, with that detective calling and all. She could have jeopardized the whole thing. But she'd woken up smarter and wiser this morning. Her mother would be proud. Nikki almost smiled.

She picked up a sheet of paper from a side table, looking for the number she needed. But before she dialed, she had a better idea. Why just settle for fixing the tramp? Why not take care of them all?

Nikki clapped the phone shut and headed for her bedroom. "Devin, get your clothes on. We got some places to go."

Anthony was surprised to see the front door of the church propped open. He entered and found Pastor Green standing in the foyer wearing a pair of denim overalls, a dripping roller brush in his hands.

"Hello, Minister Murdock. Watch your step." He smiled almost as if he'd been expecting him.

Anthony maneuvered around several open cans of paint and trays, stepping back on the crinkling plastic to admire the pastor's handiwork.

"That's a nice shade of white. Why didn't you let me know you were planning to paint the hallway? I could have helped."

"Thanks for the offer and the coffee. Actually, a contractor was supposed to do this weeks ago. I guess I got tired of waiting and figured there was no reason I couldn't do it myself."

"I understand that. You've always been a take-charge kind of person." Anthony chuckled as he rolled up his shirtsleeves. "I'm taking a lesson from you, Pastor Green. From now on, I'm not going to allow anyone or anything else to control my destiny but God Himself. Not one person, not one situation, not even a dollar sign."

"Praise the Lord." Pastor Green smiled, but his eyes were serious. "I woke up early this morning praying for you. I prayed and prayed until I had peace that you were okay. I can see from the fire in your eyes that the Lord is seeing you through. God has a purpose and a calling on your life, Anthony. Follow Him straight to real blessings." He turned back to the wall, the sound of rhythmic brush strokes taking the place of words in the quiet corridor. As Anthony reached for a small brush sitting atop a can, the pastor spoke again.

"Don't worry about the paint, Minister Murdock. I can do it. There are other things that need your attention. God is fighting the battle, but the war is not over yet."

Anthony stood still a few moments, watching the elder man's back as he painted a second coat near the basement steps. Suddenly, in midstroke, he turned around.

"You haven't talked to Terri, have you?"

Anthony slowly shook his head. He did not want to upset her in her delicate condition. It had been enough seeing her fume in her seat at the banquet the night before. Anthony figured she just needed some time and space, and that she would probably call or come home later that day. Her absence worried him, but the thought of his baby boy brought a generous smile to his face. Pastor Green did not join in the cheeriness.

"You need to talk to her, Anthony. Tell her everything." With those words he resumed his painting. "Can you press Play on that CD player on your way out?"

Anthony was almost out the door when he turned back to start the CD. Within seconds the hand-clapping, feet-stomping chords of a gospel choir filled the paint-scented hallway. As Anthony walked out the front door, he noticed a black Jaguar slowly passing by. Without warning it suddenly sped up although a sharp curve was in its immediate path. After the curve, which took the car out of view, he heard the engine relax.

Anthony shook his head. He had to agree with Marvin, his office mate at Haberstick Associates. Drivers were getting out of control in Shepherd Hills. Why somebody would want to speed up before a curve and slow down afterwards was anyone's guess. Anthony only knew that this was a driver he wanted to avoid.

Terri was quiet as Reggie smiled at her. He turned on his blinker and waited to make a left turn onto his street. Houses that resembled mini-castles dotted the green landscape before them. Mature trees stood like watchtowers on the sprawling acres between homes. Wanting to break the silence, Terri blurted out the only thoughts she allowed herself to dwell on.

"Nice neighborhood." They were traveling northward on the winding road.

"Thank you. I enjoy the privacy people around here give. And the meticulous upkeep of the individual properties is second to none. You should consider living out here." He looked at her from the corner of his eye, letting the silence push her to respond.

"Actually, Anthony and I did consider this area before we bought our house earlier this year, but we decided to settle for a home that was still within our originally proposed budget. If I had known that I was six months away from making partner"—*and being married to a millionaire*, she couldn't help thinking—"I would have put up a bigger fight." The Murdocks' estate, at slightly less than a half million dollars, was worth a fraction of the value of the homes whizzing by the car window.

Reggie nodded, looking pleased with her answer. But the smile faded from his lips as the iron gate to his expansive property came within view. The talk of homes and nice neighborhoods had done little to gloss over the unspoken awkwardness, which Terri, wringing her hands, could not contain. And speaking Anthony's name had only intensified the discomfort.

"Did you enjoy your breakfast?" He approached the gate.

"Very good. Between that meal and this smooth ride, I nearly fell asleep on the drive here." She hoped she sounded convincing, but when she looked at him, she knew that he knew.

Reggie knew that she was awake enough to have seen Anthony standing in the doorway of Second Baptist Church when they'd driven by a few moments earlier. He knew that she was well aware of his attempts to speed by at the last minute. And he knew she had looked back.

When the Jaguar circled the roundabout, stopping directly beside the double front doors, Reggie didn't bother to cut the ignition.

"Terri, I think you are a beautiful, classy, one-of-a-kind woman. A woman who knows she deserves only the best. A woman who knows the best is yet to come. A woman I will wait for. When you are ready to accept all that I can offer you"—he looked hard at her—"and I know that acceptance will be soon, I'll be here."

Terri was quiet, looking straight ahead. *That darn Anthony.* Why couldn't she just let the fool go in peace? *Because I always have to have the last word.* She knew what she had to do.

"My car is still over Cherisse's house. Would you mind dropping me off? I have some business to take care of."

∾

At eleven A.M., the business of the day was just getting started on Cherry Tree Court. Given the illegality of their trade, the workers had a surprisingly strong work ethic, willing to make money seven days a week, three hundred sixty-five days a year, through weekends, holidays, rainy days, and snow. Even the postal workers who walked quickly through this housing development could mark the time and day of the week by the activity of the street businessmen, who peddled their powdery wares on the corners and stoops of their own neighborhood with violent efficiency.

Eric Johnson sat by a window on the top floor of the three-story brick-and-concrete building he called home. He had lived in the projects all his life, unwilling to move even after securing a steady salary through CASH that afforded him the luxury of residential choice. He could have rented a home farther down the boulevard where the rats were fewer and the stoops led to two residences and not five, but his was a matter of mission.

"If I move," he would explain to people who raised eyebrows when they learned his address, "how would Ms. Peaches and Mr. George know that ten years of hard-core drug abuse don't bind them to a life sentence? How would Lil' Moe, Peanut, and Ray-Ray learn that being born on the street don't mean you got to live on the street? If I move, how would them little kids coming up on Cherry Tree Court know there's a life that's different from everything and everyone they see right now? I am a living testimony of one who surpassed the basics of survival. I'm succeeding. They see me and they know things can be different, better. It's hard to deny hope when it's standing flesh-and-blood in your face."

But today Eric was not up for any speeches. He wasn't up to much of anything. After last night's meeting everything had gone further downhill. After he'd given up trying to convince Mrs. Malburn-Epworth and Ernest Rutherford that he was one-hundred-percent drug free and not misusing their donations, he came home to find his answering machine blinking with over thirty messages, angry volunteers and pledge partners vowing to forgo support of anything that had his name attached to it. Eric stopped listening after the seventh message.

"People ready to judge you, before they even talk to you, believing every rumor without a reason." Eric looked back out the window.

A group of eight- and nine-year-old girls were singing outside, their hands joined in a mesmerizing motion of slapping and clapping. Eric could not help but chuckle as a little boy who looked like a brown, overgrown cucumber cut through their circle on a pink tricycle, screams and threats abruptly ending the cheery chorus. He kept his eyes on a group of teenage boys huddled by a black Infiniti, their loose denim jeans barely covered by the white T-shirts that draped their skinny frames like cotton curtains. Eric looked for Mr. Matthews, a gray-haired man who kept a front seat on the block, his throne a metal lawn chair under the sparse shade of a single tree. He was there, sipping from his brown paper bag, laughing hysterically at a joke Ms. Peaches was sharing from her stoop. There was more laughter across the street, where some teenage girls, many of them with infants in tow, were taking turns dancing to a radio propped up in a window.

"These are the people I'm fighting for. This is the reason I can't give up. I'm in this too deep." Eric put his shoes on, pulled a shirt over his head. He walked out of the complex, unsure where he was going, what he was doing, but knowing he had to do something.

As he jogged down the concrete steps, one of the youths leaning against the Infiniti came to attention and broke away from the group.

"Hi, Mr. Johnson." He approached Eric with a curt nod, a cap sitting loosely on his braids. "I ain't with them. I just came out here to keep an eye on Keisha while my mom's at her weekend job." He nodded toward a little girl with two puffy pigtails sitting silently on the curb, a dirty, naked doll tucked tightly under her arms.

"I know, Snap." Eric nodded, although he didn't miss the two color-coded vials peeking out of the boy's pocket. He knew that Snap's mother, like many others in his development, was not at work, but at one of the abandoned row homes turned crack houses down the street. "Your mom's doing the best she can to take care of you two."

"Yeah, whatever." Snap's attention was diverted for a second as an Escalade with tinted windows booming with a heart-fibrillating bass came almost to a stop in front of them.

"That's Peetie and 'em." One of the Infiniti boys shouted toward them. All eyes turned to study Snap.

"It's cool." He nodded as the car picked up speed and turned a corner. Snap was rising in the ranks; Eric felt another piece of his heart breaking.

"So you think you'll make it with me to church tomorrow?"

"I would, man, but I got some things I need to get done. Maybe next week."

It was the same question every Saturday, the same response.

"Anyways"—Snap studied Eric with the eye of an experienced dealer—"you all right these days?"

"Yeah, why?" Eric knew questions from Snap were a rare order.

"I don't know, just been hearing things." The youth took a sip of fruit punch from a plastic bottle before tossing it in a nearby gutter.

"Well, whatever you been hearing, I can tell you it ain't true."

"What's going on, Mr. Johnson? Somebody messing with your rep?"

"Ain't nothing for you to worry about. CASH business, that's all." Eric wanted to leave the conversation.

"Naw, man. You done looked out for me and my sister too much for me to let someone mess over you without at least looking into it. I got your back, Mr. Johnson."

"Snap, I don't want—"

"Don't worry. You know why they call me Snap? 'Cause when I snap my fingers"—he snapped as he spoke—"things get done."

Eric shook his head as he walked away. The unrest inside him intensified.

～

Anthony pulled to a stop in front of the Vital Records Department of Shepherd Hills just after eleven. He knew he was taking a chance. What government building was open on weekends? But he followed his gut, an urging telling him to go anyway, and got confirmation that God was leading him in the right direction before he even finished parallel parking in front of the one-story office building.

A woman dressed in sweat pants and tennis shoes came out of the building, a pencil tucked behind her ear. Her hair was pinned in an elaborate upsweep, and a pair of dangling stone earrings clanked with her every move. She sorted through some keys in her hand and was locking the glass front door as Anthony walked up to her.

"Excuse me, miss"—Anthony extended a hand to her—"do you work here?"

"Mmm-hmm." She didn't bother to look up at him as she gave the door a final tug. "Office hours are Monday through Friday, eight-thirty A.M. to four P.M. If you need a copy of a marriage, birth, or death certificate, you need to fill out Form LL4W, check box three, and mail it along with a check or money order for twenty-five dollars and you'll receive what you want within ten to fifteen business days. Or you can come back during our office hours and pay fifty dollars and receive it in thirty minutes."

She was walking away as she talked. Anthony followed, his head nodding the entire time. *Maybe she'll help if I offer her a hundred dollars. That satchel of money is still in the trunk.* Anthony rejected the thought as fast as it came. Jesus works over the table, not under.

"I understand, Ms. . . ."

"James. I am Mrs. Florence James, chief administrator

and supervisor of the department, and I'm running late for my gym class."

"I understand, Mrs. James, and I am not trying to inconvenience you. It's just that I have an urgent situation that you may be able to help me with. Please."

Mrs. James looked at Anthony over the rims of her frosted, square-framed glasses. "I'm sorry, hon, but I'm not even supposed to be here right now. I just came this morning to finish some last-minute filing for an audit scheduled Monday."

"All the more reason you can help me. Your files are in their best possible order, so pulling what I need shouldn't take more than a second. I don't even need a copy, I just want to look at it, and I'll still pay the fifty-dollar fee. I promise I won't take more than two minutes. Please." Anthony's words sounded desperate but his demeanor was not. *Confidence*, he told himself.

She sighed as she unlocked the door to her SUV. "Write down your name, number, address, and what you need and I'll make your request the first I look at on Monday morning, after the audit. I'm sorry, but that's the best I can do."

"Thank you for your help, Mrs. James." Anthony quickly fished for a pen and paper and scribbled down his information. He held the car door open as she got in and closed it once she was comfortable.

Just as he was unlocking the door to his own vehicle, he heard a voice calling after him.

"Wait, Mr. Murdock, I might as well help you. My aerobics class is almost over anyway." Mrs. James was out of her car, sliding another quarter into the parking meter.

~

Reggie and Terri rode in silence the entire trip to Cherisse's condo. When she got out of the car, she gave him a half-smile in response to his.

"I'll be waiting for your call, Mrs. Murdock." Terri could almost feel the bass in his voice.

"Thank you, Reggie. For everything. You made both my evening and morning very enjoyable."

"Hopefully, soon, we can add 'night' to that list. Forgive my forwardness, Terri. You have that effect on me."

Terri rolled her eyes as she turned away. For such a smooth brother, he really had some corny lines. But as fine as he was, *as rich as he was*, that was a forgivable trait. Terri looked from her Lexus to Cherisse's balcony and back. The blinds on her windows were still drawn. For Cherisse that could mean anything, but for Terri, who had noticed the Denzel Washington look-alike checking Cherisse out before, during, and after the banquet, that could only mean one thing: Cherisse had some take-home from the dinner last night.

"At least one of us had more than appetizers," she mumbled to herself as she sped out of the development. "It's been too long since I've had a full-course meal."

Terri thought back to the "diet days," as Cherisse called them, before she was married, when Anthony decided he could no longer ignore his convictions and the buffet she'd been indulging in suddenly had a Closed sign posted until their wedding night.

At the time Cherisse could not understand why Terri continued to stay with a man who was "starving" her to death. Truthfully, Terri could not explain it to herself, either. There was just something about his resolve that made him more irresistible. A man who valued her enough to decide to wait so she could have *his* best was a man worthy of hers. She'd jokingly told Cherisse later that once the Closed signed was turned over and the buffet was reopened, it became an all-you-can-eat affair that never left her feeling guilty or weighed down. The food was always fresh, with enough variety, spice, and flavor to keep her satisfied breakfast through dinner, snacks included.

Over the past few months, however, the buffet, for some inexplicable reason, had grown cold and stale. The pilot light in the kitchen stove had gone out and the burners weren't working. And now, Terri was convinced, the buffet had been opened to the general public.

Terri put her foot on the accelerator, nearly blind to the passing world around her. She just had one thought: Seeing the look on Anthony's face when she exposed him for who he was *right in front* of Pastor Green would be the sweetest, most filling dessert ever.

Chapter 12

Nikki was just about to walk out the front door with Devin when her telephone rang. Dressed in a short denim skirt and calf-high black boots, she stood on her tiptoes trying to get a good glimpse of the caller ID over the kitchen counter.

"Now you decide to call," she muttered. "Too late." She was determined to make all of them pay for wasting her time, treating her as a convenient commodity and not as the crucial contributor she knew she was. It was time for every man who ignored her, or used her for all the wrong reasons; every woman who took from her, or added to the drama of her tumultuous life, to know that they'd picked the wrong person to play with.

"Y'all ain't just going to pick me up and put me down when you feel like it. Come on, Devin, let's go." She slammed the door shut behind them, tripping over the corner of a straw welcome mat a neighbor had put too far out in the hallway.

"Oops." She kicked it out of the way as she and her son descended the apartment stairwell to the busy boulevard in front of them.

"Hold my hand! Don't you run out into the street!" she screamed, grabbing Devin by the wrist. Within moments, they both were settling down on the wood bench where the number-fifty-seven bus was due to come in ten minutes.

She stuck her hand in the pink feathery handbag she was carrying. Good, the spare key Eric Johnson had given her was still in the side pocket. She was glad she never told *him* she had it, or he would have asked her to use it a long time ago.

"I'm a genius." Nikki smiled to herself. As long as the bus came on time, she should be at the office of CASH within the hour.

"Thank you, Jesus." Anthony could not stop praising Him as he walked down the darkened corridor to the room where marriage licenses were filed. Following Jesus with no hidden agendas was opening more doors than he could have ever opened on his own.

Florence James, the supervisor of the Vital Records Department of Shepherd Hills, escorted him through a musty hallway, switching on lights and unlocking doors as they walked.

"What's one of the last names on the marriage license you need, hon?"

"Murdock. Either Charles A. Murdock or Stephanie Ann Murdock." His parents, both out of his life before he reached eighteen.

"They were both from Shepherd Hills County?" She

tapped expertly on a computer keyboard. Hundreds of names followed by coded numbers scrolled down the screen.

"Yes." Anthony remembered vividly the countless times his mother exclaimed how glad she was that her own mother had left the South well before she was born.

"I don't think I would have lasted in the country" was the one sentence he could remember her saying all the time, turning down any and all opportunities to go back and visit her family roots in Sharen, South Carolina. Because of her, he had never been to the birthplace of his mother's people. She had turned up her nose at anything southern, except the food. If it wasn't for Aunt Rosa's kitchen genius, Stephanie Ann probably would have turned against her as well.

"Sorry, hon, but I'm not getting any matches for a marriage license in those two names."

Anthony wrinkled his forehead as he stepped closer to view the screen. "Is that all the Murdocks you have listed? Is there another index?"

Florence James looked at Anthony over her glasses as she spoke. "We upgraded our system a few years ago so that all of the licenses and certificates we have in storage are catalogued on this computer. We type in a name and access a code number that tells us exactly where the license is located in our archives. Our files are among the most comprehensive in the state. If a license is not listed in this system, then it does not exist."

"Okay . . ." *Think, Anthony, think.*

Mrs. James pecked at a few more keys. "Do you know either one of their Social Security numbers?"

"No, that's what I was hoping to get off the marriage license. I have very little information about my mother and absolutely none about my biological father."

"I see. Do you know your mother's maiden name?"

It was the same as his Great-Aunt Rosa's. "Bergenson."

She was quiet as she tapped again on the keys before slowly shaking her head. "No, sorry. I'm only showing a Stephanie Ann Bergenson with a Harold Cook, married in June of 1979."

"Harold was my stepfather. They married when I was five." Anthony shook his head as well. "My parents had to have been married at some point. I distinctly remember my mother having my last name, because I was upset that I was going to be the only person in the house with a different last name after their wedding."

"I don't know what to tell you, Mr. Murdock." Mrs. James turned off the computer, her eyes glancing at a wall clock. "The only thing that I can think of is maybe they got married somewhere else. We only keep records of marriages performed in this county."

The church bell tolled twelve as Terri rounded the last curve toward the parking lot. She'd made a quick stop at home to change first before speeding back to where she'd last seen Anthony. The car hit the gravel lot with a skid and slammed to a stop. Neither Anthony's car nor Pastor Green's blue Buick LeSabre were there.

She cut the ignition, unsure of what to do next. It was quiet, except for a light wind that rattled some dead tree branches stacked at the edge of the lot.

Terri watched a rabbit hop across a patch of brown grass. It sniffed at a few wildflowers and then edged its way alongside the church, cutting across the main entrance and disappearing into a group of trees that bordered the church cemetery. The open front door of the main entrance caught Terri's eye.

"Somebody's here." She decided to investigate.

The smell of fresh paint filled her nostrils as she stepped into the foyer. Drop cloths and plastic sheets lined the floor and the single pew that sat in the corridor near the stairway. She saw a couple of empty paint cans lined up against the unfinished wall. Pastor Green must have gone to get some more paint, she realized. Maybe Anthony was helping him. With that thought a long string of maybes crowded her mind, pushing out other thoughts, chipping away at the certainty that had been building alongside her anger.

Maybe Anthony really was here meeting with Pastor Green every time he said he was. Maybe she had misread his intentions, his actions. Maybe he was planning a good surprise for her and she was ahead of his timing. Maybe she was blowing things out of proportion. Maybe her doubts were unfounded. Maybe everything really was okay.

She walked down the basement steps, ducking her head as she entered the lower hall. The paint-spotted plastic was loud under her feet and she was careful to avoid wet patches. For once, Terri was glad she'd put on tennis shoes.

The pastor's study was open and the lights were on. Gospel music played softly from an unseen CD player. Donnie McClurkin—she recognized the CD as one Sister Porter had given her last Christmas. Terri took a quick look behind her before stepping in and looking around. She didn't know what she was looking for, but she was compelled to keep moving forward.

A half-eaten breakfast sandwich and cold coffee sat on the desk next to a stack of sermon notes. Typewritten pages, study guides, Greek Bibles, Hebrew texts, journals, notebooks. Terri flipped quickly through the stack, seeing nothing of particular interest to her. She ran her fingers along the leather-bound volumes lining the two medium-sized bookcases behind Pastor Green's desk. Greeting cards and plaques filled almost every available space on the wall. Terri smiled at some of the messages of gratitude and honor scribbled on the flowery pages and inscribed on the metal tablets. Pastor Green was a well-respected man. Terri couldn't argue with that.

She sank into the overstuffed desk chair and rested her head against the red, bumpy leather. *So this is what it feels like to be a minister.* She picked up a pen and tapped the stack in front of her. Her office was bigger, less cramped, with no basement mildew smell.

"All right, enough. I need to know what's going on with my husband." As she spoke, her eyes caught the corner of an envelope sticking out of a pile on Pastor Green's desk. She immediately recognized the print on its face.

"I saw this before. This is that letter I gave Pastor Green the other night after I found it in my old car. Anthony wrote this letter."

She picked up the envelope, fingering it on all sides before slowly lifting the flap. *It's not really a violation of privacy. The letter was already opened and the writer is my husband. He shouldn't be keeping any secrets from me anyway.* She thought of a million different reasons defending her right to read the letter, but curiosity alone served enough justification. Her eyes soaked up each word.

Dear Pastor Green,

This is a hard letter to write, but it must be done. I want to let you know that I am stepping down from my ministerial duties at Second Baptist Church effective immediately. Several months ago, I made a choice that has weakened my walk with the Lord and severely injured my conscience. While it would be easy and preferable to secretly pray for forgiveness and move forward like nothing happened, the decision I made has significant consequences that will not go away until publicly addressed.

As I deal with the fallout of my disobedience, I feel that it would be in the best interest of the congregation for me to remove myself from my leadership position. The role I played in the scandal I must disclose will most likely discredit my witness and affect my relationships. I do not want to be responsible for tarnishing the work and image of the church by staying in a high-profile place once news of my actions is disseminated. Thank you for your understanding. Please pray for me.

Anthony M. Murdock

Terri read the letter twice, then once more to make sure she was believing her eyes. Her husband was admitting to a scandal. It was written in black and white, in his own handwriting, confessing that he should not be a minister anymore and that his choices were going to affect his relationships.

In anger, she rolled up the paper in a tight ball, aiming for the trash can.

"No." She caught herself. "I need to hold on to this. This is my proof. There's no way he'll be able to deny that he's been cheating on me."

With a calmness that almost scared her, she folded the letter and put it in her pocketbook. By the time she walked out of the church, she already had a full game plan in mind. She turned on her cell phone and dialed quickly.

"Hello, Reggie. Do you know any good lawyers?"

"I was just looking one up for you."

The number fifty-seven bus was crowded for a Saturday afternoon. Eric marveled at the hordes of people left standing behind in the choking fumes as the bus pulled away. He was fortunate to have gotten on the bus himself. Two buses filled beyond capacity had already passed without stopping.

He did not mind standing, even after the rare occurrence of a young man offering him a seat in the elderly and handicapped section. Eric knew that his past years of drug use had made his body age well beyond its thirty-eight years, but the generous act of respect still surprised him. *Do I look that old?* He chuckled to himself. He was one of the lucky ones. Premature aging was one of the milder outcomes of long-term drug abuse. Many of the addicts he knew from yesteryear were in jail, HIV positive, or long dead.

The bus hit a sharp bump on the road, making everybody jolt backwards. Eric held on to the pole as most of his body bumped into the tight ball of legs and arms and breath around him. The coolness of the day had not found its way onto the bus. Stuffiness wrapped around the swaying bodies like a flannel blanket in July.

"You've got to love traveling in this forty-six-seat stretch limo, don't you?" A kind-looking woman with rosy undertones in her brown skin sat near where he stood. A bag of groceries filled her lap.

Eric smiled. Hers was the first genuine smile he'd gotten all day.

"You look familiar to me," she continued. "I know I've seen you somewhere. Do you attend Saint Peter's Cathedral?"

"No, but I recently gave a presentation for CASH there. That's probably where you remember me. My name is Eric Johnson."

"Eric Johnson of CASH?" Her smile quickly faded and her eyes turned to the window. She said nothing else.

"Everyone, please take a step back," the bus driver called out. Backs pressed against backs and space was made where there was none as several more passengers squeezed onto the bus. Hands held on to every available stationary object. Eric was relieved when his destination came into view. He rang the bell and got off, staring at the massive warehouse building before him as he crossed the street to enter. Sometimes just sitting behind his desk at the office of CASH gave him the extra push he needed. It was a tangible piece of evidence that his prayers were being answered.

"I'll have to send some new prayers up now." He sighed as he took the elevator up to the fourth floor.

Eric knew someone was out to sabotage his efforts. He knew someone had access to his mailing list and was determined to use it to undermine his name. He knew

someone had a single purpose to destroy everything associated with CASH. He knew all of this, and yet he was
still not prepared for what he saw when he opened the
doors to the office suite.

Everything was in shambles. The furniture, old and
worn as it was, had been pushed over the edge of its us-
ability and lay broken in pieces throughout the room. The
computer had been smashed, papers and leaflets were
shredded and tossed about the room like crumpled trash,
and jagged, black graffiti covered the walls and floors with
harsh, unspeakable words and pictures.

Eric slid into a slump beside the door, unable to find
words or even identify an emotion. In the quiet chaos he
thought he heard the voice of a child. Before he could
make sense of it, Nikki Galloway and a small boy emerged
from the adjoining conference room. After a split-second
look of shock, immediate tears washed over her face.

"Oh my goodness! Can you believe this? I was feeling
better when I woke up this morning, so I came in here to
make up some of the work I missed yesterday, and this is
what I found." She recapped a black marker out of Eric's
sight as she spoke. "This is terrible! I can't believe it!" she
screamed, and then realization dawned on her face. "You
know what?" Her voice softened. "I think I know who is
responsible for this, Eric. Eric?"

He was still sitting on the floor, his head buried in his
hands.

Anthony left the Vital Records Department with more
questions than he'd had when he went in. But wherever
there were questions, there were also answers, he was certain. It was just a matter of going to the right source. *And*

with You, Lord, as my source, how can I fail? It felt good praying that prayer, knowing that his Source was not affected by the stock market, downsizing, or any other temporal factor that could leave him short-changed. He was convinced that his trip to the department had not been fruitless. It had been necessary to lead him to the next thing.

"Jesus, I know You have my best interests at heart. I love You, and I want to do things Your way, so I'm trusting You to guide my steps."

The next step took him back home. Searching for the licenses and certificates that recorded his parents' lives and times made him wonder about his own proof of existence, namely his birth certificate. He had not thought about it until after Mrs. James had relocked the front door of the office, but now it was the single thought in his mind. Certainly his birth certificate, a document he had never bothered to study and had not even seen since he took his driving test at age sixteen, would have some kind of information about his parents.

Standing in the two-car garage adjacent to his house, he groaned at the racks, crates, and boxes before him. Many of the cardboard and plastic bins were still sealed, the contents of them deemed nonessential since the move into their home several months ago. Anthony knelt on one knee and picked up the first stack of boxes. Left to right, top to bottom, that was the order he would follow.

He was nearing the end of the fifth box, second row, when a rustle in the bushes near the garage entrance caught his ear. He turned but saw nothing.

"Squirrels." He returned to sorting out the blue-and-white-checked dishes surrounding him, placing them back in the unmarked box. Humming as he worked, he almost missed the second rustle, but he did not miss someone calling his name.

"Anthony!" It was a sharp whisper, more of a muted yell, and Anthony did not recognize the voice. He dropped the gravy bowl in his hand, the splintering shatter of it making the rustle in the bushes turn into hurried footsteps on the black pavement.

"Who's there?" Anthony stood with a ladle outstretched in his hand. He looked down at the silver utensil, poised between his fingers in full attack mode, and could not hold back a quick laugh at himself.

"Who's there?" he called again, this time walking out of the garage.

"Not so loud." It was Councilman Frank Patterson, a man he had not seen or spoken to in six months. Their last encounter had been in a supermarket parking lot when a stack of green went from Anthony's hand to his with a promise from the politician to vote against CASH in the next council meeting. Councilman Patterson, a long-time elected official who was often at odds with Walter Banks, had been an easy bribe.

"I don't know why you would want to do this in the middle of the day." The councilman brushed some leaves off of his suit jacket as he scowled at Anthony.

"Do what? Why are you whispering?" Anthony looked past the stout, red-cheeked man. "Why are you here?"

Frank took a quick glance back to see what Anthony was looking at behind him. "Look, enough with the questions. Just give me the money so I can go."

"Money? What money? What are you talking about?"

"You know, the five grand." Frank grew impatient. Anthony had no response, only a look of bewilderment.

"Oh no—no you don't." The council member looked at Anthony sideways. "They told me you might do this."

"They who? Who told you what? I still have no idea what you're talking about." Anthony's befuddlement quickly turned into amusement as Frank became more agitated.

"They said that you would try to play dumb so you could keep all the money to yourself. Look, I know you have it, so give me my part and I'll vote the right way, just like last time."

"Somebody sent you here to collect a bribe?" Anthony caught on. He still had the five hundred thousand dollars in his trunk. Whoever the "they" was knew it.

"This is good." Anthony shook his head, amazed at the smoothness of the scheme trying to take him down. "Look, Mr. Patterson, I'm not involved with whatever's going on here. I should never have gotten involved six months ago, and I'm in the process of getting out. If you care at all about your community and your conscience, you should too. For what will it profit a man if he gains the whole world, and loses his own soul?"

"Don't start with the moralizing, Murdock. You better be careful about what you say. If you start trying to come clean, you'll make too many other people look dirty. I don't think they'll like that." Frank gave Anthony a fierce stare as Anthony stared back unperturbed.

"I think they are right. You do just want to keep all the money to yourself, don't you?" Frank's cheeks turned redder.

"Who is this 'they'?"

"Don't play games with me. You don't know who you're

messing with." Frank Patterson stepped away. "Don't think you're going to get away with this. I know you have my money."

Anthony went back to the boxes after the council member disappeared into a silver Audi parked near some shrubs. He was wondering if anyone else would be coming his way when he noticed a manila folder at the bottom of a crate. *Anthony* was scribbled across in Terri's curvy handwriting. He opened it immediately and found his birth certificate mixed in with other legal forms, tax information, and myriad insurance papers.

He studied the fading print, his eyes stopping abruptly at a single line.

"Why didn't I notice this before?"

The fresh ocean air seemed to bring out all of the vacationers on Martha's Vineyard Saturday afternoon. Kent, wearing sunglasses and a green windbreaker, stood in line with the others waiting for the next tour at a historic lighthouse. As tourists around him talked on endlessly about the centuries old building, he scanned the small visitors' center for a pay phone.

Kent had been waiting all day to break away from Mona. Opportunity came when she decided to hike a public walking trail with a woman she met at an art gallery the day before. It was a hard sell, convincing her to leave his side. She was suspicious of his intentions when he encouraged her to go to the trail. She agreed to the split only after he promised to do some casual sight-seeing that would keep him in relaxation mode.

"I want you to have fun. If it's not listed in a travel brochure, don't do it."

"Yes, Mona, but you must promise me the same." He gave her a quick peck on the cheek as they departed in different directions, agreeing to meet later in the day for dinner. Kent walked to the nearby lighthouse attraction and waved good-bye from the end of the line. Once she was out of view he searched for the pay phone. He used his calling card to make the long-distance call.

"Malloy speaking."

"Gary, it's me."

"Kent, how's your vacation going? Are you getting some rest?"

"Yeah, sure. Just checking in about the case. Any new developments?"

"Nothing major, although I keep crossing paths with that preacher you mentioned before, Anthony Murdock. And he's been keeping suspicious company with that black politician, Walter Banks."

"Yeah? I knew politics was involved with whatever scam Murdock's trying to pull."

"I'm agreeing with you. You've been saying that all along. I should have been listening."

"I need to come back."

"No, Kent. Stay where you are and keep your wife happy. I'm keeping an eye on both Murdock and Banks myself now. Don't worry. If and when things go down, I'll let you know. You got your cell phone on?"

"No, it seems to have disappeared."

"Well, check back with me when you can. And we're still looking into who was behind that hit-and-run."

"Thanks, Gary."

Kent hung up the phone, but the unsettledness that had driven him to make the call had only increased its fury. Something he couldn't put his finger on was gnawing away at his nerves.

"Maybe I really do just need to relax," he muttered to himself while picking up a few pamphlets from a welcome table. He studied a calendar of events posted with an array of things to do. After picking out a couple of activities for the rest of the weekend, he got back in the lighthouse-tour line.

"Mona will be happy."

Kent turned to the two senior men behind him and joined their discussion about the best fishing holes on the East Coast.

A silver Audi sped away as Terri made the right turn into the driveway. She did not miss Anthony disappearing quickly into the garage.

"So he's got more than one woman coming in and out of my house?" Terri was certain Gloria Randall had neither the means nor the mind-set to own such a flashy car. She pulled her Lexus right behind Anthony's BMW. He was not going to find a way out of there before she finished with him.

"You!" She screamed at his back, her finger pointing, shaking with rage. No words came for a second as Anthony turned to face her, a folder tucked into his hands.

"Terri? Hey, baby, how are you? Seems like I haven't talked to you forever, and we really need to talk." Anthony had a calm smile on his face that turned into a slightly questioning look as Terri wiggled out of his embrace. "Is that a new car?" he asked.

Hot tears fell down her face as words failed her. And then, after a deep breath, her voice was a controlled stabbing. "I want a divorce. I know everything. I know what you've been up to. I read your letter." She flashed the open page she'd taken from Pastor Green's study as she spoke.

Anthony's jaw dropped. *The letter! How did she get that?* More importantly, how was he supposed to explain everything right then? This was not the scenario he'd had in mind when he'd pictured breaking the news of his crimes to Terri. She was not waiting for an explanation.

"I don't know why you decided to get involved with all these different people, but the very first time you made that choice was the day you chose to end our marriage. What kind of ring are you running? You are worse than a whore, because at least a prostitute gets paid for what she does. You, on the other hand, are paying out to get what you want."

"Terri, I've been set up. I'm not the one running—"

She cut him off with a hand. "Yeah, I was at the banquet the other night. I know about all your money. You were keeping it a secret from me so you could keep handing it out to everyone else. How much are you paying Gloria? Gloria Randall? Why of all people did you have to get her involved with your sick self? And how much did you give the driver of that Audi that just left? Yes, I saw the quick getaway. You thought you could keep everything a secret from me?" She thought of every name she could call him and then realized she was thinking them out loud. Anthony shuddered under the creative combination of obscenities and names she put together.

"Listen, Terri, I—"

"How could you do this to me? Did you ever stop once

to think about how I would feel? How could you do this to us? All that we built up together? Our house, our savings, our plans for the future! You've thrown it all away, and for what? I hope you're prepared to lie in the bed you made, 'cause you certainly ain't laying in mine anymore! Forget the fact that you call yourself a man of God. You ain't even a man. You ain't even worth one more second of my time." Her back turned, a middle finger in its place as she tore away.

"Terri, wait!" The shock in Anthony's voice took a second to catch up with his feet. Terri was already getting into her car when he reached her. "Terri, listen. You're right, and I'm so sorry, baby. I was wrong to get caught up with the money and I only made things worse by getting others involved. Believe me, I'm sorry. But Terri, you've got to give me a chance to fix things."

The motor started with a roar as she yanked the door shut. Anthony shouted through the closed window.

"I'm trying to fix things now, or rather Jesus is showing me what to do. I know it will be hard, we may lose everything, but we can work through this. Together. I've been a living Samson, but Delilah can't trick me anymore. I know that sounds crazy, but let me explain. Terri—"

She had the car in reverse, her hand whipping over the passenger seat, her head facing the back window.

"With God's help we can get through this! We may lose everything, but I promise we'll get it back, and much more, God's way! Terri, wait! I need to talk to you! Don't go! Don't leave like this! What about our vow to stay together no matter what?" He watched her back out onto the street and pull away with a loud screech. His voice fell to a whisper. "What about the baby?"

Anthony's eyes followed the red Lexus until it and Terri disappeared out of view. He refused to let despair or panic find a seat inside of him. He was determined to stand and fight. The battle had found its way into his home and he was not going to let himself get beaten up in his own front yard. *Confidence*.

"Show me what to do, Lord." Anthony looked down at the folder still in his hands. The birth certificate. He found the words that had caught his attention right before Terri came. The birthplace of his father, Charles A. Murdock. It was not Shepherd Hills. He was born in Sharen, South Carolina. Anthony did not remember his mother ever mentioning that Charles was from her parents' hometown.

"What do I do?"

Start at the beginning.

Anthony still had to return to Sister Porter's house and meet with Councilman Banks that afternoon. Find time to eat, schedule time to rest. If he left by midnight, no later than one the following morning, assuming no traffic, he would be in Sharen in time for Sunday visiting hours at Haven Ridge Nursing Home.

"Listen to me." Nikki half pushed, half dragged Eric to one of the few seats that still had all four legs. "I think I know how we can get to the bottom of this. I can help you." Even as she spoke, she wiped black marker stains from the palms of Devin's hands and kicked a crowbar out of view.

"Nikki, I appreciate your concern, but I think it's best if you let me take care of all this. I know CASH has some enemies, particularly from the business community, who want to use the land we're claiming for their own profits.

I've learned from experience that they'll stop at nothing to beat us."

Nikki's face wrinkled as he spoke. *He thinks this is about business. Stupid.*

"Eric, I really think I can help you." She got down on her knees to get her eyes level with his and gave him two slow bats with her lashes, complete with sparkling tears. "Please, Eric, let me help you." Her voice was soft, almost a whisper, as she gently took his thick, dry hands into hers, careful not to scratch him with her new nails.

"Nikki, I—"

"Devin, get your butt back here!" The sudden outburst allowed Eric just enough opening to ease from her grip, but her voice softened and eyes glistened once more as she turned back to face him. "I'm sorry, Eric. What were you saying?"

"I appreciate your concern, but there's really nothing you can do. Why don't you go on home? All this broken wood and glass, it's not safe for your son to be around this."

Nikki was not going to give up so easily. She needed Eric on her side for her plan to work. "It's not about what I can do, it's about what I know."

"What do you know, Nikki?" Eric decided to humor her as he began picking through the destruction, sorting trash from salvageables.

"I went to a dinner last night"—she picked her words carefully—"and all these people there were talking about their new businesses. At first I wasn't paying too much attention, but then I kept hearing them talk about the location of all their upcoming building projects, and it sounded like the same place where Bethany Village is supposed to be built."

Eric slowly put down the white trash bag he'd filled halfway. "What was this dinner? Did you catch any names of these businesses?"

"Well, it was some kind of fancy dinner for this group called the Black Entrepreneurs Alliance. I didn't get all their names, but I know that there was a man with a jewelry store. He had like all this gold and diamonds, I mean some serious bling. And then there was some kind of tax-service business. Oh, and then this man talked about a big, fancy hotel he was building—"

"The Empress Hotel. Reginald Savant." Eric cut in. "I've heard of the other businesses you mentioned, but I know specifically about the hotel. I did not know they were all related, but that does not surprise me. Six months ago, when CASH lost the bid over the Stonymill expansion project, Reginald Savant approached me with other locations where CASH could build. He presented me with this whole elaborate package, like he'd done a lot of research, but when I looked into the lots he offered, they were of such poor quality I wouldn't build an outhouse on them."

"So you know Mr. Savant?" He was falling for it head and feet first. Nikki kept the solemn look on her face as she urged him to continue.

"When I found out about his proposed hotel, I understood why he was so adamantly for the Stonymill light rail stop. What I did not understand was why he took such a personal interest in the affairs of CASH, especially since we were competing for the same land. I never trusted that man. Too smooth, too polished, like it was a very well-practiced act. I've never trusted people like him."

"I hear you on that. I hate phony people, and that Reginald Savant seems about as phony as they come."

"But Mommy, I thought—"

"But like I was saying," Nikki quickly interrupted, pulling Devin into the side of her leg, "they was all talking about their building projects and I heard someone say, 'But what about CASH' and I think that Reggie guy said something like 'That's being taken care of.'"

Eric was quiet, letting the words sink in as Nikki looked on expectantly.

"Reggie may be phony, but he strikes me more as a businessman than a tough guy." Eric looked around the room. Splintered wood, shards of glass, scattered paper. "He seems like the type of man who wouldn't want to dirty up his fingernails or mess up his pretty suit."

"You don't think he'd try to bring CASH down?"

"I'm sure there are many who want to bring CASH down. That's why I'm depending on Jesus to bring us through. I've got"—his voice broke as he listened to himself—"I *had* the prayers of many and the support of local churches. And having some political backing hasn't hurt us either. Walter Banks has made it clear to the city council time and time again that CASH has his utmost support."

"That doesn't surprise me." Nikki thought as she spoke. "I used to work in his office, and the things he did, the schools and families he helped, he seemed like a man of the people." She wondered if the outcome of her present assignment would be better or worse than that of her previous assignment.

Nikki had stopped working for the councilman abruptly, but it was necessary. Things had gotten too risky. She had started making too many mistakes. Good thing she'd left when she had, or the whole plan could have been blown.

"Yeah, I thank God for him. He's been my biggest ally. He has always—What's wrong, Nikki?"

A look of confusion had suddenly appeared on her face.

"He's supporting you? That can't be right." She was remembering Walter Banks standing on the stage next to the rich preacher, nicknamed Target X by *that man.*

"He was at the dinner last night. The emcee introduced him and a man named Anthony Murdock as the biggest political and financial supporters of all the businesses there." Nikki stopped talking. Why was Walter Banks out there supporting the BEA? Her plan wasn't going to work. *I should have just keyed up that pretty black Jaguar and slapped the mess out of that woman.* She was having second thoughts.

"Someone called the police?" A uniformed man stood in the doorway.

Eric smiled for the first time in hours. "Yes, I did."

Nikki froze as Eric circled around her to the office door. She really had not thought this through. She turned with her sexiest smile to face the two police officers entering the broken office suite, wondering how she'd missed Eric dialing 911. She'd only left him once for two minutes to take Devin to the rest room. It never crossed her mind that Eric would get the police involved.

"Whew, what happened here?" One of the officers spoke, carefully stepping over the shards of glass and chunks of wood. The static of their walkie-talkies seemed to add more confusion to the overturned room.

Before Eric could respond, another officer appeared at the door.

"Bill, Kevin, thanks. I'll take over from here." The officer smoothed his red hair and motioned for them to leave all in the same movement. "You two can help with that domestic dispute ten blocks down."

He waited for them to leave before speaking to Eric. "Mr. Johnson, I'm familiar with CASH and the positive community work you're hoping to accomplish. That's why I wanted to handle this myself. There's too much corruption going on in this town, and I don't want your cause to slip through the cracks. We'll get the thugs who did this." He gave Eric a warm smile and a tight handshake.

And then he turned to Nikki, who had become consumed with sweeping the office floor the moment the first officers showed up. She dropped a dustpan, picked it up, and dropped it again, careful to keep her eyes away from his.

"I, um, will help whatever way I can, with helping find who did this, I mean. And cleaning up." She blinked nervously, her eyes still avoiding all contact. "Oops, you know, I almost forgot, I'm supposed to drop Devin off at a birthday party, his friend next door. Let me see if they can keep him and I'll be back later." She rushed through these last words, pulling Devin by the coat sleeve and dragging him toward the door.

The officer looked less than humored. "I'll get your name and number from Mr. Johnson here so that I can talk to you as the investigation proceeds, miss. In the meantime, if you run into any more trouble while you're out, call the precinct. Ask for me, Sheriff Malloy. There's no telling how far the person willing to do this kind of damage to the office of CASH will go." He gave Nikki one last look over as she skittered out of the room.

Chapter 13

Terri stared up at the stone-and-brick façade, the multi-leveled porches, the stately columns. From behind the iron gate, she could make out the beginning of a pathway near a second entrance that led to a gazebo peeking from behind the massive estate. It was quiet, save for a few birds screeching from the treetops that shaded the sprawling grounds.

"Nice. Very nice." She pressed the power button to the driver's-side window and as the glass pane disappeared with a muted thud, she reached for the intercom. But before her painted fingertips could press the small orange button, a bass voice came through the speaker.

"Come in, Terri." The gate slowly swung open.

She entered the long roundabout, feeling like she was driving down a street and not a driveway. After what seemed like a scenic drive through the countryside, she pulled to a stop behind Reginald's Jaguar. A man with short blond hair and faded blue jeans was wiping the black metal to a smooth, shiny polish. She did not see when and where Reggie appeared from, but there he was, opening the car door for her.

"Hello again, Terri. I knew you would be back soon. You're just in time." He helped her to her feet as he spoke, his voice wrapped in a smile. "Okay, Eddie," he called back to his car as the two of them walked to the double front doors. "When you finish with that, you can see if Leon needs your help with the south lawn."

He turned to Terri as he pulled down the brass handle on the front door. "I'll have to take you on a tour of the property. I found Leon doing amazing work with the grounds surrounding the Quadrangle Towers. He was working for an independent contractor back then, but I offered him money to start up his own business. He's been maintaining my property ever since. When I find the best, I keep them near me, and pay them well so they don't stray away. Terri?"

She still stood in the doorway. Her mouth was slightly open, but no words were coming out. The open gallery before her was flanked by a double winding staircase. A crystal chandelier the size of a compact car dipped gracefully from the ceiling. The oak floors were stained a deep brown, and a taupe carpet that looked as though it would be velvet to the touch began where the hardwood ended.

"Let me give you a quick tour of the house." He slipped off her coat and handed it to a young woman Terri had not noticed standing behind her.

"Thank you, Yvette. If you can, please prepare a light meal for my guest and I to eat on the patio. Come on, Terri, let me show you around."

He took her by the arm and led her to a large room to

the left. "This is the living room." He let her take in the sight in silence for a moment. Splashes of burgundy and champagne colored the walls and the woodwork.

"The sofas and chairs I had handmade by a designer in D.C. Velour and Company—I'm sure you've heard of them."

"Yes, we were going to use them for one of our commercial projects, the restaurant for the Hendricks Group. But that would have taken us well over budget." She scanned the room, admiring the contemporary layout with her designer eye. "Perfect."

Reggie nodded at her conclusion as he led her back across the foyer into the dining room.

"The only antique I allowed in the house." He spoke as he knocked on the dining room table. "I prefer modern furnishings, but I could not pass this up. I saw it in a window of an antiques dealer during one of my trips to London. At twenty-five grand, it was really quite a steal."

He took her through the rest of the first floor, providing detailed commentary on the rug in the family room, the renovations to the library, and the museum-quality temperature controls of the art gallery adjacent to the conservatory.

He led her through sliding-glass doors to an elegantly set table on a stone patio. A man in a tall chef hat stood by an outdoor oven and grill, which had been built in to blend with the stone architecture of the outdoor dining area. Terri's mouth watered at the smell of barbecue, smoke, and wood chips. The chef turned briefly from the flames to face them, a long silver fork in hand.

"Honey barbecued spareribs for your dinner this evening, sir. Yvette is preparing a corn casserole and fresh collard greens. Everything will be ready soon. I've turned the woodstove on for your warmth and comfort while you wait."

"Thank you, Tyrone." Reggie turned back to Terri, who was sipping a drink Yvette had just placed before her.

"Good, isn't it?" Reggie stretched back in the cushioned chair. "I promised myself that when I could afford to hire my own personal chef, he or she would have to be a specialist in good old-fashioned down-home cooking. I found Tyrone and Yvette in the kitchen of a little restaurant down in Louisiana. They gave me a plate of shrimp jambalaya and I gave them an offer for a better life." He took a sip of the bubbly orange liquid in his glass.

"How did you do all this?" Terri studied him with an admiring smile. "How did you make your millions?"

Reggie swirled the liquid around in his glass with a quiet chuckle. "I told you: I'm a firm believer in entrepreneurship, but I never thought to go it alone. I'm all about networking, and building on those networks, because that way you raise not only yourself, but also everyone around you. Let me show you something."

He propped open a briefcase that had been sitting next to the table. He was quiet as he sorted through a bunch of papers, his face serious as he placed a bound leather portfolio in front of her.

"Let me introduce you to the Black Entrepreneurs Alliance. I know you heard about it last night at the banquet, but let me show you the hierarchical framework."

Terri traced the gold engraved letters before opening the folder. She skimmed through the contents, flipping through and stopping at random pages.

"So all of these businesses belong to you?"

"They don't belong to me as much as we are all related to each other. For political reasons, we had kept quiet about our enmeshed interests up until this point. We knew that our plans directly competed with those of some local charity groups, and that's bad publicity in the eyes of the common man. But now with Walter Banks, who was our most vocal opponent, giving us public support as you saw at the banquet last night, we are confident that our display of unity will only help our bid before the city council to grant us the building permits we need."

"This is impressive. I did not realize how much you were contributing to this community." Terri looked away. "But I'm still not understanding where Anthony's getting all his money from."

"Ah, Anthony." Reggie finished his glass and set it down with a loud clink on the aluminum table. "Your husband has proved to be an excellent negotiator and businessman. I guess he excels at some things"—he reached for Terri's hand as he spoke—"and fails at others. I hold nothing against him so long as his personal life doesn't clash with business."

"Hmmpfh." Terri sucked her teeth and let out a loud sigh. She did not want to think or talk about Anthony anymore. She quickly changed the subject. "For all these businesses that are represented, I see no females in the mix."

"Again you prove your keen eye. It does not surprise me that a successful, career-minded woman such as yourself would make that observation. Terri, I've been wanting to talk to you about that very thing. How would you like to be the first female business owner in the BEA? You have all the merits and credits we require for membership."

"That may be true, but I don't own a business."

"At the moment you don't. And I know that you just made partner at your firm. But have you ever considered taking your expertise, your creative designs—your clientele—to your own office space, your own interior-design firm?"

"To be honest with you, my biggest career goal was making partner at Raylin and Blake. I never thought beyond that."

"Terri, don't limit yourself or your abilities. Too many black people settle for working for someone else, never thinking big enough or outside the box labeled 'employee.' Let your dreams and passions be your boss and your paycheck. At least promise me you'll think about it. And remember, I am here to help you in every way that I can."

Terri was quiet for a moment, listening, until a thought occurred to her.

"I know you are working on the Empress Hotel, but you never did tell me how you came to be so, well, rich. So tell me, how did you do it?"

Reggie placed the portfolio back into the briefcase and made room for the heaping plates of ribs and greens being placed in front of them before he spoke.

"Real estate, Terri. The road to my wealth is paved with real estate."

Anthony knocked on Kellye Porter's door just after one. He felt good about his timing because he was not the only visitor. Several cars were parked in front of her house, including Pastor Green's blue Buick. This time, unlike earlier that morning, he would not be intruding. Sister Ethel from church opened Kellye's front door, her small frame draped in black from head to toe.

"Oh, Minister Murdock, isn't it just awful!" Tears ran away from her eyes in all directions as she collapsed into his arms with a loud sob. He supported her as they entered the living room of the small rancher.

Four or five other people he recognized from Second Baptist were sitting there, along with a couple of strangers and the woman who'd answered the door earlier that morning. Pastor Green sat center in an oversized armchair draped with a lace scarf. He was wearing a suit, no traces of his early morning paint job on him. Soft conversation and the smell of fruit punch and coconut cake filled the room. Sister Ethel stifled her sobs as they both took a seat on the sofa. Anthony looked around for Kellye.

"She's in the kitchen." Pastor Green seemed to be reading his mind.

"We can't seem to talk her into staying still." The woman who'd answered the door that morning spoke directly to Anthony, who noticed that she'd been staring at him since he came in.

"Hi, I'm Mabel Linstead." She suddenly thrust a hand out to give him a quick shake. Her grasp felt like a slippery ice cube. "Bernard was my brother." She sat back in her seat, but her eyes stayed on him even though she said no other words. Anthony thought he noted a quick flash of anger in her eyes. Maybe he should apologize again for knocking on the door as early as he had. He wanted to ease the awkwardness.

"So, I hear some southern in your voice. Where are you from?"

Mabel did not answer, and for the first time she looked

away. She mumbled something about needing to help Kellye in the kitchen and promptly disappeared. A woman in her early thirties with the same square-shaped face as Mabel quickly piped up.

"I'm sorry. I'm Denise, Mabel's daughter. Please excuse my mother; she's having a hard time adjusting to my uncle's death. He was her younger brother and it was just the two of them. She was always protective of him, as she is with everyone she loves." Anthony nodded at the friendly gesture, still trying to decide how best to get the information for which he'd come.

"You are from the South, aren't you?" He echoed her friendliness.

"South Carolina." She smiled.

"Really? That's where my family is from. In fact my great-aunt moved back home there a few years ago."

"What part?"

"Sharen. It's a little town on the southern coastline. I've never been, but I hear it's a nice place."

"It most certainly is." Denise's smile widened, show-casing deep dimples in dumpling-sized cheeks. "That's where we're from. My uncle Bernard was born and raised there before he came up here to marry Aunt Kellye."

"Really? I never knew Minister Porter hailed from down there." Another Sharen, South Carolina, descendant; Anthony could not help but wonder about the connection. But Denise did not leave him to his thoughts for long.

"What's your great-aunt's name?"

"Rosa. Rosa Bergenson."

Denise looked thoughtful for a second. "Where have I heard that name?"

But before she could continue, Mabel came back into the living room, cutting her off by offering a platter of lunch meat, cheese, and crackers.

"We've just about finished making arrangements. Thanks, Pastor Green, for your help. The funeral is going to be on Monday at two. The wake begins at one-thirty." She acknowledged everyone in the cramped living room.

As Mabel continued giving information about the viewing and interment, Anthony took the opportunity to catch Kellye in the kitchen.

"Hi, Sister Porter." He gave her a firm hug and planted a quick kiss on her cheek. "How are you feeling today?"

She offered a tear and a smile as a response.

"You know that I am praying for you and if there is anything I can do at all, please let me know."

She was quiet, tearful as she went back to scrubbing an old stain on a vinyl tablecloth. Anthony leaned against the sink, praying silently for direction.

"Sister Porter, is it all right if I go up in your attic? I left something the other night I was here."

At her nodded approval, he cut back through the living room, headed down the hallway, slipped into the guest bedroom, and pulled down the attic door. A light layer of dust sent him coughing up the narrow stairway. Within seconds he was standing in the center of the airless room. Other than an overturned stepladder and a few scattered books, everything was the same as it had been the other night.

Footsteps echoed down the hallway. Anthony looked at the door behind him, expecting someone's face to appear in it any second. He would have to hurry. He did not want—nor did he know how—to explain to anyone what he was doing. The green shoe box with the letter Bernard Porter wanted him to have was on the other side of the attic. He could see the lid halfway off where it sat on the bottom shelf of a low bookcase.

The footsteps were coming closer. He looked at the door. He looked at the box. He had to take the chance. He was on his knees reaching for the box when a sharp voice startled him from behind.

"Just what do you think you're doing?" It was Mabel Linstead. She stared down at Anthony, both hands on her hips, any hint of cordiality long gone.

Anthony gave her a friendly smile. "I helped Sister Porter in here the other night, and I left something that belonged to me behind without thinking."

He left it at that, hoping she would not ask what was so important that he had to dig through the dusty attic of a grieving widow with a house full of the bereaved. Quickly standing, he headed back to the attic door. Mabel was close behind him. When he got back to the living room, he took a seat next to Sister Ethel, ate a fried chicken drumstick, and talked a little with a couple of choir members and a deacon who were there. When more knocks came at the door, he sneaked back into the kitchen to pay Kellye departing respects. She was steadfastly examining and wiping spots off some sterling silver flatware she'd found with some Thanksgiving-themed serving bowls.

"Sister Porter, I'll be back to see you later. You're getting a full house and others can use my seat. Please, go rest. You don't need to worry about any of this stuff right now." He gave her a knowing hug. "At least try to sit down."

"Thank you, Anthony." The whispered words were the only ones she had uttered since his arrival.

Anthony patted her back as he left the kitchen. He quickly but politely said his good-byes to the other guests and headed for his car.

Before he started the ignition, he pulled a white envelope from under his shirtsleeve and put it in the glove compartment. Mabel had never noticed him taking the letter out of the shoe box.

The delivery truck driver checked then rechecked the address.

"Yep, it's the right place." He shook his head. It was enough that he had to deliver this on a Saturday. But why the sender didn't just put *Police Headquarters* as the recipient instead of the roundabout name and address typed on the label, he didn't understand. Then again, anytime a sender did not even put his or her own name or return address on a package, why would he expect a straightforward recipient address?

The driver swung out of his seat and carried the package through the front doors of the precinct. He approached a serious-looking blond at the reception desk.

"A Gary Malloy work here?"

"That's the sheriff. I can sign for his packages."

"Actually, I have specific instructions for him to sign it." Strange, the sender doesn't want to be identified but wants confirmation. The driver shifted feet as he placed the small package on top of a counter. "Don't worry, we scanned it. There's nothing dangerous inside." The blond disappeared with a sigh and a few moments later a redheaded uniformed man approached him.

"I'm Sheriff Malloy."

"Then this is your package. Sign here, please."

Malloy raised an eyebrow at the delivery, signing quickly as the driver watched.

"Have a good day." He was gone.

"Take messages for me." Sheriff Malloy shouted back to the receptionist as he took the package to his office. Very rarely did unmarked packages get delivered specifically to him at headquarters. When it did happen, it was almost always related to a high-profile open case. Ripping apart the cardboard box, he already knew it had something to do with that preacher-politician scandal. A shiver of excitement ran through him.

Inside were several documents, handwritten and typed pages, all carefully ordered and detailed by Anthony Murdock himself. Sheriff Malloy studied each page, "off the record" transactions the young man had noted. Questionable receipts, memos, all dating around the time the Stonymill expansion project submitted by AGS Railroad to the county council beat out the proposed bid by CASH. Six months ago.

"That boy was right in the middle of this deal, calling all the shots," he murmured to himself. "A lot of money went through a lot of hands, even more than I realized. There's more money out there than people are letting on." He was genuinely surprised.

Seventy-five thousand to this person; eleven hundred to that; three hundred grand to another. All of them names he and most of the community of Shepherd Hills knew and respected. Sheriff Malloy shook his head as he rubbed his own empty pockets. "One day I'll have some money of my own," he comforted himself.

"He took some good notes." Malloy continued mumbling as he added a few notes of his own to the pages. Pencil marks next to Anthony's black ink. He'd have to remember to erase them before the papers were submitted as official evidence. It should be an open-and-shut case. He wondered if Anthony even suspected that he had signed his own downfall with the detailed notes he'd recorded in his own hand.

"You would have almost come clean if you had not signed this receipt accepting two-point-five million on Tuesday." He came across the paper Garfield Haberstick had made Anthony sign upon his acceptance of the check to found the BEA.

The press would have had a field day with all of this information. Sheriff Malloy wondered why the sender hadn't mailed the package to the *Shepherd Hills Herald*, the local newspaper, or WSH 12, the major local television station. The result would have been just as effective.

"It's all in my hands now." He looked at the telephone, wondering if and when Kent would call.

Anthony found Councilman Banks sitting in his office with his head bent down and resting between two fingertips. When he saw Anthony standing in front of him, he put a slight smile on his face.

"Hi, Anthony." He sighed, leaning back in his chair. "I can't say my day has been too productive so far. I'm trying to stay positive, but every time I take a step forward, it seems like satan is there to push me two steps back. I just got a call from Eric Johnson of CASH. He heard about last night, me being onstage with you at that dinner. I know I sounded like a double-sided fool trying to convince him that it was all a major misunderstanding. I told him that he has my complete support. Did you hear about a rumor going around saying that he's been using CASH donations to revive a drug habit?"

"Huh?" Anthony did not hide his surprise.

"Yes." Walter shook his head as he spoke. "Apparently most of CASH's supporters ducked out of an important meeting he had last night. He said someone with access to his mailing list sent out a letter perpetrating that lie. I feel bad that I was not there myself, but he understood when I told him what happened. Our foes are relentless. We need to hurry up and get all this resolved before more ugly lies and rumors surface."

Anthony knew Walter was thinking about the future of his career as he told him about Eric's misfortune. They were all in this together. *All because of me*. Anthony stopped the deluge of guilt before it intensified further. God had already forgiven him and was working it out as they spoke. Anthony pulled out Bernard's letter and passed it to the councilman.

"Tell me if anything jumps out at you when you read this."

Walter put his glasses on, reading silently with a slight frown. He sighed when he finished, putting his gold-rimmed frames back in a black case.

"I don't know, Anthony. Was I supposed to see something in this?"

Anthony quickly told him about his conversation with Minister Porter concerning his biological father. He shared how Bernard had made Kellye promise to give Anthony the letter, the desperate plea one of his last requests.

"Let me see it again." Walter's concentration was obvious during the second read. After a few moments, he remarked, "The only thing that jumps out at me is the fact that Perkins Street is underlined. Maybe we should take a drive that way and see if there are any connections."

They drove together, Anthony at the wheel of his car, Councilman Banks in the passenger seat. Starting west and heading east, they went the distance of Perkins Street, stopping at the end where an old warehouse building made a corner with weed-filled railroad tracks. The tracks were being renewed toward the construction of the Stonymill light rail extension.

Anthony looked up at the building that sat alone at the end of the ten-mile street. Broken glass and splintered wood frames were in many of the windows. The steps were cracked, cement crumbling in piles in several areas. Other than an occasional car or bus that passed, the corner was empty and silent.

"You would never believe that building was once a thriving warehouse for many of the companies that used the old AGS line." Walter looked up at the elaborate architecture. Many of the gargoyles and statuettes that dotted the columned framework were broken, heads and fingers, limbs and toes missing or badly worn.

"Let me see the letter again," Anthony asked after a long silence. He read it aloud to make sure he was not missing anything:

"'January 12, 2003

'Steelworkers' Guild #29
'409 Central Avenue
'Shepherd Hills, MD 29473

'Mr. Bernard Porter
'7493 Blue Wheel Court
'Shepherd Hills, MD 29473

'Dear Mr. Porter:

'This letter is in response to your request to have your prescription plan reviewed. As is true with all retirees of Toringhouse Steel, prescription co-pays are either 7% or $15 of the purchase price, whichever is less. As your union, we can only petition in your behalf if we have the original employee folder that details the specifics of the union's agreement between employer and employee at that time. As you were last employed over twenty years ago, your file would have been maintained in our former Perkins Street headquarters.

'During the move to our new office ten years ago, several employee files were misplaced, or otherwise lost. Unfortunately, your file appears to be among the missing. Therefore we can only help you if you have an original copy of your employee file that includes the date of your hire in 1956. Sorry for any inconvenience.

'Sincerely,
'SG#29'

"Former Perkins Street headquarters." Anthony muttered the words before looking back at Walter, who was studying the letter intently over Anthony's shoulder.

"Do you know the exact address on Perkins Street the union for Toringhouse Steel had ten years ago?"

Walter shrugged. "No, and from what I understand, that union just folded a couple months back due to Toringhouse Steel's filing for bankruptcy last year. If you want, I can have Gloria check into it first thing Monday morning. I've found that she's quite good at digging up hard-to-find information."

Anthony pressed a finger to his lips. "Yeah, that might be a good idea. I'm not sure what Bernard wanted me to pull from this letter, but I can't rest until I turn over every stone." He looked over at Walter, who suddenly turned to him with new life in his face and voice.

"You know what, Anthony? I believe the office of CASH is in that building. If I remember correctly, Eric told me his headquarters were in the old warehouse by the railroad tracks. Maybe that's the connection Bernard was making. He knew that all of this was somehow related to the fight against Bethany Village."

"Yeah, maybe, but what does that have to do with my father?" They both stared back at the six-story building in silence.

She tried to enjoy the kisses he planted on her, first on her cheek and neck, then her collarbone and shoulders. His hands were like black feathers, tickling the sides of her waist, just under her arms, until they began searching for other places to land.

It was when his fingers found bare skin under the edges

of her shirt that she felt herself pulling back from his touch. She sat upright in the bed. He sat up slowly, his eyes serious and filled with longing.

"What is it, Terri?"

She collapsed back into the black silk sheets as whiffs of smoke and rose tumbled from the burning candles surrounding the king-sized poster bed. Although sunset was still a few hours away, the room was a playground of darkness, curtains and shades drawn, the black and silver fabric and décor creating an impression of the midnight hour.

"I don't know. Everything is happening so fast. It almost feels wrong." She stared at her purse, tossed on the floor by the door, her cell phone peeking out along with her makeup bag. Anthony had been trying to call her all day. She had sensed the phone ringing even after she silenced it. What else could he possibly have to say to her? The anger was unbearable.

"There's nothing wrong with us being right here, right now. You're going to go file the divorce papers on Monday morning with the attorney I found for you, and I'm going to give you a life that surpasses any you've imagined." Reginald ended his words with a gentle stroke that started on her chin and ended at her hips.

Terri felt herself shiver under his caress. She closed her eyes and then opened them to find his easy smile coming back for her face. The man was so sexy. She lifted her head up to his and gave him the kind of kiss that had up to that point been reserved only for her husband.

They were both fingering the hooks and elastics of undergarments when a loud slam made them bolt upright in the bed. Several of the candles went out as a sudden burst of air chilled the room.

"I'm sorry, Mr. Savant. We tried to stop her, but she pushed past all of us." Tyrone was rushing through the doorway, followed by Yvette, Leon, and Eddie. The bedroom door squeaked back and forth on its hinges

"What the—" Reggie's long, black muscular legs swung out of the bed as Terri pulled the sheet up to her neck. Neither of them focused on the foursome at the door. Their eyes were glued to the heavily weaved blond standing at the foot of the bed. She was shaking and pointing and shouting.

"You! I knew you were up here with that raggedy skank!"

"What in the world is going on?" Terri did not realize how loud she was yelling. "You again?" She screamed at the woman, recognizing her immediately as the woman from Bible study the other night. Who could forget that nappy wet and wavy? "Reggie, who is this? Do you know her? What's going on?"

Reggie was the only calm person in the room.

"Now, now, ladies. Wait." But his words were lost in Nikki Galloway's sudden lunge toward Terri's hair. She grabbed a handful of the short tresses and pulled Terri out of the bed by her roots.

"I don't know what you thought you was about to do with my man, but you're about to find out what I'm going to do to you."

Nikki threw a slap in the direction of Terri's face but Reggie interceded.

"That's enough." He grabbed Nikki by the wrists, pulling her out of the room as Terri quickly buttoned up her shirt.

Tyrone and company still stood gaping at the door.

"Ex-*cuse me!*" Terri finished readjusting herself, picked up her purse, and headed for the hallway. Nikki and Reggie were arguing in a corner.

"Terri, wait." His bass voice was two octaves higher. "Miss Galloway mistook the business relationship between me and her as something more. I assure you it has never been more than that."

"Negro, why you talkin' about me like I ain't even here? I know I ain't just business to you. Come back here!"

Nikki's continuing rampage of words was largely ignored as she followed Reggie, who was following Terri down a back stairway. The tears streaming down Terri's face felt like pepper mixed with fire as she stormed to her new Lexus. Reggie caught her arm just as she opened the door. She tried to pull away, but he pulled her face into his hands, looking directly in her eyes.

"Terri," he said, leaving his words at that.

She could not stop the tears. "I have never been so embarrassed and humiliated in my entire life."

It was true. She had never imagined a low lower than the experience she'd had at the banquet with Anthony. But here it was. She stared at the small crowd coming out the front door, Nikki's mouth again leading the parade. These people had just seen her in her drawers, about to get down and dirty with a man who had "business relationships" with a woman who could pass for a free hooker. The thought brought a shame beyond definition. It wasn't just these circumstances. It was everything.

"Terri, please believe me. We need each other. This wasn't a good start for us, but I promise everything will get better." Reggie seemed oblivious to the commotion. He was standing there barefoot in his underwear, for goodness' sake. What kind of fool turkey was this man?

And then, just as intensely as the tears had fallen and the sobs had sounded, came a burst of laughter she could neither explain nor control. She laughed so hard the onlookers stared at her as though she were the one standing outside in nothing but a pair of black boxers. It was all so ridiculous she couldn't wait to drive back across town and tell Cherisse.

"Mr. Savant, your car." Nobody missed Eddie's words. Terri drove off, leaving Reggie to rescue his Jaguar from the inspired artistry of Nikki Galloway.

Anthony woke up exactly one minute before his alarm went off at midnight. He had managed to squeeze in about four hours of sleep. Stretching, he walked to his closet and pulled out a pair of khakis and a long-sleeved cotton shirt. He wanted to be comfortable for the trip but still look nice enough to win Aunt Rosa's approval. Her mind may be slipping in the haze of Alzheimer's disease, but he knew that every now and then she would peek through the fog and comment on reality.

As Anthony quickly prepared and ate a turkey-sausage biscuit, his thoughts were on what he would say to his great-aunt. He hadn't spoken to her in months, hadn't seen her in a couple of years. He knew he was wrong for not checking in on one of the few family members he had left, but it was hard seeing her go forward in years as her mind went back.

Rosa Bergenson had been a pretty woman in her youth, with deep black hair that naturally curled around her pear-shaped face. Her skin had the texture of finely spun silk and was the color of sweet straw in August. Highly arched eyebrows accentuated the intensity that lurked in her deep brown eyes. The beauty she carried so regally as a young woman had retained its grace into her winter years. Gray hair became a silver crown upon her head, and her skin, though slightly wrinkled, held no other blemishes. Only her eyes proved her age and her illness, the sharpness to them losing its edge to a glassy, often blank, blackish blue.

Anthony tried to call Terri on her cell one more time. He'd been trying to reach her since their confrontation in the garage. The shock of her words found no place in him. He'd already prayed and left his marriage in the Master's hand. Anthony was convinced that once he shook Stonymill off of him, she would find it in her heart to forgive his greed. They would be able to focus on the coming baby and be a drama-free family.

He fought to hold on to his peace, smiling to himself although she was not picking up her phone. Her voice mail was already full with messages he'd left earlier, pleas for her to come back home to talk. He tried Cherisse's number again, and again no answer. He was not deterred. It will all work out. *Confidence.*

Half an hour later, he was behind the wheel of his BMW once more, the gas tank on Full, a cup of steaming coffee in the cup holder. It was a ten-hour drive to Sharen, South Carolina, a ten-hour drive to his dear great-aunt Rosa. That meant he had ten hours to pray for enough watts to work in Aunt Rosa's memory to shed some light on him.

Chapter 14

Tossing and tumbling were doing nothing to help Eric sleep, so he was almost happy when the telephone rang. It gave him an excuse to get up at four A.M.

"Mr. Johnson!"

"Who is this?" Eric did not catch the voice initially. He thought of all the phone calls and messages he'd been getting the past two days. The fallout from that false mailing had only increased.

"It's me, Snap. I'm at the phone booth outside." Eric looked out a window and saw Snap waving under a street lamp at a booth halfway down the block. As he reached back for the phone, the encounter he'd had with the young street hustler early Saturday played in his mind like a movie tape on fast speed.

He'd known Snap since he was a preschooler, watched him grow up on the street, both of them fighting their own personal demons. But with all the history behind and between them, he'd never gotten a phone call from him. A feeling of dread crept upon Eric.

Pray.

The command was as intense as it was sudden. Just under his breath, Eric slipped into a prayer so fierce only the Holy Ghost could understand his words.

"Snap, is everything okay? Why don't you come up here to talk?" Really, why didn't he? Eric wondered. What was so urgent that Snap could not take the extra three minutes to run up the street, up the steps, and knock on Eric's door? Why the phone call, and why right now? Eric tried to stay positive, although he knew from experience that phone calls at four o'clock in the morning rarely brought good tidings.

"There's no time. Look, man, I been tryin' to find out who's behind them rumors about you. I know it's early, but I had to tell you to watch your back, Mr. Johnson. I been hearin' some serious—"

Eric cut him off with a question he abruptly felt compelled to ask. "Snap, have you asked Jesus into your heart yet?"

"Huh? Look, man, I'm tryin' to tell you—"

"Do you believe that Jesus died for your sins and came back to life so you could have a right relationship with God?" Eric interrupted again, his words spilling out over each other. He could not remember a time when he'd felt this much urgency.

"Eric, listen to me!"

"You need to confess Jesus as your Lord and Savior. Right now!" Eric surprised himself with the force of his words. Where was all this coming from?

"I'm hearin' you, man, but you need to listen to me!

Aw, shoot!" Snap turned away from the phone. The deep rumble of an approaching speeding car filled the night air. When Snap spoke again, his words were breathless and fast.

"You know a chick named Nikki?"

"Snap, what's wrong?"

"Don't—"

But before he could finish his sentence, a screech of tires cut him off. Eric could smell the burned rubber from his window. Before another word, another thought, another prayer, gunshots rang out like supercharged popping corn. A spray of pops and pings shattered glass and bounced off concrete. Eric could almost hear the standing chorus of screams from unseen mothers and fathers inside their homes, trying to cover their little ones who were sleeping near windows. He knew from experience that the people on his block were once again trembling, hiding, ducking down out of stray-bullet range, even as he himself dove to the safety of his floor.

When the shower of metal stopped and the car sped back into darkness, Eric whispered knowingly into the phone.

"Snap?"

There was no answer.

He waited until after the sirens stole the silence, until after his room was washed in a flood of blue and red flashing lights, until after the newest heartbroken mother's scream for her son added another high-pitched timbre to the community's ongoing wail. And then he allowed himself to look out the window.

Seventeen years of life, seventeen years of hard labor but no birth, lay stretched out in a pool of blood on the street below him.

Minutes later: yellow tape, white chalk, the crowd standing on the corner, the sleepy eyes peeking from behind window shades. It was the usual scene. The officers, wearing gloves and badges, picking up bullets and drug vials, no longer shaking their heads. It was the usual scene. But even as Eric surveyed the routine scene unfolding before him, he knew that there was nothing routine or usual about Snap's murder. The timing was too coincidental. His gut told him so.

Snap got killed trying to tell him something about Nikki.

"Don't." Eric said the boy's last word out loud. Don't what, though? Don't give up on her? Don't ignore her? Don't dismiss her? Don't ever fire her? Don't trust her?

Eric fell to his knees.

"Jesus!"

Groans and cries replaced words.

Sunday morning Kent Cassell agreed to attend a local church at Mona's insistence. Other tourists on the small island of Martha's Vineyard flocked inside the historic sanctuary, admiring the centuries-old architecture. It was a traditional service with a pipe organ and hymns, responsive readings, and a scholarly sermon.

Kent, who did not consider himself a religious person, found a comfortable solace in the voice of a mezzo-soprano who led an eight-part choral arrangement of the classic hymn "Great Is Thy Faithfulness." Mona seemed similarly moved. He noticed a tear gracing her cheek as she closed her eyes and listened to the soloist. When she opened her eyes and caught Kent glancing at her, she took his hand and they refocused on the service together.

The young preacher, a new graduate of divinity school, gave a thought-provoking talk on predestination and free will. Kent listened intently until his mind drifted back to Shepherd Hills. He wondered what gospel that preacher Murdock gave from the pulpit on Sunday mornings. A gospel of deceit and lies, Kent was sure.

He was convinced that Anthony and that phony politician were working together to dupe weak-minded people out of their money. That was how Kent viewed religious nuts and fanatics, easily swayed simpletons who lacked the strength and sense to think on their own. He never understood people who trusted their lives to unseen "forces" or "powers" and freely gave of their purses and wallets because a man in a long robe standing in front of them told them to do so.

When an offering bucket passed by him, he dropped in a dollar strictly out of politeness and not out of religious principle. He'd willingly paid to tour a lighthouse: why not offer a buck to keep the historic church building healthy?

After the benediction was given, he followed Mona out to the vestibule and tried to join along with her a spirited discussion about destiny and fate, but he could not get his mind off of Anthony and Councilman Banks. He slipped away unnoticed to a pay phone in an adjacent church hall.

Using his calling card, he dialed the police headquarters in Shepherd Hills and pressed extension two. He knew Sheriff Malloy would be there, as he was every Sunday morning, catching up on the week's paperwork.

"Malloy speaking." He answered promptly on the second ring.

"It's me again. Just checking to see if there are any new developments."

"Actually there is. I'm glad you called. I've been waiting to hear from you."

Kent's heart beat faster as he felt the usual nervous excitement that flooded his senses whenever a case was about to break. "What is it?"

"I got a package yesterday filled with papers compiled and signed by Anthony Murdock himself, implicating him in fraudulent business dealings in that Stonymill expansion project. From what I can see, we have almost enough to indict him and several other businesspersons and politicians on federal bribery charges."

"Including Councilman Banks?"

"So far I haven't been able to come up with any misdeeds by him, but I'm still looking."

Kent could hear the sheriff rummaging through a pile of papers. He felt disappointed, wanting to know what was missing so both Anthony and Banks could be exposed for the lying, crooked thieves he was convinced they were. There had to be something more. Something wasn't adding up right. Maybe he and Malloy were making the wrong assumptions about how Anthony was working. Maybe there was a plan in place that they had not even begun tapping into. Kent wanted to see those papers himself.

"There you are!" Mona was standing behind him, a little New Testament in her hands. "You're on the phone?"

"I was just checking our finances, but I'm about to hang up."

"Call me back when you can." Malloy had heard Mona in the background.

Kent said nothing as he hung up the telephone. He had to figure out a way to get a copy of those papers from Malloy. Mona was oblivious to his furrowed brows.

"This free-will debate is pretty intriguing." Her eyes were lit up with the excitement of a newfound interest as she pointed to a verse. "Tell me what you think of this."

Kent looked, but his heart was not in it.

Anthony pulled into the gates of Haven Ridge Nursing Home just after eleven on Sunday morning. He parked in the gravel lot and let the peaceful scenery envelop him. He'd been on the road for almost eleven hours, stopping only twice at two interstate rest stops, the first to eat, the second to get a quick twenty-minute catnap and stretch.

This was his first trip to the birthplace of his family. Sharen was a beautiful township of varying landscapes, from gentle rolling hills of forests and dipping valleys of grass; to fertile farmlands and formidable old plantations. And then there was the rocky coastline where thunderous waves drowned out the screech of seagulls.

Anthony wondered why his mother never wanted to visit Sharen. The countless times his great-aunt Rosa returned for family reunions and funerals, his mother had refused to go with her and was adamant that Anthony not attend either. He had stayed true to her stubbornness and never visited Sharen himself, even after her death. Now he wondered if the reasons for her rejection of Sharen extended beyond her disdain for "country folk and their country ways."

He sat still in the car a moment, listening intently to a trill of nearby birds, as if the answers he needed were somewhere in their chirped notes. The quietness of the rural countryside contradicted the flurry of questions that piled up in his mind like so many rear-ended cars. He had spent the past eleven hours with constant thoughts of his childhood, trying to summon up memories of his father, who, his mother said, had walked out on the two of them before Anthony's first birthday.

The story was that he'd left their Shepherd Hills apartment to pick up milk and never returned home. The police ruled out foul play, and after learning about the tumultuous home life he and Stephanie Ann had shared, the police concluded that Charles Anthony Murdock had left to start a new life away from his wife and child. Their small joint savings account was licked clean to the bone by an out-of-state withdrawal.

Stephanie Ann and her young son would have gone homeless and hungry had legendary Aunt Rosa not stepped in with a roof large enough for the three of them to share and a stove that never stopped turning out culinary masterpieces. Aunt Rosa had moved up to Shepherd Hills when Stephanie Ann's mother took ill and stayed after her death to help her young niece raise her infant son. She'd purchased a home on the outskirts of Shepherd Hills, not too far from Second Baptist Church.

Aunt Rosa's shingled bungalow was one of Anthony's first memories. It was the first home he could recall living in until his mother remarried and a first-floor den in Harold Cook's two-story condo became Anthony's new bedroom.

Anthony smiled at the memory of his blue-and-red Superman-themed bedroom at Aunt Rosa's house. His mother made the curtains herself out of old cape costumes, and he had blue Underoos that matched the S-inscribed comforter on his bed. He remembered Aunt Rosa walking in on him one day as he attempted to leap from his bureau to his bed.

"What are you doing?" she had screamed, the harshness in her voice tempered by the laugh lines in her face. Anthony chuckled at the memory, thanking God Aunt Rosa had not told his mother half of the things she'd caught him doing.

He looked out his car window at the massive plantation turned convalescent home. Through a curtainless window he could see a Sunday service going on in what looked like a rec-room area. Soft piano keys filtered out the window to Anthony's ear. "Blessed assurance, Jesus is mine/oh what a foretaste of glory divine." Was that Aunt Rosa's soprano voice blending in with the others?

A smile spread across his face as he entered the building. He signed in at the visitors' station and immediately singled out Aunt Rosa. She was at the far end of a circle of wheelchairs and walkers surrounding a podium in a large open area to Anthony's left. A man who looked just as old as the senior saints he was ministering to stood on the podium, a Bible open in his deep brown, wide hands. Thick, knotty curls covered his head like a silver cap.

"Okay, everybody." His voice was soft and rhythmic like the coastal breeze. "Let us look today at the Word to see what God has to say to us. Brother Gregory, do you need some help?"

A heavyset nursing aide rushed to the
leaning too far out of a metal chair. She re
and placed his cane firmly in his palms.

"Keep this in your hand and on the floor so you
fall." She whispered, but everybody could hear her hoarse
words. Brother Gregory looked confused as he kept his
eyes on her, his bottom lip, hands and feet shaking from
what looked like Parkinson's disease. The nursing aide
stayed beside him as the speaker continued.

Anthony marveled at the crowd of worshippers. Many
sat or lay with their bodies disfigured, their words disor-
dered, their movements disjointed. But their faces said joy
and peace. Light and wisdom and gratitude were in their
eyes. They had sojourned and endured for many years, and
after it all, they still concluded that it was worth the sac-
rifice to begin their week in the Lord's presence with songs
of Zion on their lips and hearts, and words of prayer and
praise. God bless them, they were not forgotten or useless
limbs in the Body of Christ.

Anthony stood in the back of the hall, not daring to
interrupt the flow of fellowship, not missing the light that
seemed to shine on even the most dejected faces once the
reading of God's Word began. The atmosphere of worship
was contagious; Anthony bowed his head where he stood.
God was good, letting him still be in the service six hundred miles from home.

He would have almost forgotten the reason for his trip
had he not looked back up and seen Aunt Rosa looking
at him. The service was now over, and the patients were
being wheeled back to their rooms. He grinned as his
long legs took him to her side. They were alone in the
room.

"Aunt Rosa." He bent down to kiss her cheek but froze when he saw the look on her face. She was not smiling. Her eyes were small slits as she glared up at him.

"Aunt Rosa?" He had never seen her like this before, not even the day he broke her vase that was a gift from her grandmother.

"Kofi Olakunde? What are you doing here?" She hissed. "Get away, I'm not going to let you hurt my babies."

"Aunt Rosa." Anthony tried to stroke her cheek but she swatted at his hand like it was a house fly on a hot summer day. She began mumbling something, but before Anthony could make sense out of her words, a wellspring of tears poured from her eyes and her hissed words became shaking sobs.

"Get behind me, satan! I'm going to forgive him! Oh, Jesus, help meeeee."

Several nurses and aides rushed to them, one carrying a paper cup filled with water, another bringing two large pills.

"I'm sorry, sir," said one of the uniformed workers, looking apologetically at Anthony as the group tried to calm Rosa down. "I understand that you are Anthony, Ms. Rosa's great-nephew." She nodded toward the sign-in sheet. "She used to talk about you all the time, but she's been getting worse lately with the Alzheimer's. Half the time she doesn't know who any of us are, and she sees us every day."

There was nothing for Anthony to do but step back and watch as an experienced clinician tried to coax his great-aunt out of the fog that had enveloped her mind. He slipped away almost unnoticed and leaned against the nurses' station.

"Lord"—he rubbed his temples—"I just need some an-swers."

"What are you looking for, baby?" A woman sitting in front of a computer at the station saw the anguish on his face.

Anthony shook his head as he replied, "I just drove al-most eleven hours to see if my aunt could tell me some-thing about my biological father who was born down here, but I don't think it's going to happen."

"What was his name? Ain't too many people down here that go unknown."

"His name was Charles Anthony Murdock."

"Charles Anthony Murdock?" She looked up at the ceiling, her mouth turned down in a frown. "I'm sorry. That doesn't ring a bell."

"Thanks anyway." He gave a sincere smile as he turned to check on Aunt Rosa. The woman called after him.

"Wait a minute." She was reaching for the telephone. "I don't want your trip to be for nothing. My sister works down at the vital records department. I know it's Sunday, but if I tell her how far you came, I'm sure she'll help you. She's in church right now so I'll leave a message on her answering machine if you don't mind waiting around for a couple of hours."

"I'll be glad to. Thank you."

The woman left a message and then pointed Anthony in the direction of the home's kitchen. There was no reason he shouldn't have a proper Sunday dinner while he waited.

~

The den in Cherisse's condo was more like a comfort-able closet, simply furnished, and looking like a showroom in IKEA. Terri had laughed when her friend had sat sprawled on the small floor, boxes, screws, metal, wood, and directions swallowing her. But when the red-and-white-striped sofa bed, wooden coffee table, and cushy red armchair were up and operating, Terri openly admired Cherisse's choices and handiwork.

"Not bad for a wanna-be designer," she had said approvingly, offering carved wooden elephants she'd found at an offbeat boutique to finish off the Delta-themed room. Terri had planned to pledge AKA in college, but when she'd found out Cherisse was going the Delta Sigma Theta route, she put all her sorority dreams into supporting her best friend, attending every party, cheering at all her step shows.

Now, with college years long behind them and apart from the occasional Delta-sponsored event Cherisse attended, Terri knew that she and her friend were true sisters for life, a two-woman sorority based on mutual trust, care, and respect.

They were lying stomachs down, elbows propped on the den floor. Although it was already approaching late Sunday afternoon, the two of them were still cozy in terry-cloth robes, white slippers on their feet. A pile of magazines sat between them on the berber carpet and music blasted from a nearby stereo speaker.

"See, here's the article right here," Cherisse flung an old *Essence* magazine to Terri. 'Why Men Cheat.'" She made her voice deep and official sounding as she read the boldfaced title.

Terri flipped through the pages, her eyes barely taking in the paragraphs and subtitles.

"Can you believe this craziness that's happened to me?" She sounded tired. "I'll never understand men. All of them are dogs."

"Don't say that, Terri. You know somewhere out there is a man or two who knows how to treat a woman. At least I *hope* it's two so that *I'll* be covered along with you," she finished with a short chuckle.

Terri did not join the laugh, instead letting out a long sigh as she sat up and leaned her head back on the sofa bed behind her.

"Well, I don't think I'll be wasting any time trying to find him. Why should I?" She stabbed a fork into a box of cold beef lo mein and let the oily noodles slide to the back of her throat. "I mean, look at me. I'm a successful black woman with a good—make that great—job. I have the house of my dreams, the car of my dreams, and you should see all the looks of jealousy I get when I pass by. Most women only wish they could sport my size four the way I do. And on top of all that, I'll have at least half of Anthony's millions by the time I finish wringing him out in divorce court."

Cherisse turned serious. "So you're really going to go through with it? A divorce?"

Terri blinked back a tear, sounding stronger than she looked. "I never thought I'd have to go down that road with Anthony, but after all he's done, what choice do I have? I still don't know exactly how many women he's been with, but I can tell you one woman he is now without."

"And you're sure he's been cheating on you with Gloria and company?"

"I told you, he admitted to me himself that he was wrong, talking about how he was 'trying to fix things now.' Now I see why he never told me about the money. He's been using it to play sugar daddy to all his women. After watching my mother and aunts go through all kinds of drama with their so-called men, I decided a long time ago that would never be me. I told Anthony before a single wedding plan was made that I would never even consider staying married to a man who abused my body, my brain, or our bed. Anthony's just fallen into category number three. So, see ya."

They were quiet for a moment, the neo-soul notes from the CD and the rustle of turning magazine pages filling the space between them.

"What about Mr. Reggie?" Cherisse broke the brief silence with a sly smile on her face. "Have you decided what you're going to do with that brown sugar? If you're not going to get a taste of him, I've got some tea that needs some sweetening."

"You better throw some ice cubes in that pot and cool down," said Terri, a smile finally breaking through on her face. "Girl, you don't want that kind of trouble. That man may be sweet to the eyes—"

"And the ears. You know that voice alone is enough to stir up some trouble—"

"But he's sprinkling that sugar around too many places. Don't forget cockroaches and mice find sugar just as sweet, and he doesn't seem to mind feeding the vermin population."

Cherisse laughed, her hands clapping as Terri recounted last evening's spectacle featuring the best of her lacy lingerie and the worst of Nikki's wet and wavy hair weave.

"But you have to admit, a man willing to bare his boxers to win you back is worth some attention."

"Cherisse, I am in no way, shape, or form ready to pursue another relationship with anyone right now."

"Relationship? Girl, who said anything about a relationship? Right now you are hurting, and a little love medicine may be just what the doctor ordered. I hereby grant you permission to take two pills and call me in the morning."

Terri giggled as her mind began to wander back to Reggie's bedroom.

"And look," Cherisse continued, "I don't want you overdosing, so you better let me handle the refills. If that medicine is as potent as it looks, I may need a dose to heal some heartaches of my own."

"You are certifiably crazy." Terri laughed, shaking her head. "Besides, don't think I didn't see that Durango parked in your space yesterday while your shades were drawn tight."

Cherisse rolled her eyes, a hint of distant sadness hidden in them. "Honey, that was some generic medicine. I haven't been able to get any of that name-brand stuff you're used to getting from Anthony."

They both grew quiet, withdrawn, but for different reasons, in different worlds.

"Do you still have that frozen lasagna and that pint of chocolate ice cream in your freezer?" This time Terri broke the silence.

"Girl, you are lucky that I love you like a sister, because you are truly eating me out of house and home. If I didn't know better, I'd think you were missing some punctuation marks."

"Huh?"

"You know, question marks, commas. Periods."

"Nope. There are no buns baking in this oven, but I'm sure about to reheat that cinnamon bun you have in your fridge." They both laughed as they made a return trip to the kitchen, but Terri's snickering stopped when she saw a calendar posted on the refrigerator door.

"What's wrong, Terri? You miss a hair appointment at Freeda's House of Beauty?" Cherisse followed Terri's eyes to the posted magnet. "Don't worry. You're still beautiful."

"I've been so caught up with work and making partner that I haven't been keeping track of dates." Terri suddenly looked pale.

"Yeah, so?" Cherisse was pouring a glass of sparkling water so she did not see the fear creeping across Terri's face.

"Cherisse, I'm about to scream. I need to take a pregnancy test."

Kent Cassell could not relax even after two full glasses of wine. He looked across the candlelit table at Mona and wondered if she was picking up on any of his uneasiness. Strangely, she appeared to be calmer than *he* normally was on a routine day. This evening he was the one on edge.

They sat at the restaurant table with a couple they'd met at the morning church service, locals, Mr. and Mrs. Clyde England. Clyde was a banker in a tiny mainland Massachusetts town, and his wife, Evelyn, was a curator at a small museum on the island. Evelyn had gentle eyes that kept landing on Clyde, who unabashedly smiled back. Obviously, they were in love. Kent was not surprised to hear that they were relative newlyweds; for both, their second marriage.

"This time around, we're going to make it because we have Jesus to hold us together." Clyde proclaimed over appetizers.

"How romantic," Mona gushed.

What had Mona gotten them into? Kent groaned to himself. Going to church was one thing. It was an entirely different thing taking the church to dinner. Mona was really sucking this act up. Kent studied her carefully. Dressed in a black pantsuit that brought out the silver in her hair, she was all laughs and smiles. She was not even fingering her pearl drop earrings, a normal nervous tic for her in social settings.

Kent did not miss the little New Testament still clutched in her hands. She had been reading it almost nonstop since they'd left the eleven-o'clock service, even blurting out verses to him as they drove to the formal seaside restaurant to meet with the Englands. Had he known dinner was going to be an evening service over crab cakes, he would not have given up as easily on his headache excuse. He could be using this time to figure out the whole Murdock/Banks case.

"Did you hear that, Kent?" Mona talked to him as a waiter refilled their glasses.

"Yeah, I heard. It's not God's will that any should perish."

The slight chuckles around the table told him he was completely out of the loop.

"Yes, God does want us to choose life through His Son, but I was just inviting the two of you to join Evelyn and me on our yacht early tomorrow morning. We're having some friends from church over for morning prayer on the Atlantic. There's nothing like having a conversation with

God while being surrounded by His sunrise on His ocean. We'll be on the water from five to eight, early and out of the way enough for you to keep whatever plans you have for the day."

Clyde was a square-shaped man with silver-blond hair and deep crow's feet that made his eyes look like they were always laughing. Kent made himself smile in response to Clyde's offer, but enough was enough.

"That's very kind of you, but I had plans to get some work done tomorrow morning."

"Kent, we're on vacation. You promised that—"

"Now, now"—Kent pushed both his hands forward in gentle stopping motions—"I did promise to avoid work at all costs, but I remembered this morning that I also promised to check in with Malloy before he went in to work tomorrow. It was the only way he would let me take time off during such an intense investigation. You can go if you want, Mona. There's no reason for you not to."

Kent held his breath, wondering if his lie would get him out of the invitation. A boat full of church people? Next thing you know they'll be talking about how Jesus walked on water and trying to baptize him.

"What kind of work do you need to get done?" Clyde was not giving up.

"Well"—Kent furrowed his eyebrows, looking down at the table as if it would speak for him—"I was going to get briefed on a case I'm working on with the sheriff in our jurisdiction, and I need to review some paperwork with him. I'm a detective, and I can only stay off duty for so long." There, satisfied? He sat back in his seat, taking another sip of his drink.

"If you only need to review papers, you are more than

welcome to bring them along with you and call him from onboard. I purchased the yacht from a bankrupt CEO, so there's plenty of private office space if you'd like to use it."

"Thank you, but that won't work. I don't have the papers with me. I was going to receive them from him tomorrow morning." It wasn't exactly a lie. He wanted to see those documents that had been delivered to Sheriff Malloy. He just had not yet fine-tuned a plan to get them.

"I have a fax machine onboard. You're welcome to use it to get what you need."

Kent looked up from his glass, his eyes peering over the rim at Clyde. He slowly set the glass back down. "Fax machine? That might work. That just might work indeed."

It wasn't a bad trade-off. Getting a copy of papers that could possibly break the case in exchange for an early morning expedition with Jesus freaks.

"Well, praise the Lord! We'll count both of you in." Evelyn clasped her hands together, smiling like an angel under her wavy auburn hair.

"Yes, praise the Lord!" Kent fished in his pocket for a lighter as he quickly spotted a nearby exit. He needed a cigarette break.

It was nearly four o'clock when Anthony finally got good news. The receptionist's sister called from a church friend's home, saying she'd checked her messages and would be happy to help the young man fill in his family tree. Her name was Hazel Groves and she gave instructions to meet her in front of the old schoolhouse turned vital records department in half an hour.

Anthony was relieved, jotting down driving directions with a quick hand. He'd spent the afternoon trying to waken Aunt Rosa's sleeping memory, but she refused even to be in the same room with him. After a while, the nursing director informed Anthony that he was welcome to stay, but would have to observe his great-aunt from another room. His presence was upsetting her too much. Anthony was heartbroken, but complied.

Driving down the South Carolina back roads was a therapeutic experience. The hum of dragonflies and the soft lull of wind swaying weeping-willow branches offered Anthony a soothing retreat as he drove with the radio off and the windows down. An occasional house, an occasional car were the only signs of human life in the scenic landscape before him. A right turn off the single-lane highway took him to a more developed area, developed in that the houses were only a few acres apart and not miles. He pulled into a gravel parking lot in front of a small, whitewashed building at a quarter to five. An old Cutlass Sierra in desperate need of a car wash was already parked beside it.

"You must be Mr. Murdock." A wiry, thin woman with skin the color of used charcoal came out to greet him. Wrapped in a crocheted shawl, she gave him a hug as if he were her son come home from war. "My, you a handsome thing, but you could use a little more meat on those bones. Didn't you get some dinner yet?" A pair of black eyeglasses on a metal chain dangled over her flat bosom.

Anthony looked down at himself thinking he could afford to lose a pound or two, but he smiled back at her nonetheless.

"Thank you for your time on this glorious Lord's Day, Mrs. Groves. Yes, I did eat, and I don't mean to keep you from your dinner. I just need to get any information you may have about a Charles Anthony Murdock." If he could just get some kind of vital statistic about his father, then maybe he'd be able to research his finances, his life. Right now, the only proof he had that the man ever existed was himself.

"Murdock? Can't say that rings a bell, but I'll check for you."

Anthony was already getting a sinking feeling that only increased when he entered the musty wooden one-room structure. As his eyes adjusted to the decrease in light, he noticed that smoke damage and water stains discolored the rear wall.

"You had a fire here?"

"Yes, some years back. I was just about to get to that. Watch your head—the ceiling is uneven in spots."

Anthony ducked as he followed her to a corner of the room partitioned off from the rest of the building. A large desk that looked like a discard from a school classroom filled up a tiny niche. Plants filled whatever space was left over and a small window spilled drops of sunlight in the otherwise darkened corner. A single flickering bulb overhead provided light to the rest of the building.

Hazel dug out a pencil and an index card while he looked around.

"It was a small fire so most of our records escaped damage, but there were a few that were destroyed. Just tell me, what year was your father born?" She put on her glasses and waited with her pencil poised for action.

"I don't know." Anthony looked around the small room. Rows of green metal file cabinets were topped with hand-printed signs.

"Well"—she studied him once over as she spoke—"you look like you're, what, in your late twenties?"

"Yes ma'am. Twenty-nine, to be exact."

"Uh-huh." She pulled out a calculator. "And assuming your father was in his twenties, maybe early thirties, when he had you, that would put him in the 1940s birth-year range. Good." She tossed the calculator back on the desk. "That narrows our search. Follow me."

She walked fast despite the full head of gray hair and the fine wrinkles that lined her cheeks. Anthony stayed close behind as she stopped at a file cabinet near the back of the building.

"We have records dating back to the early 1800s, census reports; birth, death, marriage certificates; even slave schedules." She pointed to different areas as she spoke. "Everything's alphabetized by last name and each file cabinet represents five years. The forties start right here."

A spray of dust flew out of the first heavy drawer she pulled open. Together, they fingered through folders and yellowed papers, stopping only when they got to a file marked *December 31, 1949.*

"We can look through the late thirties that we have and the early fifties if you like."

Anthony appreciated Hazel's willingness to help. They worked in a comfortable silence, the only noise coming from the rustle of papers and the squeaking metal drawers. Hazel went through file cabinets with dates well before and after the original estimated range. At eight o'clock she turned to him, an apologetic smile on her face.

"I'm sorry, Mr. Murdock, but it looks like we have no

records of him. The only Charles Murdock I found was born in 1908 and died in a house fire in 1934. For some reason, his birth and death certificates were put in the wrong folder; otherwise I would have never even seen them. But it doesn't matter anyway. Both those dates were long before you came on the scene."

Anthony blew out a long sigh, partly out of disappointment, but also because the dust particles floating freely in the air seemed to be choking his lungs.

"It's okay, Mrs. Groves. I believe that God will lead me to what I need to know when I need to know it. Thank you for your generous time. I did not expect to be here this long."

"Oh, it was my pleasure. It's not often that I get to be near such a handsome young man like yourself. Your wife is a very lucky woman." She looked down at his wedding ring. "If I was twenty years younger, and you were available, I'd take you home right now and bake you one of my rhubarb pies. That's how I snatched up my old Henry." She grinned wide enough for Anthony to see two teeth missing from her smile.

Anthony let out a partial chuckle, unsure how to respond. But then his face became serious as hers suddenly did, her eyes looking deep into his, her mouth scrunched up like a question mark.

"You know, I can't put my finger on it, but something about you looks familiar."

"My mother's family is from here. In fact my great-aunt, Rosa Bergenson, is a resident at Haven Ridge Nursing Home."

"Yeah," Hazel spoke slowly, "maybe that's what it is, family resemblances. I know some of the Bergensons.

Good people. Even still . . ." She studied Anthony as he walked back to his car.

"Good night, young man." She waved from the wooden porch, her other hand holding her shawl around her. "Be safe and come back again sometime. Sharen is your history, your home. You sure you don't want any pie?"

Chapter 15

Nikki couldn't stand being alone with him in his office. Here, she really did feel like a piece of work, another check mark on his to-do list. But it was Sunday, and the evening at that. Nobody would be around to see them here. His office, as much as she detested it, was safe ground.

"You need to stop ignoring me. You can't just treat me any kind of way. If it wasn't for me, your plans wouldn't be going half as good." She snarled as she rebuttoned her shirt. Her eyes bored right into his, doing her best to hide her resentment, her shame. Maybe she really did deserve better than this.

"I'm sorry, Nikki, if you have been feeling ignored. You know how I feel about you, but it's been important for me to stay the course. We're too close to completion now. Don't mess this up."

Nikki did not mistake the tone in his voice. Her gaze dropped as she mumbled her words.

"I'm sorry about everything I did yesterday. I wasn't thinking. I was just . . ." A sigh ended her sentence. "Look, I gotta go. I left Devin with a neighbor this morning. She's probably wondering where I am." She turned to leave, making sure to keep her head up high as she let her swaying hips escort her out of the room. She had her pride to keep.

"Nikki?"

She turned around for a second to see what else he had to say.

"Thank you."

"My pleasure," she said, imitating the deep, rich cadence of Reggie Savant's voice. *Stupid fool.* She so much wanted to come out on top, beat everyone at their own game. But now she wasn't sure how.

There was nothing else for her to do but pick up Devin.

The wait in line at the pharmacy had been more than excruciating. The wait standing over the narrow white stick on the bathroom sink was enough to push Terri over the edge.

"What's it say?" Cherisse called from the other side of the door. "Remember, one pink line means no and two pink lines mean yes."

"I know, I know. I have the directions right here and you read them to me five times on the way back from the pharmacy." Terri bit down on her lip until blood threatened to break through her skin.

"So? Are you pregnant or not?"

"Will you wait? Come on now, give this thing a chance to work. It's only been ten seconds, and the box said it could take three minutes."

Ten more seconds passed by in silence and then Cherisse yelled through the door again.

"Anything?"

There was no response.

"Terri, talk to me. What are you seeing?"

Some more long seconds went by and then the bathroom door squeaked open. Terri was holding the stick away from her body as if it were radioactive material. She held up the two pink lines for Cherisse to see before flicking the pregnancy test into the bathroom wastebasket.

They walked back to Cherisse's den in silence. Terri collapsed onto the daybed, pulling her knees up to her body and laying her head on top of them. Cherisse sighed from the nearby armchair.

"There is no way I'm giving that man a child."

"I know."

"I've worked too hard and got too much going for me to be dragged down by dirty diapers. I don't have the time or desire to be cleaning up anybody's poop, Anthony's or his baby's."

"I know."

"I don't have a choice. I'm taking care of this tomorrow."

"I know, Terri. I know."

~

His best attire, a brown double-breasted suit, white shirt, and checked-print tie, were draped over the kitchen chair. A pair of brown loafers and wool socks sat outside the hallway closet door. Eric Johnson looked at the clothes, inspecting for any missed wrinkles or stains, and then smoothed out a sheet of crinkled paper. It was a speech he'd prepared weeks ago to present to the Shepherd Hills City Council. There was no point in throwing it in the trash, he assured himself, ashamed that he had resorted to that action earlier in the day. He may be the last one standing on his side out in the battlefield, but he was still standing. The war was not over yet.

Daylight had just slipped away from the Sunday evening. That gave him only a few more hours to perfect his presentation for the council. The vote for or against CASH's bid to build was scheduled for Tuesday morning, and Eric had one last chance to make a positive impression. He was scheduled to speak sometime during the Monday legislative session. If he was there alone, then so be it. But he would be there. God had brought him too far to quit.

He read and reread his speech far into the night, making notes, adding lines, crossing out words. A rapid knock close to eleven-thirty jerked him out of his concentration. It must be his neighbor, Miss Angelique, needing flour, or some eggs, or milk, he figured. She had a knack for showing up at his door all hours of the day or night, asking for a teaspoon of this, a cup of that. Eric quickly pulled on a pair of gray sweats and opened the door with a metal canister full of flour in his hand. A cop stood staring at him.

"Mr. Johnson, I need to talk to you." Sheriff Malloy pushed his way past Eric into the small living quarters. His eyes glanced over the stacks of papers and brochures piled throughout the kitchenette and living room.

"Is there a problem, Sheriff? Any news about who destroyed my office?"

"No, I don't have anything new. Right now I'm working on a homicide that occurred around four o'clock this morning. Are you familiar with a Dontay 'Snap' Peterson?"

"I know who he is. Was." Eric fought back the lump in his throat. Focusing on CASH throughout the evening had been enough distraction to keep his mind and heart off the shooting. Eric was not ready to revisit the heartbreak just yet. There were too many pieces.

"Peterson was in that phone booth by the basketball court down the street. You can see it out of your window." The yellow tape and chalked outline was an easy view beyond the chipped windowpane that separated the living room from the sleeping area. "According to phone records, Snap was in the middle of a call when he was gunned down. Those records indicate your phone number as the one he dialed. Do you live alone, Mr. Johnson?"

"Yes."

"So it's safe to assume that Snap was talking to you when he was gunned down."

Eric paused a moment before answering yes, unsure where the conversation was headed.

Malloy must have picked up on Eric's hesitation, for he quickly added, "I just want to know if you heard anything right before he was killed. You are our last contact with him, so you may be able to help us in our search for the killers. We know that it was a drive-by. Were you looking out the window as you spoke to him?"

"My phone cord is too short to reach the window."

"I see. Did you hear any voices or peculiar noises during your conversation with him, or did he say anything that led you to believe that he thought he was in imminent danger?"

Eric shook his head. "Everything happened so fast. Snap was . . . He sounded a little on edge, but that's not uncommon for him. He was somebody that always seemed to be watching his back. As far as voices or sounds go, the only thing I heard was the screech of the tires right before the gunfire and the shots themselves. I don't know how much help I can offer you beyond that."

"Okay." The officer scribbled some notes in a pad and then looked back up at Eric. "Thanks for your time. I'll probably be contacting you again soon."

Eric walked him to the door. "I hope you're able to find out who did this. Snap had his issues, but I believe—I know—he had the potential to do and be better."

"Yeah, it's a shame." Sheriff Malloy was on the top step of the landing before he suddenly turned back to ask Eric one more question.

"Tell me, what were you and Snap talking about? Why was he calling you so early in the morning?"

"Personal problems." Eric left it at that, not wanting to divulge more information than what he knew himself.

"His? Or yours." There was no question in his final two words.

"Snap and I talked a lot. I tried to be there for him, and in his own way, he was there for me." Eric saw the change in Malloy's eyes. Any hint of friendliness had iced into a steely blue.

"Have a good week, Mr. Johnson."

Eric watched as Sheriff Malloy descended the steps and then looked out his window to see him leave not in a squad car, but in a dark-colored Thunderbird.

"What was that about?" Eric wondered aloud as he picked up his speech again.

Anthony searched for a place to lay his head on the vast stretch of highway before him. He did not know what had made him think he would be able to begin a ten-and-a-half-hour journey without getting some shut-eye. He finally found a small motel, the Vagrant's Inn, about a two-hour drive outside of Sharen. He checked in and collapsed onto the double-sized bed, afraid to pull the frayed green comforter down for fear that he would have to get back in his car to find another motel. The room was about the size of his garage with a bathroom that made him want to use the Spot-A-Pot across the street at a construction site, but he was grateful to have some time to catch up on both sleep—no matter how uncomfortable—and his own investigation.

It wasn't a bad trip. It had been worthwhile, he assured himself. At least he'd been able to see Aunt Rosa, although she'd had no clue who he was. And he had eliminated stones to turn over in the quest to research his father. He would just have to start picking up pebbles, sift through sand if necessary, to get the information he needed.

Anthony firmly believed God was nudging him to learn about his father and his finances. He was sure his feet were being directed as he kept his mind in a state of prayer and seeking. It all had to come together somehow.

Before he closed his eyes, he offered up a prayer of thanksgiving. "Thank You, Jesus, for loving me enough to forgive my shortcomings and giving me a chance to pursue what is right and honorable before You. I know that however this ends, I'll be closer to You on all accounts. I long to stay in a place of transparency with You so I may know that my heart reflects Yours.

"Lord, whatever else I need to know, whatever else I need to learn, I know it will get me to the place You want me to be. Father, as a new generation of the Murdock family enters this world, I pray that any seeds of unrighteousness that have been planted throughout our family line will be exposed and uprooted so we can have a family tree that is fruitful and pleasing unto You."

Anthony stretched out across the bed, feeling the weight of sleep falling heavily upon him. He strained to keep his eyes open to concentrate as he finished praying. "There may be more bumps and painful turns on this road, but I know that at the end is a destiny that is for Your glory and my good. My lifelong pursuit of money has led a broken me to You, but now I am whole and rich in Your mercy, wealthy in Your grace. Thank You for showing me who I am so that I can trust You to be who You say You are—the Way, the Truth, and the Life. Be my all, Jesus. In Your name I pray, Amen."

As he drifted off to sleep, he wondered what Terri was up to. He'd stopped dialing her cell phone just before he'd gotten to Sharen, deciding that the next time he spoke to her it would be to tell her good news. With the baby, there was no need upsetting her more. He fell asleep dreaming about him and Terri and the baby bouncing through green fields of tall grasses and dragonflies. Together, the three of them. There was no way she meant what she said about a divorce. They would be together. The three of them.

Kent came to with a start as Mona nudged him awake. Sitting on the deck of the *Trinity*, the water bobbing the fifty-seven-foot yacht in early-morning darkness, only beckoned Kent back to dreamland. The soft-spoken prayers and scripture readings did little to halt the lull. Only when a sudden soprano burst forth with a song about the beauty of the earth did he lunge forward.

"Who—what?" He looked over at Mona seated next

to him. She looked completely caught up, her eyes glazed with tears, her hands clenched together in her lap.

They were sitting in a rough circle: the Englands, a couple of older businessmen dressed in suits, a middle-aged woman with her hands resting atop a Bible, and a married couple who looked to be in their late sixties. The sun was just beginning to surface over the water, yellow and orange rays spilling across the ocean like an opened bag of marbles. The glassiness of the sea met the purple-tinged sky in a single demure kiss. Kent took in a breath of salty air, struggling to stay awake.

"We are glad to welcome new friends with us this morning to enjoy the glorious sunrise," Clyde said as the song turned into a melodic hum. "We praise God for each new day. Morning by morning new mercies we see. I thought for a quick meditation today we could talk about the mercy God shows us through His providence."

Mona squeezed Kent's good knee and smiled. She really seemed to be enjoying these spiritual talks, he noted. A woman who'd tried everything from Yoga to self-help books to calm her short-wired nerves, Mona was soaking up these Bible studies and discussions with a calm exuberance he'd never before seen in her.

They all turned to Philippians 4:19. More out of politeness than interest, Kent looked at the passage over Mona's shoulder. She still clutched the little New Testament given to her the day before.

But my God shall supply all your need according to His riches in glory by Christ Jesus.

Kent looked at the words, tried to listen to the short devotional discourse Clyde was giving, but soon found his mind drifting back to the questions he'd been unable to leave behind in Shepherd Hills. When the others began to join the discussion, offering their thoughts and life examples of divine intervention, he quietly excused himself and slipped away.

He easily found the small room Clyde had told him about with the fax machine and worktable, nestled between the main salon and the guest cabin. It was a high-tech office aboard the otherwise plain-looking yacht. Whoever had owned this before really invested a lot of money in his business, Kent concluded. He slipped on his glasses and picked up the receiver, quickly dialing the number to the precinct. It was early—Malloy might not be there yet. The phone rang and rang. He hung up and dialed again. This time it was picked up on the second ring.

"Hello?" A woman answered.

"Jessica, it's me—Kent." He recognized the voice of the receptionist who sat at the desk right in front of Malloy's office. "Is the sheriff in?"

"He hasn't come in yet, and probably won't be here until later this afternoon. He left a message on my voice mail saying that he had some fieldwork to do this morning. Is there anything I can help you with, Mr. Cassell?"

"You don't have to call me mister," he grumbled. He hated being reminded of his age, especially when the reminder was from a pretty young blond like Jess. "Look, are you in Malloy's office?"

"I'm standing right by his cabinet, trying to reach a folder I left in here."

He tried not to imagine her reaching for anything, her long, thin arms a graceful curve over her body. He needed to focus on getting those papers.

"Do you know anything about a special package the sheriff's received recently?"

"That delivery he's been hoarding in his office? I sure do. You know Ms. Hope, the cleaning lady? She said he was locked in his office for most of the weekend studying it. It's sitting right here on his desk."

"Is there any way possible you can fax it to me?" He heard a shuffle of papers before she spoke.

"It's a lot of pages, but I can send it if you don't mind waiting."

"Not at all." He gave her the number and sat down to wait. Within twenty minutes, he had the entire seventeen-page document in his possession.

The cabin door swung open.

"There you are!" Mona beamed. "Why don't you come back? The views and the conversation are inspiring. I'm sure there's something you can add to the discussion. There've been plenty of times things have worked out for you in a way that couldn't be explained, don't you think? Why don't you come up and talk about it? At least listen."

Kent knew it was pointless to argue. He was surprised he'd gotten away for as long as he had.

"Okay." But even as he spoke, he noticed a different style of handwriting on the papers written by Anthony.

"Why would Malloy write on evidence?" he mumbled, recognizing the sloppy scribble. He turned to the next page, and the next. More notes by Malloy. It was not just the fact that he'd written on Anthony's records; it was *what* he had written.

Kent thought back to the conversation he'd had months prior when Malloy had informed him about the investigation the FBI was heading up, delving into possible public corruption by political figures in Shepherd

Hills. Malloy had told him then that the FBI wanted the local authorities to help. Kent was initially surprised that he, and not someone who still officially worked for the department, was given the case. But Malloy had insisted that it would be better if someone outside the precinct headed it up, and Kent, who'd started his private-eye business after retiring and removing his bid for the sheriff's seat, would have the time and experience to pursue the matter. It had never occurred to Kent that outside of Malloy, he might be the only law-enforcement official in Shepherd Hills who knew anything about the case.

Kent quickly dialed the number to the regional FBI office near Shepherd Hills and fielded a couple of questions to an agent.

When he hung up, he rested his head in his hands and then sat back with a heavy sigh. Mona was still standing at the door, a calm seriousness settling into her delicate features.

"We need to go back to Shepherd Hills this morning. Right now. I think someone is in danger." He stood, bracing himself against the padded swivel chair in front of the fax machine.

Mona started to say something, sighed, and then looked back at Kent. "Do you want to let Sheriff Malloy know you're coming back into town?"

"No. Let's just go."

Anthony chewed slowly on the scrambled eggs and let the sweet aroma of hot chocolate fill his nostrils. Sitting next to a window inside a crowded diner, he scanned the rest stop, knowing that would be the extent of his sight-seeing in southern Virginia. He was a little over halfway home. Within another five hours, he would cross the Maryland state line and be on the final leg back to Shepherd Hills. He was determined to get back in time for Minister Bernard Porter's funeral. He probably would miss the wake at one-thirty, but he hoped he would be seated inside Second Baptist by the time the funeral started at two.

As he crunched on a piece of toast and jelly, he checked the time on his cell phone. It was a few minutes after eight-thirty. Time to check in with Councilman Banks. Anthony hoped Walter had managed to have a peaceful Sunday. He wished he had better news to tell him. This goose chase into his father's history was bound to leave Walter more unsettled. Gloria answered the office phone on the first ring.

"Anthony, I'm so glad you called! I've been stressing out all weekend after what happened Friday night. I feel like there's something I should be doing to help the two of you out of all this chaos. I can tell that you both were here over the weekend. You left some food containers on my desk."

"That's my fault, Gloria." Anthony chuckled. "I've been so focused on cleaning up the big mess I made that I'm neglecting the little ones. But on a serious note, I'm sorry that you are even involved with all this. Please try not to worry. God is in control and nothing's going to happen without Him knowing about it first."

"I know, it's just hard being in a place of helplessness. But I am feeling a little better now. Walter left a note on my desk that he would need my help with some research this morning. I'm waiting for him to come in so I can get to it."

"Oh, I know what that's about." Anthony remembered the drive down Perkins Street he and Walter had made on Saturday afternoon. "He was going to ask you to look up the old address of the union that served the workers of Toringhouse Steel before it went bankrupt. Not its last location when it folded a few months back, but where it was ten years ago."

"I will work on that immediately. Address. Union. Toringhouse Steel. Ten years ago." She wrote as she talked.

"And if you have time, can you get some general information about both the union itself and Toringhouse Steel? I don't know exactly what I'm looking for—I guess anything that looks interesting."

"I'll look up whatever it takes to help you."

"Thanks," Anthony said as a waitress gave him a receipt and change. "I won't be back in town until early afternoon, but I'll have my cell phone on if you need to call."

"I'll contact you as soon as I find out something."

"Excuse me, ma'am," Anthony called after the waitress as he clicked off his phone. "Here, you gave me back a dollar too much."

"Oh, aren't you a good man. Most people would not have thought twice about keeping that little bit of money."

"Been there, done that. Ain't going back."

Terri sat alone in the doctor's office. It was pretty busy for an early Monday morning. She must not have been the only one who'd had an eventful weekend. Just the Monday before, she had been sitting across from Reggie at the Westcott Room at their first meeting. She never realized how profoundly the entire direction and focus of her life could change in seven days.

She looked around at the mix of women around her, knowing that most were there for routine checkups. A young couple sat cuddled with their arms around each other, a baby name book sitting across their laps. Same room, worlds apart. Terri looked away.

With the hustle and bustle filling the small waiting area, she was surprised at the ability of the receptionist to squeeze her in the schedule on such short notice. But she had been coming to Dr. Levinson's office for years, and found the staff willing to accommodate her pleas. She still could not believe that she was pregnant. Maybe her long-time doctor would have a different story for her. She hoped so.

Her cell phone ringing caught her off guard. She had been reluctant to turn it on, refusing to check her messages, not wanting to risk hearing Anthony's voice. When she did not immediately recognize the number, she answered.

"Terri, I'm glad you are finally taking calls."

It was Reggie.

"Before you say anything, I want to apologize again for Saturday's debacle. I'm hoping that you will be able to forgive me for allowing you to endure such a humiliating scene. I still feel that I have a lot to offer you, if you are willing to open both your personal and professional interests to possibility."

Before Terri could respond, a young woman wearing a pastel uniform and carrying a chart called from a nearby doorway.

"Mrs. Murdock, you can come back now."

"Reggie," she spoke softly into the phone, "I have to go."

Terri followed the nursing assistant to the exam room. After undergoing detailed lab work, she was left alone to her thoughts and fears. Dr. Levinson was a doctor who believed in providing the best care for her patients. High-tech machines and the latest obstetrical medical equipment lined the walls alongside more traditional blood-pressure cuffs and boxes of latex gloves.

Terri sat in silence, waiting for Dr. Levinson to make her appearance, wishing that Cherisse had not gone in to work that morning. She really could have used a hand to hold. When the doctor finally came in, she was smiling, a stack of books and magazines in her hands. On top was a tiny pink paperback book titled *Pregnancy*.

"Good morning, Terri, and congratulations. Welcome to the beginning of your new life."

"No." The finality in Terri's tone quickly changed the demeanor of the middle-aged brunette.

"No?" She was suddenly serious, stacking the books on a shelf out of Terri's view. "Terri—"

She waved a hand to cut her off. "I really don't need to talk about it. I've already made up my mind. I am not having this baby."

Dr. Levinson snapped on a pair of gloves and rolled a large machine toward her. "Let's see what we have here, see how far along you are." She called in another staff member as she explained to Terri that she would use a specialized ultrasound for early pregnancy to help date it.

"Is this really necessary?"

"Let's just see what we're working with so we can narrow down your options for termination, if that's really what you want."

"It is."

Dr. Levinson and the staff members were quiet as the whir of the machine and the occasional peck on computerized keys filled the beige-and-pale-green exam room.

"Okay, you said that you think it's been over six weeks since your last cycle, and this ultrasound is consistent with that, showing a gestational age of four weeks, five days. Let's go over your options."

"Let me see what you're looking at." Terri was curious as they turned the ultrasound screen to face her.

"See that round blob? That's your baby." Dr. Levinson pointed. "There's the amniotic sack. You're too early to make out much more than that, but we can zoom in if you like."

She pressed a button and the blob was magnified. Terri raised an eyebrow at a slight flicker in the sack.

"What's that? Is it . . . moving?" She pointed a finger.

"Huh? Oh, that's just the heartbeat." Dr. Levinson scribbled notes on her chart as she spoke.

"Heartbeat? This early?"

"The heart starts beating around twenty-one days after conception. That's about a week after your period's late. Okay, let's go over your options. You're so early you could . . ."

Dr. Levinson's words became drowned in Terri's ears as she heard and felt her own heartbeat pounding in her head. She stared at the screen, trying to imagine a life with another heart to tend to while salvaging her own. Could she do this without Anthony? Would Reggie care enough to be around? Why did this little blob with a heartbeat have to come and make things so darn complicated?

". . . And so we can take whichever route you are most comfortable with. Mrs. Murdock?"

"Excuse me. I need to go talk to someone." Terri's voice was barely audible as she quickly redressed and headed for the door. For once, she wondered if Jesus was available.

Chapter 16

Shepherd Hills City Hall was a stone rectangle in the middle of the downtown district. Squeezed between a soaring office building and the courthouse, it looked like an afterthought that had been designed by an architect obsessed with castles and fortresses of the Middle Ages. At exactly 9:01, a blue-and-white mass-transit bus pulled to a stop in front of the hall, letting out a horde of people who immediately dispersed in all directions. As the crowd thinned out, Eric Johnson stood in front of the stone building, a battered briefcase in hand. He knelt down for a brief second to wipe a fresh scuffmark off his three-year-old church shoes and then set his eyes on the mission for the day.

It was the last council session before the vote. As of tomorrow morning, CASH would either be calling the construction company to begin building, or it would be calling on Jesus for a new game plan. Eric felt in his heart and soul that it was time to build, so why was he so nervous?

It was more than the usual jitters that crept up on him when he was about to enter an official-looking building where people dressed in money and status might smell him out as the former homeless drug addict he was. Eric looked down at himself, from his feet on up, his long shirt-sleeves covering the telltale needle marks on his arm. There was no reason for the sudden burst of insecurity and shame. God had graced him to look as important and worthy as the polished young professional walking by him at that minute.

"I *am* just as important and worthy," Eric said to himself as he adjusted his tie. "I am because Christ is."

He started up the massive stone steps toward the front door, stopping just shy of the rotating entrance. It *was* more than the self-conscious jitters because those were fading away and he was still feeling like something was wrong. He stepped into the lobby, alert and observant as he went through security. The men's room, a few paces from the main council floor was his first destination. As Eric walked in Councilman Banks walked out.

"Eric." He grabbed both hands into his, a warm gesture although he appeared to be troubled. "I'm so glad to see you. I think this is going to be a tough day, and your presence is right on time. I've been hearing about sudden changes of minds of several council members who previously promised to support CASH alongside of me."

"Sudden changes, huh? Just like last time. I'm not surprised. Our enemies have had a busy weekend. It's been so bad, I can't even begin to tell you how terrible it's gotten. You know about the vandalism and the rumors, and that's only the beginning. I knew I was stepping into the heat the moment I stepped off the bus. I felt it.

Thanks for the heads-up, Councilman Banks." They shook hands again.

"I have to run over to my office to pass along some information to my secretary. I'm still trying to get to the bottom of who's trying to set me up to look like I'm against you. I'm working on a lead from a young man from my church who's been caught up in this confusion. You may have heard of him, Anthony Murdock?"

"I know who he is. He was recommended to CASH as an excellent contact for PR and marketing. At first he seemed enthusiastic about the project, but then all of sudden he seemed to catch the same germ that's been making so many council members turn sick against us. That was several months ago."

"Don't hold it against him, Eric. Anthony's a fine man who is trying to do the right thing. At this point, I think we're all trying to hold on to this roller coaster for dear life."

"Yeah, I guess. I'm just hoping that this ride ends soon. And that it's a happy ending."

"It will be. We've got to believe that it will be."

As they parted, Eric knew Walter was being optimistic for his sake. He had not missed the strain on Walter's face, the new gray hairs that had sprouted on his head. The last few months had taken their toll on him too.

Please help him, Jesus. Eric prayed silently to himself. *Please help us all.*

A few moments later he headed for a lobby area where many of the legislators mingled with constituents. He noticed a small group of people standing in a corner. At center stood a well-dressed man with sparkling diamond cuff links and a fine Italian suit. Though his back was to him, Eric recognized the easy laugh and finely oiled bass voice immediately. It was Reginald Savant, the multi-millionaire real-estate investor and the visionary behind the Empress Hotel.

A couple of other well-groomed and trimmed faces Eric did not recognize were standing beside him shaking hands with the small group of council members. As Eric drew near, Frank Patterson, a councilman who never returned his calls, abruptly stopped talking and threw his mouth into a cup of boiling hot coffee. Reggie turned to see what the distraction was.

"Mr. Johnson"—Reggie's singsong voice never skipped a beat—"it's good to see you. How are you today?"

"I'm blessed." Eric spoke, but his eyes were not on Reggie. They were on the startled pecan-skinned blond standing beside him. Nikki gaped as Eric brushed past all of them, picked up a doughnut at a refreshment table, and headed back toward the hallway. He needed a moment alone to collect his thoughts.

"Eric!" Nikki ran out after him. "I was going to call you to let you know where I was." She was out of breath.

"Not right now, Nikki." He kept walking.

"Please, listen. I'm trying to help you. Remember what I told you on Saturday? About Reginald Savant? I figured if I got on the inside of his circle, I could get information that would help you out."

"You got on the inside pretty fast, didn't you?"

Nikki paused for a second, standing still as Eric continued walking. She quickly caught back up with him.

"Look, I had been suspecting something was up for a while. That's why I came to work for you. Remember, I used to work in Councilman Banks's office so I know how hard you've been trying to make Bethany Village happen. After that last vote went wrong for you, I figured I could better help the cause by joining the front lines and working for CASH directly."

"Nikki." Eric did not realize how loud he was talking. "I hired you while we were sitting at a bus stop and you were weeping and crying about being laid off. What are *you* talking about?"

"Huh? Oh. I—uh." Suddenly she broke out in tears. "Eric, everything's going all wrong. I need you to believe me. I'm trying to help you." Two long sobs followed her words. Eric grabbed both her arms.

"Tell me, Nikki, who are you really working for? Me or Reginald Savant?"

"Eric"—she blinked up at him—"I need you to trust me. I admit I haven't been completely honest with you, but I had my reasons. I promise you, I am on your side. I want you to win."

Gloria was glad when the window finally slid back open. The woman on the other side looked friendly enough, although she had made Gloria and the few other people standing in front of her in line wait for over half an hour as she took a mid-morning break. Gloria was in the Shepherd Hills Courthouse, the Office of Public Records and Recording, doing her best to get information about the old address of the former local steelworkers' union. It had been an unsuccessful phone trail thus far that morning, and she was anxious to pull up something that would help Councilman Banks and Minister Murdock out of their troubled circumstances. If they were being set up, there had to be a way to find out who was behind it all. Another fifteen minutes went by before she was finally able to reach the window.

"Good morning." Gloria tried to sound cheery, knowing how it felt to be on the receiving end of a rude greeting.

"How may I help you?"

"I need to get all the public records you have on the Steelworkers' Guild Number Twenty-nine and Toring-house Steel."

"Whew! I hope you brought a wheelbarrow with you, miss. That's like asking the plastic surgeon for the medical records of Michael Jackson." The woman had a scraping laugh.

"Well, I really just need to find out where the steel-workers' union was located ten years ago." Gloria smiled, thinking how the woman reminded her of her older sister. They both had a way of finding humor in anything. It kept the day from getting too dry.

"Okay, that helps narrow the field. I'll pull only the folders from 1993, and you can get whatever you need from that."

When the woman resurfaced ten minutes later, Gloria could not help but wonder if there was a way to narrow down the search even more. Three charts, each four inches thick, were plopped onto the counter in front of her.

"I hope this helps, honey." The woman smiled as Gloria carried the folders to a nearby desk.

"Jesus, You got to show me how to do this." Even as she prayed, she was hit with an idea that made her want to smack herself in the head. "All I need to do is find a piece of their letterhead in here and get their address off of that. Should be easy enough." She smiled at her own ingenuity and threw back the heavy pages, stopping randomly at one.

9705 Perkins Street, Suite 600, Shepherd Hills, MD 29473. She wrote the address down and reclosed the file.

"You can leave those right there. I know that pile is heavy. I'll get it on my lunch break," the woman at the window shouted down to Gloria, who had just stood and braced herself to return the load. Gloria eagerly complied with the woman's directive, pushing the papers to the side and straightening them in a stack. As she patted down the thick pages, her eyes caught the corner of a sheet sticking out.

"Oh, this looks like the contract of sale for their old office suite." She started to push the paper back in when she suddenly froze, nearly tearing it out of the bound chart.

"Excuse me." She nearly knocked over the next person waiting at the window. "I'm sorry, but I need to see any public records, if any, that you have on the Black Entrepreneurs Alliance."

"Just a moment." The woman smiled, although the waiting patron gave Gloria a nasty look. A little while later, Gloria flipped through the single thin folder the woman placed in front of her.

"There was more, but someone checked it out first thing this morning. I'm glad you asked for it or I may have never noticed that it wasn't returned."

"Do you write down who checks out documents?"

"Yes, um, let's see." The woman skimmed over a notepad. "Yes, it was . . . Benjamin Franklin?" She looked back up at Gloria, embarrassment clouding her hazel eyes. "I'm sorry, I guess I wasn't paying much attention. I need to go fill out an incident report for the missing records."

As she turned away, Gloria searched for Anthony's cell-phone number in her purse. When she couldn't find it, she dialed Councilman Banks instead.

"Mr. Banks, I hope you can talk."

"Gloria, I'm glad you called. There's something I want you to look up for me."

"Anthony already told me, and I've already done it and I've got news."

"You're amazing, Gloria." Walter chuckled. "You are by far the most dependable employee I've ever had. What have you found? Wait, let me see if I can get Anthony's cell on three-way so he can hear too." There was a pause and then a phone ringing. Anthony answered hello through sharp static.

"Minister Murdock, can you talk?"

"Walter, hi. I'm just rounding an exit. Give me a second."

After a brief moment, all three greeted each other.

"Anthony, where have you been? I've been trying to call you on your cell phone since yesterday." Walter did not hide the concern in his voice.

"I'm sorry. I was out of range. I'm just coming back from South Carolina trying to dig up info about my father."

"Did you learn anything?" Walter sounded hopeful.

"Well, let me put it to you this way: I hope you and Gloria have had better success on your end."

"Anthony, Gloria thinks she's found something." Walter's hope turned into outright excitement. Both men turned silent so Gloria could speak.

"Listen, I'm up here at the Office of Public Records, and you won't believe what I just found out. I hope this helps you and Mr. Banks somehow."

"What is it?" Anthony felt his heart pick up a few paces.

"I have the old address to the steelworkers' union. It looks like it's in the same building CASH is in on Perkins Street, up on the sixth floor. But look, I also found out who bought the space from them ten years ago."

"Oh? Who?" Anthony and Walter asked at the same time.

"Remember the name of the business owner on those Stonymill documents I got that didn't have any clear-cut information?"

"Wait a minute." Anthony strained his brain trying to get a mental picture of the papers he and Gloria had pored over Friday afternoon. "I remember the brothers who owned the tax service, Reggie Savant and the Empress Hotel, the jewelry store. Who am I forgetting?"

"There were a couple of others, but the one I'm talking about was called Pride and Fidelity."

"That's right. Isn't that the company we couldn't find a name for, or any other information?" Anthony had to speak louder over the static.

"Exactly. We only found the name Razi once somewhere on the documents. That was the only reference of a name on all the Stonymill stuff I got from city hall on Friday."

"So this Razi character who is associated with Pride and Fidelity and the BEA owns the old offices of the steelworkers' union." Walter was in attack mode. "We need to find out who he or she is and what role they are playing in all this."

"Well, check this out. I tried to get current public records of the Black Entrepreneurs Alliance to see if they disclosed any information about this person and their business, but the records I needed were missing. Someone checked them out first thing this morning under the name of Benjamin Franklin. The only records available have absolutely no mention of either Razi or Pride and Fidelity."

"This is crazy. Someone must be onto our personal investigation." The static on Anthony's phone made him barely audible.

"Gloria, you haven't noticed anyone following you?" Walter sounded anxious again.

"No, well, I haven't been looking." For the first time in the conversation, Gloria's excitement diminished.

"My phone's breaking up. I'm going to have to talk to you when I get back in town, probably after Minister Porter's funeral," Anthony interjected.

"And I'm due back in session in a few seconds," Walter said close behind.

"I'm going to go over to the office on Perkins Street to see if I can find anything."

"Gloria, I don't think you should go by yourself. Why don't you wait until my session is over and we can go together?" Walter pleaded.

"I agree with Walter. Don't go. Wait until I—" Contact with Anthony was lost.

"I'm going, Walter. I feel like I need to do it. If someone's onto us, we need to act right now. If it makes you feel any better, I do keep a bottle of pepper spray on my key chain."

"Gloria, I have to go, but I beg you not to go alone to that building. I know that Eric from CASH is down at city hall, and I'm not sure where or if there are any other active offices in that old warehouse. I hate the idea of you being alone in there. Please, wait until I or Anthony—or both of us—can go with you. I'd go now, but I really can't miss this session. You've helped so much, and this really is not your battle to fight."

Gloria sighed heavily into the receiver. "I guess you're right. Maybe it would be unwise for me to go."

"Of course. Promise me you won't go."

"Okay, Walter. I promise that I'll wait for either you or Anthony to check it out."

"Thanks, Gloria. I'll be finished here by four. We can meet at my office and go together, or we can meet Anthony after the funeral so he can go with us too."

"Okay." Gloria sighed. "I'll just go over to the library and see if I can get any research on all this done there. How's that?"

"Perfect, and I'll give you a call as soon as I'm out of session so we can make the next move together, preferably with Anthony."

They hung up after talking briefly about some unrelated office business. Gloria checked the time. It was already almost noon, a perfect time to take her lunch break. If she wanted to run errands on her *own* time, that was her prerogative. The first errand on her list was to catch the bus to the office of Pride and Fidelity on Perkins Street.

Terri sat back in her leather desk chair. She had come to her office after leaving Dr. Levinson's. For the past few hours she had done nothing but stare at her phone. Her door was closed, the blinds on the large windows drawn. If she had not given a message to the main receptionist to be left undisturbed, nobody in the office would have known she was there.

"I wish I knew who to talk to," she said to herself, consulting her feelings and emotions for guidance. Anthony. Baby. Reggie. Work. Entrepreneurship. The issues presented themselves not as questions but as statements, facts of her reality. She closed her eyes, thinking to pray, and opened them, uncertain how to.

Finally, she picked up the phone and dialed slowly.

"Hello." The simple crisp baritone of Reggie's voice awakened a subdued longing in her.

"I just want to be happy. That's all." Terri's voice was weak, worn as she uttered her hopelessness into the receiver.

"Terri, is that you?"

"I don't know what to do anymore about anything." She was beyond tears, her eyes as dry as the breath in her words.

"Terri," Reggie's voice was soft and soothing through the phone, barely above a whisper. "This past week has been terrible for you. Anthony ought to be ashamed for putting such a lovely woman as you through all this."

"Reggie, I just found out that I'm pregnant."

"Oh? Oh." Reggie was quiet only for a second. "Terri, you do not need to think or worry about anything right now. Let me handle that. What you need is some relaxation, some head-to-toe pampering. That's it. I'm sending you to a day spa, the finest on the East Coast. I want you to do nothing right now but relax and enjoy the royal treatment a queen like you deserves. Let your loyal subjects deal with the dirty work. Where are you?"

"At work." She had no energy to fight his demand.

"Is there somewhere you can safely leave your car? I'm going to send a limo to get you and take you to the airport. First-class service all the way."

"I'll drive to Cherisse's."

"Then it's done. Let me make some calls and finalize arrangements. All you need to know is that a limousine will pick you up from Cherisse's condo at two o'clock. Enjoy these next few days of pampering. You do not need to make any deep decisions right at this moment. Let me take care of you."

"How do I explain this to my partners? I have so much work to do."

"When you're self-employed, you answer to no one but yourself."

"Reggie, I'm not sure that—"

"Uh, uh, uh." Reggie cut in. "You are not to be thinking or trying to figure anything out. Let me handle everything. Just remember, two o'clock, Cherisse's condo, limousine." A dial tone filled Terri's ear.

For the first time in her adult life, Terri laid aside every conviction she held about independence, self-determination, and standing on her own two feet. She was tired and nauseous, confused and drained. She wanted nothing more than to find a place to rest her hurting heart and head. Reggie's arms were wide open.

Fingering the keys to her new Lexus, she left, speaking to no one, looking forward to the promise of rest that would begin in Cherisse's parking lot.

"Kent, slow down!" Mona gripped her seat belt with both hands. "I know you want to get back to Shepherd Hills as soon as possible, but you might be able to do your job better if you're alive!"

They were speeding down Interstate 95, weaving in and out of traffic—when it was actually moving. Kent cursed rush hour, wondering if everyone was heading for the same place he was.

"Get out of the fast lane!" He honked at a car that was cruising just below the speed limit. The driver honked back.

"Darling, how are you going to explain this to the cop who will stop you?"

"I have a badge. I'll tell them it's an emergency. I need to close a case. They'll understand."

"What I don't understand is why *you* have to do this. Why can't you just call someone down in Shepherd Hills and give them the information you feel is so life-and-death?"

They just missed clipping an SUV. Mona stifled a scream.

"I told you, I don't know where my cell phone is and we don't have time to stop. And even if I did make a phone call, I have no way to prove what my gut is telling me."

"What is your gut telling you that's making you risk our lives so greatly?" Mona's knuckles were white as she re-clenched the New Testament in her lap.

"Well, for starters, I think I've been investigating the wrong people, and if I'm right, there are at least a couple of people down there who are in grave danger."

"Danger of what?"

"That's what I'm afraid of. Oh, shoot!" Kent put his foot on the brake as the cars in front of him came to a complete stop. Orange construction signs dotted the paved expanse before them.

"At this rate, we won't be home until late this evening." He fingered through the faxed papers with Sheriff Malloy's marks over Anthony's print, and then tossed them to the backseat.

"I don't know if that will be in time."

Kellye Porter sorted through the basket full of dark-colored clothes. The sheets and towels in another basket were newly folded, and one of the two loads of whites was in the dryer. Four loads in three hours. Bernard would have been all over her; she smiled to herself. In the early days of their marriage, he used to take freshly cleaned and air-dried clothes, hold them to his nose, and compare the captured scent of sunshine to his own captured sunbeam.

"You are a ray of light that has refreshed my life," he would whisper into her ear while nuzzling her neck. Years later, even after she finally convinced him that an electric dryer would make life easier for both of them, he still called her Sunshine every time he saw her washing clothes.

It was the day of his funeral.

Kellye looked at the white dress she had picked for the occasion hanging on a wire hanger near the dryer. Pressed and starched, it looked like angel clothes suspended in mid-air. The thought made her wonder how many angels he had seen in heaven already.

"Sunshine is always bright, not dark," he had whispered to her so many times from his sickbed, their fingers intertwined, as a comfortable silence became their daily conversation. He made her promise never to wear black at his funeral. She never liked or wanted to continue the talks he initiated about his home-going service or the life she would live once he was gone, but now she found herself engrossed in every written and remembered detail, his final wishes followed as much as possible to a tee. Dwelling on his requests surrounding his departure gave her a sense of connection to the man she could no longer hold. She could not embrace his body, but his desires could embrace her. Knowing she was honoring his last hopes seemed to keep him alive just a little longer.

She was just about to put the last load of clothes in the washing machine when her fingers brushed against the crumpled edges of stiff paper.

"What's this?" Her fingers dug into a pocket, then pulled a terry-cloth garment out of the pile for inspection. It was the robe of her sister-in-law, Mabel.

The stiff paper turned out to be an old photograph. Kellye's fingers shook as she slowly smoothed down the edges of the worn picture. It had been extraordinarily difficult to go through all of Bernard's pictures earlier. She had let Mabel pick out the obituary photo. She must have missed this one, Kellye concluded. She blinked back a tear, and as the serious-looking faces came into focus she brought the picture closer to her eyes. These faces looked familiar, and she felt like kicking herself when no names came to mind. A younger, headstrong Bernard stared back at her from the center of the picture, flanked on either side by equally young and headstrong men. One face in particular troubled her as she searched for a name.

"I was just looking for my robe."

Kellye had not noticed Mabel coming down the basement steps. The older woman came beside her and loosened the maroon robe from Kellye's grip.

"Something wrong?" Mabel could barely get out her words.

"I know what it is," Kellye said, suddenly smiling. "It's the eyes." She pointed to the picture. "This man here looks just like a young minister at my church, Anthony. Real nice young man. You met him, Mabel. He was here Saturday. If I didn't know better, I'd say this man could pass for his father." She was still smiling as she pointed quickly at the photo before tossing a dirty dish towel into the washing machine.

"If you didn't know better?" Mabel knew instinctively she should have left it alone, but she wanted to make sure Kellye was not onto anything.

"Yeah, I know, it's amazing how everyone has a twin out there. I guess Anthony's was in another generation. That picture looks like it was taken before I even met Bernard, back when he was still living in Sharen."

Mabel's smile and caution faded as she snatched the picture from her and clenched it in her fist.

"So you really don't remember him?"

"Remember who, Mabel?" Sister Porter did not seem bothered by Mabel's sudden change of mood. She turned the dial on the washer and poured a scoop of laundry detergent in the tub.

"His father. Anthony's father. You really don't remember who he was?"

Kellye was heading back to the basement stairs, her white dress draped over an arm.

"Anthony's father? Why would I know his father? I remember his step-dad, Harold, but beyond that I—" Kellye froze mid-step as she threw a hand to her mouth. She looked back toward the photo and then again at Mabel. The anger in Mabel's eyes was smoldering and unmistakable.

"My Jesus! *He* was Anthony's father? He was Anthony's father." Disbelief and confusion locked into her face as she looked pityingly at her sister-in-law. "Mabel," she whispered between her fingers, "are you still holding on to that after all these years? I wonder if Anthony knows that—"

"Leave it alone, Kellye." Mabel's voice was low, almost threatening. "It's almost all taken care of. Please, just leave it be."

"But what difference does it m—"

"Just leave it be. We have a funeral to get ready for today."

"You're right, Mabel. But it seems to me that a casket is not the only thing that needs to be buried." Kellye rushed up the steps with fresh tears in her eyes. It wasn't just grief anymore. It was grief plus. Something was terribly wrong. She felt it. She knew it. But trying to talk to Anthony would be too ambitious a goal to accomplish on this heavy day. She would call him tomorrow. If that man in the picture really had been Anthony's father, he had the right to know, she figured. Maybe that was the information Bernard had been trying to tell Anthony. She sighed in relief as she remembered that she had honored one of Bernard's last wishes. That box in the attic, she'd seen to it that Anthony received it. Anthony already knows the whole story, she assured herself.

But even as she went through the dreaded duty of getting dressed for her late husband's funeral, she could not shake a nagging feeling that everything was not okay.

"I'll talk to him tomorrow," she murmured, trying to calm herself as she stared at her white-clothed reflection in the bedroom-door mirror. "I'll talk to him tomorrow and make sure he knows the whole story. Tomorrow will be fine. If Anthony has spent the last twenty-nine years not knowing about his father and what he did to the residents of Sharen, what difference will one more day make?"

It was not until she, Mabel, and Denise were sitting in the black limo from Winston's Funeral Home on their way to Second Baptist Church that she realized something else was bothering her.

"Mabel," Kellye whispered from behind the paper fan and white handkerchief she was holding, "do you still have that picture on you?"

The dull clink of the elevator signaled its destination. The sixth floor of the building at 9705 Perkins Street. Gloria waited for the doors to slide open, and shrank back when they did. The sixth floor was an open dumping ground; chairs, trash, and furniture were spread across the large floor like the skeletons at an ancient ruin. Her heart beat faster as she tried to adjust her eyes to the dim light offered only by the erratically placed windows of the warehouse building.

She checked her watch; it was already a quarter past one. That gave her only a few minutes before she had to report back to Councilman Banks's office. He'd promised to come here himself after he finished with his session down at city hall later in the day. Maybe she should have listened and waited. She held back a scream as a wad of papers shifted in a near corner. Rats. She knew the sound.

"Don't have much time, so I better work fast to find something." She checked her purse for the name she had scribbled down at the Office of Public Records and Recording. Razi.

"There's got to be something here that explains why this person would want this suite and what he or she is doing in it."

She quickly scanned the room, letting her eyes do the walking before her feet began the tour. This would have been a good time to be rid of those pesky extra pounds. She frowned to herself. Covering her nose and clenching her purse, she darted through cobwebs and coughed in dust as she began a quick trot around the massive open suite.

At an upturned desk near a window, she noticed something she had not seen anywhere else in the room. Order. She stepped semi-athletically over some broken shelves, forging a path to the wooden hutch. A telephone and a stack of papers sat atop it, and a pen lay on the floor. A quiver of nervousness edged up her spine as she moved closer to investigate.

The window offered a mini flood of light onto the work space. Gloria looked out through the glass pane at a spectacular view. She could see most of Shepherd Hills from where she stood—trees, buildings, homes, land sprawled out for miles. She had never realized that the county was true to its name, hills and valleys dictating development.

She could also see unused, weed-filled railroad tracks just beneath the building. The warehouse sat on a dead end. She closed her eyes for a brief second, trying to imagine the area as it had been decades before, busy with blue-collar industry, loud, smelling like sweat, smoke, and the other stenches of hard labor. She opened her eyes and saw the desolation that had claimed the area. Even at one-thirty in the afternoon, no traffic, no pedestrians, no hints of life were around. Had she read her watch right? She needed to put a move on it.

A quick shuffling through the papers left her wondering where to begin with her jotted notes. Although there was no clear contact or identifying information on Razi, she was starting to feel like she was merely scratching the surface of Razi's wealth. Who or whatever it was, its ownership extended far beyond the sixth floor of the old warehouse. Razi's name was attached to the sales and utilities bills of several businesses and structures, including the steelworkers' hall that had been transformed into the Diamond Mount where Friday's banquet had been held. Razi held major shares of AGS Railroad, which was responsible for the expansion of the Stonymill light rail line. Many houses, lots, buildings—most related somehow to the now defunct Toringhouse Steel and its branch-offs—all had attachments to Razi.

Gloria set the stack of papers back down and walked around the desk to a metal file cabinet that had more papers sticking out of its drawers. As she went to open one, her feet brushed against a manila folder sitting like an upside-down V on the floor. Its contents had spilled out and lay scattered around it. She scooped it all up, reading the name on the folder's label.

"What is this?" she muttered to herself, freezing when she saw the first piece of paper inside. It was a photograph of a serious-looking black man with a huge afro and an orange-and-black dashiki.

"The eyes." She took the picture closer to the window to get a better view. Anthony had said something about researching his father, and this man certainly could pass as a DNA-test candidate.

She flipped through the folder one page at a time, her eyes getting slightly wider with each read.

"This man was quite the con," she muttered as the pages and yellowed newspaper clippings crinkled softly in her hand. She gave one last look through the stack, noting only that most of what was there either referenced or came from somewhere in South Carolina.

"There's got to be something that I'm missing." She checked her watch. She should have left minutes ago, but one more quick look-through wouldn't hurt, she decided.

She spotted a wood stool behind the file cabinet and quickly headed for it, but it was not until she was almost completely seated that she realized it had a bad leg. Using a nearby shelf for leverage she caught herself, trying to hold on to the papers and grab the dusty ledge at the same time.

"Ouch!" A cup of hot coffee spilled onto her arm, scalding her wrist and fingertips. "Where did this come from?" She gasped, her realization that someone else was there coming a second too late. Before she could regain her balance, a strong hand clenched tightly around her mouth and heavy rope bound her arms behind her. She used all her strength to kick back with her legs, but the way she was sprawled on the floor gave her a severe disadvantage. Before she could make sense of what was going on, she was alone again, attached to a pipe that ran the height of the room. Silence filled the space and nobody else was there.

She sat shocked for a long minute, until a slight trickle of blood caught her attention. Pain thumped near her wrist, and she realized for the first time that she had been cut. Her artery had been missed by millimeters. Suddenly her mind caught up with her heartbeat, a million thoughts thundering like a high-speed train. She had to get out of there. Whoever it was was going to come back, and she knew it wouldn't be to apologize.

Though her hands were tied behind her back, there was just enough slack in the rope for her to grope the immediate floor. Good: her purse was reachable. She knew she had a nail file in there, and she convinced herself that even a dull edge could help her slice away at the thick twine.

It took her more than ten minutes just to unzip the black leather bag, and another fifteen to find the metal nail file. She began sawing away at the cord with a vengeance, her strength limited by the strained position of her arms and the pain near her right wrist. When another twenty minutes had gone by, and she had only made a slight nick in the rope, she banged her head against a shelf beside her. It fell on top of her bloodied hands.

"Jesus!" Hot tears blinded her vision. Nobody would even know she was missing yet. Councilman Banks was down at city hall thinking she was at the library, and if Anthony was back, he probably would not be trying to call her from the funeral. She had to get out of there and get in contact with both of them. If she was in danger, maybe they were as well. There was nothing she could do but feel for the nail file and resume whittling away at the rope.

Chapter 17

Anthony breathed a sigh of relief. With every change in his BMW's odometer, he drew closer to the skyline of the Shepherd Hills downtown district. It was ten after two. He would only be a few moments late for Minister Bernard Porter's funeral. The winding road that led to Second Baptist Church was a short three exits away. Figuring an hour and a half for the funeral, another hour for the burial, he should be able to drive over to the warehouse on Perkins Street by five.

He was turning on his blinkers to change lanes when he saw red-and-blue lights flashing behind him. A police car. Anthony checked his speedometer. He didn't think he was speeding. Were his lights not working? He tapped the blinkers again as he slowed to a stop on the shoulder of the expressway. He cut the ignition and put both hands on the steering wheel. No need to turn a routine police stop into a Rodney King rerun. He could see the officer approaching in his rearview mirror. It was Sheriff Malloy.

"Good afternoon, Sheriff. Is there a problem?" Anthony was courteous.

"Shut up and get out of the car! Keep your hands where I can see them!"

"What's going on?"

"I said get out of the car, Murdock!" Sheriff Malloy quickly pointed a gun at him.

"Whoa, whoa, okay, I'm getting out." Anthony stepped out, each movement slow and exaggerated as he kept his hands spread out in front of him. Cars were beginning to slow down on the freeway beside them, onlookers pointing, speeding up only when they saw the gun aimed at Anthony.

"Lie facedown on the ground!"

Anthony obeyed, but Sheriff Malloy still pushed him down on his way to the pavement. Blood spattered across his teeth as he hit the black tar.

"Stay still!" Malloy continued his assault, hitting, smacking, spitting as he pulled out handcuffs, using them to whack Anthony hard just under his ear. Anthony felt like his bones were forming fault lines.

"Wait a minute, what's going on?" Anthony demanded. "What are you doing?"

"Shut up, Murdock! You know what you did. You are under arrest for public corruption, embezzlement, and bribery of state officials. You have the right to remain silent . . ."

The sheriff proceeded with the Miranda rights as he roughly shoved and pushed the compliant Anthony to his cruiser, using the full force of his hands and a knee to thrust him inside. "I hope you have a good attorney, because you're looking at some serious time, Reverend Murdock!"

He watched as the sheriff dug through the trunk of his car, pulling out the bag of money that had been hidden in its belly for too long. Even as his body ached from the ruthless blows he had suffered, he felt as if a burden had been lifted off his shoulders as Malloy tossed the brown bag onto the passenger-side floor of his police cruiser. Anthony was quiet as the cruiser pulled away with him in it. A part of him had been expecting this very moment ever since the late-night "Samson" study session. *For Samson to overcome, he had to go down with the enemy.*

But even as a calmness controlled him, a realization put him on high alert. Malloy was driving in a direction away from the county jail.

"Where are you taking me?" Anthony demanded from the backseat, his wrists hurting from the clasp of metal around them, his head and neck aching with pain. "I have the right to know where you are taking me."

"Shut up!" Malloy shouted through the grate that separated them. "There's a special holding cell for criminals like you, a place far away to keep you from spreading your brand of corruption any more throughout this city."

"I want to speak to my lawyer. I don't know what you're doing."

"I said shut up!" Malloy brandished a gun. The cruiser's lights and siren were not on, and Sheriff Malloy seemed to be driving casually to the outer areas of the city. He suddenly veered off road at some old railroad tracks. Anthony stayed quiet, alert, his mind pleading for direction, insight. Safety.

"Where are you taking me?" Anthony asked again as Malloy pulled to a sudden stop. What looked like an old, abandoned checkpoint station sat leaning to one side.

Anthony studied the green-painted splintered wood, trying to make sense out of what was going on.

"Where are we?" he demanded again.

"Didn't I say shut up?"

Anthony never saw the billy club coming, but the sudden strike on his skull plunged him into spinning darkness.

Terri raised her car seat back to its upright position. She'd been sitting in her car, really lying down in it, in Cherisse's parking lot for a couple of hours. It was a little after two o'clock. The limousine should be here soon. The idea, this trip away from her problems, seemed a little farfetched, Terri knew, but she was not prepared to think right now. She wanted nothing more than to curl up into a tight ball and wish the world away. Closing her eyes was a start.

"Terri!" A sudden hand grabbed her through the window. "Terri, are you okay?"

"Cherisse." She had no fire to speak.

"Oh my goodness, girl, what are you doing? My neighbor called me at work and told me someone was sitting in my parking space in front of my condo for almost two hours. When they described your Lexus, I knew something was wrong. What are you doing? Did you go to work? What happened at the doctor's office? I've been trying to reach you all day! What's going on?"

Terri could not handle all the questions. "I'm about to go away for a little while."

"Go away? With who? Where?"

"Reggie's sending a limousine to come take me to the airport. Should be here any minute." Terri rubbed her eyes, yawned, and rested her head back on the seat.

"Terri, I don't know if I'm liking this idea. It seems so sudden. I know you're feeling kind of bad right now. You might do better staying in a familiar setting with friends until you can see more clearly what to do next. Are you sure that you can trust Reggie like this?"

"The limo's here." Terri pointed weakly at an old Cadillac limousine, which looked like it had seen better days, turning onto the lot. The windows were tinted and it crept along slowly, almost erratic in its direction.

"Ew." Cherisse wrinkled her face. "The brother makes how much? And that's the best he could send you?" They watched as the limousine began a sloppy turn into another development. "Where is he going?"

"He must not see us over here." Terri forced herself out of the car and waved her arms. The limo jerked back toward them, stopping just past Terri and Cherisse.

"Terri, I don't have a good feeling about this at all. Something doesn't feel right. I don't think you should go."

But the chauffeur, a skinny man with a wide hat and dark glasses, had already gotten out of the limo and was holding open the door, waiting.

Terri was quiet as she skirted past Cherisse.

"Terri"—Cherisse grabbed her shoulder—"are you sure about this?" When Terri shrugged out of her grip, Cherisse called after her. "At least call me when you get to wherever you're going. I'll feel better. Okay?"

Terri said nothing as she disappeared into the vehicle, the door slamming loudly behind her. The limousine sped off.

It was Eric's turn to address the assembly. He stood in the lively room, taking his time to reach the solid mahogany podium. As he faced the legislators, he scanned the crowd for friendly faces of support but saw none. Being alone made him feel more nervous than usual. Some of the lawmakers looked ready to hear his presentation, though he questioned their motivation as they studied him from head to toe, pens in hand, brown and white faces solemn. Others looked preoccupied, checking Palm Pilots, conversing with neighbors, brushing lint off of clothes, doing any- and everything not to acknowledge his presence. A couple excused themselves to accept phone calls; one headed for the rest room.

Okay, Lord, this is it, Eric silently prayed. *This is the last chance I have to address the city council before they vote tomorrow whether to give that tract of land to CASH or to all those other businesses. Father, please, Your will be done.* With that prayer, Eric cleared his throat and spread out his speech before him. The room quieted as he looked down at his paper.

"Good afternoon, ladies, gentlemen, honoraries, dignitaries, esteemed officials of—uh—elected officials of esteem and honored representatives, guests—uh." He cleared his throat. "Good afternoon, everyone." He looked up from his notes to see many of the faces smiling, snickering at him. This was not how he'd wanted to start.

"I come before you today to explain why we . . . why you . . . why I need . . . I'm here today to talk about CASH and what it will do for this community." He stammered as he read. When he looked back up, the faces that were not smiling were beginning to turn in other directions, pulling out papers to read, pens to doodle.

"Forget it," he mumbled to himself. He balled up his written speech and stepped to the side of the podium.

"Many of you here today look at me and wonder what I have to offer this county. You're looking at me standing before you and saying to yourselves, What on earth does a non-degreed, ex–drug addict that you probably passed in the streets not so many years ago have to offer the people of our community? Well, let me not keep you wondering. Let me remove the guess, end the rumors, and stop the speculation.

"I am here today to offer the community of Shepherd Hills hope. I am here to propose a second chance, maybe even a first chance, for people in our county who feel like chance has walked on by. Now, I know that you are expecting me to stand before you this afternoon and beg and plead with you to let CASH build. By now, all of you know what Bethany Village is, what it will be comprised of, the population that it will serve. I know that you are expecting me to present charts and diagrams, slide shows and statistics. But you have already received all that over the past few months; all of you have seen the handouts, received the letters, fielded my phone calls.

"So what I'm presenting to you now is *your* chance to provide hope to someone who thinks there is none. Tomorrow, you have the power to begin a building process that extends far beyond bricks and mortar, with results that will measure profits in the awakened purpose and potential of people's lives.

"I'm presenting to you your opportunity to be part of an uprising. An uprising of addicts who will get clean. An uprising of youth who will value education and won't lose their lives taking lessons from the streets. An uprising of people who've been pushed to the edges of society, pushing their way back in with new jobs, new chances, new leases on life.

"What dollar amount can be placed on dreams come true and hope renewed? How do you compute the bottom line of a human being's restoration?

"If you believe that it shouldn't be done, there is nothing else I can say to you. If you believe that it can't be done, then let me offer you some living proof: Hello everyone. I'm Eric Johnson and I am *here* today."

He picked up his briefcase and walked out of the hushed room, making no eye contact with all the eyes that followed him out to the hallway. Once there, he let out a deep breath, almost doubling over in the release of air. A cup of water, a bite to eat might calm his bubbling nerves. Eric felt numb as he headed for the nearby cafeteria. A small crowd of people had gathered around a television set.

"What? I know him. He goes to my church. He's one of the ministers." A young woman in an apron and net cap pointed to the tiny black-and-white screen.

"What's going on?" Eric moved closer to see. "Did something happen?"

"Police brutality, my brother, caught on tape." A hefty man with flowing dreadlocks was shaking his head. "The news just cut in with some amateur video somebody taped over on the outer loop. That redheaded sheriff is out there acting like a maniac as usual, but he messed up this time. His victim, I heard, is a minister, so you know Jesse Jackson and Al Sharpton are probably on their way down the interstate as we speak."

Eric looked at the video, showed over and over again.

"Ooh." The man next to him grimaced. "Look at that upper cut, and the man ain't even resisting."

Eric watched as the video was shown again in slow motion with second-by-second commentary. The frame stopped precisely at the moment when the officer lashed a pair of handcuffs at the motorist's neck. The picture was magnified, the look of pain and anguish on the man's brown face frozen for further remarks by the news reporters.

"Isn't that Anthony Murdock?" Eric recognized the baby-faced features.

"That's him." The food worker nodded. "Like I said, he's the youth pastor at my church."

"What did he do?"

"I don't know. They're not saying, and I can't imagine what he did to get beat up and arrested like that."

Cherisse was still looking off in the direction the limo had left although five minutes had passed. With a loud sigh and a shrug of her shoulders, she fumbled for her house keys in her purse. There was no point in waiting outside for Terri to return from wherever she was going; that could be days. She was going to have to spend her evening friend-free. She was just starting up the manicured walkway toward the steps when a gleaming white stretch limo pulled to a stop beside Terri's parked Lexus.

"Huh?" Cherisse turned back to investigate. As she rushed over, Reginald Savant stepped out of the rear door. He turned and scanned the entire length of the parking lot until his eyes rested on Cherisse. A scowl was on his face.

"Where's Terri?"

"Uh, in the limo you sent her?"

"The limo I sent her?"

"Yeah, you know, the raggedy rust-mobile that just whisked her away a few minutes ago?" Cherisse pointed down the tree-lined street. The afternoon traffic was beginning to pick up.

"Raggedy rust-mobile? What are you talking about? This limo was the best I could find on short notice. The only thing missing is a Jacuzzi in the backseat."

"So you come rolling up here in a suite of luxury on wheels while my girl gets the best of 1985 on hubcaps?"

"Cherisse, what are you talking about? I have come here myself in this limo to pick up Terri and escort her personally to the best day spa this side of the country. I know I'm a little late, but some things were beyond my control. Can you just tell me where Terri is so we can go? Her flight leaves in thirty minutes."

"And what I'm telling you is that she already left in a limo she said you sent."

Reggie and Cherisse looked at each other a hard minute, until realization set in.

"What kind of limo was it again?" They both jumped into the oversized Lincoln.

Terri did not like the way the driver smelled. She felt like she was locked in a grandmother's closet, suffocating under the sharp scent of mothballs and mildew. And where did this chauffeur learn to drive? The way he was bucking and shifting, Terri wondered if he had ever been behind the wheel of a car larger than a Volkswagen Beetle. Maybe this was not such a good idea. *Are you sure that you can trust Reggie like this?* Cherisse's voice replayed over and over in her mind. If this was his idea of a trip to relaxation and luxury, then she was going to have to reevaluate his judgment.

Terri tried to make herself comfortable in the torn vinyl seat, but the yellow stuffing was bunched up in a hard knot against the small of her back. This was ridiculous. She was two seconds away from telling the driver to turn around and take her back home when she noticed that they had passed the exit for the airport.

"Excuse me." Terri rolled her eyes as she called out to the driver. "I'm sorry, but I think you were supposed to take that last right."

"Don't tell me what to do, tramp!" The driver snatched off his glasses and freed the triangular cap from his head. Loose, wavy blond hair tracks fell out. "I can't believe you had the nerve to call Reggie when I'm standing right next to him and he's going to make arrangements for *you* to get the royal treatment!"

Nikki Galloway. Terri reached for the car-door handle, but speed and nausea held her back. "Stop the car. Right now. Let me out." She spoke calmly. This girl had too many loose bolts Terri did not want to rattle, not at sixty-five miles an hour.

"No. We are going to finish this once and for all. I've got a job to do, and I'm not going to let you get in my way." Nikki laid her foot on the accelerator and the car bucked like a crippled stallion. "Oops."

"You can at least tell me where we're going." No need to fight the girl in a moving car on the freeway. Terri was patient. She could wait. "Where are you taking me?"

"Don't worry about it. Now shut up."

〜

His head felt like it had been split in two. Anthony's eyes blinked open. He wanted to massage the back of his skull, but something was keeping him from doing that.

"Wha—" He sat upright, realizing his hands were still cuffed. "What's going on?" Anthony struggled to make sense out of the world whizzing by him at top speed. It took him a few seconds to conclude that he was back in Sheriff Malloy's cruiser, only this time the lights and siren were on full blast. He was about to close his eyes and let his aching head succumb to the piercing noise and bright flashes, but he realized the car was slowing down. Straight ahead was the police headquarters, and a mob of cameras and reporters surrounded the entrance. His head hurt too much to figure out what was going on.

Malloy suddenly veered away from the front driveway of the headquarters, turning instead into an alley that took them to a back entrance. Before the car came to a complete stop, it seemed he was getting out and pulling Anthony with him through a door. Next thing he knew, Anthony was on the floor of a holding cell. Several officers surrounded him, all talking at once. Anthony could not make sense out of the confusion as he felt like he was being passed around from one hand to another. Someone was wiping his head, his mouth. Voices shouted over each other and Anthony tasted his own blood. He closed his eyes and just as suddenly as there had been chaos, he was alone in the metal block.

"Can I make my phone call?" His eyes were barely open, his voice a dry whisper as he spoke to no one in particular.

His answer came in the exclamations of Councilman Banks.

"Anthony! Are you okay?" He was standing there, reaching both arms through the jail cell, as if the mere act of extending his arms could equal the warmth of a hug. "I came down here as soon as I saw it on the news! Don't worry. I'm getting you out of here right now. I'll make sure you get the best lawyer, and the cop who did this to you will be switching places with you before you can spell lawsuit!"

Anthony could see the deep anger in Walter's eyes, hear the fury in his throat. This was the no-nonsense Banks, the-don't-play-with-me-I'll-get-the-job-done activist attitude that had won him his seat on the council time after time.

Even as he spoke, Sheriff Malloy was approaching the cell. "Don't think that just because Mr. Murdock is on one side and you're on the other that you're out of the woods with me, Walter. I've got what I need for Anthony, but I'm still working on you."

"Do you really think I'm taking a word you say seriously after what you have done to him?"

"And just what have I done? Nobody can prove anything!"

"There's a video being aired on the five-o-clock news throughout the state that in the public's mind will be proof enough."

Sheriff Malloy fell silent at Walter's words. He had been forced to change his original plans once he realized the media had caught on to him. He'd had no choice but to bring Anthony to the station.

"I'm posting bail for you, Anthony. I don't want you to worry about any of this. I'm getting a plan together now to deal with this nonsense. There's no way that you will ever set foot in a courtroom. Let him out. This should not have happened." The last comment was said to Malloy, who was fingering through a large set of keys.

"Take him." Malloy studied Anthony's disheveled and wounded frame through the metal bars. "I had nothing to do with his condition," he asserted as if it were truth. "Don't think this is over."

"I know it's not." Walter glared at him.

Half an hour later, Anthony walked out of the headquarters behind the councilman through an emergency exit.

"I don't feel like dealing with anyone, the press, the media. I knew exposure was coming, but I don't have any statements prepared." His voice was strong, although his body ached. *Confidence.* "The only person I want to talk to right now is my heavenly Advocate. I'm going to need the best legal services of my life, and the way I see it, the same One who pled my sin case before a righteous Almighty God will help me through these charges."

Walter was preoccupied with planning.

"I've already started contacting lawyers for you. One in particular from Baltimore"—he looked quickly at a business card—"said he could meet with both of us tonight. I figured you wouldn't want to be dealing with the general public so I arranged for him to meet us at a safe, private place halfway between here and his office, about thirty minutes away."

"That sounds good." Anthony's nods were firm, focused. Before the crowd of onlookers and microphones and cameras could catch on, Walter's Lincoln Town Car had disappeared into the rush-hour traffic.

I'm standing between the pillars. Now it's time to start pushing them down. Lord, give me Your strength in Jesus' name. Anthony closed his eyes, then quickly reopened them. He had to stay alert.

"Thank you, Jesus!" Gloria's hands were shaking as she cut through the last thread of the thick rope. Her hands were free. She massaged her wrists, wincing at the sharp pain that still throbbed through them. She gave a quick look around for her shoes, grateful that the one-inch-heeled black leather pumps would not slow her down too much.

"Now I can get out of here." She grabbed her purse and headed for the broken exit sign. Stairs. There was no way she was going to stand still and wait for an elevator. She was outside before she had a second thought.

Gloria felt helpless standing at the bus stop. Few cars and fewer people were around, so she started walking.

"Excuse me, ma'am. Do you need a ride?"

She never heard the taxi come, but when the car door opened she was convinced that cab drivers were angels.

"Where to?" The driver started the meter.

What was closer? She checked her watch and calculated the distances instantaneously in her mind. "Take me to Second Baptist Church on Valley Road." Anthony should be at the funeral by now. If he wasn't, then she'd continue on to Councilman Banks's office.

The yellow cab pulled in front of the sanctuary just as the mourners emerged from the front door. Six men held on to either side of a silver casket; Pastor Green in a flowing black robe led the procession. A long, single line of women carrying flower arrangements of varying shapes and sizes followed close behind. Gloria pressed her lips together and held back a tear at the image of sweet Kellye Porter walking expressionless, supported on either side by two women she did not recognize. A rich alto hum floated in the otherwise quiet breeze.

She waited for the last of the procession to pass before joining the end of the line. They were all headed to the cemetery behind the church, where tall white crypts over-shadowed engraved memorial markers on the sloping grass. Gloria scanned the crowd for Anthony as everyone formed a semicircle around a green canopy. Kellye and the two women with her sat in metal folding chairs under the shade; the flowers, the pastor, and funeral attendants sur-rounded the coffin.

As tissues dabbed eyes and a solemn hush wrapped around Pastor Green's words, Gloria peeked over a shoulder to read the obituary on the program. She had never known Minister Porter's relatives outside of Kellye. They had no children, as Gloria had suspected. She was reading the list of survivors in the final paragraph of the obituary. Besides Kellye, only two other names were listed: a sister, Mabel Bernice Linstead; and a niece, Denise Towanda Razi, both of Sharen, South Carolina.

Razi.

Gloria almost snatched the folded paper from Win-ston's Funeral Home out of the hand of the woman in front of her. She stared back at the two women flanking Kellye. The interment was over, and all three were heading back in her direction. As they passed, she could not help but wonder whether the older of the two un-known women was glaring at her.

"Sister Porter." Gloria quickly grasped the grieving widow in a gentle yet firm hug. "You are in my prayers. All of you." They were standing in between two slightly sloped mounds, simple white crosses on either side.

"Thank you, sweetheart." Kellye softly blew her nose.

"I did not know Minister Porter hailed from down South, but I should have known. He had a way about him that wasn't as hurried as it is up here in the Mid-Atlantic."

"Yes, Uncle Bernard definitely had his ways." Denise chuckled quietly, the dimples in both cheeks showing before she drew back into serious contemplation. "But I loved that man like a father, although I did not see him much. He was the closest man I had to a father since my own moved to Texas before I can remember."

"Moved to Texas?" Kellye jerked her head back. "Mabel, I thought you said that Roger passed?"

"Roger? I thought my father's name was—"

"Listen, that's a chapter in my life that's been closed for three decades." Mabel cut in with an uneasy smile. "I did the best I could as a single mother with no help from anybody." Anger tinged her words. "Now I just lost my brother, and I don't feel like bringing up any other man that I lost from my life, the hows or whys. If y'all don't mind, I think we should go on and sit down for that dinner the kitchen committee of your church prepared. That fried chicken and cornbread sure smell good."

She began to leave, walking away as if the matter had been settled. Both Kellye and Gloria studied Denise, who stared back at them with tears in her eyes. Obviously, hurt was there, too.

"Mabel, I want to see that picture you were trying to hide from me earlier." Kellye's voice was low, but loud enough for Mabel to hear. "I'm not convinced that chapter ever ended."

"Oh, honey." Mabel turned around with rage trembling in her jaw. "Trust me, that chapter ended. There're just some parts that need to be rewritten. And the pen is moving now."

Chapter 18

T hat man has some nerve. I will see to it myself that these are the last days he flashes that badge." Walter talked nonstop as he drove, hoping that Anthony would remain calm and encouraged as they drew strength from each other. "Is that ice pack helping? Maybe I should have had that lawyer meet us at the hospital. I'm sure the judge who tries this case will want to see medical records." The upbeat chorus of an old gospel quartet played softly on an AM radio station as Walter stared at the ugly knots rising on the back of Anthony's head, the blood on his neck and face. "Frankly, I'm tired of that sheriff thinking he can just do what he wants, when he wants to. I'm glad he's finally getting called out."

Anthony was quiet as the day was just beginning to finger the early evening hours. The traffic on the outer loop was at a head, bumpers edging on bumpers, car horns sounding like the unconducted warm-up of a brass band. Walter checked his watch again.

"At this rate, we're going to miss that lawyer. I need to get off this highway." He took a sudden exit heading west, away from Baltimore.

"Are we still meeting him halfway?"

"Yeah, I'm going to have to take the back roads and loop around. Don't worry"—Walter was reassuring as he smiled—"we'll get to him soon." The smile faded as he refocused on driving.

"I can't believe this." Cherisse and Reginald were standing next to their stretch limo at a gas station–convenience store, a cell phone flipped open to Cherisse's ear as she talked. "I can't get through to anyone. Nine-one-one keeps putting me on hold, Terri's not answering her cell phone, and now I can't even contact darn Anthony." They both looked through the glass window at a television flashing under a Fresh Donuts sign. Replays of the beating Anthony took from Sheriff Malloy flooded all the local networks.

"I'm surprised at how much you seem to care about Terri's disappearance. I would never have expected this response from you." A scowl was etched on Reggie's broad features.

"What? What are you talking about?" Cherisse glared at him as she pressed Redial. "Terri has been my girl since college. We always have each other's back. My only regret today is that I let her trust you enough to get in that broke-down piece of shadoozle you claim you did not send. I should have kept her from going." Cherisse bit her lip, struggling to hold back tears. "I feel like I need to take my own advice that I told Terri the other day, and have a little talk with Jesus myself. Can we pray?" Cherisse pleaded, her eyes staring desperately into Reggie's.

"And I would think that this scenario would be exactly what *you* would want." His scowl deepened.

"What *I* want? Why would I want my best friend to be in danger?" She hung up and pressed Redial again, but was greeted by another busy signal. "Darn it!" A quick tear slid down her nose.

Reggie seemed unmoved by her distress. "I don't know, it just seems odd to me that a woman determined to tear apart a marriage to get another woman's goods would be so upset to see her on the way out of the picture. Seems to me that you would be rejoicing to see Terri gone without getting an arrest warrant tagged to your name."

"What? Me tear apart a marriage? You're the one who's been trying to get Terri's bounty by flashing yours all over the place."

"I was just trying to spare her the sorrow, give her something to hold on to, once she found out about you and Anthony."

"Me and Anthony? Me? And Anthony? Are you serious? You thought me and Anthony had something going on?" Cherisse recoiled. She knew her boundaries, loose as they were.

"Well, yes. I was told—"

"Who in the heck told you this? Why would somebody be putting out lies on me and Anthony like that?"

"So you're not having an affair with Anthony Murdock?" Reggie looked confused.

"No!" Cherisse was horrified. "I want to know who—"

"Look, we don't have time to argue right now. We need to find Terri! Is nine-one-one still putting you on hold?"

≈

"Where are we?" Anthony looked up at the log cabin he and Walter pulled up to. Tall, mature trees spread thick limbs as far as Anthony could see. After driving down the rural road for almost forty minutes, Anthony was surprised to see something other than green branches. The house had a rustic quality to it, contrasting with a gold Escalade parked by the door.

"Don't tell me that big-time Baltimore lawyer lives all the way out in these backwoods?" Anthony looked around as he limped up onto the porch. He massaged the back of his head as fresh pain seared through it, and used a dirty paper towel to wipe new blood off of his face.

"No." Walter smiled, picking through a set of keys. "I own this place. It's my personal retreat when I get tired of dealing with politics. I like to come here and be alone with God. Some of my best quiet times have been sitting out back where a small stream ends. Reminds me of my childhood fishing days down in Georgia. Not Atlanta; I was from the sticks. You know my story, had to leave the small town to make it in the big city and ended up settling down right here in Shepherd Hills."

"That's something." Anthony shook his head, trying to imagine Walter Banks sitting in a fishing boat in one of his pin-striped suits. "I'm just not getting that picture." He chuckled as he stepped into the cabin with Walter. "I honestly did not know that side of you, Mr. Banks."

"Yeah, well, a lot of people don't." The councilman flicked on some lights and both of them blinked to adjust to the sudden brightness.

"Oh boy." Walter looked around. "Guess I haven't been here in a while. Excuse the mess. Here, let me wipe a place for you to sit and I'll go back out front to see if that lawyer is coming. That driveway can be an easy miss. I'm just going to go flag down any car I see coming. He should be here any moment. I'll be right back."

"That's fine. I've been wanting to check my messages anyway. I haven't done it since I came back from South Carolina this afternoon." He prayed that Terri had been trying to reach him.

"Good luck finding a signal."

Walter stepped back onto the front porch as Anthony flipped open his cell phone and began pacing the pine-scented living room to no avail. His nationwide service plan had failed once again. He was about to give up checking messages when he noticed an old-fashioned telephone sitting on an end table in the generous room. Fortunately, it was only a reproduction of an older model. Anthony was relieved to see that it had a touch-tone keypad that would allow him to review his home phone number's voice-mail messages.

He skipped through a message from Marvin asking if he could have one of Anthony's desk organizers. The next message was from a woman who sounded like the assistant who worked for the supposed Detective Kent Cassell. Anthony shook his head, wondering how law officials could be so crooked.

"The detective would like you to come down to headquarters tomorrow morning for questioning. Be there by nine. Oops, eight. And come in through the door marked Exit. I mean, Emergency Exit."

Anthony shook his head. That message had been left the day before, Sunday, when he was down in Sharen, South Carolina.

He pressed 1 to listen to the third and final message.

"Uh, good morning, Mr. Murdock. This is Florence James from the Vital Records Department of Shepherd Hills. You were here on Saturday, trying to find out information on a Charles and Stephanie Ann Murdock? I'm sorry your trip was not more helpful, but I did come across something today. The auditor asked to see our name-change files, and I don't know why I did not think of this on Saturday. I don't want to take up all of your answering machine, but I did want to let you know that I did a check on Social Security numbers under our changed-name index, and I came across a man whose birth name was Charles Anthony Murdock.

"Apparently, he must have gotten caught up in the Black Nationalism Movement back in the sixties and began to go by the name Kofi Olakunde. Your mother must have changed back to her maiden name or something after he was out of the picture. I wish I could give you more information, but that's all I've been able to find. If you still want their Social Security numbers, you can come back to the office, fill out form 295782 and bring a money order, check, or cash, twenty-five dollars. Hope this helps. Bye, now."

Anthony held the phone frozen in his hand. *Kofi Olakunde. Kofi Olakunde.* He had just heard that name somewhere recently.

"Jesus, please." He racked his mind, straining to place the name, and then memories fired away like bullets. Aunt Rosa. The nursing home. Alzheimer's. When his mother was angry at him, she always told him that he looked just like his father. *Kofi Olakunde.* The vital records department in Sharen. Hazel Groves. Anthony fished in his wallet for her phone number. He had noticed yesterday that she wrote it on the napkin that covered the piece of rhubarb pie she'd talked him into taking. He had felt like a crazy man, opting to file the dirty napkin in with his business and credit cards instead of throwing it away, but now he knew that keeping it had been divine intervention. Providence. He dialed quickly.

"Hello?" Her voice was rich with southern cadence.

"Hello, Mrs. Groves. This is Anthony Murdock. I was with you yesterday at—"

"Anthony? Oh, I know who you are." She smacked her lips as she spoke, her words mingled with food. "Yes, Anthony Murdock. I was just sitting here thinking about you, sugar. I hoped I would hear from you again. Did you like the pie?"

"Yes, it was delicious. Thanks for everything. I'm sorry I took up so much of your time yesterday, but listen, I need to know—"

"Oh, sugar, it was my pleasure to help you. I was just talking about you too, telling all the ladies on the senior choir that you were such a nice, kind, handsome, respectful, God-fearing young man, the likes of which seems to be disappearing from down here in Sharen. You need to come back to visit. And bring your wife with you, too. She cooking good for you, sugar? A man like you deserves a good hot meal every night. Now I—"

"Mrs. Groves," Anthony cut in, "do you know anything about a Kofi Olakunde?"

"Kofi Olakunde?" She screeched. "Now what do you want to know about that no-good, dirty rotten thief? Why did you even bring that name up? There are people down here in Sharen who'd rather cuss in the Lord's house than speak that thing's name."

"What did he do?" Anthony spoke quickly, both of his hands wrapped around the receiver.

"That little devil said he was going to run for mayor down here back in the early seventies. He said he was going to do for us what them white politicians couldn't and wouldn't do. He was all about black power this and black power that, was going to go start an evolution or revolution or pollution or something. Then he took all our money and disappeared.

"I had neighbors who gave him their little bit of life savings, insurance-policy funds, parts of their children's college tuitions they'd been accumulating for years; all kinds of cash was given to him, all for the cause, the great black hope. He had everyone believing that he was raising money for the common good, but he wasn't concerned about anybody but himself. That was a dark moment in Sharen history. We lost so much money as a community that it took nearly a decade to get over it. I think there are some who still haven't, to be honest with you, but don't nobody talk about it much no more. How did you come across his name?"

Anthony was quiet for a moment before answering. His answer to her was as much a statement to himself. "Kofi Olakunde was my father."

"What do you mean he was your father? I thought you said your daddy's name was Murdock, Charles Murdock."

"It was. He changed it."

This time Hazel was quiet before responding. "I guess that could be. I remember him standing up there on that platform talking 'bout how he was an orphan who grew up in foster homes. His parents supposedly died in a house fire. Hey, remember we came across a Charles Murdock who died in a fire back in 1934? That must have been his father, your grandpop. Kofi must have changed his name before we really got to know him. I knew your eyes looked familiar, but I would never have thought that you came from that clown, sweet as you are."

Anthony did quick addition in his head. "So that means he was around forty when I was born."

"Don't get me started on that. Kofi was always hanging around young women. Girls, if you ask me. I think I remember your mother, Stacey, Stephanie, something like that, right? She was a quiet little thing who used to visit down here all the time with her mother, but she disappeared with him that last summer he was here once the rumors started coming out about her growing belly. She had to know what he did and was too ashamed—or afraid—to come back to Sharen, 'cause if memory serves me right, I ain't seen her since. I never knew she was Rosa Bergenson's niece. Rosa never talked about such things."

"My father left us with nothing."

"Wouldn't surprise me, crooked devil like that. Probably put all the money somewhere trying to figure out what to do next. You know, there were two things people used to talk about before it all simmered down."

"What's that?" Anthony turned around as the screen door squeaked open. Walter was coming back in, a steady smile on his face. Anthony held up a finger as he turned his attention back to the phone.

"Well, first, couldn't nobody get the story of Kofi's death right. We always heard that he was found on some train tracks up north somewhere back in the mid-seventies. The police never figured out if he stood there himself or if somebody pushed him, or so the story goes. And the other mystery nobody could agree on was whether or not he had a partner. If he did, I don't know how much that partner benefited from the scam. Kofi disappeared too fast. What was that, honey?" Hazel turned away from the phone.

"Sorry, Anthony. My husband just walked in and heard me talking. He said there used to be talk about a partner that Kofi did wrong by, a man from Georgia named—say it again," she paused. "Wonj—, no, Wayn—, no—Henry, get on this phone and say that name, please." There were some fumbling noises and fussing as Anthony heard the phone exchange hands.

"I got it, woman. Will you let go?" There was more fumbling until the man's voice, scratchy and slow, spoke loudly into Anthony's ear.

"Wanjala Razi. The partner Kofi supposedly stiffed was named Wanjala Razi. Don't know what his real name was. His momma probably named him William, or Wade, or Walter, or something real simple like that. Yep, they had all of us fooled. Here, Hazel, take this phone. I gotta go get the . . ." His voice faded into the distance before the line went dead.

Anthony felt the blood draining from his face as he eased the handset back into the base.

"Is everything all right?" Walter looked concerned as he studied Anthony's face. "Who were you just talking to?"

"Uh," Anthony looked around the sparse living room. He did not know where he was, and now he was not sure he knew why he was there. "I was just checking my messages and returning phone calls."

"Anything interesting? Anything related to our difficulties?" Walter flashed a warm smile as he offered Anthony a paternalistic pat. Anthony looked at the councilman's hand resting on his shoulder. The dead end of the phone cord peeked between his fingers. Hazel had never hung up. Walter ended the call.

Kellye Porter clutched the photograph in her hand. The heaping plate of fried chicken, green beans, potato salad, and cornbread lay untouched in front of her. Several of the church mothers surrounded her, silent in their support other than an occasional word of prayer sent up in her behalf, not realizing her grief was mixed with angst about another trouble.

In the church basement, the metal chairs were a sea of black as the friends and family of Minister Bernard Porter sat dining around rectangular tables. Gloria stood outside the circle of comforters surrounding the widow's seat, her eyes never leaving the diners at the head table: Kellye, Mabel and Denise, and Pastor Green. From the looks on all of their faces to the noticeably empty seat beside the quiet pastor, Gloria could sense unrest in the crowded room.

Kellye, who sat still even as the other mourners were beginning to file out of the small church hall, finally spoke out loud the concern that was etched on her face.

"Where's Anthony?" Her voice was a faint whisper as she laid the worn photo on the lace cloth before her. Pastor Green studied the photo from where he sat, a question forming in his eyes. When nobody responded to Kellye's concern, she did not hesitate with a response of her own.

"One of Bernard's dying wishes was for Anthony to

know about his father, and after the story you just told me, Mabel, now I know why he was so insistent."

Mabel sat tired and emotionless next to her sister-in-law. Just before the dinner had been served, she had relieved a load, a secret she had been holding on to for too long. Now Kellye, Denise, and Gloria looked burdened under the weight. Kellye was still talking.

"There is no way we can leave things like this. You know that, Mabel. And even if you don't, Bernard would not want me to sit and do nothing with this information. I have to go to the police. Bernard would want this taken care of right away. I have to go now." She spoke with finality and certainty as she began gathering her things. Nobody disagreed with her.

"Pastor Green, thank you for everything, but I have to make sure Bernard can rest in peace. Can you receive my visitors for me? Come on, Mabel, Denise. Gloria, I need you, too." Kellye took comfort in knowing that Bernard would be pleased with her actions, even as a rare anxiety gnawed at her gut feelings. Urgency came with her decision to head to the police headquarters.

"Ladies, we need to hurry."

It was almost five o'clock when Kent Cassell skidded to a stop. Mona stayed frozen in her seat as Kent jumped out, anger on his face as he pushed through the press, the cameramen, reporters, journalists with pencils and notepads who surrounded the entrance of the precinct like flies on trash.

"Excuse me, sir, can you share your comments on the alleged act of police brutality that occurred in Shepherd Hills today?"

A young Asian woman with black-rimmed glasses stuck a microphone in his face when she saw his badge. He pushed away the padded mike and kept marching onward, not slowed by his bad knee or the onslaught of reporters. Within minutes he was rapping, then banging, on the glass door of Sheriff Malloy's office. The sheriff sat turned away from his desk, his back the only offered view.

"He won't come out or open the door for anyone." Jessica, Malloy's assistant, was sitting like a scared rabbit at her desk. Her voice squeaked out just as frightened.

Kent turned away before turning back with his hand clobbering the metal frame.

"Malloy, open this door right now!"

The sheriff squeaked around in his chair and when he saw what was in Kent's hand, he immediately let him in.

"Where did you get those papers?" He looked drained, removed, as if he had come to the last leg of a race that had already been won by someone else.

"No, the question is why would you mark up evidence with notes that incriminate you?"

"Nobody can prove anything."

"Gary, the date and time that I received this fax is clearly marked on these papers. The notes you made predict when and where Anthony Murdock was going to be before the fact, and they're written as if it's for your benefit, like you had a plan outside of what he even knows."

"It doesn't matter anymore." Malloy looked down at his desk, shaking his head. "It was never my plan to get involved in any of this, but once I found out about the money, I thought it would be a quick, easy, painless way to get a paycheck bigger than any I've ever seen. Everything was going fine, or so he said. Just trust me, he kept telling me, and I tried. But when that crazy girlfriend of his started going off the plan over the weekend, I didn't want to take any more chances. She was getting so careless, even that young street hustler was—"

"Snap Peterson?" Kent interrupted. He had heard about the homicide on the car radio. "You had something to do with that." It was as much a question as an answer. The sheriff squeezed his hands together.

"My career was on the line. We were right there, and that darn woman was pulling everything apart. I thought I could arrest Anthony and take care of things myself. But"—he looked out the window at the growing crowd. Protesters with signs and banners were filing off of a bus— "I guess *I* lost control."

"Where is Anthony Murdock? Where is he right now?"

"I don't know."

"What do you mean you don't know?"

"He left here with Councilman Banks over an hour ago, and I could not tell you where they went."

"So you just let them go?"

"What else was I supposed to do?" Sheriff Malloy closed his eyes and swung his chair back to face the wall.

"We need to find them right now!"

Reginald and Cherisse were almost at the police station. Despite the luxurious appointments of the Lincoln limo, both of them looked uncomfortable in their seats.

"If nine-one-one won't come to us, then we need to go to them."

Cherisse had seen no need to disagree with Reggie's plan. Now she wished they had only thought of it earlier. The blocks surrounding the precinct were already being barricaded off as crowds of protesters showed up from all around the region.

"I still don't understand why that cop was giving Anthony a beat-down like that." Cherisse pressed her lips together in a thick worry line as she watched concrete barriers being used to section off the main thoroughfare. Officers in riot gear were lining up around the perimeter.

"We're going to have to walk the rest of the way." Reggie got out as quickly as humanly possible from the limo. He held the door for Cherisse and then took her by the hand as together they pressed through the growing crowd. They shoved through in silence until Reggie briefly let go of Cherisse's hand to raise his arm in a desperate wave.

"Gloria! Gloria! Miss Randall!" Reggie's bass thundered over the shouts and protests until it caught the ear of Gloria and the three women with her. They were almost a half block ahead of them.

"Gloria Randall!" Cherisse narrowed her eyes at the woman who was looking around at the yell of her name. "*That* chubby checker is Anthony's mistress?"

Reggie gave Cherisse a double-take as they wrestled around the flow to catch up with Gloria and company.

"Anthony's mistress? You think so? I thought she was just Councilman Banks's secretary. Remember up onstage at the banquet Friday night? I don't know why the councilman looked so surprised when the emcee announced his support for the BEA. That man approached *me* months ago with a guarantee not only of his vote, but of most of the council members' votes as well. To hear that man speak, you'd think he owned this city."

"And you think Gloria is only Councilman Banks's secretary, not Anthony's lover?"

"That's the impression I got, anyway. He said she was a good worker, but I don't know how well I'm trusting his judgment right about now. Anybody that would recommend that crazy Nikki Galloway as a personal assistant has got to be off his rocker." Reggie was running out of breath as he led their way through the throng.

"Wait a minute—Nikki is your personal assistant? Terri swore that woman was your girlfriend!" Cherisse had to catch herself from stopping in her tracks at such a critical time.

Reginald gave Cherisse a triple-take. "You haven't met Nikki, have you?"

"Out to lunch, huh?"

"Forget out to lunch. She called out for the day. Check that—she ain't even got *it* to call out of!"

It was good to share a laugh, albeit a quick, nervous one, in a moment when the world had seemed to lose its correct rotation. They had almost caught up with the others when a group of demonstrators blocked their way again.

"In all seriousness, Nikki wishes, maybe even imagines, that there's more between us than business, but now I've cut that off too. She's entirely too unpredictable and completely unprofessional—and that's the best that I can say about her. I had been sending her to meet with CASH—you heard of Bethany Village, I'm sure—and from what I overheard her saying to the director today down at city hall, I think she had another agenda going on than what I had asked her to initiate. I thought she was presenting him with some lots I own that he could use alongside the businesses of the BEA."

"I can't hear you. Wait a minute!" Cherisse tried to shout over a man screaming into a bullhorn. The crowd was growing more restless. She and Reggie were jostled around by a group of young men running with car tires in their arms. A glass bottle shattered at Cherisse's feet.

"Step to this side." Reggie gingerly but quickly pushed her around him. Gloria and the three women with her had stopped in the near distance, but all of them looked confused, searching Reggie and Cherisse's faces for familiarity. Reggie continued talking as they pressed closer to them.

"I had been telling Councilman Banks that the BEA could benefit from a partnership with a non-profit, and vice versa, but he insisted that I try to sell CASH some acres I invested in at his request. I never looked at the real estate I bought from him, being so eager to keep such an influential man happy. I'm not even sure what we were offering Eric Johnson, the director of CASH. Now seeing Walter Banks's judgment of good help, I wonder about his judgment of good land. I'm starting to believe that Nikki was playing both me and Eric, but I haven't figured out why."

"Do I know you?"

Reggie and Cherisse had finally reached Gloria. Two of the three women standing with her were dressed in dark church clothes; the other was in white. All of their eyes were swollen and red from crying.

"I recognized you as Councilman Banks's assistant, Miss Randall. We've spoken on the phone and you were onstage Friday night. I'm Reginald Savant."

Gloria instantly knew who he was the moment his silk voice fluttered out, but she had no time to be gushy.

"We're trying to get to the police station. We have an emergency."

"We do too," Reggie said, looking at Cherisse, who was biting her lip, holding back tears once again. "I was hoping that you could contact the councilman so we could use some of his clout to get an immediate response."

One of the women who looked like she had just recovered from a tearful outburst suddenly broke down again. "How is it that everybody seems to know all about Walter Banks except me, and he's my own father?" A deep moan rose from her throat.

One of the other ladies grabbed her in a tight hug.

"I'm sorry. I was just so mad about trying to get through this life all by myself with no help from anybody, that I was glad when he called me. I hadn't heard from him since the night you were conceived, and after all I went through trying to raise you by myself, I was glad to take the money he offered me."

Tears washed Mabel's face anew as she continued holding Denise.

"It seemed the least he could do was give me an easy retirement since he gave me such a hard life. It seemed simple enough, keeping a great-nephew from contacting an old woman at a nursing home, keeping him from learning through her about his father. I blamed Kofi for everything, and I guess I was just mad at Anthony for being his son. I never knew it would get this far." She wiped more tears from her face as she kept talking.

"Walter was so nervous about Rosa recognizing who *he* was, but she never did. She only met him once briefly down in Sharen, as did Bernard, and that was almost thirty years ago. Walter looked a lot different back then."

"He most certainly did," Kellye Porter agreed, looking down at the worn photo clutched in her hands. Three men, all in colorful dashikis and super-sized afros, filled the four-by-six frame: Bernard, Kofi, and Wanjala, whose face was covered with thick, untrimmed hair.

"Sweet Bernard, he never made the connection until he tried to look for some insurance information he needed at that old warehouse on Perkins Street, Walter's other headquarters." Mabel had let go of Denise, though an arm was still wrapped around her shoulders as they continued to push through the crowd. "I don't know what he found there, but I think I told him more than what he knew when I spoke to him last week." More tears trickled down her cheeks. "It was the last time we talked."

"Walter's other headquarters? What are you talking about?" Reggie was confused, but nobody responded because they had finally made it to the front of the police station. Several guards stood around the entrance and the clamor of reporters kept all of them from maintaining their balances.

"We have an emergency and need help right away." This time Reggie's words caught everyone's attention.

"Sir, I'll have someone help you when we can." A stern-faced walnut-colored officer holding a shield talked over Reggie's head after looking him up and down from his post on the steps. "A lot is happening right now with this alleged police misconduct case." This he said as officers pushed back squawking reporters and fist-waving demonstrators.

"The victim's wife has been kidnapped."

All six of them were immediately escorted to the man running things at the moment, Detective Kent Cassell.

Chapter 19

Between the hormones swirling in her system and the three hours of nonstop bucking courtesy of Nikki Galloway, Terri was ready to vomit. She had given up on waiting for the car to stop at a reasonable place to get out, choosing to take her chances of escaping once they got to wherever they were going. Terri figured the repeated circling around Shepherd Hills would have to come to an end at some point, and Nikki was a small girl. Injury by moving limo seemed like a more damaging alternative than injury by swinging string bean. Terri was not afraid; she was annoyed more than anything.

The landscape of trees whizzing by did nothing to soothe her rocking stomach. She did not know where she was, and at the moment she felt so sick she was not sure that she cared. She just wanted to go home, return to a normal life. Yes, even a Sunday morning service at Second Baptist with Anthony at the pulpit seemed tolerable to her now. She wondered if that life would ever return.

"I'm going to throw up," she whispered, doubled over in the expansive backseat.

"Shut up! We're almost there!"

"So what was the deal between you and my father?" Anthony stared Walter square in the eye. "What kind of game have you been playing with me, Walter?"

He did not know what it was or where it came from, but he felt it, a sudden whack on his head in the same spot Sheriff Malloy had already pre-tenderized. Anthony buckled under the pain, falling to the hardwood floor under the force. He nursed his wound even as he searched for something he could use to defend himself. But there was little he could do. Walter stood over him, a gun gleaming.

"Don't you dare talk to me like that." There was something in Walter's eyes Anthony had never seen before. Hate. A sudden kick in the center of his forehead took Anthony by surprise. Wasn't it enough that the man had a gun pointed at him? Anthony was shaken but struggled to stand, his movements slow and painful under the watchful barrel of the gun. Walter kicked him back down to the floor.

"So you're going to beat a man who's already down. That's not much of a fair fight." Anthony had steel in his eyes.

"Don't talk to me about fair. I can tell you what's not fair. I came up with that plan down in Sharen. I wrote your father's speeches, built up his campaign. I had those people trusting him, hailing him as a hometown hero. He was working for me. That was *my* money. He was only supposed to get twenty-five percent. But then he disappears, and what am I left with? Nothing."

The gun became animated in Walter's hand as he spoke. Anthony swallowed hard, thought hard. He was not going down like this. He eased back to his feet, his eyes on the black metal before him. Anthony backed up little by little until his back bumped into an end table. The councilman followed him with every step. He had to keep Walter talking as he tried to figure out how to get out of there alive.

"So you found him and killed him?" The words sounded unreal coming out of his mouth. This was Walter he was talking to, his mentor, his friend.

"No." Walter shook his head and glanced down at the gun.

Is that nervousness in his eyes? Hesitation? Anthony wondered, trying to make sense of the look on Walter's face.

"I spent two years and three weeks looking for that man and then I found him just in time to watch him kill himself down in the rail yard of AGS. It took me another fifteen years to figure out what he did with my money. That's seventeen years I spent broke, dirt poor, without the money I planned so perfectly to get. Hundreds of thousands, you hear me? Do you know what that's like? To know you have a windfall out there but you're still living like a pauper? To know that your financial success was stolen by a quote-unquote partner who disappears like water in air?" The gun became steadier in his hands. Anger seemed to be replacing the nerves.

"I am not responsible for my father's actions." Anthony kept his eyes centered on Walter's, determined to stand tall and strong like Samson did as he pushed the pillars on the Philistines. *Samson went down with the enemy.* Anthony turned his focus off of the fear that was trying to inch back into him. If Walter was the last person he saw in life, Jesus would be the first person he saw in death. He was convinced, holding on to that thought for courage.

"You're right, Anthony. I never said you were responsible." Walter gave in to a slight smile. "I just thought it *unfair*, as you would call it, that I spent years of my life struggling because of your father and he just slides away into eternity. After all I went through, it only seemed *fair* to me that somebody should pay."

Walter took a step closer to Anthony as he spoke. "When I found out he had a family that he walked out on, I befriended your mother and stepfather in the hopes that one of them would come across the money. When they died, my last hope was that maybe when you turned eighteen or twenty-one, some large trust fund would appear in your name somewhere and I would be able to stake my claim. When that didn't happen I did my own research, and I found accounts your father opened at a whole bunch of different banks. The money meant nothing to him because he was dead, nothing to you because you did not know about it. And because it had sat so long in interest-bearing accounts, it had nearly quadrupled in value. I'm talking millions."

"The money wasn't enough? You got what you wanted, so why did you have to make my life miserable?" Anthony crossed his hands behind his back. His fingertips quietly brushed the end table behind him for something, anything, he could use against a nine-millimeter. He stopped at what felt like a toothpick. Hey, if little David could take out the giant Goliath with a small pebble from a pond, anything was possible.

"I could not just let you go because you were about to

make me lose my money." The anger was boiling into controlled rage.

"What are you talking about?" Anthony pinched the toothpick between his thumb and forefinger. This was ridiculous. What was he going to do with a toothpick? He was not MacGyver. He let it drop.

Walter was responding. "I invested all of the money I found in Toringhouse Steel, AGS Railroad, and virtually everything else steel-related in this part of the state. When Toringhouse went bankrupt, I was not too bothered because AGS was planning the Stonymill station, and that promised to be a success. But when I heard that you were considering using your business strength to support CASH's efforts against the Stonymill light rail station six months ago, I knew I had to keep you from getting involved."

"I was just one man working at one marketing firm. How was my taking up Bethany Village going to make or break you?"

"You have never realized the power of your influence, Anthony. In the years that I've known you, it seems like everything you touch turns to gold. I could not let you get involved with CASH because then Stonymill would never have taken off, and what was left of my investments would have dwindled away to nothing. I'm sure of it!"

Anthony was taken aback at the councilman's assertion. Walter seemed more certain about Anthony's authority and power in the Kingdom of God than he was himself.

Didn't I say I'd make you the head and not the tail? Didn't I say that the man who delights in My law, everything he does shall prosper? All these years he had been focused on his own agenda for success, and all he had to do was recognize the promises of God, His favor, at work in his life. Anthony's heart rang with praise to the Faithful One even as his eyes stared down the barrel of a handgun. *I'll either be saying Hallelujah to You face-to-face in a moment, Lord, or You better believe I'll be shouting down the aisles at church on Sunday morning,* Anthony thought to himself.

"Something funny, Mr. Murdock?"

Anthony did not realize he was smiling. Walter's finger tightened around the trigger; obviously he was peeved that Anthony found a reason to look happy even with death staring him in the face. Anthony knew he had to step more carefully. No need to rush up the rungs of heaven's ladder. Keep the man talking.

"Stonymill was six months ago. You dangled your money and I went for it. You won. Why all this new business with the check and the BEA? Couldn't you just leave well enough alone?"

"Once Stonymill was taken care of, I knew that I had to take care of you for good. That had been too much of a close call. I was not going to take a chance and let another Murdock have a free stab at my money."

Anthony could see the hesitation in Walter's fingers as he kept the gun pointed at him. He kept the questions coming. "So you expected me to fall for the money? That's the only way your plans would have worked."

"You are your father's son. I recognized that money-hungry gene in you a long time ago. With the right bait, you were an easy hook. I only wanted to get you behind bars and away from my money. When I found out about Reginald Savant's wishes to have the BEA, I knew that I could take his generosity and use it against you.

"Reginald thought I had talked you into willingly leading the organization, and that the money was for pure philanthropic purposes. He knew nothing about the bribes. He gave me the money to give to you, wanting to take no credit for jump-starting black businesses in this community. He simply never realized how perfect his plans and timing fit into mine."

"I give you credit, Mr. Banks. You planned everything well." Anthony wondered if Walter wanted praise and recognition for his craftiness.

"Everything was coming together perfectly." Walter began to sound bitter. "Even when Sheriff Malloy started sniffing around my finances, all I had to do was flash him some green and he promised to follow through with getting you locked up for everything. Like your father, I expected your conscience to catch up with you. I expected that you would turn yourself in at some point, then Malloy was going to throw the book at you. I don't know what came over him today. Him and that darn Gloria. I never expected her to dig up so much stuff, but she's not a factor anymore."

"What's that supposed to mean?" Anthony gaped. *Had Walter done something to Gloria?*

Reflective for a moment, Walter rested the gun on his thigh.

"It was never supposed to come to this, but I don't know what else to do." Walter slowly raised the gun again. This time both hands fingered the trigger.

"Walter, look—" Anthony was trapped, the end table behind him, Walter before him.

"Please, Anthony, don't make this any harder than it

has to be. And don't worry about Terri. I've already made sure that she'll be taken good care of by Reginald Savant."

Terri and the baby! There was no way Anthony was going to bow down to death. He was not finished doing the work God had called him to do. *Jesus!* he silently prayed, asking for supernatural strength, or at least divine intervention.

A squirrel scurried outside the front door, causing Walter to look away for one quick second. Anthony took that second to bear all of his strength into Walter's side, grabbing his wrists, reaching for the gun. They wrestled together in sweat and groans until both had landed on the floor, sending a ceramic lamp crashing with them and the room into darkness. Anthony's hands were wrapped around the barrel, but Walter still had control of the trigger. They wrestled some more, the noise of the fight echoing loudly in the isolated space.

There was a quick pause when both simultaneously caught their breath. During that brief moment of inactivity, both of them noticed a loud scuffle on the front porch. A sudden screech and a pounding bang vibrated on the floorboards.

What kind of squirrel was that? Walter aimed at the heavy oak door that was suddenly swinging open. Anthony's eyes widened with the realization that he and Walter were not the only two engaged in hand-to-hand combat. A flurry of arms and legs, fists and slaps rolled through the opening door.

"What the—" Walter pulled the trigger. A loud crash, part gunfire, part breaking wood, reverberated throughout the cabin. Blond hair tracks flew in as a bullet smoked out.

Before any sense could be made, Anthony scrambled to the doorway.

"Terri! Oh God no!"

They were sitting in an empty conference room at the police headquarters, all of them. Cherisse and Reggie sat next to each other; Cherisse with her head bowed, Reggie with his tie loosened, staring blankly at a newspaper. Denise and Mabel were locked arm-in-arm at the oval table. Kellye stood at a window, staring straight ahead. A stoic gaze replaced the tears in her eyes. Gloria crunched loudly on a small bag of cheese curls Mona had offered her from a vending machine. Outside, chants and shouts filled the street below the headquarters. Despite the occasional shatter or threat, the police had control of the crowd.

The door to the office squeaked open and all eyes turned.

"Anything?" Reggie's voice echoed through the quiet room.

"He owns a lot of properties, and not only in Shepherd Hills. They could be anywhere within a hundred-mile radius." Kent Cassell had a stack of folders under his arm. "Gloria, if you ever need a job, you can be my assistant. The work you did uncovering Wanjala Razi has taken this case further in six hours than I'd gotten in six months."

"Has it taken us to Anthony and Terri?" When there was no reply, Gloria resumed nervously chomping on another cheese curl. "Then it wasn't good enough."

"It's not over yet." Kent was firm in his words, his sharp blue eyes zeroing back down on the files in his hand.

A woman tiptoed through the door behind him. It was Mona, and she carried two large Thermoses in her hands.

"I brought some coffee in case anyone wanted some." Her voice was barely above a whisper. "I wasn't sure if there was anything else you needed," she said to Kent. "I tried calling you on your cell phone, but I forgot you didn't have it." She began pouring the steamy liquid into some mugs she had gathered around the station.

"Yeah, my cell phone." Kent shook his head as he flipped back through the papers. Then he froze, his eyes locking into Mona's. "My cell phone! Did you say you called my cell phone?"

"Yes." Mona suddenly looked uncertain, her eyes darting around to everyone in the room. "But I think I kept dialing the wrong number. The last time I called, the woman cursed me for ten minutes. Kent, darling, what is it?"

The detective had disappeared down the hall.

The edges of the evening sunlight had folded down into darkness. From the front porch of a log cabin in the middle of nowhere, Anthony fought the urge to fold down with the day.

"Hang in there, babygirl," his voice was gentle, endearing as he whispered into her ear. "We're going to get out of this together." He held Terri by the hand, stroking her relaxed hair as his eyes surveyed the thick foliage of the surrounding forest. He did not want to get them lost and stranded in such an isolated place, especially at night, but he knew that he had to get the two of them away. Nikki and Walter were not going to stand there and argue forever.

"I don't want to hear any more about your darn plan!" Nikki's voice screeched louder than Walter's. He had her by one fist, the gun still dangling in his left hand. "She and I are here now, so you're just going to have to figure out what to do. I'm not taking that thing back to Reggie! You said that I could have him!"

"Everything will be all right," Anthony whispered as Walter began a long, violent tirade in Nikki's face. He kissed Terri's hairline as he fashioned out a plan. There were a couple of cars right in front of them but Bonnie and Clyde had the keys, so that wasn't an option. The woods surrounded them on every side. It was dark, but it was going to have to be do-able. Anthony looked down again at his wife hunched over the wooden steps.

"Terri." Concern glowed in his eyes. "Do you think there's any way that you can walk?"

"What are you talking about? Of course I can walk. Why wouldn't I be able to walk?" Terri's face was buried in the wood planks, her eyes closed as Anthony gently lifted her head to face him.

"Your stomach, Terri. The bullet hit your stomach."

"Bullet? What bullet?" Her eyes shot open as her mouth dropped. "*That* was a gunshot? I thought that darn limo was still backfiring. Who the heck is shooting guns around here?" She looked past Walter and Nikki, who were in the middle of a pushing and shoving match.

"So you're not hurt? Why are you holding your stomach like that?"

"I was trying not to throw up, if you must know."

"What?" Anthony looked confused momentarily, and then a smile spread across his lips. "Oh, the baby."

"Yes, the baby." Terri closed her eyes again, but flung them back open. "The baby? How do you know about the baby?"

"The surprise, remember? Terri, your clues weren't exactly quantum physics."

"My clues? Are you crazy? You thought—"

"Look, Terri, I'm not going to go back and forth with you anymore. Let's just talk. We haven't done that in a long time. You are my wife, and I love you, and I want to show my love for you the same way God shows His love for me."

"So now you love me." Terri was sitting up. "If that was true then why would yo—"

"Terri, look at me."

"If God really—"

"Terri, look at me." Anthony held her face close to his so that all she could do was look into his eyes. He held her like this, quiet, no words, no diversions, nothing but two wayfaring wanderers meeting at the same straight path. A tear blinked out from her lashes.

"What is it, Terri?" Anthony whispered as he tenderly massaged her wet cheek. "What do you see?"

"I see . . . love. And I see Jesus in you."

"And you're about to see him face-to-face. I'm sorry, Terri."

They never noticed that Nikki and Walter's argument had come to a close. Walter stood over the two of them, the gun pointed at the top of Terri's head. Nikki sulked nearby.

"It should have never come to this"—he glared at Nikki as he spoke—"but I've got too much to lose."

Just as he was about to pull the trigger, a cell phone began ringing. Walter looked with impatience as Nikki began digging through her purse. She was still searching pockets, unzipping zippers, as the shrill notes of the cell phone became drowned out under piercing sirens. Blue-and-red flashing lights cut through the darkness in the near distance.

"You can get a signal out here?" Anthony smiled as he helped Terri to her feet. He felt it deep down in his spirit. The nightmare was over.

"Nikki! I told you to keep that phone off! Don't you know they can trace that signal to wherever you are?"

Nikki rolled her eyes as she pressed Talk. "Hello?"

"You've been *answering that phone?*" Walter was horrified.

"Yeah, why?" Nikki rolled her eyes again, but then looked down at the cellular phone like she was seeing it for the first time.

"Oops."

"That's all you can say?" FBI and state troopers were slamming into the driveway.

"Uh"—she paused—"it's for you?"

As she passed the phone to a stupefied Walter, Terri could have sworn Nikki winked at her.

Chapter 20

One Year Later

A nd Lord, may every oppressed, enslaved soul find freedom within these gates; every sick and hurting body find grace within these walls; may the homeless and the destitute know that they have found a pillow, and every foot that would go astray find the path to life here. In Jesus' name, we pray, Amen!" Pastor Green shouted a word of high praise into the microphone as the tape was cut and the balloons were released.

Anthony followed with his eyes as the multi-colored dots dispersed above their heads. It was a perfect, blue, cloudless day for the opening dedication of Bethany Village's first wing. As the senior director of public relations and marketing of CASH, Anthony had made sure that the celebration was grand enough for the highest dignitary's standards, yet touchable enough for the meekest child's embrace. He welcomed the unusually sun-filled September day as an approving nod from God.

Eric Johnson, standing between Gloria Randall—his administrative assistant—and Pastor Green on the podium, gave Anthony a thumbs-up. The smile on Eric's face was overflowing. Anthony had found his niche, his calling. The pay surpassed dollars.

"Hallelujah!" He joined the others in celebration as he gave Terri a quick squeeze around her waist. She was fussing over Adrienne, as had become her custom over the past three months, but took a moment to smile up at her husband's face.

"You did good, Anthony. Your father would be proud. Your whole family would be proud." Her voice softened. "I'm proud of you." She kissed him lightly on the lips before pulling the fuzzy pink blanket tighter around the sleeping infant. Before she could reposition the pink and white DADDY'S LITTLE GIRL bib under her chubby chin, a sharp poke on her arm jabbed her back to attention.

"Oh my goodness, she looks more and more like you. You too, Anthony." Cherisse squealed as she took the infant. "Give me my baby. I could hold this little angel all day."

"You'll be fighting with Sister Porter for that privilege." Terri laughed. "Ms. Kellye has pretty much adopted Adrienne as her own. She's always saying that Adrienne and I are the daughter and granddaughter she never had. I don't mind. God knew I was going to need all the help I could get, running this business from home."

"And how's your new business faring these days?"

Cherisse's voice was high and squeaky, as if she were talking to the baby and not Terri.

"Better than I ever imagined, girl. Anthony helped me fix up a work space comfortable enough for me to develop my designs yet professional enough to invite over clients. I never thought it would happen in that tiny little house we had to move into, but it has. Thank you, baby." She gave Anthony another kiss on the lips. He ran his fingers through her hair but froze when he turned around to see Cherisse.

"Whoa, when did this happen?" He covered his eyes as if shielding them from the sun. "Reggie, come on now. Diamonds don't come that big. You tryin' to trap my sister with some cubic zirconium you found at the dollar store."

"Don't hate." Cherisse joined the laughter. "God's getting you through all this debt and taking you to a season of *true* prosperity that'll surpasses any you thought you had."

"Whew!" Reggie used the program in his hand to fan Cherisse. "My woman is on fire! I'm telling you, those financial seminars you've been giving over at Second Baptist have been teaching *all* of us a thing or two about God and money. I need to have you as a speaker for one of the BEA meetings."

"Yeah, how are things going with that?" Anthony pulled at one of Adrienne's chubby, curled fingers and she rustled in her sleep.

"Man, I tell you. God don't play when it comes to showing off His favor. Brother Eric just finished looking at the plans for the training center and vocational institute that's going to link our organizations. Thanks for your input and your contributions. It amazes me how much you've given to Eric despite your own financial set-backs."

"Hey, the Word says give and it shall be given unto you. I'm holding God to it, and you know what? He's been faithful." He nodded at Terri, who gave him a supportive smile.

"Look, Terri, I know I helped you max out all those credit cards, and even though you said selling the cars helped, it's only right of me to pay my share of the bills, interest included." Cherisse squeezed her friend's shoulder.

"Can I get an amen?" Anthony joked.

"Ooh, that's cold, especially coming from a man who's only seen God's mercy these past few months. Please extend some to me, for everything." Cherisse turned serious as she reached out a hand to Anthony.

He gave her a hug. "Every night as I watch the updates on the trials and see all those faces—Walter, Haberstick, Patterson, all of them—coming across the TV, all I think is but for the grace of God, there go I."

"That's the truth," Terri said while dabbing drool off the baby's lips. "You need to write a thank-you note to Gary Malloy for beating you up on national television. The state didn't even try to press charges against you."

"And then they turned around and made you their star witness," Cherisse added.

"Even Sheriff Cassell can't deny that evidence of God's presence and power." Reggie grinned. "No matter how hard he tries."

"I wouldn't worry about him," Terri spoke again. "You know Mona's living out the Word for him now. And considering *our* testimonies"—she nodded her head at Reggie and Cherisse—"he'll be giving his life to Jesus like we finally did this past year."

"Amen to that and thank you, Jesus!" Anthony looked at his wife, his awakening daughter, his friends, his community, his life. As they headed for the cake and punch table covered with confetti and fresh flowers, he took a quick glimpse back up at the sky. One single balloon was still barely visible, the tiny red dot seemingly determined to defy reason as it continued its journey upward.

"Stay on track. You'll get there," he whispered as it disappeared into the heavens.

Reading Group Guide

1. Anthony's sermon on Sunday seemed to preach as much to his own spirit as to the congregation. Have you ever spoken words to someone else that proved to be a Word to you as well? If you had that opportunity now, what Scripture text would you be "preaching"?

2. Terri doesn't comprehend Anthony and others at Second Baptist Church who are seemingly *obsessed* with Jesus and the Bible. "They don't understand that there's more to life than religion," she complains. She thinks they're fanatical; someone else might call them faithful. What do you think? What kind of churchgoer are you? What do Scriptures such as Romans 12: 1–2 and Hebrews 10:24–25 suggest about the kind of churchgoer we *should* be?

3. Pastor Green prays for Anthony, saying, "Do what you've got to do to make things right, whatever it takes."

Does that prayer inspire you? Encourage or challenge you? Or terrify you? Why?

4. Throughout this novel, characters deal with the issue of wealth and the power, status, and stumbling blocks that are associated with money. In Chapter 2, Pastor Green speaks about spiritual status and blessings in relationship to material blessings. What do you think about his spin on a "prosperity gospel"? How does it relate to Jesus' attitudes about money (e.g., Luke 18:18–27)?

5. "Better is little with the fear of the Lord than great treasure and trouble therewith" (Proverbs 15:16). What has been your experience with the principle laid out in this proverb (which Anthony recalls was one of his Aunt Rosa's favorites)?

6. Being mindful of his own desperate need for a second chance, Eric gives that chance to Nikki. There's another expression related to second chances: "Fool me once, shame on you; fool me twice, shame on me." How do you know when the generosity of a second chance may result in a "fool me twice"? Do you offer a second chance based on faith or reason or some combination of both? Why? How does our willingness to trust people reflect our trust in God?

7. Terri compares her pursuit of peace, esteem, and status through wealth, success, and possession with the peace evident in the worshippers at Second Baptist. Do you have peace? If so, what is its source? If not, where have you sought it—in the past and now? What does Scripture say

about the source of true and lasting peace? (See John 14:27; 16:32–33; Romans 5:1; 15:17; Colossians 3:15.)

8. In answer to his own question "Who do I trust?" Anthony remembers the words of Proverbs 3:5. Whom do you trust? Why? What is the evidence of your trust? What does it look like to place your trust in God?

9. Sister Porter offers counsel to Terri about her faltering marriage with Anthony by quoting Ephesians 5:21–33, and noting that even Paul called the marriage relationship a mystery (v. 32). How have you experienced mystery in a relationship—with a spouse or with Christ? Is that mysterious element a source of celebration or frustration to you? Why? How might you work to remove the frustrating aspects and retain the celebratory ones?

10. Eric faces an all-too-common dilemma: the church and its people have let him down. At first, it seemed they just didn't follow through on their promises, which would be disappointing enough. But then it becomes clear that they have believed a false report and judged him harshly on that basis. How do you respond when other Christians let you down? How does the relationship about Paul and John Mark offer counsel or encouragement (see Acts 15:36–41; 2 Timothy 4:11)?

11. Anthony repeatedly asks such questions as "How did I end up in this place? Why is this happening to me?" When have you asked such questions about your life situation? What answers did you find? How were those answers key to ensuring you didn't repeat your mistakes?

12. Anthony is tempted to "overlook" the extra money in his pension; he can easily justify doing so! But his spirit is uneasy. Why? How do you handle financial "windfalls" from a bank error in your favor or incorrect (excessive) change from a cashier or other mundane sources? Why should God care about such little amounts of money? (See Proverbs 16:11; 20:23; Micah 6:11; Luke 16:10.)

13. Anthony finds inspiration and motivation in Judges 16. Read it yourself. What does the story of Samson say to you in whatever challenging situation you may be facing? How might you be called to claim a Samson-like victory in that circumstance?

14. Ironically, both Anthony (in his fraudulent actions) and Terri (in her adulterous desires) are saved by exposure. How is such exposure an answer to Pastor Green's prayer? In what way(s) has God allowed exposure of your sin to save you from perpetuating that transgression—or worse?

15. Anthony gradually discerns that his financial issues are the product of a generational curse, handed down from his biological father. What experience do you have with generational curses? What does Exodus 34:5–7 seem to say about them?

16. "Terri laid aside every conviction she held about independence, self-determination, and standing on her own two feet. . . . She wanted nothing more than to find a place to rest her hurting heart and head." It isn't necessarily a bad or wrong thing to do or desire—but it can be

dangerous if we don't choose our "resting place" wisely. When have you felt that way, and what resting place did you choose? (See Matthew 11:28–29; Hebrews 4:9–10.)

17. Eric had carefully prepared a speech for city council, but when the moment came, he balled it up, tossed it aside, and spoke from his heart. Scripture says that the Spirit will give us words to speak when our own fail (Mark 13:11; Romans 8:26). When have you experienced such inspired speech? Where does human preparation leave off and the Holy Spirit take over?

18. In this story, as in real life, preachers and politicians are often lumped together in a category marked "suspect and/or corrupt." What do the two groups have in common that make them vulnerable to corruption? How do scriptural catalogs of leadership qualities (e.g., 2 Timothy 3:1–13) offer counsel and caution to those in leadership—both in the church and in the world?

Reading Groups for African American
Christian Women Who Love God and Like to Read.

BE A PART OF
GLORY GIRLS READING GROUPS!

THESE EXCITING BI-MONTHLY READING GROUPS ARE FOR THOSE SEEKING FELLOWSHIP WITH OTHER WOMEN WHO ALSO LOVE GOD AND ENJOY READING.

For more information about GLORY GIRLS, to connect with an established group in your area, or to become a group facilitator, go to our Web site at **www.glorygirlsread.net** or click on the Praising Sisters logo at **www.walkworthypress.net.**

WHO WE ARE

GLORY GIRLS is a national organization made up of primarily African American Christian women, yet it welcomes the participation of anyone who loves the God of the Bible and likes to read.

OUR PURPOSE IS SIMPLE

- To honor the Lord with <u>what we read</u>—and have a good time doing it!

- To provide an atmosphere where readers can seek fellowship with other book lovers while encouraging them in the choices they make in Godly reading materials.

- To offer readers fresh, contemporary, and entertaining yet scripturally sound fiction and nonfiction by talented Christian authors.

- To assist believers and nonbelievers in discovering the relevancy of the Bible in our contemporary, everyday lives.